Jemez Spring

Jemez Spring

Rudolfo Anaya

UNIVERSITY OF NEW MEXICO PRESS ◆ ALBURQUERQUE

Ana

Printed in the United States of America
11 10 09 08 07 06 05 1 2 3 4 5 6 7

LIBRARY OF CONGRESS CATALOGING-IN-PUBLICATION DATA

Anaya, Rudolfo A.
Jemez Spring / Rudolfo Anaya.
p. cm.
ISBN 0-8263-3684-1 (Cloth : alk. paper)
1. Baca, Sonny (Fictitious character)—Fiction. 2. Private investigators—New Mexico—Fiction. 3. Terrorism—Prevention—Fiction. 4. Albuquerque (N.M.)—Fiction. 5. Mexican Americans—Fiction. 6. Spiritual life—Fiction. I. Title.
PS3551.N27J46 2005
813'.54–dc22

2004020729

Book design and type composition by Kathleen Sparkes
This book is typeset using the Centaur family
body type is Centaur 13/15
display type is Decotura

Jemez Spring *completes Sonny's*
adventures through the four seasons.
For all the faithful who waited
for the quartet to be done,
this is for you.
An abrazo of love.

Who is worthy to open the book
and to loose the seals thereof?

~ Revelations 5:2 ~

1 »

Do dogs dream?

Sonny awakened slowly, opening his right eye first, then the left. He stretched like a rubber band until every nerve and muscle twanged. His vertebrae cracked and he relaxed back into the warm blankets.

Beside him, Chica stirred.

Do dogs dream?

That's the question, Sonny thought. He yawned and looked at the light filtering through the window.

The denizens of the City Future weren't discussing the depressed economy, terrorism, Iraq, tapping the Rio Grande for water, the silvery minnow, drought and fires, or politics. For weeks now the regulars at Rita's Cocina had tossed the dog question back and forth. The discussions had grown heated, some arguing yes and others adamantly denying it.

Sonny rubbed his eyes and looked at his watch. Dead battery.

I dream therefore I am, he thought. In last night's dream he had only one eye, like Cyclops. A one-eyed man lived in ordinary time, like Polyphemus. Odysseus had blinded the giant and the poor

Cyclops ran out of his cave, crying I am blinded! Noman has blinded me! Chingao! Noman has blinded me!

Sonny had taught the Greek myths to his literature classes at Valley High. That seemed ages ago. He always acted out the part, working like hell to get their interest. But the ancient Greek stories were far removed from the memory of the land-locked Chicanos of the valley where the phrase *we sail with the tide* had never been heard. So he told them the cuentos his grandfather had taught him, incorporating them into New Mexico history. The history of la gente was embedded in the oral tradition, but it had to be mined if one was to know the ways of the ancestors.

The teachers were alchemists, turning raw material into gold, but they had to compete with teenage interests: cars, video games, rap music, after-school jobs, family troubles. And hormones.

"I was a good teacher," he said to Chica, rubbing the head of his one-eyed dachshund. Raven's demons had scratched out her left eye. So much loss in that winter-solstice nightmare where Raven killed don Eliseo.

For the past three months Sonny had been reading don Eliseo's books. He couldn't sleep, so he read till two or three in the morning, and the more he read the more he understood that ordinary people go through life thinking they see, but what they're seeing is only the surface of things. The trick was to see beneath observed reality, and for that one needed to develop a new kind of sight.

"The Egyptians painted the all-seeing eye on their temple walls," he said to Chica. "Horus had one eye cut out by his uncle Seth. Seth had killed Osiris, the Ruler of Eternity, as the ancient Egyptians called him. It was the eye of Horus that restored Osiris to life. A lot of powerful magic there."

Seth cut Osiris into pieces and threw him in the Nile. Isis and her sister had brought Osiris back to life; that is, they gathered the dismembered body and sewed it together. The first mummy. One thing was missing. His penis. The organ had been thrown into the Nile where a goldfish ate it. Centuries later, a poet Sonny knew wrote that the missing organ had washed up on the banks of the Rio Grande. History belonged to those who wrote its poetry.

So many allusions to sight in the old stories, he thought, and still, most of us go through life half asleep, one-eyed men, tuertos searching for the truth, a purpose, the meaning of life. Somnambulant, we stumble down the road, unto the burning sheets of the malpais. Unconscious. Why?

If you are unconscious you feel less pain, he thought.

Yeah, that's it, we don't want to feel the pain. A man can get along with one good eye, lead the ordinary life of Polyphemus, until along comes Odysseus and drives a stake through it.

Bile rose in his mouth. Raven had driven a stake through his heart.

"Maybe I opened a few eyes," Sonny whispered, thinking nostalgically of his teaching days at Valley High.

But the classroom was confining, so he quit and learned PI work from Manuel López. He liked the independence.

All seemed normal until he moved to La Paz Lane and met don Eliseo. The old man became a mentor. The bond between them grew strong as the old man taught Sonny how to walk in the dream world. The world of the shaman.

Chica shook off her covers, stretched, and yawned.

"You know, don't you Chica?"

The small dachshund had followed him into that fateful winter-solstice nightmare where she lost her eye.

Did his dream become hers?

I dream therefore I am. People in deep comas continued to dream. Death came when one could no longer dream. But what if, as the Bard asked, the dead also dream? There's the rub. La vida es un sueño y los sueños sueño son. Life is a dream and on the other side waits another dream. Maybe?

Do dogs dream?

Several weeks ago Sonny was having a drink at Sal's Bar—actually he was sipping on a Pepsi—and taking a ribbing from some of his

North Valley amigos, weekend cowboys who once a month gathered at Sondra's Magic Acres stable to ride along the river bosque on borrowed horses. Reliving the Old West. Pretending to trail ride. They spent more time downing beers than riding. Chicano male bonding.

Quite innocently, Sonny had said, "My dog dreams."

The amigos knew Sonny had been depressed lately, but claiming his dog dreamed was too much. An argument ensued, the staunch Catholics in the group protesting against dreaming dogs. After all, a dog cannot recite the Nicene Creed.

"It's, 'I believe in God,' not 'dog'!" Mike challenged.

Sonny shrugged. What did Mike know? He was from Tucumcari.

"Yeah, d-o-g is not g-o-d," Vivián, the attorney in the group, added.

Anagram madness. A shouting match broke out between those who agreed that dogs could dream and those who said no. Two off-duty Bernalillo County sheriffs hustled them all out of the bar. The "dogs don't dream" amigos hadn't spoken to Sonny since. The innocent comment had taken on serious proportions.

The story was then spread by the barmaid, a woman of philosophical bent who used to teach Shakespeare at the university, an aficionada of Lone Star beer. She told the story to her customers and it spread along the valley like an unchecked virus. Suddenly conversations erupted into arguments, shouting into fisticuffs, and friendships ended.

The debate, which soon became known as the Great Dog Dream Debate, spread into the neighborhoods, into the restaurants, into city hall, into the schools.

An Alameda Elementary School teacher invited Sonny to her class. The students fell in love with Chica, the dreaming dog. The dachshund became the poster dog of the Dogs Dream camp. The following day a group of Dogs Don't Dream parents boycotted the school, pulling their children from classes. Sonny became persona non grata to a small camp of anti-dog-dream neoconservatives.

In the meantime, scientists at Sandia Laboratories recorded a rise in the decibel rate over the city. A long mantra-like hum had settled over Alburquerque. *Zaaaaaaaaaaa uuuuuuuummmm,* something akin to a Buddhist chant. In some of the barrios the hum became *aaaaala, alaaaatuya, daaaaale chingasooooos.*

The hum seeped into homes, inciting family arguments. The city libraries reported a run on dog books, people trying to figure out which came first: the dream or the dog. The police department reported a surge of fender benders. DWI's rose; so did divorces.

The metaphysical argument invaded classes at the University of New Mexico, where just before spring break the philosophy department sponsored a symposium. If it were proven that dogs did indeed dream then the entire history of western civilization might have to be rewritten.

It didn't get that far. Baptist students on campus boycotted the lectures, claiming that, like the Harry Potter books, dogs dreaming were the work of the devil. But what if the dog is baptized, fully submerged? an innocent voice had asked, a sylph sitting at the back of the room, and the debate took on a Reformation frenzy.

Dogs were like women, the fundamentalists argued, meant to serve the master. On this we agree with the Taliban: the man is the head of the household. Then the feminists on campus boycotted the boycott, shoving and pushing broke out at the picket lines, and the university cops had to break up the confrontation.

Recalling the events, Sonny slipped back into that sleep of the just-barely-awake, until a hullabaloo of crows, raucously cawing and crying as they ripped through his garbage can, roused Chica. She tossed off her blanket and, barking furiously, ran through the kitchen and out her dog door to challenge the birds.

Flocks of crows invaded the valley every winter. By day they scavenged in back yards and at the city landfill; by night they roosted in the cottonwoods of the river bosque.

The morning sun had just cleared Sandia Crest, filling the Rio Grande Valley with a golden hue, the same aura that often shines on Jerusalem, a sheen on Temple Mount.

Last night the crescent moon, the Water Carrier moon of the spring equinox, a goddess to lovers of long ago, a bowl moon to New Mexicans, had tipped and spilled its contents, dusting the Sandia Mountain with a thin coat of snow. In the valley the spray had fallen as a holy mist that barely dampened the tired but awakening earth.

Sonny blinked and looked at the east window. He kept the curtains slightly parted so a slice of sunlight landed on his bedroom wall, a crude calendar marking the movement of the seasons, from one solstice to the next.

Just like the sun calendar at Chaco Canyon, don Eliseo once pointed out. Here is the light on December 21, here June 21. In between, sacred space, life unraveling, our days on earth, and in March the spring equinox, time of earth's renewal. Remember, time on the clock means little. It moves in a line. The time that encircles you is the time that provides a center. The soul is like an antenna, gathering the unity of cosmic time.

The old man had been a friend of the Pueblo Indian people, attending many of the dances and ceremonies. Don Eliseo had taught Sonny how to construct his dreams, as one would tell a story or act in a play. Sonny learned he was a dream person, one who could create his dreams and play a role in them.

If I dream a butterfly, I am that butterfly. If I dream a dog dreaming, I am that dog dreaming. If the dog dreams me then I am in that reality and not this.

One had to be master of the dream if he were to understand the message inherent in the dramas that unfolded in the unconscious, that realm so deep in the psyche that only its images gave hints of its geography. The ancients knew this. It was written on the walls of Karnak, etched on the petrogylphs all over the Southwest.

Being an actor in the dream was the only way to stop Raven and his mad plan. Raven was also a dream person. That's why he was dangerous. If he controlled your dream, he could drown you in the chaos that was his nature.

So, dreams had to be opened, as we open our eyes after sleep. Dreams not brought into the light remained gook, troublesome dark stuff, detritus floating in the cosmic waters from which the first consciousness sprang, those first retinal cells responding to light.

But any damn psychologist knows that, Raven had once cursed. He didn't like their ilk peering into his psychic space.

The trick was to participate in your dream as if you were the main actor. A person who could create his own dreams was a brujo, a shaman. Unfortunately, the world at the beginning of the twenty-first century no longer believed in the role of the shaman. Such persons were suspect, labeled witches or druids, shunned, set apart from their fellow human beings, ostracized.

Sonny didn't care about the labels, but he did wonder if he wanted to enter the dream world again. Going into Raven's dream had cost don Eliseo his life. They had gone looking for Rita's unborn child. Sonny believed that Raven had caused Rita's miscarriage. And during the past few months he further convinced himself that Raven somehow kept the soul of Rita's child a prisoner.

He swore he had seen the soul of his unborn child in Raven's nightmare. He was sure the light he saw shining was the soul of Rita's baby. Raven had said as much. For three months all Sonny could think about was how to rescue the unborn child from Raven's dark circle.

He knew the miscarriage had put dread in Rita's heart. They had struggled through the winter, nurturing Rita with the remedies Lorenza prescribed, herbal teas from China, osha from Taos, massages, anything that would ease the loss. And they worked long hours at Rita's restaurant, serving meals to the working people of the North Valley.

In work they found some respite, but at the end of each day Sonny would drive her home, kiss her goodnight, then return alone to his apartment. Rita was still grieving.

He knew she needed time to recuperate.

"I appreciate what you do," she had told him. "Really. Having you at the cafe is more than . . . well, it means the world to me. I'm not afraid to be alone at night. It's just something I need to do. Give me time."

So Sonny waited, and three months later they were both stronger. She laughed and teased him more often. "Any day now," she had whispered yesterday.

"Any day now," Sonny muttered, jumping out of bed, hoping a shower would wash away the night's images. He had seen a man drowning in a large tank that resembled a baptistry.

Wish I could just flush bad memories down the toilet, he thought, or wash them away in a hot shower.

But what was engraved in the soul was eternal. And Memoria was a tough old dame. She bedded in the cells of the body and just lay there forever, awakening at the oddest times and flooding the mind with the damnedest memories.

Memoria also lived in the petroglyphs scratched into the volcanic boulders on the West Mesa escarpment. The ancient symbols were the memory of the Anasazi. A few of the Pueblo elders whispered stories. One glyph, they said, was carved on a boulder called the Zia Stone. That sacred symbol was a unifying sign that would reveal the mystery of the universe, the meaning of life. It had been given to the ancestors long ago.

Searching for the Zia Stone, Sonny and don Eliseo had explored ancient Anasazi haunts in the windswept mesas and canyons of the state. Like penitents searching for a holy sign in gothic cathedrals, they sought the glyph that held the answer to life, a unifying theory of the universe.

Learn to enter the dream, don Eliseo said, and Sonny had followed the old man into the dream world. He became a winter shaman, a brujo who could construct his dreams. And to what end? To meet Raven. He was always there, always waiting.

"Revenge," Sonny whispered, flushing the toilet. "I want my revenge. I will find a way—"

The struggle with Raven had gone on too long. Maybe don

Eliseo was wrong. Maybe a well-placed bullet between the eyes would kill the bastard. What the hell is a dream good for if I go there only to meet my shadow?

He showered, toweled himself dry, and shaved. He put on a pair of freshly pressed jeans and a blue cowboy shirt, still thinking of revenge.

Don Eliseo appeared, as he often did when Sonny's thoughts stampeded.

Won't do you any good, the old man said.

You keep saying that, Sonny replied. Why?

When your thoughts are confused Raven has the upper hand.

I can take care of Raven! Sonny retorted. I know what he wants. The Zia medallion. I'll tempt him. Hold it out to him, then shoot him—

Damn it, Sonny! the old man shouted. There you go! You're not thinking straight. You can't kill him with a bullet!

"I'll find a way," Sonny said aloud, pulling on his well-worn boots.

No time to shine them, he thought, slipping the Zia medallion around his neck, the gold medal engraved with the Sun symbol, an amulet as magical as the precious stone once suspended from Abraham's neck. Mojo power.

The medallion was Sonny's now. There had been no contact with Raven the past three months.

He walked into the kitchen, started the morning coffee, fed Chica, and was pouring himself his first cup when his cell phone rang. Something told him it was no good; still, he answered it.

"Sonny Baca?"

"Yeah."

"Augie. Augie Martínez, state police."

Augie, Augememnon Martínez, son of an influential Santa Fe politico who on a cruise of the Greek isles fell in love with a dazzling Greek beauty, brought her home, and took her as his wife. He retired from politics, raised goats in Nambe, sold goat cheese, and years later died, leaving behind his wife and a bunch of kids, restless creatures who fled home as soon as they realized there were oceans to cross.

The mother, too, grew restless, the people of Nambe said, because she missed the sound of the surf, the sun setting on the sea. She took to wandering the hills around Nambe, a gypsy with green eyes, always pushing the herd of goats just over the next hill, until one day she didn't return.

Only Augie remained on the wind-scarred hills of the Española valley. He finished school and joined the state cops, seeking some stability in the corps, or perhaps seeking his mother, who began to appear in the oral tradition of la gente of the Nambe valley as La Llorona, the crying woman. Did she cry for her children or for the sound of the sea?

"I've got a homicide on my hands—"

Sonny filled his cup of coffee and waited. In his dream a body was floating in dark, swirling water.

"Who?"

"The governor—"

"Dead?"

"Yes."

"Where?"

"Jemez Springs. Someone drowned him in a tub at the Bath House."

"Why call me?"

"We found black feathers . . ."

The hair on Sonny's neck prickled. A shiver passed through his body. Don Eliseo was right! He had been too confused to figure it out. Equinox! Raven was back!

"Raven," he whispered.

"That's what we figure. You haven't heard the news?"

"No," Sonny answered, turning on the small TV set on the table. The picture slowly solidified into the blurry image of Dick Knipfing reporting from the Jemez Springs plaza.

"We have a big mess on our hands," Augie continued. "The

governor's dead and somebody planted a bomb up on the mountain. It's a weird contraption but the lab boys from Los Alamos say it's radioactive. The shit has hit the fan, Sonny."

A bomb, and the feds knew Raven was in possession of a plutonium pit. But he had lain low during the past three months. Now he was out of hiding.

"I can't discuss it on the phone. Fucking news media is everywhere. The chief wants you. You know Raven better than anyone else—"

"Where are you now?" Sonny asked.

"I'm in Jemez Springs, interrogating people. The chief wants you to take a look at the bomb."

Why? Sonny thought. That didn't make sense. Anytime Raven left feathers at the scene of a crime, he was setting a trap. Raven wasn't going to be up on the mountain, he was going to be around the corner. But where?

"Let the Los Alamos boys handle the bomb," Sonny said.

"They will, but we need you," Augie insisted.

"Sorry," Sonny replied, "I don't think Raven would leave the feathers and stick around." He offed the phone. So Raven was back. And he had planted a bomb. Why on the Jemez mountain?

To get you there, the old man said.

Yeah, Sonny thought. Something big was going down in Jemez Springs. The faces of the reporters on the old TV set looked concerned. The Alburquerque news hounds were hot on the unfolding events.

He rose and went to the window. March was already drawing the first green shoots out of winter's compost, hyacinth borders in pink and deep purple, apricot blossoms, yellow jonquils, the lime-green seeds of the elm trees, sienna-red cottonwood buds, swollen with promise.

Raven lived in the hot compost of the unconscious, because Raven's world was mythic, levels and circles deeper than Dante's inferno, dark epicycles where he composed his stories, images with which he tortured the unwary. To understand Raven one had to go into his world, a world so deep in the psyche a one-eyed man might get lost. That was the rub. The dream that revealed the dark images could liberate, or destroy the dreamer.

There was a saving grace. In the dream world everyone had friends, allies who appeared in all sorts of disguises, bringing messages from that hidden glob of memory that has been passed down since mother nature first conceived of a cell that could gather light. *Primal images,* the psychiatrists called them. Messages in the cells. The trick was to bring those images into the light of day. The dark shadows of the soul had to be birthed into the world. Every man, woman, and child was a creator who could build soul from the psyche's darkness. Every dog?

So he's back and he's planted a bomb on my mountain. Maybe he really is up there. Maybe today's the day we end this struggle that has gone on too long.

He closed his eyes and leaned over the table.

"All I want is to marry Rita, help her at the restaurant. I want to take care of her . . ."

But deep in his guts revenge seethed. He knew he would be going after Raven. It could be no other way.

He stood at the window, allowing the warm rays of the sun to penetrate him. Cupping his hands he held the light, let it shine as deep into his soul as possible. Then he felt what he hadn't felt since the winter solstice. Something palpable in the light rays, the Lords and Ladies of the Light entering his soul.

"Señores y Señoras de la Luz, bless all of life. Bless the children of Iraq, Afghanistan, Palestine, Africa, Colombia, our barrios. Bless the sick, those in prison, those who need food. Bless the dead governor . . ."

He turned, offering the light in the four sacred directions, scattering the light cupped in his hands and wishing for himself only clarity of soul.

Like most rituals, the prayer had become routine, but today the fingers of light cut to his heart. He heard music, and he trembled. The essence of sunlight passed through his body like an electric current. The brilliant Lords and Ladies of the Light touched him, entered him, and for a moment a clarity beyond the light revealed itself, leaving him dazed.

He looked out the window and squinted.

One eye open.

2

He picked up the dreamcatcher, his weapon of power, the round spider-webbed instrument with a juniper handle. Because of the handle it could be mistaken for a tennis racket, but the netting had a hole in the middle for bad dreams to pass through and disappear. Good dreams were caught in the web and thus retained in the memory of the dreamcatcher's owner.

Don Eliseo had constructed the shaman weapon, and Sonny used it to fight Raven during the winter-solstice dream, a nightmare really, in which he forced himself into Raven's evil circle, the misty chaos where dark, fiendish bird-like demons, or vampires, kept watch, horrendous creatures who had scratched out Chica's eye.

Only don Eliseo's final sacrificial act had saved Sonny from being swept into Raven's chaos, that river of a thousand currents from which there is small hope of return. Sonny struck Raven with the dreamcatcher, making him disappear through the hole in the web into the nebulous undercurrent that is always the essence and energy of the dream—or the nightmare.

Was chaos a dark, raging river, a Lethe that emptied into a stagnant lake where all was forgotten? Oblivion, the lake at the murky bottom where thoughts of home did not exist. Or was chaos the very essence of a person's psyche, a deep, undefined energy that gave rise to the images of dreams and nightmares, a place that could be called the unconscious unconscious? A geography of the mind not yet mapped? If there was a river of life, was there also a river of dreams? A river called chaos?

But Raven, everyone knew by now, could not be killed. Not even the power of the dreamcatcher could dissipate that terrible and wondrous energy. He wouldn't stay away forever. He was back.

Good, Sonny thought as he walked outside. I've been waiting. Chica followed at his heels.

Take a jacket, Rita would say. She had given him a colorful Chimayó jacket, which he kept in a plastic bag tucked behind the truck seat. He wore it for special occasions. Today his well-worn denim jacket would do.

Last night's weather front had dropped a light snow on the high peaks of the Jemez and Sangre de Cristo mountains. The Cloud People had danced into northern New Mexico, scattering the scant moisture, passing quickly over the mountaintops, creating hope in the hearts of the Jemez Pueblo farmers. The entire region was years into a severe drought. Forest fires had eaten away at Arizona and Colorado, fires that a few years back had nearly destroyed Los Alamos. As summer progressed the fires flared up in the Northwest. It would take many snow and rain storms to break the drought.

In the heart of the sky, a skinny Water Carrier moon shone pale, a sliver that resembled a bowl. It had tipped and rained its meager contents on the dry earth.

It was time for cleaning the acequias, time for plowing and readying the fields. In a few weeks the river water would be diverted into the irrigation ditches. In Jemez Springs Melvin would be pruning his apple trees.

Over Alburquerque the thin clouds that scudded across the vernal equinox dawn would dissipate, winging their way over the Sandias like raggedy old women. The afternoon would warm up nicely.

Sonny sniffed the air, spermy and spongy with the aroma of the thawing earth, the sweet smell of cedar burning in someone's wood stove, mixing with the aroma of tortillas baking on a hot comal. Overhead, the call of crows in the bare cottonwood trees mixed with the chatter of children gathered at the bus stop.

A few hardy old men, Sonny's North Valley vecinos, had arisen with the sun to look at their gardens and dream of April planting.

These old-timers still planted backyard gardens, a small milpa of corn here, a chile plot there, tomato vines and calabacita plants. But for the most part Frank Dominic's prediction had come true: the once fertile valley was being taken over by developers who subdivided the land into lots that sold at a premium. People with money were building large adobe mansions on the last of the valley's agricultural fields.

A way of life was dying for the old Hispanos of the valley. The fertile lands the Españoles and Mexicanos had settled during those terribly cold years at the end of the sixteenth century now belonged to people who did not know the land's history.

Across the street there was a For Sale sign in front of don Eliseo's home. His sons had come a few days after the old man's death, a real estate agent trailing along. Elysium Realty—a lot in heaven. The old rambling adobe had been in the Romero family for generations. Now it and the old man's cornfield were up for sale.

What did I tell you, Sonny, the old man said, the kids don't care about raising corn anymore.

Sonny sighed. "I know."

Chica whined, perked her ears, and looked lovingly at her master.

"Don Eliseo," Sonny said, reassuring her.

She understood that he talked to the spirit of the old man. Sonny had been reading late one night when a gust of wind blew the door open and in walked don Eliseo. Chica whined. She sensed the spirit in the room. She turned and saw Sonny's book drop from his hands.

"You?" he cried.

For tense moments Sonny seemed frozen, staring into a dark

space, or at the shadows cast by the window's curtains stirring in the cold breeze. Was it a dream?

Who were you expecting, the old man answered, the Lone Ranger? You better close the door, it's blowing outside. March wind.

Sonny stood and closed the door. In a trembling voice he said, "I didn't know—"

Chica whined again. She understood whatever the spirit said was audible only to her master.

Then Sonny sat down, and for hours he seemed to be listening intently to the sound of the wind raging outside. Finally he fell asleep on the chair, and he slept soundly, the first time in a long time.

So the spirit of the old man was accepted by both Sonny and the dog. It was a comforting appearance, for it helped settle the restless energy that had consumed Sonny. Spending the nights alone was not good for him. He read books until the early hours of the mornings, devouring the many volumes, searching for the revelations the past had once offered seekers after truth.

Sonny placed the dreamcatcher on the rifle rack and called his bilingual dog. "Anda, vamos."

Chica barked and eagerly scooted into the truck and up into the seat. This was the life, riding shotgun with the master, sniffing the wind, her brown dachshund ears flaring back like sails, barking at neighborhood dogs as they drove into the day's adventure.

Sonny looked down the street. Yes, change had come to the valley. Soon the small farms would be gone, the old people would die. La Paz Lane, where Sonny had lived the past four years, would be a memory.

Todo se acaba.

Sí, todo se acaba.

It wasn't just the city, it was the entire region. Up for sale. The Southwest was the fastest growing region in the country. Sun. Desert air. Golfing in January. Phoenix was a nightmare in a once-pristine desert, Tucson followed suit, Las Vegas burgeoned like a fat whore, and the Las Cruces/El Paso/Juárez border city kept expanding across sand dunes. All would run out of water in a few years.

Along the Rio Grande, it was the same story. The fragile land was bulldozed, deep wells were drilled to satisfy the needs of a growing population, and the river was diverted for the city to use. The silvery minnow swam toward its extinction.

We need water! the developers cried, and deals were cut in city hall to satisfy their thirst.

Water became the gold of the desert, and he who controlled the supply could make the rules.

In Alburquerque expensive homes stretched up the slope of the Sandias; on the west side of the river, tract homes spread nearly as far as the Rio Puerco. Never mind there was a water shortage and the aquifer that fed the city was drying up. The city was on a roll, burgeoning with growth, vying for new business ventures, drunk with a vision of itself as a City with a Future.

Thank God for the Indian Pueblos, Sonny said. They'll keep the city hemmed in. They can't build on Sandia and Isleta land.

Don't believe it, the old man replied.

The Pueblos won't let the developers in, Sonny insisted.

Yeah, what about the casinos? Las Vegas in your back yard. Five-star hotels, fine dining, All Pro golf courses. Money talks; those who want to hang on to the old ways walk.

Where will it stop? Sonny wondered, starting his truck and turning on the radio. Something big was happening in Jemez Springs, the Spanish-language station announced between corridos, the songs that told the stories of the Mexicanos. But not a word on the governor's demise.

Sonny drove down La Paz Lane. He waved to Toto and Concha, who were out raking leaves, readying her garden for planting.

Chica barked in greeting.

"Hey, Sonny! How's it hanging?" Concha called.

"ATM!" Sonny called back.

"Que Dios te bendiga! Say hi to Rita."

"I will. Don't work too hard."

"Hey, Sonny! How's Chica?"

"Still dreaming," Sonny called back.

"Atta boy, cowboy! Ten-four!"

Sonny laughed. Retired neighbors, octogenarians, still clinging to their homes, but when their time on earth was finished everything would change, their culture and the culture of their ancestors would die.

Was the governor's death related to the ominous feeling in the air? Spring should be a time of renewal, but for life to sprout, there first had to be death. But the dead governor was no Christ.

You got that right, the old man said. Like most politicians he's a product of genetic drift. Some weird gene in their DNA makes them do what they do.

Genetic drift, Sonny repeated. Maybe it's just a need for power.

Yes, the old man agreed. The world moves back and forth; now it's in our backyard. People migrate to the Rio Grande Valley. Clovis hunters left their spear points in Sandia Cave. Folsom Man. I read about them. Then the ancestors of the Pueblos came down from Chaco, etching glyphs on rocks, signs for the kachinas. And hidden somewhere in the boulders that dot the West Mesa escarpment, there lies hidden one large, magnificent rock: the Zia Stone.

A Sun Stone. A large meteorite on which the ancestors of the Pueblos carved a symbol of universal truth, a unifying sign of being and harmony. It holds the meaning of life. I tell you, Sonny, if bulldozers plow up the West Mesa they will bury the Zia Stone forever. We won't be able to connect the past to the future. You read about those al-cemistas. They were looking for the Zia Stone. In their own way.

In Europe the alchemists had searched for the formula that turned lead into gold, the dross matter of flesh into spirit. In the Americas the elders of the Anasazi had contemplated a unifying symbol that would unite organic and inorganic life, earth and cosmos, the universe dancing to one drumbeat.

Farther south the priests of Tula, of the Olmecs, and of the Mayas had recorded the movement of the moon and the sun, the epicycles of Venus, carving the flow of time into their calendars. Archeologists worked to decipher the symbols on the stelae, to tell the story of time, how it all begin, the ages of men. But a unifying symbol was missing; the Zia Stone was missing.

In order to dominate nature, man had stepped outside the great chain of being; he could no longer hear the music of the spheres. The new alchemists at Los Alamos National Labs were too busy converting plutonium into bombs. Soul and spirit were split apart, bombarded in vacuum chambers, reduced to quantum particles.

Quantum mechanics had forgotten that a quantum spirit moved in the material world, atoms seethed with activity, and the energy itself was the consciousness of the universe.

Sonny knew his history. He knew the Pueblos had smelled the Spanish coming. Bearded Spanish and Mexican men trudging up the Rio Grande in 1540, finally settling near Española in 1598, farming the Sangre de Cristo valleys, raising sheep. Pastores spreading east to the Llano Estacado, high into the sierras for summer pastures, hundreds of thousands of sheep. The Pueblos and the Navajo learned to eat mutton.

That was their first mistake. Then they learned to weave wool and make blankets. They learned to use iron pots and knives. That did it. Learn to use somebody else's tools and your way of life will change forever. Learn their language and your kids grow fat and lazy, your women learn wild dances and gamble too much at the casinos. The men will leave the land, leave the old ways. Once you're on the Booze Way you might as well call it quits. The beauty given to you by the ancestors will die.

But history doesn't take sides, and some would say adapting to new ways was the way to survive.

Survival was the theme of the land. The Anglos arrived and the crushing wheel of change rolled on. A new argot filled the air, which to the Nuevomexicanos might as well have been Greek, but to survive they had to learn the new gobbledygook. Learned to say "jalo," "tank you," "how mush," "haw-r-ju," "see you later alligator."

New laws came, new courts, new police, and the land slipped from one hand to another, and the way was lost.

Sonny remembered, and he knew Memoria could sometimes be a cruel comadre.

Change is constant, he thought. "And Raven has returned."

Could he really enjoy the crisp spring air, the smell of compost, the apricot and peach trees blooming with the fragrance of a woman awakening to love, clothed in robes of luminous pink, soul flowers born of the bud's flesh. Tall lilac bushes shrouded with regal purple blossoms. In one yard a fragile redbud tree.

Along the river stood the towering cottonwoods, unleafed but with their buds preparing to burst. And Clyde Tingley's elms, lime green with seeds, all in hosanna of spring. Dressing up.

But up in the Jemez Mountains, in the little magical village of Jemez Springs, the governor lay dead, the image Sonny saw in the dream. But why would Raven kill the governor? That was the question of the day.

The parking lot of Rita's Cocina was full so Sonny drove around to the back. Entering the kitchen always provoked hunger pangs, a burst of saliva. He stopped and sniffed, allowing his coyote sense of smell to take in the aromas. Butter melting on hot tortillas, warm and crisp, piled high around plates of huevos rancheros, crisp bacon sizzling on the griddle, curling next to the one-eyed eggs, sunny side up, crackling and sputtering, exuding the protein smell of life. The rich, exotic smell of the Colombian coffee that Rita loved. Papas fritas, pots of just-cooked beans that melted in one's mouth, carne adovada, and red chile—ah, red chile de ristra, the Crimson Queen. The New Mexicans splashed chile colorado on everything, even on Thanksgiving turkeys and Christmas hams.

Comida sin chile no es comida. His mouth watered.

"Hey, Sonny," Diego called, leaning over the hot stove. "How's it going, bro?"

"Good," Sonny replied.

"Listen, I got an idea. You know they say the country's getting too fat. Pues, we have some Chicano heavyweights. Gordos. So why not go all the way?"

Sonny listened. Diego always had a new scheme.

"Chicano Sumo wrestlers! We feed them extra tortillas, menudo, chicharrón burritos, and we go all the way with panzones. Hey, we can compete with the Japanese!"

Sonny laughed and gave his friend a high five. "Porque no?"

"Pues, you know what César Chávez said: Sí Se Puede."

Diego's wife, Marta, greeted Sonny with a smile and a "buenos días" as she waltzed past him, holding a tray of food above her head.

Chicano Sumo wrestlers, Sonny thought. Why not?

From the dishwasher Cyber called, "Hey Sonny, guess what? I'm thinking of joining the circus."

"Cool."

Rita appeared. She greeted Sonny with a kiss and a smile.

"He saw Cirque du Soleil on TV," she said.

"Yeah, Circo de Slow-lay," Cyber repeated.

"Du," Sonny corrected.

"Tú?"

"No, du."

"Me?"

"Sí, tú. Say 'du.'"

"Do what?"

"Cirque du Soleil."

"Yeah, circo de slow-lay."

"Not *de,* du."

"Do what?"

"Who's on first?" Sonny said and let it go.

Rita smiled. "I'm glad to see you," she said and picked up Chica.

"Hey, me too," Sonny replied.

A finely crafted silver chain hung around her neck. It held an oval silver pendant that embraced a glowing azure stone, sky-blue lapis, so polished Sonny could see his reflection in the stone.

On her wrist hung seven silver bracelets, each etched with signs of the zodiac, each blessed on a special saint's day, each hinting at a power in nature, an animal spirit.

Her eyes glistened with the water of life.

"Did you sleep?" she asked.

He looked into her eyes, windows into her soul. He felt complete when she gazed at him in the quiet moments of their love.

In another time, another culture, she would have been Ishtar, the Akkadian goddess of love. Here she was the center of his Zia Sun universe, a hard-working businesswoman with a kind and loving soul.

I'll be poetic, he thought, woo her with all the beautiful words ever written by the poets of the world, especially the poets of India who extol the woman's body as a temple.

Or Hamlet, he thought. Soft you, now, the fair Ophelia, beneath the boughs of a purple flowering tamarisk, on the banks of the quiet flowing Rio Grande, I will love you . . .

He ran his tongue over his lips. Her kiss had left a tinge of her red chile con carne.

"You taste good," he said, thinking maybe the undiscovered petroglyph, the Zia Stone of ancient lore, was really the heart of the beloved, and the symbol written on it was her name. One only had to open the third eye to see it, the wisdom of gnosis, the Hindu third eye.

In the dining area the old jukebox that held only fifties records blared out Little Richard's "Good Golly Miss Molly."

"You look beautiful," he said.

He put his arms around her. An erotic fragrance, her own particular woman perfume that he knew so well, or a feeling, or something he couldn't identify, passed from her to him, and he held her for a fleeting moment in the aromas of the kitchen, because with Rita sex and food often came together. Arousal could be a steaming plate of huevos rancheros for breakfast, a Navajo taco or enchiladas for lunch, an organic salad for dinner, a bowl of menudo spiked with hot red chile, onions, and oregano on Sunday mornings.

"Sorry. I slept late."

"You need the rest, mijito," she whispered. "By the way, the mayor's here. There's something going on at Jemez. Que pasa?"

Sonny shrugged.

"They called you."

"Yes."

"It's Raven, isn't it?" She knit her brow.

He nodded. He couldn't just pretend he didn't know the way into the dream world, he couldn't just wish it away. Once the gift of the shaman was there, it just was. He might sit for years helping her in the restaurant, cook menudo from his mother's recipe, man the cash register, visit with the customers he knew so well—all North Valley friends. He would pretend normalcy, but sooner or later the phone would ring, a breeze would stir, a crow would call from a telephone pole, a message would come for the winter shaman and he would have to go. She knew that.

"What about the meeting in Algodones?"

"I might get back in time."

A group of Pueblo men intent on preserving their water rights had asked Sonny to join them in Algodones. The newspapers had labeled them Green Indians because of their pro-environmental stand. All they really wanted to do was protect their ancient water rights. Those rights, once taken for granted and protected by codices going back to the Spanish entrada into New Mexico, were under attack.

"I love you," she whispered. "Whatever the day holds."

"I love you. My fair Ophelia," he whispered.

She smiled. "That's a sweet thing to say."

"I mean it."

"I know, but doesn't Ophelia go crazy and drown herself?"

He blushed and looked down at his feet. His boots needed a shine.

"Maybe you could be my Helen of Troy."

"Oh no. She was too beautiful. Besides, she left her husband for Paris. I would never leave you, mi amor." She touched his cheek.

"Hey, what if I said you're my chile and beans."

"I like that best," she replied. "Now to work. Lorenza's not here today. She called early this morning. She might not return in time to attend the Algodones meeting."

"Where is she?"

"She went to Las Cruces to help a friend. A writer whose friends swear the image of Pedro Infante appeared on a tortilla. You know how Elvis appears, now it's Pedro. First he was spotted in El Paso, now in Las Cruces on a tortilla they were baking for their Pedro Infante Club party. We all have our spirits, que no?"

"Yeah, we do," Sonny agreed. "I'll take Chica."

"I'll fix you two a lunch."

"Great."

He wished they could cancel everything and spend the day together in Jemez Springs. But she had to be ready. Something fragile had broken in her during the miscarriage, and that would take time to mend.

She needs time, Lorenza had told him. Right now she's just dealing with the cafe, living on the surface of the world. Her love is still there, perhaps stronger than ever. You just be ready.

"I will be—"

Rita turned. "What?"

"Nothing. I love you."

She winked.

Sonny walked into the dining area, which was buzzing and crackling. Jemez Springs was the morning's conversation. What the hell was going on?

In a corner table sat the mayor, Fox, and a couple of his cronies from city hall, men who wore two faces.

Chicano activists called the mayor Fox because his favorite TV show were reruns of the *X-Files*. La plebe loved to nickname politicians. Once baptized the name stuck for life, and those who recognized the crafty man's politics said he played like a Zorro, so Fox it was.

Today the Fox was sniffing around Rita's Cocina.

The mayor looked at Sonny and signaled.

Yeah, Sonny thought, genetic drift. Now I'm caught in it.

3

Rita's Cocina was packed with an assortment of North Valley paisanos, including a chorus of retired elders. Los viejitos ate breakfast at Rita's then headed for the North Valley senior citizen center, their agora, to discuss the politics of the day. Today they would sit glued to the TV set, ignoring the primped-up, purple-haired comadres who tried to get them to play bingo. Instead the old codgers would watch the sketchy news they were getting from Jemez Springs. A terrorist plot in the air. They loved it. Any news was fodder for their plática.

Retired, bent, slurping their coffee, they talked, a continuous buzz, bees in a hive. "En aquellos tiempos la gente vivía en paz." "Hoy no sabe nada la plebe." "Chingaron bien a Saddam. Pulled down his statue. Nothing lasts." "You know, todo se acaba." "You got that right!"

Plática, the oral tradition of the forum, ancient as the Nuevomexicanos who first settled the Rio Grande Valley. In the shadow of the Sandia Mountain they had settled to farm, to raise sheep and kids, and to leave their bones in the penitente earth once their plática was done.

Plática was a cultural ritual, old as the Greeks at the agora, old as the Sumerians who told stories of the flood and the creation of first man and woman long before those stories were recorded by the Hebrews. Stories older than the telephone and TV. The oral tradition was alive, gone digital, buzzing through telephone wires and cell phone frequencies up and down the valley, from Taos down to Las Cruces and to Chihuahua. Down to el Valle de Tejas all the way to Brownsville where the river emptied into the gulf. Plática infused the poetic marrow of every community.

Sonny listened. The buzz roamed here and there, reminiscences of the way things used to be, world problems, the devil loose in the world, terrorism, Iraq and North Korea, the Santa Fe legislators spending their taxes, Social Security going broke, help with prescription drugs. And today, something happening in Jemez Springs.

They turned to look at Sonny.

"Buenos días te dé Dios, Sonny," one said. Ladino greetings.

"Cuidado con los dog dreams."

"Si los perros sueñan, entonces los gatos también."

"Gato dreams."

"Pussy dreams," chortled Clyde. "Ha, ha, ha." The oldest of the clan, rumored to be taking Viagra, at eighty.

"Entonces todo los animales sueñan."

"Entonces la vida es un sueño."

"I dream forty-year-old mamasotas," Clyde said, stroking his waxed mustache.

"Forty? They run you ragged, Clyde."

"La problema no son las mamasotas, la problema son los terrorists. Como lo que pasa en Jemez. What is it, Sonny?"

"Yeah, what's happening?"

"Pendejadas," Sonny answered.

"Bueno, que Dios te bendiga."

"By the way, Sonny," one touched his arm. "We can't remember the Spanish word for oar? Tú sabes, paddles. For a boat."

Sonny didn't know. The ancestors had been gone too long from the sea. They had no need for an oar in desert New Mexico. The words of the sea culture were forgotten, as the words of every culture are destined to be forgotten. And so they created a new language, Spanglish.

"You can say, 'se fue en el barco con paddles.'"

"Porque no."

"I want to know the Spanish word," the vecino insisted. "I'm writing a poem."

"I'll look it up in my Velasquez," Sonny promised.

"Gracias," they nodded and went on sipping their coffee as they talked, turning over and over the dog dream question.

Sonny paused to look around.

The cafe was packed with the workers of the City Future. Electricians on their way to wire a job. A mexicano crew of roofers, mostly men from Chihuahua, Sonny surmised, about the only workers that would do that hot, heavy work all day long. Plumbers working in the new North Valley mansions that kept sprouting like tumbleweeds. Drywall men, their pants covered with chalky dust. Painters in paint-splattered overalls, which if framed and hung on a wall would fetch de Kooning abstract art prices. A couple of Bernalillo sheriff's deputies, one a very nice-looking Chicana who smiled at Sonny. Sirena. They had attended Rio Grande High together, and Sonny had almost scored one night. Those were the heavy-duty hormone days of almost going all the way.

"Hi, Sonny," she said. "How's your dog?"

"Still barking," Sonny replied, returning her smile.

A few horsemen who kept stables along the river sat at a corner table, and by the window a smattering of the ubiquitous North Valley yuppie rich: attorneys, doctors, and businessmen and women who worked downtown. They ate huevos rancheros while they read the *Wall Street Journal.* Eating at Rita's Cocina was a shot of culture for the North Valley yuppies.

Republican immigrants, Sonny thought, sniffing the air, glancing at the blonde in blue who looked up and smiled.

From a corner table, a haggard-looking mayor signaled for Sonny.

Sonny sniffed again. There was no threat in the air, only the honest smells of hardworking people, paisanos. The yuppies acknowledged Sonny's presence as he walked toward the mayor's table. They knew about his exploits, considered him a hero for catching the mad scientist from Ukraine who had tried to build a nuclear weapon at Sandia Labs. And Sonny had started the "do dogs dream" controversy, and like all good baby-boomer professionals they thrived on controversy.

"Good morning, Mr. Baca," said the blonde. She was a big-shot attorney in the biggest law firm downtown. "Is this the famous dreaming dog?"

"That's her," Sonny replied.

"Howcuuuutydoggie, cutiecutiecutie. Here dogggieee." She threw Chica a piece of leftover tortilla from her plate. Chica looked disdainfully at the woman. I don't take scraps from the likes of you, she snapped.

"She already ate, thanks." Sonny moved on to the mayor's table.

Sonny knew Fox secretly supported Frank Dominic, the City Future's big tycoon who had set up a corporation to buy water rights in the state. Dominic's goal was to privatize the water rights of the entire Rio Grande Valley. The new czars weren't into oil, they were water despots. This was the same man who had proposed the city siphon off Rio Grande water, not for drinking, but to create a Venice in the city. He had a plan to build canals from Downtown to Old Town, a new image for the City Future, a casino on every corner.

"Hello, Fox," Sonny greeted the mayor.

"Sit down," Fox answered, scowling. He didn't like to be called Fox. He hadn't shaved in days. A random pattern of red chile spots adorned his tie.

"How's tricks?"

"I don't do tricks!" Fox replied.

Sonny sat and Marta delivered a cup of coffee and a steaming plate of huevos rancheros, the old-fashioned kind with blue corn flour tortillas, Rita's brand of beans flavored with chicos and her famous Nuevomexicano red chile con carne. Plenty of crisp hash browns on the side. Carbohydrates for the long day ahead.

Chica jumped up beside Sonny.

"This the dreaming dog?" Fox snarled as Sonny speared the two eggs so the yellow mixed into the beans and chile.

"Yeah. Chica Chicana. Wonder Dog. She can fly."

"Bullshit," Fox scoffed.

"You asked," Sonny shrugged, then smiled as he dug into the food, satisfying the enormous hunger he felt. He figured he had gained a few pounds since Christmas. No sex, so he was eating a lot. Making vicarious love to Rita through her comida. In the morning she was a spicy plate of huevos rancheros, enchiladas with refried beans at lunch. Hot tortillas at every meal.

He glanced at the cash register where she was ringing out the yuppie blonde. She smiled. Sonny returned the smile. Someday soon she would be ready. Like the Canadian geese and sandhill cranes flying north in February, love had to return to the North Valley, it just had to.

"...you have to tell me," the mayor was going on, "what the hell you mean dogs dream? You can't know. You can't get into the dog's head."

"She gets into mine," Sonny answered.

"Some of the city workers are betting their paychecks. Does she or doesn't she dream? Why don't we get a psychiatrist to check her out?"

Sonny frowned, looked at Chica then at Fox. A bureaucrat could run a city, but not dream. Fox was smart but he didn't know the invisible world of dreams. Fox had never been master of his own dream. Fox was no shaman.

"Do you dream, Chica?"

Chica barked and wagged her tail furiously.

"See?" Sonny burped, sipping Rita's rich coffee blend, better than Starbucks, and wiping up the carne adovada on his plate with a piece of tortilla.

"That's no answer! Let's test the dog."

"Not on your life!" Sonny petted Chica. The last thing he would do is put Chica through any dream exam. Her dreams were hers. "What's happening in Jemez?" he asked to change the subject.

Fox shrugged. "So you know."

Sonny nodded.

Fox leaned closer. "Remember the Bible, Sonny. There's a prophecy about the mountains. Because the enemy stands against you, even the ancient high places are in our possession. God speaks on the mountains, Sonny, and the only way to save them is to make a deal with the devil. Let us handle Raven."

Fox bared his teeth. Sonny drew back. Fox quoting the Bible was scary.

A paranoid prophet gets you nowhere, the old man told him once, because he doesn't even know he's paranoid. This, after all, was the Chinese Year of the Ram. The sign was stamped on Fox's forehead.

"How do you know it's Raven?"

"He contacted us. He wants to deal. I suggest you don't get in the way."

"What about the governor?" Sonny asked, baiting the mayor.

"Too bad," Fox replied, "but he was no dream man!" He handed his check to one of his cronies. "Did the FBI call you?"

Sonny shook his head. "State police."

"It figures. They know very little." He leaned closer and whispered. "Someone murdered the governor, but it's not Raven. It's a terrorist plot. It's big, Sonny. We have to proceed with caution, not muddy the waters. Raven can help us. In fact, we have a press conference scheduled at six at the Hispanic Cultural Center."

So, thought Sonny, Raven was already calling the shots. The bomb Augie mentioned was probably a hoax. To get him up on the mountain. Get him out of the city while he made his deals with the politicians. And both events were diversions. What Raven really wanted was to confuse, and in the confusion grab the Zia medallion.

"You better change your tie," Sonny suggested.

"Look, Sonny, it's not just politics I'm talking about. What happened to the governor is just the tip of the iceberg. If you get involved it's going to hit you like a bucket of—you know."

"You're saying I should stay out of it?"

Fox nodded. "Yeah, stay out of it. You don't want to mess with the big boys. My father used to say, the only words you'll never hear in New Mexico are *We sail with the tide.* You just missed your boat, Sonny."

Fox grinned, turned, and hurried out, followed by his flunkies.

Sonny burped again. Lordy, Lordy, a satisfying breakfast, but sitting with Fox had left a bad feeling in the air. It was rumored Fox and the governor were business partners with Dominic. Fox had taken Dominic's money when he ran for mayor, and if the governor was dead that left Fox in charge of the henhouse, or the water house. If Fox didn't want him involved in the governor's murder, that was all the more reason to get involved.

He's no dream man, Fox had said. A dead governor can dream no more. Did they want the governor out of the way?

His cell phone buzzed and Sonny answered.

"Sonny, Augie. Where are you?"

"Having breakfast."

"You were there when Raven infiltrated Los Alamos Labs."

Yes. Raven had waltzed into the labs, or flown in like a brujo. He had stolen a plutonium pit from under the nose of Los Alamos security.

"You know the core of a nuclear weapon is still missing. So what if Raven sold it to Al Qaeda?"

Sonny paused. Raven would form alliances with anyone out to create panic.

"Don't believe me? What if I told you I have an Al Qaeda operative prisoner?"

"You have an Al Qaeda agent?" Sonny repeated. That got his attention. What the hell was an Al Qaeda operative doing in Jemez Springs?

"Here's what I'm guessing. Raven was paid by Al Qaeda. The FBI's been following this agent. All of a sudden he shows up in Jemez Springs. Walks right into my hands. You know what this means. Promotion for me. I call the shots."

"And the Al Qaeda man is there to blow up Los Alamos."

"To blow up the whole fucking mountain!"

There was a strain in Augie's voice. State cops like Augie didn't panic just because somebody knocked off their boss.

But two and two could equal Al Qaeda and Raven. Chaos was visiting the world. Today it was in Jemez Springs, and Raven would be there.

"It's a radioactive contraption. The lab boys have verified that. It's sitting in the Valle Grande. You can see it from the road. Right now they don't know if it's got a live pit, or some of that dirty nuclear stuff Al Qaeda has."

Sonny glanced at his watch. The battery was dead, but it was spring equinox time all right. Raven time.

"All we know is there's a timer in the damn thing. Ticking away. If it blows, the lab boys think the Thing—that's what they call it, the Thing—will blow the mountain apart. Not only Los Alamos and the labs, but it might create a new volcano. Hit the hot stuff. I mean, half the state could go up."

Sonny sighed. Augie was prone to exaggeration. The Thing really wasn't to scare the Los Alamos Labs, it was for Sonny. Raven had begun the game for the day, and Sonny sensed tragic consequences ahead.

"Raven left a message for you. Lab boys found it in the bomb. I'll wait for you at the Bath House." With that, the phone went dead.

A frown crossed Sonny's face. Damn Raven! Yes, the games have started. I'll see him dead!

You can't kill him, the old man said.

I can! Sonny replied. I will!

You've been dreaming revenge, Sonny, and that's no good. Maybe he's already gotten to you.

Bullshit, Sonny scoffed. My mind's clear. He paused and thought awhile. And suppose he has. Don't we all have a shadow inside? Doesn't that part of the mind always make trouble? Isn't half the world troubled? Time to get rid of him, once and for all.

The old man shook his head. He knew even a shaman can be confused by spirit voices, and Sonny heard voices. In fact, it was often the dream shaman who suffered most from disruptive voices. Even the saints and holy men heard the devil's temptations. The struggle raging within the soul was a battle to still the voices.

"Maybe I am—" Sonny whispered.

He creates illusions, the old man said. Be careful. Don't look up in the sky for answers. Look inside. Shadow and light, it's all inside.

"Sonny."

He looked up into Rita's eyes, eyes of love, and the ship he had to sail that day rocked in the water of her eyes, water of life.

"Don Eliseo?" she said softly.

"Yeah . . . he's quite a philosopher."

"You two make a good pair," she said, placing a bag with chicken tacos and a thermos of coffee on the table.

"You heard him?" Sonny asked, for the first time seeking confirmation.

"No. He belongs to you. Your helper."

"I have to go," he said.

"I know."

He stood and kissed her. "I'll go by the cabin."

Years ago, before real estate prices went out of sight, he had bought a cabin by the river in Jemez Springs. He and Rita had spent Sundays there, fixing it up. Then came the summer of the Zia medallion, the large gold amulet that would belong to Sonny or Raven, whoever won the contest. Raven tried to blow up a WIPP truck loaded with toxic plutonium waste; Sonny stopped him. In October he reappeared during the Alburquerque Balloon Fiesta, and again on the winter solstice.

Raven was a predictable threat. Always lurking in the shadows, he especially picked the solstices and equinoxes to do his dirty work, days of great ancient power, days when the sun was most related to the earth. Today the sun crossed the plane of the earth's equator. The vernal equinox. The world could fall one way or the other.

No doubt about it, he was making trouble on the mountain.

"Maybe you'll have time to take a mineral bath."

Since Christmas Sonny had been driving up to the Jemez Springs Bath House to sit in a tub of the hot, healing water that flowed from a nearby spring.

Now the governor was lying dead in one of the tubs Sonny had used.

"If I have time."

Rita touched his cheek. "Did I tell you you're looking great? Stay that way." She paused then whispered. "I'm ready for one of those hot baths."

That surprised Sonny. It's what he had been waiting for. For her to say the word. "They have a tub for two."

"Maybe Sunday."

Sonny felt a gentle knotting in his stomach, a welcome tightening in his throat. She was coming back from the trauma. The time of the spring equinox would be a time of love. Buds, flowers, and sprigs of grass were being pushed up from the dark earth by the spirit within.

From the jukebox Little Richard continued to shout. Diego shook the box and the arm of the old record player lifted, a new record falling into place. Fats Domino.

Sonny smiled. "Sunday sounds great. Weather's clearing—"

"And you?"

"I'm strong as ever, really. The numbness is gone."

There was nothing she could say that would keep him home that day. If Raven appeared she knew Sonny had to go. She didn't know the depth of his need for vengeance, but she knew he had been waiting to make a stand. After all, who really knows what drives a man? Destiny? Fate? The daimon within?

"Cuídate," she said. "I love you. I'll wait—"

She hugged him and quickly returned to the cash register.

Sonny looked after her. There were tears in her eyes. Did she know what he had planned for the day? Did she sense he had to get Raven? The voices he had been hearing were shadows from his dreams, and don Eliseo had said a man fears voices when he cannot see the person who is speaking.

"Hey, Sonny, adonde la tiras?" Diego asked, bussing the table.

"Jemez."

"Cuidao con las Inditas."

"I already got one," Sonny replied.

Like Cleofes Vigil used to say, when the Españoles came they found all these beautiful Inditas de los Pueblos, Navajosas, y Comanches, and the lust of men who would never see the ocean again being what it was, ipso facto, the mestizo was born. Expanding the gene pool, something nature loves. We are los manitos de las naciones de la Sangre de Cristo, Cleofes used to say. The citizens of the city states del Rio Grande del norte. Each village a polis.

The Chicano mestizo. A man on whose body was written a history of suffering. A future of great beauty. A woman throwing off the shackles of a long oppression.

Sonny walked out to his truck and opened the beat-up ice chest. It was empty except for three cans of warm Diet Dr. Pepper rolling around the bottom. Sonny tossed the tacos and thermos into the cooler.

The bed of the truck held a shovel, some rope, an old sleeping bag and a tattered tarp, a very old pair of muddy boots, a collection of empty diet-soda cans, a frayed battery cable, and an odd assortment of wrenches, pliers, duct tape, and a coil of baling wire. With duct tape and baling wire he could fix anything. Chicano welds.

He and don Eliseo had gone fishing up in the Pecos a couple of years ago and the old man swore the sleeping bag and tarp were all a king needed to sleep well. If it rains you pretend you're a rock, he said, until the rain passes. A rock with eyes.

Got everything a PI needs, Sonny thought, satisfied.

Today's the day, he thought as he and Chica headed north on 4th Street toward Bernalillo, tuning the radio to KANW. The news was leaking out: an Al Qaeda terrorist had been apprehended. But no mention of the governor.

So the governor was dead. It was rumored that he visited the Jemez Valley because he was seeing a woman at the pueblo. A very nice-looking Jemez woman, a sculptor whose pottery was known and collected internationally.

So the governor had a liaison. He claimed he went for the baths to get rid of stress, but did he really go to visit a woman?

None of my business, Sonny thought.

I don't like this, the old man said. He had been quiet, perhaps mulling over Sonny's motive. Now he spoke of caution.

Raven's threatening to blow up the mountain, Sonny replied. You want me to stay home and do nothing. Raven's up there, waiting. That's what Fox meant with his allusion to the Bible. Fox knows.

The old man said nothing. Sonny was lying to himself.

Look, Sonny continued. We know even a small explosion can change the course of the underground water. That hot mineral water worked magic for me. I can't turn my back on the mountain.

He'll be waiting.

So what! He's always waiting. Let's end it today.

That's what you really want, isn't it?

Yes!

It's not that easy.

It's him or me.

And you think I can help?

You're my trump.

You're wrong, Sonny. You're not thinking straight. There's not a thing I can do.

4 »

Sonny listened to his scanner. The state police had closed Highway 4 between Jemez Springs and Los Alamos, citing a jackknifed gypsum-carrying truck blocking the road. The news media didn't buy it. Too many government cover-ups had made the newshounds wary. Sonny guessed that SWAT teams from Kirtland and Los Alamos were already on the mountain.

But not a word about the governor.

The Bath House didn't open till ten, and it was still early in the morning. Did that mean the governor was in the tub all night? Not discovered till morning? And where was Augie when the gov drew his last breath?

Fear death by drowning. Sonny remembered his close encounter in the river when he was twelve. Swept under by a treacherous current, he had swallowed a lot of water before he could grab hold of cottonwood roots along the bank and crawl out. He had been under long enough to feel the fingers of dissolution working in the water, long enough to hear the siren's call.

A plaintive cry, the wind sweeping past the open window, filled the cab of the truck, reminding him the river was full of spirits. La

Llorona and her son El Coco walked the dark pathways of the river forest. She cried for all the children the river had carried away.

Sonny shivered, turned the radio off, and looked toward the blue Jemez. The day was hazy, with ribbed clouds still drifting eastward, the tail end of last night's weather front.

Long ago the Nuevomexicanos had lived on the mountain, pastores grazing sheep in the high pastures. They settled the San Diego Land Grant and learned to be vecinos with the Jemez Pueblo people. With time, more lovers of the mountain made their way up the river valley and the canyons to call the place their home. Men and women who liked to make it on their own, full of independent zeal, pilgrims whose reward was the sound of the breeze sailing through the trees. But even tough mountain men and women got lonely. Sooner or later they came down from the mountain to Jemez Springs, to church, or the library, or to the cantina. Sooner or later everybody got lonely.

Was the governor's wife a lonely woman? Sonny had met her once or twice. He couldn't remember what she looked like. And perhaps it wasn't other people's loneliness gnawing at his heart, it was his own sense of being alone. His need to avenge the death of Rita's child had driven him against the wall. Only getting Raven would bring respite.

He remembered he had promised to call his mother. He took the phone and scrolled to her name. Her phone rang and she answered.

"Hi, mom—"

"Sonny, where are you?"

"I'm on my way to the cabin."

"How are you feeling?"

"I'm good. Just had breakfast with Rita—"

"That woman is incredible. So, have you set a date?"

"Maybe we'll get the judge at Jemez to marry us, honeymoon at the cabin—"

"Oh, no, Sonny. I want a big wedding. The family has to come. All our friends. Promise me you won't do anything rash."

"You're the one who keeps telling me to settle down."

"I know, hijo, I know. You do what you think is best. But a mother just wants to be there. I'm old fashioned, I know. Armando will never get married. Wild women, cars, and gambling—speaking of gambling, Max is taking me to lunch at the Isleta Casino. The man has given me a new life. Don't worry, we don't gamble, we just go for lunch. Those poor people at the slots make me sad. Did you hear about the woman who met the devil?"

"No."

"She was from Belen, I think. She lost everything at the slot machines. Even mortgaged her home. The machine had just taken her last dollar, and she was in a panic. How could she tell her family she had lost their home? Anyway, a handsome man dressed in black appeared. He gave her three coins. She bet the coins and each one paid her a fortune. She cried with joy. She tried to thank the stranger but he was gone. Only burning sulfur filled the air. Anyway, she hurried home to share her luck with her family, but when she got there the police were waiting. They were there to tell her an hour ago her three sons had been killed in a terrible accident. The woman went crazy. Her arm grew stiff. When they pried open her hand there were three burned spots on her palm."

"The three coins," Sonny said.

"If you make a deal with the devil you have to pay. I feel awful for that woman. It could be someone we know. I guess some people just don't have a choice—"

"You mean they're addicted?"

"Life is a gamble, isn't it? She lost her sons."

"But the lottery pays for scholarships," Sonny said. He didn't play, but if people wanted to gamble that was their business.

"Are you feeling well?" she asked.

"I'm good, really. You have fun at the casino."

"We just go for lunch, mi'jo. Cuídate. Call me when you get back."

"I will. Have fun."

"Oh, Sonny, it's not going to the casino that makes me happy, it's being with Max. We fit. You know, like you and Rita fit. You could be anywhere with her and be happy. Que no?"

What she said cut to his heart. Yes, she was right.

"Bendición, hijo. I'll call you tonight."

Sonny offed the phone. He wiped his eyes. Damn, a tough PI shouldn't get soft, he thought. But his mother spoke the simple truth, a truth she had engraved in his heart when he was a child. It was part of the creencia of the Mexicanos, to be kind. Yes, being anywhere with Rita would be his happiness.

She obviously hadn't heard what was happening in the Jemez, where in the caldera of the mountain, the cradle of Valle Grande, a bomb was ticking away. In the city people were going about their business, paying no heed to the possibility of danger. Or maybe too many terrorist alerts had just numbed sensibilities.

Overhead the equinox sun traveled across the blue sky, creating in its journey the quadripartite day. Equal lengths of night on each side of the equator. Day of perfect balance.

The earth turned its face to the light, so degrees of time were born on the maps of argonauts, seasons marked by the solstices and the equinoxes. And in the center a vertical axis, a gold column to heaven, Jacob's ladder, the same tree of light seen by those who went through near-death experiences. The axis mundi connected the earth's plane to the gods, although some would say that axis was simply a revelation of the spinal cord and its seven seals. An experienced soul could climb to heaven on that ladder of bones, or plunge to the land of the dead below.

The universe, the ancients said, was delineated by four spaces. In the face of chaos, Homo sapiens had need to give form to his universe.

We seek unity, Sonny said. He coaxed the old man into storytelling.

That's the promise of the Zia Stone, the old man said. The glyph on the stone forms a quincunx. Let's say it's like four trees at each corner, and in the middle a fountain. Tree of Knowledge, Tree of Life, Tree of Hope, Tree of Sadness and Pain. Fountain of Eden's water. However you envision it, the quincunx is a symbol that unifies the universe. Four parts of the universe and the center. Four organs in man and his center, the soul. Four humors, the ancients said. Man corresponds to the cosmos. We are children of the universe. Stardust and earthdust. But in the beginning we also knew chaos. We are children of chaos, too. We need a center, a home, a place from where we can communicate with the gods. The ancients raised dolmens, temples, pyramids. The tops of pyramids, church spires, and mountains are closest to the spirit world. Raven wants that power. From there he rains destruction, pulls us all into the ancient sea, the chaos before the Light, before the Logos.

King of the mountain, Sonny said.

Yes, the old man said. Raven likes to play games. He's a trickster. Always remember that. Shape shifter.

What is he today?

He's gone high tech, the old man answered.

I don't get it.

The bomb is a hoax. He's playing at getting the politicians to play his game. You heard the mayor, there's already a press conference planned. In the meantime he's going to play with your head. He wants the Zia medallion.

What does he want from the politicians?

Power. But it's also a game with them. He doesn't give a damn about their power. Men used to put on the skin of animals or masks of animals to get the animal's power, to hunt the animal. Today it's the high-tech machines.

So that's where he is.

Yes.

And the mountain?

It's the beginning of the game.

I see, Sonny said.

He drove slowly through Bernalillo. Once a quiet hamlet on the banks of the Rio Grande where Hispano families raised corn, beans, chile, and children, the place now buzzed with fallout from Rio Rancho. Up on the West Mesa, Rio Rancho was spreading like a fire out of control, covering the sandhills with brand-new homes, from the Rio Grande all the way to the Rio Puerco.

The aggressive Anglo world meeting the once bucolic Indo-hispano world of the valley. A new conquest. Culture clash was real, even if the local chamber of commerce said otherwise.

The valley used to be full of vineyards and cornfields. People from Jemez, Zia, Santa Ana, San Felipe, Sandia, Santo Domingo went to Bernalillo to trade. Camino del Pueblo buzzed with activity. After the war everything began to change. Work for wages replaced the old barter system; neighbors no longer worked together. They went to work for the almighty dollar. To assimilate a culture you don't go to war, you provide low interest rates. And you grab hold of city hall. Once the newcomers controlled city hall the old ways would go out the window. History records wars and conflicts, but the real colonization takes place by imposing law and language. The Americanos' law and language were swords cleaving the land. The land was lost and traditions crumbling.

Now the Nuevomexicanos have to build museums to teach the kids about their culture, Sonny thought as he crossed over the bridge. Below, the surging river was a sheen of light, a flood. Hundreds of acre-feet of water had been released from Cochiti Dam, and the water sang its freedom. Along the banks the bosque of bare cottonwoods had sprouted russet buds. Chica smelled the crisp air and barked.

Sonny smiled. To enter the river's presence was to enter a different time zone, where time turned into space. That was the magic of the land, spirit entering matter.

Sonny knew the river. He had grown up in the South Valley, and he and his boyhood friends had spent their summers along the river, fishing, roaming, swimming. The time of childhood was magical because the spirit entering the river was a presence they could feel.

Sometimes it dazzled in the glory of bird wings, the color of the roiling water, the brilliant green of the alamos. Other times it was the cry of La Llorona, the wailing woman. She held a dagger in her gnarled hands, and she chased the boys home when dusk fell.

Every river is ruled by a god, the ancients believed.

The Spaniards called the Rio Grande el Río Bravo, as brave as a thundering bull. Perhaps it was a bull, or an ancient Sumerian god delivering its life-giving waters, providing a home for the almost extinct silvery minnow. The toro sacrificing its life-giving blood so man might turn the water into his fields and grow his crops. And man the acolyte of the river.

Before the Cochiti dam was built the floods of spring arrived like a herd of brave bulls, a thundering whoosh of hooves roaring down the streambed to fertilize the cities with life-giving waters.

A presence imbued the river, an essence that was the spirit of the stream. When the dying day delivered its life to the shadows a change came over the bosque. The air grew cool and still. Night hawks, evening's graceful minions, swooped low along the water, their starred wings signaling the end of day. Then the shadows tumbled down the arms of the towering cottonwoods, and the smell of the earth rose from the rotting compost. The spirit of the river spoke, filled the dark paths, touched the shoulder of the wary.

Without the river the cities on its banks would wither away, so man built dams to control the flow, to take the water as his own. Men had come to believe that nature was not complete unto herself, that she should not be left alone.

The Rio Grande Conservancy controlled the flow of water, not the ancient god Enki. They had opened the gates at the Cochiti Dam, and for a few weeks the river would look as it did in the old days, before the dam was built, when the snow melted on the high peaks of Colorado and on the Sangre de Cristos of Taos and Santa Fe. Then the spring runoff came roaring down the valley, the rushing water cleaning out winter's stagnation, like an angioplasty opening clogged arteries, washing the winter plaque away.

The river was the alchemist of the valley. The water was the gold rush that swept away the compost, dissolved the leaden weight of winter, invigorated the natives with fresh oxygen and ozone, delivered nitrogen to the alamos, filled the acequias, irrigated fields and orchards. All the elements of spring met in the river, impregnating the slumbering earth. The river rocked and rolled in its emotional life, and the dance brought joy to the hearts of its sons and daughters.

Somnambulant man saw only the surface of the river. But beneath the skin of water lay the web of veins and arteries that fed the river, the underground water that could be felt but not seen. That was the secret of the desert rivers. The Rio Grande stretched its arms up into the Sangre de Cristo Mountains and drew down the hidden waters, tapped each small spring, every rivulet of melting snow, summer rains, morning dew, night mists, gathering every drop, creating the fingers and hands of mountain streams, strong arms that came tumbling down the arroyos and canyons into the basin, forming the shoulders and body of the great river.

Now the river was dying. Too many cities siphoning off the water. Too many needs for too little water. By the time it reached south Texas it was a dead river. The creatures of the river were also dying. Pollutants were clogging the heart and soul of the river. The dance was ending.

Sonny crossed the bridge and drove up the incline past Jackalope and the Coronado Monument, the place where Coronado had spent the winter of 1540. From here the adventurer and his scraggly crew had looked down on the frozen river and on thin columns of smoke rising from a thousand Pueblo Indian homes. Aztlán, the Chicanos said, land of the Hyperboreans, lost tribe of antiquity. Our home, said the Tiguex pueblos, fearful of the barbarians camped on the west side of the river.

It was winter, the time of storytelling. But time had been disrupted. White men with coarse hair flowing from their faces walked the earth, muttering in a strange tongue. These were not the kachinas who came to bless the villages, these were strange creatures who demanded buffalo blankets and corn. Men lusting for the warmth of women.

Sonny crested the rise and got his first view of the blue Jemez. The softly rounded volcanic peak wore a scarf of last night's snow. The equinox sun was entering the space of the mountain, the first quadrant of the day. Overhead a striated bank of clouds ribbed the blue sky, the remains of last night's storm, now streaking east toward Texas.

There were distinct parts of the road Sonny enjoyed. The drive to San Ysidro was breathtaking, a panorama of flesh-colored, sandy hills dotted with juniper and chamisa. To the north the long, flat blue mesa, to the south Cabezon Peak, in front of him the first view of White Mesa.

At San Ysidro he would turn into the red canyons that crawled like wrinkles down the face of the mountain. And dominating the landscape, the gentle Jemez Mountain, the ninety thousand acres at the top of the collapsed volcano known as the Valles Caldera National Preserve.

Ages ago when the volcano blew its top it scattered ashes as far away as Kansas. The huge crater became a lake. Now it was a vast grassy meadow that fed the largest herd of elk in the state. Lucky visitors sometimes ran into the herds crossing Highway 4, a sight to inspire wonder.

The mountain was also home to mule deer, black bears, mountain lions, dozens of species of birds, and streams replete with trout. An animal paradise.

For the Jemez Pueblo people the mountain was a place of sacred sites. Some twelve thousand years ago groups of hunters and gatherers had walked on Redondo Peak, the second-highest peak of the mountain. In the mid-nineteenth century parcels of the mountain were granted to the Cabeza de Vaca family. Sheep roamed the meadows. A century later the mountain was heavily logged.

In the warm sunlight that filled the cab, Chica squealed, perhaps dreaming of August when the purple sage blossomed in the sandhills and frantic honeybees gathered the sweet sage nectar, refining it into a honey that old men from Belén sought as an aphrodisiac. Sonny had made the drive hundreds of times, and still the view filled him with peace. He belonged here. From the moment he bought the cabin he felt he had been here before, long ago. Transmigration? Did he believe? He had been reading a lot lately, trying to figure it out. Don Eliseo laughed at him.

It ain't in books, mijo, it's in front of your face.

A glisten of scales on the side of the road caught Sonny's vision. He pulled over and slowly backed up. Most of the traffic on 550 was flowing south, into Burque.

He got out and stood looking at the large rattler that lay crushed, writhing as it died, scales shining in the morning light.

"Damn," Sonny muttered. He looked around, sniffing the air. The sharp metallic smell of death touched his nostrils. There was another scent, a feral scent.

A crow perched on a juniper called. Not good, Sonny thought. The snake had come out of hibernation to lie on the warmth of the asphalt and had been run over. Or it had been rushed out of its damp, underground home by someone's need. Whose?

There were no marks from scavengers on its body, but he knew he couldn't leave the snake on the side of the road. The crows would tear it apart; the snake spirit would become a burden.

Gotta take Señor Vívora so he gets a proper burial, he thought. He took his leather gloves from the truck, carefully picked up the snake with the shovel, and placed it on the bed of the pickup.

A coyote trotted up the wide, sandy arroyo. It stopped to glance at Sonny, as if approving, then disappeared. Sonny got back in the truck and drove on.

At White Mesa the road curved, and he slowed down to enter San Ysidro. The village budget depended on ticketing speeders, and Sonny wasn't in a contributing mood. He turned north toward the pueblo, past the P.O., the village offices, the church.

San Ysidro had fallen on hard times. Every time Sonny and

Rita drove through he caught sight of one fixer-upper or another, crumbling adobe homes or double-wides that needed repair.

Fixer-upper heaven. Yeah.

He slowed down as he approached the pueblo, matching his rhythm to a faraway drum beat. The old adobe houses seemed to melt into the earth. Sooner or later everyone and everything had to melt back into the arms of mother earth. That's why the new frame/stucco houses going up on the outskirts of the pueblo looked so incongruous. How do you dissolve wood frame, propanel roof, steel window frames?

The pueblo kept the seasons, each one distinct. Spring was for plowing, the cleaning of the ditches, the running of irrigation water, planting. The cycle of the seed corn described the cycle of man's life, the cycle of sun and moon. In summer the greening, the corn's male tassels drooped with male pollen, and the old men went about collecting the sanctifying dust.

In autumn ristras of red chile hung on the walls, the ears of corn were dried or made into chicos, the blue corn ground to make atole. Time of the hunt. And in winter, rest. Time for storytelling.

Wrapped within the seasons were the ceremonies. The outside world knew little of the ceremonial cycle; the Jemez Pueblo kept to its traditional past. Outsiders stopped at the stalls to buy oven bread or visited the homes that sold pottery and jewelry. Outsiders came to the pueblo feast-day dances, and to the Matachines dances on Día de La Virgen Guadalupe in December. These dances were shared with the outside world, with the vecinos from the small villages that dotted the mountain.

Sonny and Rita attended the dances, felt the dance energizing the earth, the call of the spirit world, and there had been a few times when he had felt the epiphany of the dance, time becoming space. Those times the spirit entered the earth and its people. Perhaps it was the Indian blood he inherited from his mother. She was the daughter of the genízaro pueblos south of Alburquerque, the villages where both Pueblo and Plains Indians had become hispanicized, where the children came in all colors, some blonde and blue-eyed as some of the original Españoles and some brown as the river earth.

The pueblo fiestas were a time to visit, a time to hear the native languages spoken. Navajos from Gallup, folks from all the other pueblos, all uttering the few words they knew of Towa. Those without the language could only watch. The ceremonies of the ancestors belonged to the people, and were kept by the people.

From the road Sonny waved at a group of men at the acequia. Something was going on at the pueblo.

Did they know about the governor? Probably. Did they know about Raven's bomb?

On the bare cottonwood branches, the crows spoke volumes.

Only one booth at the Red Rocks rest area was doing business. He and Rita had bought oven bread from Mrs. Cota for years. There she was, tending the fire with fragrant pieces of piñon, the coffee boiling. Lard bubbled in the cast iron pot, ready for the fry bread.

Sonny pulled over and got out of the truck; Chica followed. The late model Subaru parked near the ramada didn't belong to old lady Cota, but there was no one nearby. A sharp breeze stirred, blowing across from the Walatowa store. The dust rose then fell, carrying strange sounds, a wailing from the mesa. Definitely something going on.

He looked up at the red rocks where spots of snow contrasted with the crimson of the cliff, all framed by an overarching blue sky. A striking, mesmerizing sight, he thought, an eighth wonder of the world. In the summer tourists flocked here, to eat fry bread with honey or the tasty tacos the women sold. March, which could still turn cold and blustery, was not yet tourist season. It was worth a trip to sit in the silence and feel the spirit of the place.

"Ti-wa-sho-beh," Sonny greeted Mrs. Cota.

"Ti-wa-sho-beh, Yang," the old lady replied.

"You have soom-bela?"

"Yang always hungry."

"Yes, coyote always hungry," Sonny said, laughing and rubbing his stomach.

"Where's your woman?"

"Like you, she cooks for people. I came with my cannu."

"Too early for fry bread."

"Coffee."

She poured him a cup. Sonny sat on a tree stump to enjoy the strongest brew east of Window Rock.

"The car?" he asked.

"Naomi." The old lady nodded toward the red rocks and turned to tend the fire.

Sonny watched Chica scouring the ground, back and forth, picking up scents.

Naomi, Sonny remembered. So, she was back. But what was she doing in the Red Rocks?

Where is she? he was going ask, but put the thought away. None of his business. A person came into the world of the pueblo and a lot of things were not his business.

He enjoyed the coffee and the warmth of the sun. Sun the father, the old abuelo. Don Eliseo had taught him to say his morning prayers facing the east as the sun rose over Sandia Crest. Then the Lords and Ladies of the Light chased away the dark mists that hung over the river.

Life was movement, the cycle of the sun entering the world, creating a dance, the clarity the living sought, the soul's food. Dark was a place. Dream place. Nightmare place.

Here in the Jemez Valley the light was a living substance, and it could tear apart the many layers of ego, the stress, the false identities, the veils of illusion some called reality. As the light entered the soul, it became soul.

We never are, we are always becoming, don Eliseo said. Painters paint light on canvas, we use light to paint our spirits. Light has will, the particles make choices, choose direction, how to go. It's not constant, Sonny. It is alive.

Yes, Sonny smiled. That was true. In New Mexico the light was alive, entering the mountain peaks, mesas, arroyos, chamisa, and every living organism—even the rocks, for light made the boulders and rocks come alive and share their song with the day.

"Ti-way-peh, Mrs. Cota," he said when he finished his coffee.

"Ti-way-peh," she replied.

He was putting Chica in the truck when a long, yelping cry rang from the cliff.

Some doings, Sonny thought, and started to get in the truck. Then a woman cried out.

"A woman," Sonny said, looking toward the red rocks.

He glanced at Mrs. Cota, but she looked away. None of your business, her demeanor said.

The cry came again, a cry for help. He had heard a cry like that before, and he couldn't just pretend it wasn't his business. He slammed the door shut and ran toward the red cliff.

5 »

As Sonny rounded the huge boulder, two hundred pounds of painted flesh slammed into him. He caught his balance, only to feel another painted man push him into the arms of a third.

"Ora, muchachos!" cried the fat man, pushing Sonny into the middle of the small clearing. There were six men from the pueblo in a circle, painted as if going to war, and standing near a juniper tree, Naomi dressed in white buckskin.

"Hey!" they shouted as they cuffed Sonny, pushing him back and forth from one man to the next.

"Hey! Sonny Baca!" the fat man called out. Sonny recognized Bear and a couple of the other men.

They were playing a game, the way hunters might strike the young initiate with the first jackrabbit he kills, smearing him with Brr-da-eh blood. The way a child might be frightened by a man masquerading as a bear, so that he loses his fear of bears.

Sonny didn't fight back. He knew the game. The homeboys in the barrio played it once in a while to test a vato, push him around to see how much kidding he would take before striking back.

Bear pushed him hard and Sonny fell face down. One fell on his back and pinned him to the ground.

They were talking in Towa. Sonny recognized Yang. Coyote. No use protesting; he had interrupted their ritual. Out of the corner of one eye Naomi came into focus, as regal and beautiful as he remembered her.

They passed something over him, and Sonny was sure he detected the odor of the dead snake, the snake with no charm.

Bear leaned down and whispered, "Don't play with snakes. Not your medicine."

"Yang might get bitten," another said.

"Or get blown up by the white man's bomb."

They laughed then moved away, out of the arbor, their bells jingling and turtle shells rattling. Like a sudden thunderstorm they had struck, leaving behind a dazed Sonny spitting sand.

He felt bruised. The primos play rough, he thought. What the hell did I stumble into? The fleshy smell of the dead snake hung in the air.

He knew Bear. La plebe in Ponderosa called him Gordo. He liked to drink beer and dance on Friday nights at the Ponderosa Bar and Grill.

Sonny turned and looked at the crimson cliffside. He blinked, not believing what he saw. The image of a quincunx appeared on the stone. He held his breath. Above him the sound of the wind moaned as it scraped against the red rocks.

Before his eyes the Zia glyph glistened like a mirage in the heat of summer. Four quadrants, and in the middle the blazing Zia sun, sun of movement traveling across the four quadrants, now moving into the spring equinox. Four seasons, four spaces, four dimensions, four times in the year the earth circled the sun, and the movement through space became a sacred journey.

On a flat surface the quincunx would represent the Garden of Eden, earth itself, home. The pueblo. The vertical axis pointed up to the spirit world and down into the world of emergence.

Sonny blinked again and the image dissolved. He sat up, rubbed his eyes, and groaned. His left eye felt bruised, but otherwise he was okay.

The Egyptians had carved their esoteric knowledge on the walls of their temples, hieroglyphs that told stories of their gods. Masked gods. Cerebus, Isis, and Horus, the falcon god who delivered whispered messages. The gods, in colorful dress, crossed the river Nile in the sacred raft. The walls of the tombs of the pharaohs were decorated in fantastic murals, images that spoke volumes to a learned acolyte.

In the land of the Zia Sun, in New Mexico, in the desert land the Aztecs called Aztlán, land the Americanos called the Southwest, land where the bones of the ancient ones were buried, where the wind whispered and crested desert sand into waves, there where the acolyte might follow the zigzag pattern of the rattlesnake, in this land the ancestors had walked, crisscrossing the land that would one day be called America, the earth whose name they kept sacred in their stories and parables, a name with so much power that it could not even be carved into the sand stones of the desert.

Long ago migrations had spread across the towering breasts and fat belly of the mother, treading with care, taking sustenance from the earth as a baby would suckle at her mother's breast. Those ancient people had carved the glyph of power on the Zia Stone, thus describing their relationship to a higher, creative power.

Older civilizations had done the same in their earliest writings. Sumerians, Israelites, and Egyptians, by whatever name in whatever place, the people had described the geography of the sacred. They felt the vibrations of a greater power infusing the earth, and they etched that relationship on wet clay tablets and sandstone pillars.

The word became the center, a new awareness of the sacred.

In the deserts and mountains of the Anasazi, the Zia glyph was cut into the face of a rock, a sign etched so deep that it became the center of the universe, the point around which the Earth rotated, the mother spinning in a dance of joy, dressing herself in various hues, a colorful costume for each season, but always swirling to a dance that could be measured by the movement of the stars at night, the moon, planets, the sun.

It was like this in medieval pictures Sonny had seen of the Garden of Eden. In the center was the sacred spring, with four rivers flowing from the garden in the sacred directions. The garden was the mandala of primal imagination.

Sonny had heard the story from don Eliseo, and he from the old people of the pueblos, they who kept the ancient knowledge.

There is a secret, they said, a glyph carved on a huge boulder that fell from the sky. Long ago it fell to earth. The sign on the stone will tell how time begin, how it will end, the story of earth, the story of man and woman. We came from the belly of the mother, we walked on the skin of our mother, always nurtured by her seed and animals, the fish, the deer. If you find this stone that fell from the sky, you will know how one time moves into the next, to give birth, to create the spirit of life.

The Zia Stone. The secret we sought.

What is the secret? he asked the old man.

The secret is that there is a secret, the old man said. We need that hidden knowledge to keep us searching. We don't know everything there is to know of the creation. There is one eternal question: Whence came we? Why? Even if we rose from the mud of ancient lakes, the ooze, the hidden waters, the question remains. What spirit penetrated the mud to create the first cells, a throbbing of life that millennia later would raise its arms to the sun, praising the light of creation? That is our human history, the seeking after the light.

Sonny turned and looked at Naomi. She smiled, glided toward him like a snake, making no sound on the sand.

"Thanks for saving me, Sonny."

"I didn't save you," he replied. Something in the way she walked or the way she said "thanks for saving me" angered him. How in the hell was he to know she was here?

"Yeah, well you never know what those guys would have done to an innocent girl like me."

Sonny stood and wiped sand from his pants. He looked at Naomi. Innocent? Not by a long shot. But good looking? Lordy, yes. She smiled. Her pearl teeth had been cared for by a very good dentist, a very expensive one.

"You did save me. I'm all yours."

"Look, I don't know what games you're playing, but I didn't save you. The guys were just having a little fun."

"They play rough. But don't listen to them. They carry on all that old-fashioned stuff, painting up like they're going to war. I told them I didn't want any part of it."

"So why are you here?"

"Because of you," she said, reaching out and brushing sand from his cheek. "You're part of the game."

Her voice was husky, her dark eyes shining. He could smell her body perfume, sage and a sweet cologne magnified by the excitement of what had just happened, sand and sweat and the pungent green of junipers whose spring juices were already rising.

"Remember me?" she said. "Did you forget me?"

No, he hadn't forgotten her. A man doesn't forget a woman like Naomi, even if the liaison was only one night filled with the impulse of youth.

"We made love."

But that was long ago, ten years ago, he was still at the university, had beers on Friday nights with a couple of guys from the pueblo. In the fall they invited him to go hunting, and that October full-moon night they got some good pot and peyote buds, and some of the pretty girls from the pueblo showed up, high up where the aspen exulted in their brilliant yellows, transparent in the light of the moon, and the girls were as transparent as flesh can get when you're young and horny.

Yes, he remembered, he could hear the drumming now. They sang into the night by the light of the campfire, serenaded by coyotes and the screeching call of a cougar that hunted in the mesa. It was a night he would never forget. The intensity that flesh can share with earth bonded him to the mountain and the night sky and the secrets revealed by the peyote as it entered the bloodstream.

A night of hallucinations. A huge black bear walked into the camp, growling and kicking up dust, then cougar, screeching and clawing at them, teaching them a lesson that perhaps in the last dream on their deathbeds they might understand. Finally, the owl, calling the stars down in a cascade of silver, the wisdom of Sophia, a man from another culture might say, but here it was a dance orchestrated by Señor Peyote. A song of the forest, night an indigo liquid in which they swam, the time of blue lights, deep purples, vivid strobes of green and orange notes of the drum floating into the night sky, joining the campfire embers and piñon smoke, rising into the galaxy-full sky.

It didn't end until the early morning frost fell over the exhausted campers, and Naomi slithered into his bedroll as he lay watching the play of stars as they tumbled and turned into colorful musical notes that fell to earth like burning confetti, pyrotechnic displays of living color that carried the song of the night, a symphony of owls calling, witches of the night roaming the mountain, the coyotes howling for joy, and the cry of a cougar in the hills. The night's aria circled the drum, then entered the drum, a dazzling gathering of Star People who rained from the night sky to dance around the campfire.

A drying thirst consumed him, and Naomi was like sweet water, water from a mountain spring that seemed to wash over him.

At the time he thought that lying on the mountaintop with Naomi quenching his peyote thirst was as close to heaven as he would ever get. When he awakened the following morning he had learned that sex was like soothing water, the woman a hidden spring, water that could be felt and not seen, like the streams of water that flowed beneath the rough flesh of the mountain, the sweet fulfilling water.

He ate a big breakfast, eggs and potatoes fried on the big skillet on top of the resurrected fire, shivering in the cold, drinking coffee, tasting the smoke and ashes of the fire. The guys kidded him, not loud, just kind of looking at him and saying, damn you're a lucky guy, Sonny. They glanced at Naomi, snoring in his sleeping bag.

He asked about her later, but she was gone. Headed for the big time, selling her pottery in New York galleries. She didn't have time for the likes of Sonny, a poor college student.

She moved out of his life and he continued at the university, and now ten years later she was back.

"I lost track of you."

"I went away," she said. "Went to school and became famous. I got married, about three times I think." She laughed. "But I'm a single girl now."

"Yeah."

Married three times, traveled the world, but she still looked sexy for a world-weary thirty-something.

He turned and started back to his truck. Naomi followed.

"I know you have a woman—"

He nodded.

"Don't you know it's spring? Time for planting."

"Too early," he said. "I plant corn May first."

She laughed. "You're part of the ceremony now."

"What ceremony?"

He was well aware that the muchachos who had pushed him around were vatos he knew and hunted with in the real world, but they sure as hell weren't going to let him into their ceremonial world. Whatever they did was their thing.

"You've got the seed," she said.

He stopped and looked at her. Oh, her ceremony. That's what she had in mind. Maybe she had gotten them together to do a cleansing thing, a purification. That still didn't tell him why he stumbled onto them. Synchronicity?

"Gotta go."

"See you up the road," she said, smiling.

She walked regally to her Subaru and got in. A grinding sound caused by a low battery filled the air.

Sonny turned to Mrs. Cota.

"Da-whona-umbeh," she said. You be careful. You wind up with that woman and there's only trouble. "Heya-owa," she whispered, tossing the words into the fire.

So that's what they called her. Snake Woman. Snake was related to water, and water was the lifeline of every Indian pueblo and Hispanic village in New Mexico. Long ago there was a rumor that one of the northern pueblos kept a giant twenty-foot snake in an underground cave. The Hopi had their snake ceremonies, dances to call the cloud spirits to bring the precious rain to the New Mexico fields of corn, chile, and squash.

Could be not so good if you had a fear of snakes and you hadn't been cleansed of the fear. Snake dreams might cause anxiety. Nothing Freudian about it, Sonny thought.

The image of the snake appeared throughout the Americas. Serpent heads with huge fangs guarded the great pyramids of Mexico and Central America. Quetzalcoatl, god of the arts and agriculture, the winged serpent, combining the creature closest to the earth and the colorful bird that could fly up into the spirit world.

If Naomi was Snake Woman maybe it was because of some jealousy clinging from a past event, envy over this or that. People called each other names. If somebody was really envious of you some chopped hair might appear in your plate of corn and squash. Just like in the old Hispanic lore, the hair was used by witches to cast a spell. *Envidia* in Spanish was a strong concept. Envidia was a worm in the heart. The singular crab in the bucket trying to claw his way out was pulled back down by the others.

Envy made sure they were all cooked together.

Human nature, Sonny thought. No one group has a corner on envy, or any other human emotion.

He looked in the bed of the truck. The snake was gone. Time to move on.

Sonny looked over at Naomi still trying to start her SUV. He understood why she drew unwanted attention. She was good looking, but more than that, seductive, a Nefertiti of the desert.

"Nonu-da-aeh," he said to Mrs. Cota.

"You be careful," she replied.

She was nearly eighty, and she didn't need to be out in the cold morning stirring the fire and getting the fry bread going, but she had done it for a long time, during hard times when the 25 cents she charged for a loaf of bread went a long way. She had put two of her boys through school. One was a Ph.D. in anthropology, the other worked for the BIA. Joe Sando, the well-known Jemez historian, had been their mentor, as he had mentored a lot of other kids.

So even a traditional pueblo like Jemez was sending a few of its children out into the world. The white man's world. Some of the elders resisted. They wanted to keep the children in the circle of the pueblo, close to the traditional values and ceremonies of the ancestors, but the world they distrusted kept encroaching.

I don't blame them, don Eliseo said. The world is too much with us, as the poet said.

Hey, where were you when I needed some help?

I took a nap. Besides, I did my share of fighting long ago.

Why in the hell are they painted up? Were they running?

None of your business.

Yeah. Sonny had learned not to ask questions about the pueblo ceremonies. People let you know something, that was up to them. But too many anthropologists had pried into the affairs of the pueblos, too many of the secret ceremonies had been publicized. Elsie Clews Parsons came to mind. Lordy, that woman had been in every kiva of the Southwest. Or she claimed she had been there. A little learning was a dangerous thing.

They knocked me down, and I felt a kind of energy. A surge of adrenaline in the blood. As if I had been knocked down by real animals, as if a bear had come close, I could smell him, feel the fur—

The old man didn't seem impressed. He had been in the Pueblo world too long.

Then I saw it! The Zia sign! Carved on the rock! I swear I saw it! Then it disappeared. What gives?

The old man smiled. Yeah, right.

I saw it, Sonny insisted, touching the Zia medallion on his chest. Don't you believe me?

Seguro que sí, I believe you. Why shouldn't I? What's the big deal? A lot of people have seen the elusive symbol. It's there, like the Golden Fleece was for those argue-nauts. Or the Ark of the Covenant for the judios. The Holy Grail, the naked Sofia. Those things are always there, just in front of you.

You've seen it? You never told me.

We see it in visions, Sonny. I saw it up in Mesa Verde one time. I went to get eagle feathers with some boys from Zuni. Long ago, before the government stopped us collecting. We fasted, stayed in the blind, sang a little, pretty soon there were voices all around, the wind speaking. That's when I saw it, carved on a boulder. I didn't know much about the Zia Stone, just heard a few stories. It was like being hit by lightning. When I woke it was gone.

In visions, Sonny whispered.

It starts there. You can't tell the skeptics about things like this. There's more of them than us. And you can't tell the church people, or any of the fundamentalists, you know, those evangelicals you see on TV. They have their own path. So we keep it to ourselves.

Until we find it?

It will reveal itself when the time is right. Maybe in Chaco, or Cañon de Chelly, or up on the West Mesa of Alburquerque. The old people left a lot of rock carvings. If those rocks could talk they would tell us many secrets, stories we need to know if we are going to survive. The world's gone mad, Sonny, people clinging to this or that holy book, and in the name of their gods they make war. I'll trust the message on the Zia Stone.

Like the Rosetta Stone?

Well, I read about the Rosetta. It helped translate one language to another. Everything we find helps translate the old hidden knowledge into our lives. The sign on the Zia Stone will help us translate time. How can we who live in time become spirit, see the beginning and the end?

Alpha and Omega?

That's Greek to me, the old man replied and laughed.

That's how he was, serious about life and death one moment, chuckling like a trickster the next. Sonny knew.

Our life on earth is short. But it's related to the life of the universe. We know this in our blood. We see the stars and think of heaven, our home, our beginning. Our ancestors knew this, they had the time to read the glyphs, patterns of stars carved on the belly of the night sky.

The zodiac?

Everything's there, Sonny, clear as a good meal of beans, chile con carne, and tortillas. We just can't see anymore, Sonny. We lost the sight of one good eye. We half-see. The old people left their calling cards, sacred signs. They came from the womb of the earth, came into the light of the sun, into life. They brought this secret with them. Everything is connected. Just like Einstein said. His formulas tie the universe together. DNA ties the body together. But what of the spirit? We need the signs that will reveal our alma, our soul. The Zia Stone might be sitting right under our noses. In the meantime, don't disturb the rocks. You might bury the revelation for another thousand years. By that time it will be too late for life on earth.

I've been scouring every petroglyph site from Mesa Verde to Casas Grande. Have I been wasting my time?

A man seeks what he has to find.

So what I saw was a coincidence, huh?

Goddamnit, Sonny, there's no such thing as coincidence! All those scientists up at Los Alamos talking about random this and random that. There's no random. The equations can be put on paper! $E = mc^2$. There's an order; we just can't see it.

The old man shook his head and stalked off.

Lordy, lordy. I've never heard him curse. What did I say? Coincidence. He believes everything is connected. A universal dream, a higher-order dream where everything makes sense. Is the dream carved into the DNA, the helix that looks like a curling snake? Did they initiate me into a snake dream? Quetzalcoatl's dream?

He looked at the imposing cliff. Something happened, he thought, and it's moving me into a new time. Was it Bear and his boys, or Naomi? Or finding the snake?

In dreams, or nightmares, every image or gesture or word or color has meaning, don Eliseo had said. Dreams aren't outside of reality, they are reality.

Sonny sighed. Too difficult for a mere mortal like me to understand. Being mortal meant he would keep on asking questions, though, like how in the hell did they know I would be here, at this time, that I would hear Naomi's cry and rush in blindly? Should have plugged my ears with wax, not heard the siren's call. Can't do that, not when there's a woman to be saved. A woman whose flesh he had tasted long ago in a dream.

"Hey, Sonny, you're going to have to give me a ride."

Naomi had taken a small bag from her SUV and was headed toward him.

"Back to the pueblo?"

"No, to Jemez Springs."

He couldn't refuse her. He was headed there, and in this part of the country you didn't refuse a ride to anyone on the side of the road. Especially if that anyone was Naomi. Lordy, his friends at the Sal's Bar would question his virility. "She asked you for a ride and you refused!" "Pendejo!" "What's the matter with you?" "You need Viagra?"

Get in, he motioned, glancing at Mrs. Cota, who shrugged.

Naomi petted Chica. "Oh, a one-eyed dog. Is this the dog that dreams? I heard what's been going on in Alburquerque. You know, I've got some of my pots at an Old Town gallery. That's what everybody's talking about. At La Placita, where they cook really good enchiladas, and at La Hacienda. Even at Monica's Portal. By the way, I haven't eaten at your girlfriend's cafe. I heard she's got hot chile."

Then she stiffened. "Hey, Sonny, you got spirits in this truck?"

"Only an old friend," Sonny replied, and smiled. If she couldn't stand the presence of the old man, let her walk.

"You're a spirit person, Sonny. Bet you dream a lot."

"Yeah," Sonny said and gunned the truck onto the highway.

6

THE FIRST BREATH OF SPRING, AND A crackling bright sun came roaring over the Red Rocks, glowing on the mesa to the west, awakening black bears from winter's sleep. Thin cirrus clouds glared down on God's earth, a swirling of the Cloud People who had spilled their meager, water-laden pitchers on the mountain. Now they gathered their skirts to move on, away from the magnetic energy of the mountain.

Too much beauty for one man, Sonny thought, studying the windswept formation of clouds and slipping on his sunglasses. Last night's dusting of snow was already disappearing, except in shaded patches. The Cloud People were racing east, over the Sangre de Cristos and the Sandias, toward Clines Corner, Santa Rosa, Tucumcari, and the Texas Panhandle, where the cold wind of March could still chill the bones of the toughest vaquero. With luck, the equinox front would drop more of its moisture as it moved into the llano.

But weather came with its mixed blessing. It was shearing time on the llano. The winter wool of the sheep had to come off before lambing. If a winter storm kept the Texas Mexicano shearing crews from doing their work, things got complicated. The old timers prayed for snow and rain for the llano grasses, but the storms had to come at the right time. And who could order the weather?

As a boy Sonny had visited the Hindi ranch in Duran. The llano and the people had made a lasting impression. But he found no books that recorded the lives of the llano people. Now the last of the large sheep ranches that had once made New Mexico the center of the industry were dying out.

Beside him, Chica slept, dreaming that in the Garden at the Beginning of Time it was a dog, one of her primal ancestors, who barked joyfully, daring Eve to take the apple! Take a bite and let's be off on an adventure, the dog had called to the bare-breasted mother of men.

If in the Beginning of Time dogs could talk, why could they not dream?

Naomi huddled against the door, staring at the cliff.

"I traveled in China," she said. "Studied some of their pottery techniques. The Chinese say chi is a universal energy. It's the same here. The canyon acts like a giant TV dish. It gathers the energy and funnels it into the earth."

Sonny nodded. Interesting. He had always felt comforted by the feminine energy of the mountain. The mountain grew from the piedmont, los pies de la sierra, soft sandy toes that rose into giant, gnarled knees, thick, voluptuous legs that parted to reveal the many openings into the Jemez, the honeycombed vulvas of the mountain, fuzzy with fragrant piñon, juniper, and pine. There was something dark and mystical about the canyons and wide arroyos that slashed their way down from the rounded breasts of the mountain, across the pillowed belly. It was the smell of blood, earth-blood, the waters of the mountain that fertilized the spongy nooks and crannies of the arroyos.

"I read Frank Waters when I was at the university," Sonny said. "He understood that energy."

"Yes," she replied. "But the old people also know about the spirit of the mountain. They just don't write books."

"Why are you going to Jemez Springs?"

"I could say I'm here to meet you."

"You were there last night?"

She nodded.

"Then you know about the governor—"

"Yeah, I know. Somebody killed him."

Sonny dared to ask, "Who?"

"You're the private investigator. You find out," she said, flippantly.

"I wasn't there."

"So why are you going? Don't tell me, it's Raven you want, isn't it?"

How in the hell does she know so much? Sonny wondered. I haven't seen her in ten years, I run into her by chance while she's playing around with Bear and his boys, and she knows about Raven.

"Yes," he answered.

He looked up at the canyon walls. Entering the canyon meant becoming part of the chronology kept by the cliffs, a time recorded since the mountain erupted eons ago. The strata of granite, red clay, and volcanic ash recorded time.

"You hear voices," she said.

Yes, there were voices up in the old deserted pueblo on the mesa. Voices that seeped down the canyon walls. The trees stirring in the breeze and the gurgling of the river carried the voices.

But in the present age everyone had been led to believe that only the neurotic heard voices. Psychiatrists tried to record their messages, hoping to learn the secrets of the deep and dark unconscious.

"Maybe I'm crazy," he said.

"No, it's a gift," she replied. "The voices are like dreams. I think in a way they lead us along the path we take. It's like we're not completely in charge of our lives. Somebody out there is always watching out for us, always helping."

Sonny nodded. It wasn't just don Eliseo he heard. In the maelstrom of his depression and anger a voice had told him exactly where to find an old gunsmith, a man who knew the workings of the Colt .45 Sonny carried in his truck. The man had cast a special bullet, one that could kill Raven.

The voice in the dream led Sonny to the gunsmith, a man left over from an earlier time. His dark, deserted hut near Algodones smelled of cordite, sulfur, and melted lead. I make bullets for every occasion, the gunsmith told Sonny, but to kill a shadow you need lead melted from the bowels of hell, and powder mixed with ash from where atomic bombs were exploded. This is the way the world is ending.

And so the alchemist of lead and heat cast a bullet for Sonny.

In the morning, there on his kitchen table sat the glistening bullet. On the lead was scratched an indentation, the form of a cross. The mandala of death, or the original quincunx from the beginning of time. With trembling hands Sonny had loaded it in his pistol where it rested, waiting for Raven.

"What about the governor?" he asked.

"He's what's called a meat-and-potatoes man. Typical politician. They get into office and start making deals."

"Water rights," Sonny offered.

"Yeah. We used to be able to get along. There was enough water. Now there's just too many people for too little water. So if you're a businessman you buy up water rights. Dominic wants to empty the reservoirs and store the water underground. He puts a spigot in the aquifer and sells you water that used to belong to everyone. The market will pay what he demands."

"Quite a scheme," Sonny said. So Naomi knew the score. Bear was a leader of the young Indians fighting Dominic, and she was running around with Bear. Yes, she knew the score.

She smiled at Sonny. "I learned about the market selling pottery. The world rotates around what the market gives and what it takes. Now I'm back. And what do our people want? They just want to go on holding their dances, doing their thing. Old ceremonies for the kachinas. It's been like that for hundreds of years. Now everything is market driven. I hate it."

"Myth and ritual are dying," Sonny said. "Except in the pueblos."

"Yes. It's a shitty little place. But it's home. The world out there chews you up and spits you out. Here, I feel a tranquility I haven't felt in ages. I feel committed."

Sonny had learned that myth was empty without ritual, and so the pueblos performed the ceremonies, the dances. Without enacting the myth, life was empty, the children would forget. Along the Rio Grande corridor, in all the pueblos surrounding the Jemez caldera, it was the old people who kept the cycle of ceremonies intact, prodding the young to remember.

"Were you involved with the governor?"

"None of your business," she snapped back. "Look, I've made mistakes." After a long pause she said, "Maybe I can't change. I'm cursed. I keep telling people what's going to happen and no one believes me. Maybe I'm just one of those voices that left the center, and now I'm just floating around. Bear listens. Bear is what I need. He's big and loud and crazy, but he's real."

She reached out and touched his shoulder. "Of course, I never got over you, Sonny."

He smiled at her and she laughed.

He looked out the window, thinking that if he concentrated on the road and the landscape he wouldn't remember what she had tasted like ten years ago.

Outside the truck the morning light fell like a mellow mist into the valley, imbuing the place with its sacred touch. The light was absorbed by the land and became the spirit of the place.

Light becomes time, the old man said. It penetrates and becomes the red rock, pine tree, dry earth, the deer and the maggot, crustaceans and humans. Light becomes a dance. The stars that sweep through the night sky dance, and the atoms that reflect the stars also dance. All is dance and music. The full moon sails over the mesa and fills the valley with a light that whispers, the waters of the river whisper back, soon the entire mountain is humming and drumming, the light of love, nights of passion, the energy gathers in lust, giving birth again in spring.

"What do you know about Raven?" he asked.

"He's got a bomb. He wants to blow you up."

"Just me?"

"Probably the whole fucking place."

"Where do you fit in?"

"Augie thinks—"

Sonny waited. "What?"

"That I was screwing the governor." She paused, then continued. "I guess that makes me a suspect. You know, I love this place, I really do. But, God, there's just too many bad things happening. What used to be fun and joyful is now called sinning. Screwing around used to be part of life. You know, real. Maybe if all the preachers went away we might just be better off."

Sonny smiled. He remembered the story of a preacher who came to preach against the sinners who lived in the valley. He claimed the sins were washing into the river. Sin in the river water was irrigating the corn, chile, calabacitas, and apples, and the people eating the fruits of the valley became sinners. One old man stood up and said, preacher man, water is our life, our soul. It does not sin. The preacher left and never returned. The people went on irrigating their fields and eating calabacitas con mais and chile verde in summer, and the women went on baking sweet, fat, juicy apple pies. All the great aphrodisiac fruits of the valley continued to be eaten with great gusto.

Near the pueblo the valley spread out gently. The river gave up its turbulent soul, becoming placid, flowing softly, allowing itself to be diverted into the acequias that fed the fields. The nurturing earth received the liquid gold. The river breathed a sigh of relief, slowed its rush and gurgle and continued sluggishly down past Zia and Santa Ana, finally emptying its last ejaculation into the Rio Grande at Bernalillo. Like one life ebbing into the greater stream of time, the river disappeared, took on a new name, and the waters of the Jemez Mountain Cloud People joined the Rio Grande, and all was as it might have been ordained at the beginning of time.

The river carved its own path, and at each turn the river put on a different face, just as a woman will make over her face for each of the four seasons of her life, for each day, for different lovers, even on the day she dies and whispers to those nearby, "My lipstick. I want my Maker to see me made up."

So the river had a persona for each season. El río, the Spanish said, but the river was a woman whose waters came pouring from the hot springs that dotted the caldera, a woman whose eyes bubbled with the water of life, a touch of mint in her breath, an apricot-blossom blush to her cheeks.

The mountain was female, its rounded caldera soft breasts—not like the male peaks of the Sangre de Cristos. The crater itself—a womb opening, the cleft of a distant ecological birth that spewed forth its hot magma, the birth stuff. The caldera reflected the sipapu of the kiva, the hole of emergence. The mountain had been born in the boiling belly of mother earth, and the birthing was not yet done. The magma and boiling water still slithered like giant serpents in the dark womb of the mountain, the dark womb of the mother.

The mountain watched impassively the works of men and women. Its waters ran deep; its fiery magma burned white. The old volcano would long outlast the scientists whose formulas created nuclear fire in the Los Alamos labs. The mountain was patient, the mountain could wait, and eons after man's tracks were erased from its slopes and hidden paths, its fire would still be burning deep, its waters rushing from dark, deep springs.

The Jemez River by all comparisons was a small mountain stream that petered out by the time it reached the Rio Grande. Nevertheless, it was one of those sacred places where time entered the earth and the spirit became song. It was Alph, a sacred river feeding the people of the valley.

Even after the desecrations of man, the river's magic was still intact. From the sage hills up to the flat mesa tops of piñon, juniper, and ponderosa pine, into the blue haze of the peaks, the subterranean waters could be felt but not seen, and from sheer granite cliffs small springs gurgled, sliding and tumbling downward, pulled by a force stronger than the mountain itself, the gravity of time.

On the walls of the canyon the intruder—he who was the visitor to the mountain, a pilgrim, a lost lover—could read the ages, and if he fell under the spell of the mountain, he stayed. He became a lover of the mountain and could confess, like all others who in their moments of joy said, This is our holy book, this we praise and protect, this river and mountain.

The lips of the canyon opened, red with iron ore, a bloody greeting, an entrance into the earth itself. No one could escape the feeling of entering, the shock of returning to the source, the first thrust as one entered at the Red Rocks, then moving farther into the wide cañada, with furry mesas on either side cramping down as the passage narrowed, and the lost lover wondered if to enter meant to stay forever, as time had once penetrated the canyon and stayed forever.

But the virginity of the earth was no longer intact. Every traveler entering the canyon was an intruder, a pilgrim lost according to the ages written on the walls, a lover lost, always returning, never quite achieving the burst of clarity that would relieve the tired flesh. And every lover knew the entrance into such dark, mysterious space quickened the breath, formed some knot of fear or incertitude deep in the belly. Those that did not thrust deep enough would never know the ecstasy the mountain offered.

Hundreds of times Sonny had crossed the bridge over the Ponderosa Creek, a bridge that separated different worlds, the bridge of La Llorona, who haunted late-night travelers carrying discontent in their hearts.

In the time of summer thunderstorms, the stream rolled and tumbled rocks along its bed, creating a sound that echoed in the canyon. Those from the plains mistook the noise for a train rumbling across the broad belly of the continent. Those from distant oceansides heard the surf beating its heart against a sandy beach. The natives knew: the laughing waters were rushing into time.

Sonny could not help but wonder on which palisade of crumbling rocks might be found the Zia Stone, the one petroglyph that held the meaning he sought. The ancient people, the Anasazi, had left their footprints on the sandy gullies, left their old pueblos on the mesas, left their drumming and songs playing along the piñon-covered foothills and in the tall ponderosa pines of the high country. Their voices could be heard. The spirits were there.

"Why so silent?"

"Just thinking," Sonny replied.

"This place does that to you," Naomi said. "I left a lot of my culture behind, traveled the world, got caught up in artsy fartsy New York. A girl's got to make a living. But I still feel the presence of the ancestors here. I'm still a Jemez Pueblo woman, no matter what they say."

For a while Sonny didn't respond, but he knew he had to ask.

"Where was the governor last night?"

"At Los Ojos, dancing. Yeah, I was there. That's why Augie called me. It's not what you think, Sonny."

"What?"

"You know, what people say. Damn pueblo is a gossip mill. So is every little town I know, so is every big city I've ever been in, from New York to Paris to Barcelona. People gossip. Gossip can kill you. Maybe it killed the governor."

"Gossip doesn't kill, people do."

"Words kill. Maybe the governor knew too many names. . . ." Her voice trailed off; then, "And eyes. Eyes can kill too. You know. You know about the mal ojo. The evil eye."

The governor knew too many names, Sonny thought. What the hell did that mean?

"This place is full of spirits," Naomi said, shivering. "Some people just don't see them. They hear them but don't see them. They go crazy. Some don't want to see them. I know you see them. Hey, why do you think I'm dressed in this white buckskin All-American-Indian fucking outfit? It was Bear's idea. Hell, I only wear this outfit when I go to an opening. People who come to buy my pots wants to see a *real* Indian. They still think *real* Indians wear buckskin. I got to take it off."

She opened her bag and took out a pair of jeans and a cowboy shirt with pearl buttons. Before Sonny could say a word she was wiggling out of the buckskin outfit, revealing in the light of the cab soft curves of flesh that would drive a landscape artist to portraiture. In his gut, Sonny felt the same disturbing hunger he felt when he needed a fix of ice cream. Chocolate.

He glanced at her and felt feathers in his blood. He glanced at his rear mirror, pulled over to the side of the road, and turned off the ignition.

"I'll wait outside," he said.

"Whatever," she replied. "I heard one of the girls at Los Ojos say 'the governor looks like a duck, he must fuck like a duck.'" She laughed.

Sonny stepped outside and looked at the river.

A neighbor in Jemez Springs had ducks. He had seen a male duck frantically chasing a female, dust and feathers rising, loud quacking and crying as every duck in the yard chased after the two, a gang bang, then a hullabaloo as the suitor finally caught the beloved, clamped his beak on the crest of her head, and mounted for a few fateful moments.

Zeus, in the form of a swan, had descended hot and lusty from Olympian heights, looking for Leda. The oldest stories tell us that the gods have always left their transcendent castles in the sky to mate with beautiful women. Zeus or Yahweh, it made no difference. A woman could draw the gods from heaven. And what progeny did such passion engender? Polyphemus or prophets?

Naomi called. "You know what? I get the feeling you're missing something. Or someone. The people say when you're sad like that and thinking about only one thing, that someone has stolen your heart. Is it true, Sonny, has someone stolen your heart?"

What does she mean somebody stole my heart?

He turned, and her reflection appeared in the rearview mirror, soft curves and a smile. He looked up at the cliffside, the towering palisades where, if one looked long enough, one could see the outline of a figure. San Diego.

Long ago in early mornings when he and Dennis went fishing on the Jemez, Dennis's grandfather, don Pedro, often accompanied them. The old man would make them stop along this stretch of road so he could get out of the car and point at the imposing cliff, which stood like Hercules holding up the bulk of the mesa and the heart of the sky.

Mira, don Pedro intoned, his thin voice raspy as the wind. In 1696, o de por'ay, de Vargas and some Zia Pueblo allies fought the Jemez Pueblo people up on the cliff. Rather than surrender the Jemez warriors jumped off the cliff. San Diego saved them from sure death. On the other side, the women jumped. La Virgen de Guadalupe saved them. It is said they floated down to safety like butterflies. You see, there is the image of San Diego. Carved on the cliffside. On the other side is the figure of La Virgen. We'll go see it someday. Before I die. A miracle, que no?

Where? they asked, peering up at the imposing rock slabs. Countless centuries of wind, rain, and ice had carved messages on the face of the cliff.

They followed the line of the grandfather's shaking finger, straining to see what he saw, until by sheer will power or faith they nodded, yes, they could see the outline of San Diego.

Yeah, I see it! Yeah!

The old man made the sign of the cross. So now the people pray to San Diego de Alcalá. Some resist and keep their traditional ways. That's the history of our land.

Hushed by the mystery they then piled into the car and continued up the road to stop at the Jemez Springs cafe for pie and coffee.

Those were innocent times, Sonny thought. Fish, drink beer, eat baloney sandwiches, return home with a few rainbow trout, which his mom would fry for him, shower, and go out with barrio friends for a beer. Eliseo, Jimmy, Arthur. Play barroom pool, return home late at night to prepare for Monday's university classes.

"What do you see?" Naomi asked. She came around the truck.

"I used to see the figure of a saint carved into the cliff. Now I'm not so sure. Sometimes instead of saints I see kachinas."

"Ah, Sonny, you're a poet," she whispered, and leaned close to him.

He could hear his heart pounding, the gentle morning breeze sliding down the canyon, the faint voice of the river. A truck passed by, then a car.

"You've been in the spirit world?"

Sonny couldn't tell her he had chased Raven in his dreams, chased him through hinges of New Mexican history, until the bastard killed his child and don Eliseo.

Sonny had seen the soul of the child, a bright light splitting in two, just before Raven murdered don Eliseo. That ball of glowing light had saved Sonny.

Now he wanted Raven. That's why he had come. Could he force Raven to give back the child?

"Bear came to help you, Sonny. Don't you see? You helped the snake and Bear helped you. You're a warrior, Sonny, but you don't make a very good warrior if your heart is stolen."

"What do you mean?"

"I just feel it. Maybe that's why I'm here. I don't trust Augie."

"Why go?"

"He threatened me," she said.

The morning breeze stirred, moving like La Llorona among the bare cottonwood trees, her torn and ragged skirt catching in the branches. The brittle grass of winter shivered and sounded like a rattlesnake about to strike.

From the cliff a raven called.

He's here, Sonny knew.

"Damn place is full of spirits," Naomi said.

"Yeah."

They got in the truck and drove in silence to Jemez Springs.

7 »

Have I changed so much? Sonny wondered. Are any of the vatos I went to school with out chasing their shadows? Was I destined to meet don Eliseo and learn his shaman ways? Why am I here and not there? *There* meant leading the kind of life some of his amigos led. They were entering their thirties now, mostly married and with kids. A few had been in Desert Storm.

Sonny ran into them, they talked, promised to call each other, but it wasn't the same. In the thirteen years since he graduated from Rio Grande High things had changed. People changed. The city was mushrooming with new immigrants from California and the Midwest; even from New York they flocked to Rio Rancho. Like snowbirds seeking warmer climates they found the Rio Grande Valley, nestled, and called it home.

The old valley cultures clung tenaciously to their roots, their land of passion. The light of the high desert and mountain region was a light of passion. As, he thought, it must be in the African savannah, on the mist-shrouded peaks of Machu Picchu or Tepoztlan, on Temple Mount or at the Taj Mahal, or on the blue Nile when the red orb disappeared in the western desert, coating the river with a rich alligator sheen and the pyramids of Giza with the hue of Ra.

The sun was the symbol and the source of the universal light, and New Mexicans were a people of the light. The old people understood light was time, and time was to be shared with family and friends.

The curves of the road entering Jemez Springs are low-rider territory, Sonny thought. That's why he was thinking about the South Valley homies. Good friends, good times. The old houses of the village spoke of a time gone by, a history those who hurried would never know.

But Sonny felt the urgency to get to the Bath House and talk to Augie. What Naomi had told him made sense. Raven had returned and was up to dirty business. But a bomb on the Valle Grande? An Al Qaeda prisoner? A dead governor? How in the hell did it all tie together? Or maybe it didn't. Maybe it was the unraveling of Sonny's world that Raven was after on the first day of spring. The path had already taken many turns. Perhaps it was just about to take more, all plotted by Raven.

Now something else was ticking in his thoughts, what Naomi said, about his stolen heart. Yes, he felt the vacuum, the emptiness. Not because Rita could not yet lie at his side—he could wait; it was her well-being that mattered to him—but because something he couldn't name had been lost deep inside, in recesses even he could not enter, and therefore could not know. If his heart was stolen, who had it?

In his dreams he heard the whispers of lost souls, voices he couldn't identify. Like the ancient mariner with the albatross tied around his neck, he felt the weight of the dreams. Try as he might, he had not been able to enter those dreams.

"What next?" he asked Naomi.

"Depends on Augie—" She paused. "I don't know what he wants."

"You need a ride back?"

"Bear will come for me. I'm his girl now."

She looked at him. It was obvious he was hurting, and she might be able to help.

"You want to know who stole your heart?"

Sonny shrugged. It wasn't like him to ask for help, but she had touched the sense of loss he felt in his dreams. She also knew something of the shaman way.

"You have a place here?" she asked.

He pointed to a cabin by the river. "The one with the apple trees."

"I'll wait there. If that's okay."

"Sure. It's open."

"Be careful with Augie," she said. "He's as deep in this as anyone."

Sonny nodded. A sense of relief made his shoulders relax. Maybe there was a reason she had come back into his life. Maybe she had come to help.

The old village homes always reminded Sonny of a time past, a village he had known in another life, perhaps the small towns south of Isleta, villages he had visited with his grandfather as a child, villages where his grandfather knew the people: Los Lentes, Los Lunas, Tome, Peralta, Los Chavez, Casa Colorada, Jarales, Las Nutrias, Sabinal, La Joya. La Joya, his mother's birthplace. The history of Rio Abajo was written in the blood and sweat of the Mexicanos and genízaros of those pueblos.

Each village in the state lay comforted and enveloped in its own mystique, its own history, its own ambience of time, space, and people interacting. The movement of the sun and its light transformed each town's geography into sacred space, a circle the people called home. That's what drew tourists to the state, a feeling of old-world tranquility, villages caught in a time warp.

The Mexicanos had learned from the Pueblo Indians by attending their fiestas. The early Hispanos learned the languages of the vecinos: Tiwa, Towa, Keres, Apache, Navajo. The Pueblos learned Spanish, and thus business was conducted. Young Hispanos going to a dance at the pueblo liked to flirt with the young Inditas, and it helped if they knew the language.

The women learned herbs and remedies the Pueblos had been using for hundreds of years. A bruja could pierce a man's knee with a stone. It helped if the bruja's victim knew a little Keres so he could get the help of a medicine man. Only he could pull out the stone and make the patient well.

The Catholicism of Spain with all its mystery entered the circle of the Pueblos. The statues of Mary, Joseph, Jesus, and the saints became ancestors to be venerated. During feast days the Pueblo men erected a choza, an arbor of green branches. Placed in the plaza during the summer dances, the choza protected the altar on which were placed the statues of La Virgen and the pueblo's patron saint. Elders sat in folding chairs on either side of the altar. The dancers and guests entered to pay their respects to the santo and to sprinkle corn meal.

Both the Pueblo way and the Catholic way were paths of the sacred, for as long as men and women could pray and believe in its efficacy, dance, beat the drums, and sing, the ceremonial song of life would continue.

That's the way it was in Jemez Springs where the whispering of the spirits on the mesas flowed down the imposing cliffs to greet the whispering waters of the river, the Jemez River, no more than a creek by foreign measure, but a river to the natives, a blessing of life-giving water washing down from the high peaks, flowing from waters that could not be seen.

The East Fork headwaters bubbled up from the Valles Caldera, the vast sunken valley of the collapsed volcano. That stream met the San Antonio Creek and became the Jemez River. All rivers, big and small, take their life from the waters that cannot be seen but in time became visible, and thus spirit moved into matter and renewed the life of the paisanos.

The morning sun shone radiant on the face of the west cliff. This was the time of the Lords and Ladies of the Light, the dancing streams of light fathered by the Zia Sun. Los Señores y Señoras de la Luz descended to bless the earth.

In the afternoon the setting sun christened the carmine face of the east mesa. Sonny had sat many an afternoon watching the evening light awaken the kachinas that lined the cliffside, images cut by the centuries into the rock face. Light and water and time flowed through the narrow valley, and it was all he needed to know of the beauty of the Universal Creation.

On the "dog dream" phenomenon the village was split into factions, the believers and nonbelievers. The Zen Center had held a symposium in its new building. The Zen of Dog Dreams. Mostly believers from California had attended. The others preferred to discuss the question over a cold beer at Los Ojos Cantina.

Today the sense of time flowing into the canyon was disrupted by the presence of police cars. Sonny stopped at the roadblock, and a state cop peered in.

"Sonny Baca?"

"That's me."

"Drive into the Bath House parking lot. Check in with Captain Martinez. He's expecting you."

Sonny nodded and drove on, waving at JoJo on the road, then turning into the village plaza. He parked in front of the library. The Bath House was cordoned off as a police scene. A village crowd had gathered at the yellow tape. Sonny took note of the state police helicopter parked in the open space beyond.

He picked up Chica, and he and Naomi made their way through the crowd. Friends in the crowd called hello. The Merheges, Dave and Fran, Ron and Dee, Melvin and Noni. The latter had been his vecinos since he bought the house in Jemez Springs, and in New Mexico a good vecino ranked right up there with familia. You could be a padrino, have good compadres, marry off your best friend, baptize a baby, and thus spread the roots of the compadre/comadre relationships, extend la familia, and thus be content to call many your primos. But compadres drifted, sometimes moved far away to work, following the old dream to sunny California, or Denver, or the burgeoning cities of the Arizona desert. On the other hand, a good vecino lived next door, the friendship priceless. Melvin had been that for Sonny, teaching him by example the village ways, always lending a helping hand.

Sonny waved back, gave the thumbs-up signal. An irritated Augie Martinez was waiting at the Bath House door.

"Let them through!" he called to the officer at the police tape. The young man smiled and lifted the ribbon for Sonny and Naomi to pass.

"About time," he said. "I see you brought a friend."

Augie had played football for Santa Fe High, Sonny remembered. A straight arrow who once turned in his teammates for breaking curfew. After that the kids called him Rata.

Sonny nodded at the television vans parked along the road. "I see you have company."

"Goddamn news media. I haven't told them anything. I heard one of the stations is flying in a cameraman. They plan to parachute him into the Valle. In the meantime, you're it. Come inside."

He led them into the Bath House. People had been using the hot mineral water of the nearby spring for centuries. Those in pain or those just looking for pleasure could soak in the tubs filled with super-hot water.

Sonny knew the healing power in the water. He had spent three months in a wheelchair, crippled by Stammer's electric charge, and when he regained the use of his legs he had headed for the hot springs of the mountain.

He spent cold January afternoons up at Spence Spring sitting in the warm water gurgling out of the ojito, the mist rising in winter evenings as snow fell softly and coated the towering ponderosa pines. January slipped into February and more and more bare-breasted ladies and their beer-drinking friends began to show up. Sonny shied away from the boisterous crowds that flocked to the spring. He preferred being alone. He could find the solitude he sought by using the Bath House. The springs of the mountain were free, but they grew busier and louder as the warm spring weather canopied the mountain. He had to pay to use the tubs in the Bath House, but here he soaked in silence, allowing the water to go deep into the muscles and nerves, unwinding the stiffness from those months in the wheelchair.

L'agua cura, the old people used to say. Water cures. Con el favor de Dios, l'agua cura.

The reception room was empty. "You wait here," Augie ordered Naomi.

She shrugged, sat in a chair, and picked up a magazine. "Don't say I didn't warn you," she said to Sonny.

Augie spun around, glared at her, then waved her off.

"What the hell does she know?" he said as he led Sonny down the steps into the room that held the cubicles, a concrete bathtub in each.

"We haven't let the news media in," Augie said, pulling aside the curtain of one of the cubicles. Sonny peered in. The man in the tub was a mass of wrinkled flesh, a large dark bruise over his right eye.

Sonny winced. "How long has he been in the water?"

"The Crime Lab people will tell us. I guess since around twelve A.M."

Sonny looked at the floor. "He was dragged in."

"I figure," Augie replied.

Sonny nodded. So the governor hadn't come to take a hot bath. Somebody planned his death.

"Where did you last see him?"

"At the bar. I left Los Ojos at around ten. He stayed. There were five university professors, foreigners, at the bar. He got to talking to them. Books, stuff like that."

"Where are they now?"

"At Los Ojos."

"Foreigners in Jemez Springs?"

"They're visiting with Ben Chávez. The writer. He's got a house down the road. They study his work. And Momaday. They love the whole Indian/Chicano thing."

"Thing," Sonny whispered. So the writers and the cultures they wrote about were things.

"Have you talked to them?"

"Yeah. They don't know diddley."

"Who found the governor?"

"The receptionist. She called the village marshal and he called me. I have her in custody—just so she doesn't talk."

"What time?"

"Around nine."

"Where were you?"

"Look, Sonny, you let me ask the questions. Right now only a few of us know the governor's dead, and it stays that way till I talk to my superiors."

"Superiors?"

"The chief—Ah, he's out of town. On his way back. In the meantime I'm in charge."

Sonny nodded. Augie hadn't meant the chief when he said superiors. So who was he reporting to?

"We don't want panic. The news people already know there's something on the mountain. Some Indians were up there, doing some kind of ceremony or other. They came down and spread the word."

Bear knew. At Red Rocks he, or one of his friends, had mentioned a bomb. Bear and Naomi knew a lot.

"Look, people are going to panic. I have instructions not to release news of the governor's death until—you know, one thing at a time."

Who killed the governor? Sonny wondered. Why? In the face of death it was best to be philosophical. If possible.

He looked at the wrinkled body floating in the water.

"He looks like one of those wrinkled Chinese dogs. What are they called?"

"Shar Pei."

"Shard Pee?"

"No, Shar—"

"Never mind. Why did you leave him in the water?"

"Our forensics unit broke down in La Cueva. He can't be moved until they get here."

"Yeah, but he's just cooking away."

The pink-fleshed governor looked well done. His fish eyes stared up at the ceiling where the mineral-laced humidity in the room gathered in globules, droplets that from time to time splashed down. Sonny dipped a finger into the water. It was still warm. Had someone been running the hot water from time to time to keep the governor cooking?

"Don't look like the governor—"

"It's him all right."

Sonny peered again then at the patch of pubic fur, which swayed like seaweed, revealing with each gentle roll a small, shrunken stub.

"Small. Maybe because it's shriveled?"

"I never paid attention."

"How does a guy with such a small, you know, get to be governor?"

"Money."

"Money talks."

"Yeah. Besides, they don't measure your private parts when you run for office."

"So, what do you have?"

"This." Augie pointed at the small shelf on the wall, which held four raven feathers. Raven's calling card.

"Raven."

"That's why we called you. He leaves the four feathers, doesn't he?"

Sonny nodded.

"There's four more up at the Thing on the Valle."

Why would Raven murder the governor? Create chaos in state government? Hardly. State government was always in chaos. A few would miss the governor, but the karmic wheel of the bureaucrats would go on grinding, the lieutenant governor, someone no one ever remembered, would have a few months in the limelight, and the poor would go on being taxed.

"This is going to be a gold mine for the village," Augie said.

"What do you mean?"

"Damn, Sonny. The business association can get a lot of mileage out of this. Think of the publicity this is going to give Jemez Springs. They can run newspaper ads, plaster billboards on the highway. This is bigger than Fort Sumner bragging Billy the Kid is buried there. Visitors, the curious, the psychotic, and the sick would come to bathe in the Governor's Tub. Yeah, call it the Governor's Tub."

And the university will offer a political science class on the effects of a governor drowning while in office, thought Sonny. A folklorist would suggest La Llorona killed the governor, and several Ph.D. dissertations would be written on the crying woman's pathological hatred of male authority figures.

"We haven't had a governor killed in office in a long time," Augie continued.

"Not since Governor Bent," Sonny said. In 1847 Indians from Taos Pueblo and Mexicans still loyal to Mexico had attacked the governor and killed him. The gringo occupation had not come without resistance from the natives.

"Believe me, the death of a governor by drowning in a tub in a small town in New Mexico could be very lucrative. Maybe they can get Momaday to write a melodrama. He lives down the street."

Sonny stepped back and looked around the room. He walked past the other tubs to the end. Everything appeared in place.

In this society even death can be lucrative, the old man said.

I thought you were asleep?

The commotion woke me.

You agreeing with Augie?

Ni tonto. I wouldn't trust him as far as I can throw him.

And Raven?

Why would Raven kill the governor?

"Yeah," Sonny cleared his throat. "Why?"

"What?"

Sonny looked at Augie. "What if it was an accident? He's had a few drinks, comes in to take a bath, trips . . ."

"Then why the four feathers? The chief agrees. It's Raven."

"Why would the governor come into the Bath House with Raven?"

"Naomi. He had the hots for Naomi."

"You think—"

"Hell, Sonny, things will play out. If she was in on this it's just a matter of time. Look, she's been running around with a group of Indians—they call themselves Green Indians. Preserving their water rights and all that. Bunch of troublemakers is what they are."

Sonny shook his head. Naomi was worldly wise, but she sure as hell wasn't into luring the governor to his death.

"Who else was at the bar last night?"

"Local yokels. But around closing time only the professors were left."

"Let's talk to them."

"Ah, they don't know shit. The real prize is the Al Qaeda operative I've got prisoner. That's a feather in my cap."

"Have you questioned him?"

"I'll let the FBI do that. Put two and two together, Sonny. Raven needs hired guns. He hires the Al Qaeda to kill the governor—"

"Why would the governor trust someone he doesn't know?"

"I think the terrorist offered information on the plot to wipe out Los Alamos. The governor followed him here where Raven was waiting. Equals four."

No, not four, not yet, Sonny thought.

Right, the old man cautioned Sonny.

"Where's the town marshal now?"

"He's pissed off. I took over and put a clamp on everything. Nothing gets out unless I say so."

Sonny felt an irritation creeping into his bloodstream. He turned and walked back into the reception area.

"Let's talk to the professors."

"What the hell for?"

"Curiosity," Sonny replied.

Naomi rose, looked at Sonny, and he shrugged. So far, it was Augie's show.

"Our lady friend was also at Los Ojos last night," Augie said. "I wonder what she knows."

"I left early!" Naomi answered.

"Did you talk to the governor?"

"Everyone talked to him," she replied.

"Maybe you've told Sonny what you know," he said in a threatening tone. "Maybe you should be in custody—"

"You arrest me and I tell everything!" Naomi replied, her anger flaring.

Sonny waited for her to let loose, but Augie's presence intimidated her.

She settled for "Am I free to go?"

"Yeah, for the meantime. Just don't leave the state." He laughed.

"I'll see you later, Sonny," she said and turned and hurried out of the building.

"Where did you pick her up?" Augie asked, looking after Naomi.

"Red Rocks."

"Hanging out with her friends. Stay away from them, Sonny, they're only trouble. We've had our people watching them for some time. Today they're having a big secret meeting in Algodones. Yeah, secret." He paused and looked at Sonny. "You know about the meeting?"

"I heard some talk," Sonny replied. He wasn't about to give any information to Augie.

"Come on, let's go see the professors."

Sonny and Chica followed Augie out of the Bath House and across the street.

8 »

THEY PAUSED IN FRONT OF THE BAR.

"Funky place," Augie said.

"Why did the governor keep coming back?" Sonny asked.

"He took baths. Massages. He said the place reminded him of home. Peaceful."

He's in peace, Sonny thought and looked down the road, then at the bar.

Sometime in the past, it was rumored, Los Ojos Cantina had been registered in the National Book of Funky places. Some insisted the ancient rifles, spurs, saddles, rattlesnake and cougar skins, rusty farm implements, bad paintings, and a thousand other items hanging on the walls deserved to be called Baroque Western Americana, but for the realists it was just plain junk. Funky was the allure of the place.

The bar's ambience held, in warm embrace, the sweat, tears, hard-luck stories, and the propositions of a thousand lonely hearts who had sat at the bar nursing their beers. The wooden seats had been polished smooth by all the barflies who had killed time bullshitting there, and the well-worn dance floor creaked with the weight of lovers who had danced cheek-to-cheek on Saturday nights, lovers and those looking for love.

Sitting in the middle of the floor, like a tired rhino, the pool table, the same pool table found in a thousand western bars, from Yakima to El Paso. Every small-town bar down the spine of the Rocky Mountains owned a pool table where many an idle player had honed his skills and bet "the loser buys the beer."

The booths, pressed against the honey-colored wood walls, were witness to the multitudes who had huddled there to eat green chile cheeseburgers, supposedly the best in the state, but then every small-town cafe in New Mexico boasted it cooked the best green chile cheeseburgers. Most of those claims were inflated. After all, the cooks in the kitchen were usually transients who moved from place to place, not looking for the best kitchen to work in, but searching to satisfy a personal, unsettling hunger in the soul.

"People think the governor just sits up in Santa Fe and does nothing," Augie volunteered. "This state is booming, Sonny. A lot of development going on. A man makes the right deals and he can make a lot of money. Once in a while the governor liked to get away. . . . You know, it's quiet here. Like stepping into a different time zone."

"Some say he came to see a woman."

Augie bristled. "Come on, Sonny, don't get into that. You concentrate on telling me what you know about Raven's tactics. I'll take care of the rest. You have a place here, don't you?"

"Yeah, it's home," Sonny said, surprising himself. He and Rita hadn't owned the cabin that long, and already there was a feeling of home. Perhaps it was the community he had been looking for. He couldn't return to the farm his grandfather once owned. Maybe here was a place where he could get away, a restful place close to the river and the earth.

"I'll be a minute," Augie said. He turned to talk to the cops standing guard over a police car. The occupant in the back seat was leaning over, obviously handcuffed, so Sonny couldn't see his face.

Sonny climbed the steps and waited on the porch. He looked up and down the main street. Normally the village would be quiet. Today the crowd gathered in front of the Bath House was buzzing. Inside the governor lay dead and rumors were running rampant.

"Home," Sonny repeated. This place has been home to some of the old families for generations. And now it was home to newcomers, people seeking a slower, tranquil way of life. The people of the West could be a restless bunch. Always searching for a yet-unrealized dream, a need to belong, a yearning for the perfect place to settle down, and in the process of settling down the people of the West fell into a love affair with the land.

It was this personal hunger that had driven many a pilgrim to settle in Jemez Springs. Like generations before them they had crossed the Rockies to the Pacific, then traveled north to Washington and Alaska, south into the Arizona desert. Always looking for a place to call home, a piece of Eden. They had survived the burning landscape, looking for a green oasis. Yes, once the burning search was satisfied, the people became one with the land.

"You can take my truck," the old ranchers used to say. "And you can have my wife. Hell, I'll even throw in the kids. But by god I intend to die on these few scrubby acres."

The early settlers of the West were like tumbleweeds. Dry and drifting, they had been rolled this way and that by the winds of spring, victims of stormy weather and barbed-wire fences. And what was the prize? A hardscrabble life for those who lived in the western mountains and deserts. Burned dry by the sun, weathered by the wind, they turned as hard as the unforgiving land.

People just don't want the frontier to end, Sonny thought. They keep replaying the conquest of the land in movies. Hadn't they learned by now? The land can't be conquered. Perhaps in small villages like Jemez Springs and Jemez Pueblo lay the answer. There a community could thrive, not the lone cowboy of the movies, but the people.

And where do those looking for a place gather? Sonny looked at the door of the bar. In the cantina. The cantinas of the West were places of respite from the hot sun, the constant dry wind and dust that choked, summer rainstorms drifting up from the gulf in summer, and winter snows that whipped down from Canada. When lightning and thunder tore the earth apart, cowboys and cowgirls headed for the cantina. Every western town owned a church and a cantina, but most often the weary pilgrim chose the local bar, a place of cool shades, the cavern where talk was easy and a temporary welcome was the price of a beer.

The drifter, the seeker in the wild land, the lost soul, all were drawn to the cantina. The church held answers, but the dissatisfied did not seek the easy answers. In the cantina you could tell your story before the sun set. In the dark confessional of smoke and booze and lonely hearts there was always someone to listen to your story. Paying for the beer was cheaper than paying a shrink, and for the moment the terrible weight of the search was lifted, the day got lighter, telling the story cleansed the soul.

Today the morning light seeped into the valley like a rain of gold falling from the fingers of Nebuchadnezzar.

Sonny shivered. Strange thoughts. I should be concentrating on Raven. Instead I feel I have to answer Naomi's question. The snake? The snake is related to dreams from the underworld. It wasn't by chance that I found it, then ran into Bear and Naomi.

He opened the door and stepped into the cool, dark bar.

The woman behind the counter smiled.

A transient herself, hitting forty and trying to look as she did when she was twenty. A lot of men had promised her dreams they couldn't deliver. She still showed some cleavage, just in case Mr. Good Fortune happened to show up that day, still teased her hair and brushed on bright lipstick. A Walgreens special, guaranteed to draw bees, the one good drone who could sweep her away, maybe to a condo on the California beach.

She looked as if she hurried to put on her mascara and lipstick on her way to work, and her teased hair cried that it had only waved at the comb.

What was her name? Sonny remembered the last time he and Rita had stopped by for green chile cheeseburgers. But he couldn't remember the barmaid's name. There was a different one every six months. They just moved on.

God bless the barmaids of the West. Was there ever a regal poem written for these working women who served as mother confessors, sisters, angels of mercy?

Those who came to down a beer or two didn't need to know her name. They entered the cantina to share in a few moments of intimacy. The rule of the Old West was wet your whistle, pay the bill, and move on. The cantina, like the small-town movie house, was only a temporary respite, a place to forget what was worth forgetting, a place to meet and talk to strangers, a cool, dark place where the unexpected lurked, where one just might find a moment of fulfillment, or lust, or joy, or take out bilious anger in the rage of a fist fight.

"Can I help you?" the barmaid asked.

Before he could answer Augie entered and called, "Hey, why didn't you wait? It's okay, lady. He's with me." He nodded toward the five professors gathered at the table. "State police business."

"Be my guest," she answered. "Nice to see you again," she said, smiling at Sonny. "I'll be in the kitchen."

"Not bad, huh," Augie whispered, looking after her. "She wasn't working last night so no use talking to her. Come on, let's meet the professors."

The five men at the table stood. They shook hands with Sonny as Augie introduced them. "Professor Mario from Florence. His colleague Michele. Also Italian."

"From Bari," the soft-spoken scholar said.

"Whatever," Augie shrugged. "Paul Taylor, looks American but he's from Geneva. Dieter is from Germany, and Jean Cazemajou from Bordeaux. Wine country, isn't it?"

"The best," the affable Frenchman answered.

"Bon giorno!" Mario greeted Sonny. "A pleasure to meet you. And is this the dreaming dog?"

"Chica, meet the professors," Sonny said. Chica barked a greeting.

Sonny placed her on the table. Michele offered Chica an Italian candy, which she took.

"One eye missing. Gurdjieff would love this," Taylor said, rubbing Chica's head.

Augie interrupted. "Mr. Baca has a special interest in what happened last night. Please cooperate with him."

"Did any of you see the governor leave the bar last night?" Sonny asked. "And was anyone with him?"

"I don't even remember last night," Taylor groaned. "Too much tequila." The others nodded and laughed. Except Michele, who glanced at Sonny. He had something to say.

"We walked back to monsieur Chávez's home in the dark," Jean explained.

"What can I say, the death of the governor is a tragedy," Mario shrugged and burped. "By the way, the Deli serves exquisite blue corn blueberry pancakes." He turned to his colleagues. "The ancient Aztecs raised dogs as we would raise sheep or cattle. To eat. In fact, the first tamales were probably made from dog meat."

"Dog tamales," Augie muttered.

"That raises the question," Michele offered. "If dogs dream, do those who ate the dog inherit the dog's dream? Is there some kind of metempsychosis, the dog dream being passed down generation after generation? You see, in many cultures the young warriors kill the old king and eat him, flesh and bones, or eat him symbolically. They do this to acquire his power. Cannibals eat their victims to gain the strength and skills of the enemy. This is symbolized in the taking of the Eucharist, eating the flesh and blood of Jesus to incorporate—"

Taylor interrupted. "But dreaming dogs don't appear in contemporary Chicano literature. Why? Because it's a recent story. I believe dreaming dogs are related to the Chupacabra mystery. Upon the deconstruction of the Chupacabra, that is, on the deconstruction of a folkloric creature with roots in the archetypal imagination whose only raison d'être was the collective shadow, i.e., fear of the lumpen, fear of the Anglo-American hegemony, and as those shadow fears imploded, they lost their hold over the collective memory and entered the Anglo world, i.e., the Chicano's desire to become more like his Anglo counterpart. Thus the appearance of the dog dream argument, a transference—"

Augie's jaw dropped. "Wha—"

Dieter poured a little of his Dos Equis beer into a saucer for Chica to slurp and joined in. "But you can't deconstruct folk memory! Does the dog wag the tail, or the tail wag the dog? You are going in circles. The essence of the dog dream lies in the artist as mythmaker. Which leads directly to the myth of Aztlán and its use as an identity marker in the *Weltanschauung* of the Chicano."

"No, Dieter," Jean contested in his mellifluous French accent, waving a finger. "The myth of Aztlán is dead. Contemporary Chicanos have opted for the American Dream, and their dream of a homeland has died. So has the belief in dreaming dogs."

Sonny smiled. Scholars on the road to Canterbury wound up in Jemez Springs. The world *was* round.

I think we're barking up the wrong tree, Sonny thought, but dared not say it for fear the scholars would take hold of the symbolism in the idiomatic expression. Do dogs that dream always bark up the wrong tree? Is the dream inherent in the bark? Is the tree the tree of life, the axis mundi? The tree in the Garden of Bliss? On and on.

There are two kinds of trees, don Eliseo would say. The evergreen and the deciduous. The latter blooms, leafs out, gives its leaves to the earth in winter. Birth and rebirth. Death and resurrection. The evergreen is always shining, the eternal promise of life. People are like trees.

Sonny enjoyed listening to the professors. He had read such stuff as a literature student at the university, and normally he would love to hear the scholars argue, but it was clear they didn't know anything. Except maybe for Michele. He knew something.

Cazemajou continued. "Like my colleagues, I have written on your local writers, some of whom have achieved some recognition in my country. But I beg to differ with my two colleagues. I am a skeptic. Dogs don't dream."

"But it is in Florence where we have closely studied the magical realism of the Southwest," Mario cut in. "Once I publish my dog-dream paper, the world of letters will appreciate this land I love as my own."

Augie rolled his eyes in disbelief. "Yeah. We can hardly wait. Come on, Sonny, we gotta get going." He turned abruptly and walked out. Sonny paused to pick up Chica.

"Thank all of you for an interesting analysis," Sonny said.

"Delighted," they replied. "May we meet again?"

"Sure," Sonny said. "Get Ben Chávez to drive you into town. Soon as this mess is over."

Michele stood and walked with Sonny to door. "I think you should know," he whispered, "when we left last night, I paused at the bridge. To listen to the sound of the river. This police captain who is with you—"

He paused. Sonny waited.

"He left the bar hours before we left. I think I saw him coming out of the Bath House—"

"You're not sure," Sonny said.

"Well no, it was dark. There is a light over the back door. I thought it strange for someone to be coming out of the building at that hour. I would not swear, but I am almost sure."

"Thanks." Sonny shook his hand and walked out.

The plot thickens, the old man said.

Yeah. What if he did see Augie coming out of the Bath House? Or is it another one of Raven's red herrings? In the meantime he's making deals with the politicos, and his word is not worth a plugged nickel.

Augie was waiting for Sonny by the police car. "I told you they didn't know anything," he said. "This is the real catch." He pointed at the man in the back seat. "Al Qaeda. He was in the bar last night."

"How do you know he's Al Qaeda?"

"The FBI's got a file on him. He's Al Qaeda all right. A big catch."

"And you think he killed the governor?"

"Let the bureau boys figure out the connection. Right now we have to get up to the mountain. Vamos."

He led Sonny across the plaza to the waiting helicopter.

"Get in!" Augie shouted above the roar of the chopper. "You're gonna see one hell of a strange sight!" They climbed in and strapped on their belts. Augie gave the pilot a thumbs-up signal, and the helicopter lifted into the air.

"We're closing down every airport and highway in the state!" Augie shouted above the roar. "Arresting every mother's son who looks like an Afghan."

Sonny frowned. "You're going to arrest people who *look* like Afghans?"

"Affirmative."

"You can't do that."

"The Attorney General says I can. You ever hear of the Patriot Act? You look like one of these Taliban vatos and you're dead meat."

"But East Indians, Blacks, even Chicanos have some of those characteristics—"

"Tough shit," Augie replied. "Hey, the governor's dead and my job is to cast a net that hauls in suspects. That bomb sitting up on the Valle is an Al Qaeda plot—"

"Do you know for sure?"

"Damn right! That thing explodes and the labs at Los Alamos and this whole state go up in nuclear fission. Raven's tried that before."

Sonny nodded. Yes, Raven had broken into the Los Alamos National Labs and stolen a plutonium pit. Right under the nose of supposedly tight security.

"So don't pull any constitutional rights on me, Sonny."

Yeah, Sonny thought, when in a hurry for results lock up the Constitution. He looked out as the chopper rose and quickly skimmed over Battleship Rock and past La Cueva, chugging and trembling into the higher altitude.

Below them the East Fork of the Jemez became a thread, a water snake delivering the hidden waters of the mountain down to the pueblos.

The pilot, an experienced argonaut, gunned his boat, and instead of skimming over the treetops and following the highway, he rose like an eagle, casting off the earth's gravity. As they flew over the lip of the caldera Sonny had a view of the crater, El Valle Grande, the ancient mountain's sunken womb.

In the kivas of the Pueblos, the sipapu was a small, round hole in the earth. From such an opening, the stories told, the ancestors emerged long ago. Seen from up high the volcano's caldera was a sipapu of the earth, a place of emergence.

"Chingao," he whispered, looking down. The round, sunken crater of the mountain formed a Zia symbol!

Sonny focused on the lines that radiated out from the caldera, the four directions stretching toward four sacred mountains, rolling away into infinity. A cosmos conceived by the ancestors. The prehistoric Americans had been here, and in the crater's green valley they saw an earth-womb, a place described in their legends. The Zia symbol defined the quadripartite earth. The yoni of the mountain was the center, birthplace of seething magma and boiling waters.

Suddenly the pilot pointed the chopper downward. He had climbed as far as he could go, and now he dropped in joy, round and round like a horny dragonfly during mating season.

"Look!" Augie shouted, nudging Sonny. "The Thing!"

There, about half a mile from Highway 4, which cut along the edge of the volcanic maw, sat the phallic spaceship, its nose stuck into the wet earth and winter-sere grass of the crater, its coat of shining metal reflecting the morning sunlight. The bomb, Raven's desire.

"The Thing?"

"Yeah," Augie shouted. "Like the movies! Fucking science fiction! Digital technology! Clones! Shit! What's real?"

Men in white, technicians from the labs, crawled around the bomb, holding their instruments to its belly, gauging it, measuring its radiation, skittering around the Thing like fearful ants. Along the highway where the lab cars and vans and SWAT Team jeeps were parked, more technicians gathered.

"Roswell!" Augie shouted and laughed, and gave the pilot a high five. "I swear it's Roswell all over! A guy could make a fortune out of this! You know the major networks are going to be here. So you play this up, make it a tourist attraction. A guy could make a million. Hit the talk shows . . . Jerry Springer, you know. Sometimes I wonder why I stay in the force."

The pilot nodded and brought the helicopter to a fluttering landing several hundred feet from the bomb.

Augie kept jabbering as they disembarked. "Looks like that first atom bomb they exploded down at Trinity Site. Fat Boy. If they can disarm it and take it down to Jemez Springs, place it in front of the Bath House, I kid you not: there's millions in tourism dollars! Hell, I should get into this."

Sonny, clutching Chica, followed Augie out of the vibrating chopper. A state police captain greeted them. Behind them stood the lab's heavily armed SWAT Team, outfitted to the hilt.

"Sonny, damn glad you came," said the captain, whose ID tag read *Stevens.* "This is Mr. Sturluson, he's the head honcho."

Sturluson shook Sonny's hand. "Call me Snore. Glad you could make it. Let's get to the point. We removed a side panel. Whoever placed this thing here left a message. I think you should look at it. First, slip into these."

They put on the protective suits and walked to the cylinder, its pointed nose stuck into the ground, its tail end sticking into the sky.

"Has fins like a fifties Cadillac, don't it? I tell you, it's too much," Augie joked.

"But not a laughing matter," Stevens said coldly.

"No it's not," Sturluson agreed. "It's hot. We don't know if it contains nuclear waste, which might be easier to deal with, or—" He paused. "The missing core."

"Why put it here?" Augie asked.

"Hard to tell. But whoever placed it here wanted us to find it."

"In fact," Stevens added, "an anonymous phone call told us where to find it."

Raven, Sonny thought.

Stevens cleared his throat. "Okay, I'll level with you. We first thought this was Raven's work. But it turns out he wants to work with us. Claims he's got information on Al Qaeda, or a terrorist organization linked to Al Qaeda."

"As I said," Augie said with satisfaction.

"At this point in time I don't care who he's working for or who placed the bomb. It's ticking, and we need to defuse it."

"And Raven's promised to help?" Sonny asked.

"As far as I know. But we don't know where he is or if he can, or will, help. Either way, we can't wait. We have to defuse this thing."

Sonny shook his head. Of course Raven would play all sides. Hire a few misguided terrorists to plant a bomb, then turn against them. Promise the government one thing, and deliver another. Perhaps the whole thing wasn't a Raven plot, but one more scenario by the CIA or FBI to entrap whatever terrorist cell existed in the state. Raven would play along with them.

Sonny looked at the highway and up the timbered slope of the mountain. A raven called, and the wind whipped the cry down to where they stood. He was here now. Laughing. Playing games.

"We don't even know if the thing has explosives. It is radioactive, and it is wired, but we just don't know—we did remove a panel."

Sturluson pointed at the opening where a panel on the side of the bomb had been removed, exposing a jumble of wiring inside, the face of a clock, the hour hand pointing at six.

Sonny shook his head. What the hell did he know about an armed nuke? Nothing, except it was Raven's game and that meant trickery. He walked around the bomb. It looked like the copy of the

Fat Boy bomb Raven had the Ukrainian scientist build in Sandia Labs. And that had been, in the end, a dud.

The brightly shining mass of metal reflected the morning light, exuding an aura so strong Sonny could smell the fear it created in the scientists who cautiously moved around it, their instruments buzzing.

Sonny thought of the *X Files* TV show he and Rita liked to watch. If this whole thing was taking place in another dimension, where were Mulder and Skully when you needed them? Maybe Augie was right and life was turning into one giant science fiction show, or a parody of it. Perhaps that's why so many yearned for a simpler time when people watched the moon and stars, measured the sun's course, the satisfying cyclical time of the seasons, time constantly transforming and renewing itself into something good. Now time was measured by the stock market, multinational corporations' earnings, and banks that took interest from the third world's economies. A false time, setting its imprint on the human psyche, sure to pervert human nature beyond repair.

"Speak of the devil, here comes the damned media!"

Sonny looked up into the sky. Outlined against the blue were two brightly colored paragliders, a cameraman suspended on each chute. Circling, hanging in the empty space, cameras silently whirring as they focused on the sight below. Their images were being beamed all over the world.

"We shut the road and they do this! Arrest every goddamn sonofabitch!" Stevens shouted, and a dozen SWAT Team officers ran toward the chutes.

"It's too late. They're already on the air waves. It's all a matter of time."

"We can't let the public know—"

Sturluson turned to Sonny. "We found a note." He handed Sonny a plastic bag. "It was inside the panel we removed. We checked it, it's clean, no radiation."

Chica growled. She smelled Raven. Sonny put her down and she ran first to smell, then to pee at the foot of the Thing.

"Don't that beat all? A one-eyed dog peeing on a nuke!"

"Beer makes her do that," Sonny said lamely.

He opened the bag and read Raven's message, in handwriting that Sonny realized looked very much like his own: *Sonny, you're barking up the wrong tree. Dreaming dogs don't lie.*

Sonny frowned, put the note back into the baggie, and handed it to Sturluson.

"What the hell does it mean?"

"He likes to play games."

"But he's promised to help," Sturluson said. "And I need help. The experts who can defuse this won't be here in time." He pointed at the clock. "Ticking right toward six o'clock."

There was little Sonny could say. He looked at the metallic skin of the bomb. Smooth as liquid mercury. Mercurial. Hermes. Messenger of the gods, except Raven's gods weren't the very human gods of Greek myths. His spirit ran rampant in the darkest parts of the psyche, dancing like dervishes deep in the unconscious. Each could be a god of destruction if not fished out of the broth of stagnant waters and brought into the air and light of the sun.

He touched the Zia medallion resting on his chest. Raven would kill for the symbol of the sun. Plant all sorts of tricks in the way, trickster that he fashioned himself to be, lord of skillful ravens.

Now he was ready to destroy the mountain, to rain death and destruction.

A Trojan Horse, with something dangerous lying in the belly of the Thing. But was it Raven's plutonium pit?

"There's one more thing," Sturluson said. "The Pentagon has lost a communications satellite. If these events are connected—" He frowned. He was in charge and right then there was very little he could do. The experts in disarming bombs were just now boarding planes hundreds of miles away. They wouldn't make it by six.

"If it goes off, Los Alamos goes. The entire area gets rained with the radioactive cloud, it spreads in the Jet Stream—a holocaust far beyond 9-11."

"Damn!"

9 »

There's something more than the destruction of Los Alamos on Raven's mind, Sonny thought as he and Augie walked back to the helicopter. He could have dropped Fat Boy right in the middle of the Los Alamos Labs, or in downtown Alburquerque. That would create immediate panic. Placing it on top of the mountain was a calculated move. Raven was making deals with the government. What kind of deals? And was Raven protected? It had been revealed that he once worked as some kind of courier for Los Alamos Labs.

Could it be that Raven was now seeking adulation from the very society he wanted to destroy? The terrorists' recent war wasn't new; it was as old as mankind. Raven the terrorist, or one of his tortured kind, had existed in every civilization on earth since the beginning of time. Had he now moved beyond running drug shipments into the country, beyond the eco-terrorism he had plotted last summer. Was he now masterminding Al Qaeda cells and other terrorist cults that prayed to the gods of intentional ruin?

The darkness of Raven's troubled soul only desired to return to the nothingness of the cosmic sea. The Zero before all zeros. The terrorist conspiracy had spread and Raven was using it to accomplish his goal. Chaos. Eternal strife. The bending of the light of the sun and the universal energy unto the final destruction. Apocalypse. Radioactive fires burning flesh and bone, cadavers with blistered skin walking the wasteland. A moaning of the last humans could be heard in the shrill winds that swept across the desolation.

Sonny shivered. Damn, a spring day in the Jemez, people going about their business, a time to fish the pools for trout that slept there all winter, the acequias gurgling with water that soon would rush through the canals into the fields, awakening the buds in dormant apple trees, apricot blossoms filling the air with the aroma of lust. Florella, the virgin of spring, was ready to bust the buds open.

Yes, it was the season of healthy lust, Eve enticing Adam with an apricot, or a pear, or a Mexican mango, or an apple grown in the Jemez valley, sweet fruits of paradise bursting with mouth-watering juices.

But Adam wasn't biting her apple. Que pasa?

Está chingado, Sonny cursed, like us.

Raven's every move was calculated to suck Sonny into the maelstrom, and in the process win the Zia medallion. Now he had called Sonny to the mountain, but the battle wasn't really there. As always, it had to be in the dream world where Raven lived, an unconscious realm laden with ancient images.

Had Raven chosen Jemez Springs because Sonny and Rita had a house by the river? They could hear the river song on summer nights, watch the galaxies move across the sky, the seasons of the moon, make love to the movement of stars and planets, make love to the music of the spheres.

That life was simple, as life should be simple, but not for Raven's kind. Terrorists thrived on chaos, and somehow the doomsday message, "The world is ending! The world is ending!" resonated with those marginalized by greedy men whose only alchemical formula served to turn every material object into money. It wasn't just the Al Qaeda terrorists who promised paradise. The banks and transnational corporations were all promising everyone a slice of ill-gotten pie. Pie baked from the labors of the poor, the undocumented, Latinos seeking work in cold, cold northern climes.

Raven traveled in the heart. He was always near, tracking in Sonny's dream. He was one of the subterranean images of the dream, a character in that dark soup. Every heart carried love, but every heart could also seethe with primal lust and violence; there was no denying that. In the deoxyribonucleic acid of every cell there also slept a third but invisible coiled strand. Call it chaos. Those frightening, unexplainable images that arose even in the most peaceful sleep made the dreamer wonder what was real and what was illusion, what was heaven and what was hell.

But why blow up the Jemez Mountains?

The water, the old man said. The hidden waters. Destroy the life-giving waters, and you destroy the dream of the Zia Stone. Create a new, unnatural volcano and fear returns to rule.

You here?

Hey, I wouldn't miss seeing Raven's newest act.

What do you think?

If it weren't serious it would make me laugh. He's really gone bananas. Se le fueron las cabras.

Is there time?

Sí, there's time. If you can find Raven. He's going to give it up, but not till he has his fun.

The chopper rose like a mad rufous hummingbird, feisty and full of chatter. Turbulence lingered on the mountaintop, the dying breath of a leprous wind that scattered a few impoverished clouds over the caldera. Clouds stringy as a bullsnake whip, clouds to make a philosopher wonder if it was the wind whipping the clouds or the clouds whipping the wind.

Crack the whip, Sonny thought, as a chain of the boys and girls, fifth graders at Adobe Acres, joined hands in the school yard at recess and the lead boy, always Chango, monkey boy who lived over at Kinney Brick and could whip even eighth graders, began to run and pull the line, like a rattlesnake unwinding, faster and faster until the line cracked and the smallest squirt at the end of the line, the rattler, was catapulted into the air, landing in the torito-goathead-strewn dirt. Blood and guts.

The morning had turned bitter. A spring wind howled after the night's scant rain. The serpent head of the fleeing clouds hovered over the caldera, the vagina of the mountain, casting its evil eye, el mal ojo, over the mountain. The cloud's dark face pregnant with anger, eyes and mouth spewing acid, spitting from venomous lips not the rain that blesses but the pollution of the world that swept up into the sky and came down as poison. A cloud with a hateful look that did not come from the heart of heaven but came from the demon world, the very world made by man, its luminous hair flaring around its sickly face.

It shouldn't be like this. The Cloud People come with gentle rain that enters the dry earth like a man might wet the welcoming thighs of his beloved, a soft caressing so sure and full of love that even the earth groans in peaceful response, as the woman moans to take the gift of seed.

Birthing was for spring. But today the world was balanced on a fulcrum, teetering on the edge of its own destruction, and even the clouds protested the wind's fury, a Poseidon of the desert.

Sonny remembered summer clouds over the mountain, huge billowing white buffalo clouds that rose and rose, until in a stampede the thunder shower let loose its bolts of lightning, a rumbling thunder that rolled across the valley like Rip Van Winkle's bowling balls, and sheets of blue rain that splattered the earth and ran wild in rivulets. The cumulus of summer, welcomed by the people of the mountain and the people of the Jemez Valley.

Love during a thunderstorm was tumultuous like that, with sperm and ovum blending into the sweet aroma that rose from the wet earth, the heavenly joy of Rita's face, those moments of climax in which her face radiated with love as she received his thrust, like swollen sunrays breaking through clouds after the blessed rain.

Someday the white buffalo clouds would return and break the drought on the land of Egypt. Someday the white buffalo would return to the plains, and the dancing would begin anew. The sun would once again be merciful.

The chopper rose and buzzed over a line of sickly pine trees, trees hurting from the drought and the parasites sucking at their green blood.

No good, Sonny thought. Ominous. No hard rains to break the drought that had consumed the state for the past seven years. Need Moses. Need someone to strike dead the pharaoh of drought. These summers past when little rain fell the cicadas had munched the valley pastures into stubble, left the apple trees bare, run rampant through corn and calabacitas, laying waste to the land of the ancestors.

There was hope. Somewhere on the mountain's flanks, somewhere in a dark canyon that led into the womb of the great lady, on a scarred volcanic boulder was etched the ancient symbol of life, the Zia Stone with its secret message, the meaning of life as it had been given to the old people, a hieroglyph so potent that sometimes at night, deep in dream, Sonny could feel its throbbing heart.

Raven thinks I found the Zia Stone.

The Zia Stone and the medallion are connected, the old man said. They complement each other.

So why here?

I think the cops wanted you out of the way. They don't want you to meet with the Indians in Algodones. People know you, Sonny. You could really help the cause. Dominic wants to break the back of that group.

The land and the water have always been up for grabs. The struggle continues.

Yes, the old man said, and you're in the way. You know Raven's ways and what he's capable of doing.

"Get a load of—" the pilot shouted and pointed down.

The chopper had been following the highway back to Jemez Springs.

Sonny leaned to look out the window. On the highway below them a truck was traveling at full speed. On the bed of the pickup sat two men armed with rifles. Bear and his boys?

"I thought the highway was closed?"

"Get closer!" Augie shouted, patting the pilot on the shoulder.

The pilot nodded and suddenly tilted on the chopper sideways. Sonny's door flew open, his seatbelt slipped away, and he felt Augie's push. With a gasp he tumbled out of the chopper. The rush of air hit him like runaway bronco. He reached out and grabbed the landing bars. For precious moments he dangled, tightening his grip on the bars.

He heard someone call his name. Holding tight he looked up into Augie's grinning face. The chopper straightened out and zoomed down the canyon, overtaking the truck below.

He heard the zing of a gunshot and saw a window explode. Whoever was in the truck was firing at them. Were they firing at him or at the chopper?

Hanging in the air Sonny felt a premonition of death. A waking dream unlike any other. He was flying, the cold air rushing past him, and he knew he couldn't hold on much longer. But he was flying, like an eagle, like a feathered serpent. Exhilaration and adrenaline pumped through his body. This was it, death. He would drop in free fall, enjoy a few seconds to reflect on his life, then smash into the road below. Like the dead snake on the road.

"Sawnnny!" the voice called his name.

He looked up and saw Augie holding out his hand.

"Take my hand!"

Sonny hesitated, then reached up, grabbed hold, and Augie pulled. Both men strained until Sonny could put his feet on the landing gear and push himself through the door.

"Damn!" the pilot shouted. "You okay?"

An exhausted and panting Sonny Baca nodded. He looked at Augie. Another bullet whizzed past as the pilot steered the chopper just over the tree line.

"I tried to grab you!" Augie shouted.

Or push me, Sonny thought. He had felt Augie's hands on his back as he went out the door. If he pushed why did he haul me up? Did the truck on the road have anything to do with it? Witnesses?

Below them the truck pulled off onto a dirt road and disappeared under the ponderosa pines.

Augie reached for the seatbelt and pushed it into lock. Then he pulled on it and it slid out.

"Damn, Joe!" he shouted at the pilot. "You gotta fix this damn thing! It's not locking!" He turned to Sonny. "You're lucky to be alive. Those guys meant to kill you."

Don't think so, thought Sonny. Bear and his boys were good shots. They wouldn't have missed. He wondered if he should thank Augie or smack him in the face.

The chopper zoomed over Battleship Rock, then over the village, like a dragonfly skimming over still waters it dropped into the valley, over the thin river where a stingy spring runoff trickled, over the tops of budding cottonwoods and elms, settling finally with a thump where they had taken off.

"Houston, Lola has landed!" the pilot said and gave them the thumbs-up signal. "Sorry the tour included getting shot at." He looked at Sonny and grinned. "I'll have that door fixed."

"Yeah," Sonny muttered.

"Good luck on defusing the bomb. Me, I'm just going to head down to Mexico. Watch the world blow itself apart from the beaches of Mazatlan. La perla del Pacífico."

"Hang glide on the beach," Sonny said. "Watch out for frayed ropes. You might drop out of the sky."

"Yeah," the pilot replied.

"I bet you a five-dollar bill those sonsofbitches were those Green Indians Naomi hangs out with," Augie said as they walked away from the chopper. "The highway's closed. How the hell did they get through?"

"Ask them," Sonny replied. He was in no mood to discuss things with Augie. "I'm outta here."

"Watch your back, Sonny. If they tried once they might try again."

"What are you going to do about Naomi?"

"Let her go. For now. Or do you mean—Okay, so I made a move on her. Tried to score. Don't mean nothing. She's too goddamn independent."

"What about the governor?"

"He had the hots for her too, but she wasn't interested."

Sonny shrugged. "And the professors?"

"I don't give a damn about them. They can't hurt a fly. What do they do? Read books. Write books. It's the fucking Al Qaeda I'm going to burn. If his mother ever sees him again he's lucky. We're at war, you know."

"The FBI wants him."

"Yeah, but before I turn him over I'm going to get what's coming to me." He paused. "I'm in trouble, Sonny. The governor was murdered on my watch. If I don't get this guy to confess, my name is mud. Look, if you hang around you can help."

"I'm through helping," Sonny said, and he turned around and walked away.

"Have it your way," Augie called after him. He smiled and turned to meet the news media, which were pressing forward like the Red Sea closing on Pharaoh's boys. A bombardment of questions met him.

"I know you've all been waiting for an explanation," Augie said, holding up his hands. "All I can tell you at this time is that we have a homicide—" He glanced after Sonny. "We haven't yet identified the body—"

Lying through his teeth, Sonny thought, as he got into his truck. He grabbed the steering wheel and tightened his grip until his knuckles turned white. Till now, he had controlled his anger and the sense of impotence that came from seeing himself dangling from the helicopter. He had trusted Augie and that had been a mistake. It could have been his last mistake.

"Son of a bitch," he cursed silently. Augie used to be a nice guy;

now there was too much war talk in his system. But why lie to the news media? Wait for forensics to do a positive ID? No, he was covering his ass until he got the okay from those he had called his superiors.

Maybe the governor was caught up in Frank Dominic's plan. There were millions to be made if the state decided to allow Dominic to buy up water rights.

Maybe it was an internal political battle that killed the governor.

And was it Bear and his boys in the pickup? Was Augie really chasing them? The Al Qaeda conspiracy was just a cover-up. Augie was the governor's personal guard, and whatever the governor knew, Augie knew.

What do you think? he asked the old man.

I think now you're probably using your noggin, the old man answered. Close call, huh?

Yeah.

Sonny relaxed and took a deep breath. He started the truck and drove out of the parking lot, down the highway to his cabin. Now he knew a wider conspiracy was taking place, and it revolved around the most precious element in the drought-stricken region: water.

The old man said nothing more. Sonny sensed he wasn't in a talking mood. Perhaps he felt time pressing on him. A few nights ago Sonny had asked the old man about the afterlife. What was on the other side of the bar? The old man shook his head and muttered something about the bardo, the Buddhist belief that there was a brief time on Earth during which the spirit of the dead wandered about, perhaps visiting old haunts, before it journeyed into another life form.

Was this the old man's time in the bardo? Or was it all in Sonny's head? What man conceived in the mind became more real than the world that could be touched, smelled, heard.

There were many ways of looking at death and what it meant. Many cultures conceived of it as a journey. The soul sought a new incarnation or its original home: heaven, the land of spirits, Hades,

Nirvana, an escape from the cycle of birth and rebirth, Mictlan, the Aztec Land of the Fleshless Ones, on and on.

Maybe the soul simply returned to the same energies that once engendered it, a return to the dreaming consciousness of the universe. The Oversoul. Every culture, every religion preached its ideas about death and its aftermath.

Maybe that's why he searched for the Zia Stone, the petroglyph that might provide a clue to the Alpha and the Omega.

But if the old man had the answer why didn't he just spill it? Maybe there was no answer and even the search for the Zia Stone was a waste of time. Everything was a waste of time. Time had suddenly entered his bloodstream in a discouraging, intolerable way. Even the spring equinox with the light of the moon sure to shine on the valley that night suddenly felt exhausting. He felt an emptiness he couldn't put into words. Yes, someone had stolen his heart. The child that died in Rita's womb, the miscarried blood flowing into the earth. For what? Why?

Were Rita's unborn babies now residing in a place like Limbo, place of infants who died? Or in a place like the bardo, awaiting the longer journey into the arms of God, if such a consciousness existed?

He turned off the pavement, onto the dirt road that led to the cabin. Passing over the acequia culvert he saw the water was flowing down to his apple trees. Melvin had come by and opened the compuerta. Thank God for good neighbors who watched over the place.

In this land, don Eliseo had said, a man is lucky if he has two things. A good wife, and a good neighbor.

Sonny had good neighbors. And he had a good woman.

The sight by the river bosque made him brake the truck to a sudden halt. There was Naomi, willow stick in hand, herding a dozen large pigs away from the apple trees, down toward the river.

"They need water!" she called.

Where in the hell did the pigs come from? None of the neighbors, as he could recall, had pigs. Big, round-shouldered pigs, every one a male as far as Sonny could tell, except for the huge, black sow in the lead. White, black, brown, a few spotted pigs, grunting, squealing, plowing the earth with their snouts, they let Naomi guide them to the river.

Maybe Joe Garcia traded his sheep for pigs, Sonny thought as he got down from the truck. Or Sam Mares, or Emmit? Naw, none of those had time for pigs.

He followed her down to the river's edge. The pigs had disappeared in the underbrush.

"Sit here," Naomi said. She sat under the webbed shadows of the bare cottonwood.

"Whose pigs?" she asked. Sonny shrugged. "I was in the cabin when I heard them. Figured you might not want them around your apple trees. Pigs can be destructive."

"Thanks."

Her raven-black hair cascaded around her shoulders. A perfume of sage and juniper berries clung to her body.

"You hungry?"

"No, I'm okay."

"I bet your lady friend sent food with you."

Sonny nodded.

"You're a lucky man, Sonny. Women like you. If I weren't already involved—" She didn't finish. "What happened up on the mountain?"

"They say Raven planted a bomb. Augie's got it tied into an Al Qaeda conspiracy."

"I told you, don't trust him."

"I should have listened to you. Come on, I've got to check the place and get back to Burque." He wasn't going to tell her about the near fall from the helicopter.

A Mourning Cloak butterfly flitted by. Harbinger of spring in the valley.

"What are you going to do now?" he asked as they walked back to the cabin.

"I'm getting out of town."

"Are you afraid?"

"It's not just Augie," she replied. "It's bigger than that. I suggest you get out too."

"Why?"

"You want Raven, don't you? It's a personal thing with you two. I read what happened at the Balloon Fiesta. I read between the lines. He threatens people, but that's just his game to get to you. It's personal, isn't it?"

Sonny nodded in agreement.

"It has something to do with the loss you feel—"

"How do you know?"

"I read people's faces. Whatever's going on inside a person is written on the face. The face reveals everything. Even when I was a child I could tell what the person was going through. Sometimes I told people what was going to happen, but no one believed me. I learned to keep it to myself."

They stopped at the cabin's door.

"How do I find whoever stole my heart?" he asked.

"You know, crack an egg in water. It turns into the person you love. In this case, whoever stole your heart."

An old custom, Sonny thought, used to be practiced on Día de San Juan during the blessing of the waters.

"That's June 24," he murmured.

"It will work for you today, Sonny. Today is a day of waters. We might all be dead by June 24, or just pitiful little images in your dreams."

A honking up the road startled the red robins grubbing by the river, sparing for the moment the fat earthworms in the thawing earth.

Bear's truck. The same pickup the helicopter had followed on the mountain. How they evaded the roadblocks Sonny could only guess.

"Naomi!" Bear called. "Come on, let's finish!"

"I gotta go," Naomi said. She walked away, then turned. "There's an egg in the refrigerator. Try it. Just be careful."

She turned, walked to the truck and got in. A war whoop filled the air as the truck caromed up the dirt road to the highway.

Sonny opened the door and looked inside, remembering all the times he and Rita had shared the place, every element in its place, even the palpable emptiness.

He opened the refrigerator door. An egg, she said. Villagers bless the river and acequia waters on Día de San Juan. In the old day communities sponsored corridas de gallo, young vaqueros showing off their horsemanship. The girls cut a lock of hair with an axe, aspects of an ancient ritual that reminded the girl that St. John the Baptist had his head cut off with an axe. On that day a young woman cracked an egg into a glass of water and the face of the man she would love appeared.

Glowing white with light, exhaling cold air like a demon's breath, the refrigerator that had once been simply a useful appliance now appeared as a white womb, cold and lifeless, except for the egg, alone, sitting on the shelf.

Had Naomi placed it there?

Speckled with blood, it felt warm to Sonny's touch. He held it tentatively, as if it were a live ember, glowing with the life within. Quickly he filled a glass with water, cracked the egg, and dropped the small yellow ball and its mucous into the water. It swirled and kicked, as if alive, turning in the womb of water, and Sonny thought he heard a voice calling to him.

He looked closely and saw an image forming.

"God!" he whispered. "Oh God!"

He dropped the glass on the floor. It splintered, the water wetting his boots.

The squirming egg grew still as Sonny hurried out of the house, banging shut the door behind him.

10 »

Spring is not a time to be alone.

It helps to have a good partner, the old man said in agreement. Someone who understands our dreams.

I used to tell my viejita, que decanse en paz, my dreams. She was a good listener. She would be making tortillas for breakfast, serve me a cup of coffee and say, *Bueno, dime tus sueños.* I think los sicologisticos—

Psychologists.

Sí. They should have their office in a kitchen. Ah, with tortillas cooking on the comal, coffee perking, huevos rancheros with red chile. You know, food and sex and dreams all go together.

You had a good wife.

Yeah, she was a good cook. Sometimes my dreams got too strange. Then she gave me a dose of castor oil. This will clean up everything, she would say. The old man laughed. Yeah, right.

She knew you could walk in dreams?

Yes, she knew. But she worried. I married a brujo, she would say. Pero, what about you? You got Rita.

Yeah, but—

But what?

I've been thinking. I thought *she* was the one who had to get over losing the child. She does, but it hit me too.

You've been thinking revenge.

Yes. Then Naomi shows up. Someone stole your heart. I can read faces, she said.

She knows things, the old man interjected. If she places your soul in one of her pots, you'll never get out. Maybe that's what happened to the man in the tub.

What do you mean?

A woman who can shape clay can shape the man, this way or that. If she puts the soul of the man in the pot, goodbye Charlie.

What about this reading of faces?

Some people have the gift, the old man said. But it doesn't do any good. You tell a person what you see and they don't believe you.

So that's Naomi's curse, Sonny thought. Still, she had started something unraveling.

He glanced at a descanso on the side of the road, a large cross adorned with colorful plastic flowers. La raza still kept the custom of placing a cross where an accident claimed a life, where the flesh was pierced and died, setting free the anguished soul. A cross, flowers, tokens of the deceased. Flesh died, but the soul wandered on, yearning to return whence it came.

In Tibet they prayed over the soul of the departed for ten days. The soul had to be prepared for its journey, prepared to be born again in flesh, in some newly fertilized egg.

Born a dog if you had led a very good life.

He smiled and rubbed the sleeping Chica. If a dog's spirit comes from a prior life, it must bring the dreams of that life with it. Dreams from many lives. The whole enchilada, the unconscious consciousness of the dreamer. If one believed in reincarnation, who knew how many deaths and rebirths Chica had been through? Transmigration of the soul, for the soul never died, it was forever an alien, wandering from person to person, or from dog to dog, until the karma was cleansed. Who knows how many dreams Chica brought from those distant past lives?

Did the Tibetan custom underlie the New Mexican custom? Nah, that was too far-fetched. But the soul's journey was the essence of the spiritual life of the Nuevomexicanos, coloring their ceremonies, customs, daily life.

Was it synchronicity? Buddhist teachings from the mountains of Tibet resonating to a brand of Catholicism practiced in the villages of the Sangre de Cristo mountains?

Perhaps, as don Eliseo said, the mountains of the world spoke to each other, across geographic and geopolitical space the spirits of the mountains spoke, in the wind that encircled the earth they spoke. Mountain talk. And like a person, a mountain could be murdered. It happened if it was over-logged and the slopes left bare. The mountain dissolved, rolled back into dust, died.

Yes, there were prayers to prepare the soul for its journey. Rosaries. Alabados. Doña Concha and don Toto had watched over don Eliseo the day he died. They sang and prayed that his soul would find peace. Heaven. The arms of God. Or reincarnation. What did those old people know?

The stream of thoughts bothered Sonny.

How did you get here?

I told you, Sonny, I never went away.

But you *are* going away?

Yes.

Sometime soon?

Yes.

That's all you know?

I was an old man, old men have old souls. Who knows the mystery? Maybe it's not a mystery at all. What you believe is in you. Here I am.

So what's the answer?

Living a good life is enough. Help your neighbors. What's bothering you?

I feel empty.

Seeing the images in the glass of water caused a thick, gooey depression to work its way into every thread of Sonny's fiber, spreading its endemic dullness along his nervous system, presenting itself as hopelessness in the heart, even spreading out from his soul into the landscape, making the land he loved with a farmer's passion look dull and dying.

Deep inside his Druid heart he felt the electric energy of life waiting to burst out of the dormant shells, the spirits of the earth yearning to push their green fingers through the dry, cold ground. Soon green men and women would appear to dress the fields, clusters of flowers would clothe the apple trees, and honey bees buzzing with wet proboscises would seek the nectar and pollen. Time for dandelions to sprout yellow, and even in this dry springtime the hummingbirds would return from Mexico to the canyon. An inner compulsion drove the feathered friends as it did all fish, fowl, flesh, and rock. The tiny birds returned because there were flowers to kiss, nectar and pollen to gather, eggs to be laid. The drive of birds and flowers to propagate would not be quenched, even if Sonny felt it dying.

Green and blooming it would come, but right then something about spring dragging her feet out of winter's compost made him shiver. Was it some errant emotion of loss? Was it the image the egg had formed in the water? What he had seen scared the hell out of him.

According to the Mayan prophecy the end of the world won't come till 2012. You have a few more years, the old man said, joking, trying to lighten the load he felt Sonny carrying.

Will the Zia Stone show us how to live? How to deal with all the caca life throws at us? War in Iraq. Hunger in Afghanistan. AIDS in Africa. Poverty everywhere. Terrorist killing terrorist. The greedy screwing the poor. Will it explain feelings we can't control?

It's just a sign on the path, the old man said. But do we pay attention? Our time has grown perverse. A few give a damn, the rest just want to live longer. On TV they cry out, I want to live forever. No wrinkles, no balding, no heart disease. Zero cholesterol. Clone me. I am beautiful. Let me be forever young in my clone. Que tontería!

Sonny listened.

You can pass on genes, but not the soul. The soul has its own song. Now we live in the time of Mr. Me and Mrs. Me. But the Me doesn't have a soul. The time of the soul is dying, and maybe that's why the Mayan people predicted the end of time. The spirit would no longer be coming into the earth, into us. Are we really more civilized than our ancestors?

Then why look for the Zia Stone? Why trouble?

Because, the old man said, feeling a tickle in his ribs, the worm of his karma turning, it will reveal the true nature of the world and our place in it. This is what we yearn to know.

Yes, Sonny nodded, there was always one more sign to be revealed in the tree of life that was his evolution. But the old man couldn't teach him everything. It was Sonny's search. Being led to the governor's murder scene was just a diversion. After all, governors and politicians had been murdered since time immemorial, but none of those homicides opened heaven's gate to a true understanding of humanity's role in the cosmos.

Whether he found the governor's killer or not was beside the point. And nearly ending his life on the helicopter was just one more warning. What really mattered was meeting Naomi. A shaman in her own right, she had confirmed the gnawing thoughts that had consumed him these past three months. Rita's children were alive. Or their spirits were alive. Now he didn't want to kill Raven, but corner him and make him give up the secret. Where were the souls whose flesh had been aborted by miscarriage?

There's always something waiting to be revealed, the old man said. Like the hieroglyphs of Copan. Those in the Valley of the Kings. The scrolls of Nag Hamaddi. The Rosetta stone. The sign on the Zia Stone.

Do those signs make us any more civilized? Sonny interjected.

Terrorism rules; we're killing the children, bringing them up on terror and dope. Half the world is hungry, and Raven has his way.

The old man sighed, truly regretting he couldn't ease Sonny's mood. But he knew that one man does not give another man knowledge. Instead he mused, as an old man is wont to do, about what life has meant.

The universe has to make room for its continuing creation, he said. It starts in a dream not spoken. A dark dream. Finally the Spirit enters its own body, the spirit of the universe wakes up one day and enters itself, like the serpent swallowing its own tail, like a virgin birth, the universe gives life to itself. What a glorious morning that must have been, eh? The sleeping universe waking from the dream. The Hindus have beautiful stories about dreamers. Someday I'll tell you some.

Sonny nodded. He liked to hear the old man. It lightened the load, but it did not erase the image of the egg in the water.

They sped along the winding canyon road, curves revealing a time past on the imposing cliffs.

The strata told how the ancient earth had spent eons of time growing out of its own dark heart. Groaning and thundering it had come, once upon a time, buckling, cracking, rising and falling, writhing in pain like a woman giving birth, the bloody red strata of oxidized minerals, the earth's placenta splattered on the side of the mesa, the scarred thighs of the mesa testimony to the time of birth, the wrinkled belly, each line of mineral deposit imbued with the breath of spirit, born of that deep dark dream that don Eliseo spoke of.

The massive tectonic plates of the earth crashed against each other, mountains rose and fell, a seed of fire rested in the womb of the Jemez Mountain. When the womb contracted it spilled forth a child, a fire child that came out kicking and screaming, its cry rolling like thunder across the gaseous sea, even to the shores of China. The earth gave birth to itself, repeating the process of the universe. Mountains were born, buckling and cracking the earth groaned and the mountain rose, the liquid magma poured forth as hot blood and an afterbirth that now glowed with spring light, an aura of crimson emanating from the gigantic boulders and palisades, the same fire glowing in the grains of sand in the arroyos.

The universe in each grain of sand—more than a mad poet's muttering, a truth. Everything was contained in everything else, and it continually gave birth to itself. From nothing came something. The heart of the cosmos was a song, a vibration, the music of the spheres, a symphony in a key humans could not yet hear, a mathematician's dream.

Sacred geography, the old man said. Sonny could barely hear him. It's been around for as long as man first sensed the spirit touch the earth. There are fissures where a hot wind rises from the belly of the earth. Springs whose sweet water can cure the sick. Olive groves where the Greek oracles spoke. Mountaintops where eagles converse with the gods. Monoliths of Stonehenge. Dolmens of Machu Picchu. Pyramids of Egypt and Copan. Gothic cathedrals. Sacred rivers. Too much for one man to understand, he said, his voice fading. Sheer earth, fecund topsoil or hellish brimstone, water sweet or brackish, devil's wind or bountiful rain clouds, all is touched by the energy constantly moving through the yoni of the universe.

"I have to kill Raven," Sonny blurted out.

The old man shivered.

"The dreamcatcher didn't work! Sure, he went through it, like an Oklahoma tornado, I felt the wind blasting me, then he was gone. Taking with him what belonged to me and Rita!"

Damn, Sonny, you gotta stop that kind of talk. What's really bothering you?

"I saw something in the glass of water! The egg split in two. It turned and turned and took the shape of two innocent souls. My unborn children have stolen my heart!"

The old man groaned.

"I can bring them back!"

No, Sonny, you can't. They're dead. Leave things—

You came back! You won't tell me how you came back, but you

did! You won't tell me, but I know I can go back into Raven's nightmare and bring back my children!

A tremor shook the old man. Sonny's wish was devastating. It could kill him.

Not even Christ—

Could come back! He did! That's the story! And he raised the dead! And you came back. You won't tell me how to go there, I'll go myself!

The old man heard a voice calling him, a force far greater than the tremendous aura of the mountain was calling him, whispering in the gurgling waters of the river. Return.

Where do the dead reside, and why can't we bring them back?

The wind, which in the Jemez canyon had been a gentle breeze easing itself down the side of the mesa, now grew violent as they drove past San Ysidro, a gusting wind sweeping down from White Mesa, a white cloud of gypsum dusting the flat, arid land.

The dry Wind of Spring raised its thunderous voice: I am the Lord thy God! I bend trees before your path!

Tumbleweeds rolled across the road, tormented specters in the whirling dust, and clouds of gypsum ponderous as white whales, crying mournfully. Lloronas of the Road weeping for lost children. Furiously, the dust clouds gathered their dusty skirts and swept down the highway toward the Rio Grande Valley.

Just past San Ysidro, the death cart of Doña Sebastiana suddenly appeared, the penitentes' skeleton dressed in a wedding gown, virgin white, cracking her whip, La Muerte, la Peluda, la Ciriaca, la Huesuda, la Comadre to all New Mexicans, stringing her bow with a deadly arrow, aiming at Sonny's heart.

She cried in a harsh voice: I am the lover who stole your heart, you cringing sonofabitch! Her hot spittle fell as drops of acid on the windshield.

Just in time Sonny pulled hard on the steering wheel and swerved to miss by one split second the Yellow Freight semi that hurtled out of the dust cloud. He fought the wheel to regain control of the truck as it skidded onto the shoulder of the road, tipping precariously on the gravel embankment until it grabbed the asphalt and straightened out.

Damn! Sonny cursed, realizing how close he had come to a head-on crash.

The eighteen wheeler swept past them, its horn blasting like a foghorn in the shroud of dust.

No use cursing, the gods have fled the land. Not even the prayers of the shaman can entice them back, whined the wind as it whipped around the mesas, driving the inhabitants of Zia and Santa Ana pueblos indoors.

Sonny breathed deep, saw the huge truck disappear in his rearview mirror, the shape of death a plume of smoke. On the eastern horizon Sandia Mountain, in a haze of dust, reared its head in anguish.

Thinking about death drew forth death. He knew that. Thus was the Lenten season of New Mexico described. The winds of spring mourned the land, the tinieblas of the penitentes cried for penance. The winds would blow during Holy Week, the saddest of weeks.

Thin, washboard cirrus clouds lay like a skeleton across the sky, the white-bone ribcage stretching from San Ysidro east, the shape of the skull sneering, its hollow eyes entrances into the vacant heart of the sky. These were the clouds of the dry season, clouds of drought, dry as dust, not a drop of water festered in the ribcage of the skeleton cloud, not a drop to drink in its massive hip bones, no juice of life in the sealed womb. The land was dying of thirst, and summer would bring a fire season that could be devastating. The river would slow to a trickle. The acequias would go dry, and farmers would watch alfalfa and cornfields wither.

A few steers huddled along the barbed-wire fence, cattle thin as the clouds, browsing on clumps of winter-sere grass.

A long time ago foreigners arrived and fenced the land, the first cattle ranchers, those who bought the land from the Mexicanos who had run sheep for generations from Cabezon Peak to the Rio Puerco. The barbed wire lay like a skeleton on the land; private-property signs appeared on the llanos of New Mexico and on the mountain pastures that the old Hispanos had used for centuries. The land grants vanished, pocketed by greedy lawyers and politicians who spoke English and made the old Spanish laws conform to the new laws of the American Occupation. The year 1848 was a bell tolling for the Nuevomexicanos. No need to ask for whom the bell tolled; it tolled for every sheep-herding paisano who now lay buried in the weed-infested cemeteries of the small villages.

A stranger had fallen drunkenly over the land, a tall, dark stranger called Dry Dust, Hot Wind, No Rain, Desert Man. The stranger called Spring Without Rain had come upon the land and dug his spurs into the flesh of the earth, his breath hot with turmoil.

Perhaps the Four Horsemen of the Apocalypse had already come upon the land, and the people did not recognize them.

And in Sonny's heart boiled the same turmoil that lay over the land. Why not? he kept asking, defying the old man, peering over the steering wheel at the skeleton in the sky.

It's not right, Sonny. To everything there is a season, as La Biblia tells us. Let the souls rest in peace.

Sonny shook his head. He wasn't going to listen to the old man. The souls weren't resting in peace, they were out there moving around. They were crying for vengeance.

Sonny would not be comforted. Tell Rita about the egg in the glass of water, he thought. He scrolled Rita's number on his cell phone and pushed "call." All he got was static. The airways were dead. He pulled over at the Zia Pueblo gas station and used the phone.

"Sonny, where are you?"

"Zia Pueblo gas station. My cell phone isn't working—"

"Sonny, it's in the news!" Her voice trembled. "Cell phones aren't working. Everyone is without service. It's Raven, isn't it?"

Raven screwing up the cell phones? Yeah, he had figured out a way to get into the wireless phone system's software. Hacker Raven. How far could he reach out? Was it regional or could he bring down the entire country? Could he shoot down the communication satellites, create international panic?

"They just reported an Al Qaeda terrorist was loose in Jemez. What's happening? Are you okay?"

"I'm fine. And you?"

"It's crazy. The place is full. People aren't going to work. I tried to call your mom, but her phone's not working. Lorenza called."

"From where?"

"Algodones. She hurried back from Cruces. They're waiting for you."

"I might make it," he said. But what he really needed to do was find Raven. "I have an idea—" he said, and stopped short. No, no sense in telling Rita that I know how to bring back her children. What if I can't find Raven? What if I can't get into his circle? What if don Eliseo was right? Doubt clouded Sonny's thoughts.

"What?"

"Nothing. I'll head for Algodones.

"Call me when you see Lorenza. Have you eaten?"

Sonny thought of the tacos in the ice chest. "No, not yet. But I will."

"Sonny, cuídate. I love you."

"And I love you," he said, looking up at the big Pueblo man who stood by the counter. He had been listening, now he grinned.

"Hurry home."

"I'm on my way."

He hung up the phone and went outside. The wind was still howling, so he quickly opened the ice chest and reached for the bag of tacos. When he looked up he stared into the eyes of the Pueblo man.

"Hey, bro, you going to Algodones? I need a ride."

The man had overheard him. First Naomi, now this. He studied the man. Was he one of Bear's boys? One of those at the Red Rocks or on the truck on the mountain? Sonny hadn't gotten a good look at the men, so he couldn't be sure.

"You overheard me."

"Hey, a lot of people know what's coming down in Algodones. Big powwow. Might miss it if we don't hurry."

One of the so-called Green Indians, Sonny guessed. But he had never met the man.

"Get in," he said, and the big man got in. Chica growled.

"You got a one-eyed dog."

"You want a ride or don't you?" Sonny snapped.

"Yeah, sure."

Sonny handed the man one of the tacos and a cup of coffee from the thermos.

"Thanks, bro. I had nothin' to eat all day. Taking care of a dead snake is important business." He smiled. "But not as important as what's happenin' in Algodones."

11 »

Sonny unwrapped his taco, and the two ate in silence. Across the open window the wind made a whistling sound, a long and plaintive *sheeeee,* the mournful cry it might make blowing across the Llano Estacado. Or was it the sound of an old woman whistling through missing teeth, a black-shrouded curandera who pulled her tápalo around her face so only her dark piercing eyes shone in a sea of wrinkled webs as she peered into the dusty, blistering wind on the sandy road from Pastura, miles from the Gonzales ranch? She had stopped to whistle for the boy, Alfonso, her companion, he of the sorrows of young Alfonso, a story yet to be told.

She whistled because the child had disappeared, perhaps around a bend in the road where he had stopped to pick ripe mesquite pods that glowed reddish in the dim sunlight. The mesquite fruit was a favorite treat in a land where there were few treats for a child his age. Or perhaps a coyote had snapped him up, carried him away to feed her pups, those not yet old enough to hunt for a meal. She whistled again, long and mournfully into the wind, *shheeeee.* But the child did not answer and she would have to move on to her appointed task, to lift a curse set by Satan himself.

A young woman in a deserted ranch on the road to Platero writhed in agony on her soiled bed, tore the sheets into shreds as orgasm after orgasm came surfacing from deep in her sex, convulsing her emaciated body, orgasms caused by a dark demon that spurred her flanks, an incubus from the darkest recesses of her psyche in the fearful form of the young vaquero who had kissed her and felt her breasts behind the dance hall a year ago. Then the image would change, take on the garb of the village priest to whom she had confessed, frightening her all the more because the priest should not be envisioned thus. Not as a goat-man displaying a huge organ that tore into her until she moaned for death to quiet her frenzy, while near the bed, sitting on an old, well-worn wooden bench, the concerned and puzzled father and mother, exhausted from days and nights of watching over their daughter's agony, sat in brooding silence, wondering from what depths came the evil spirits possessing their daughter's flesh.

These were the stories Sonny heard as the wind whipped past the partially open window. The winds of New Mexico carried many stories.

Sonny listened to the mournful sound and looked at the dust rising and falling in the heat of midday. Dry bone weather. Georgia O'Keeffe, if she were alive, would be haunting the dry arroyos of Abiquiu, looking for the ash-white pelvic bones of dead steers to paint, or the many-pointed phallic antlers of an elk dragged by coyotes to that place where she walked. Old Bone Woman walking the arroyos of Abiquiu, herself suffocating from impulses repressed long ago, painting dry hip bones that had never held a fetus, never parted wet with the blood of birth to cough up a child. Maybe that is why she brushed on sterile canvases the white-shaven bones of dead cows and the erogenous pistils of flowers, crimson and swollen, about to burst, thus hoping to understand—or make amends with—what dark memory?

Or were the paintings visions of a world denied to her? Paintings from her womb, a birth nevertheless, for all the world to view.

Lordy, Lordy, Sonny thought, if it weren't for the full delicacy of Rita's carne adovada taco, the marinated meat picante with the red chile, a specialty of Rita's Cocina, a taste awakening memories of her kisses, the wind and the time of day would consume him right then and there in the stories they whispered, for the day gathered many stories on its journey, and it gave way to no man, beast, or rock.

He could be blown away with the dust and tumbleweeds, like the old man was already blowing away, hardly a murmur of his soul left under the tarp in the bed of the truck.

Sonny worried about the old man. He had a secret he wasn't revealing. He needed to get him home. Maybe there in the earth of the valley he loved he would renew his energy, he would speak and reveal how he had come from the other world and would point the way.

And I need to get home, he thought, and yet he knew it wasn't going to be soon. Not with this guy sitting in his truck, a guide to Algodones where, hopefully, Lorenza waited.

He shared his taco with Chica, who swallowed it in one bite and wagged her tail. Nobody but Sonny let her have carne adovada tacos. They brought good dreams, and sometimes indigestion.

Sonny finished and got out to place the wrappings and the thermos in the ice chest. He guessed the primo was a Santo Domingo man. He had that sturdy look, and he wore a regal Santo Domingo heishi necklace. Maybe a cacique, or a holy man.

When Sonny got back in the truck the man spoke. "You got a big pistol," he said. "Saw one of those in Nam. A lieutenant used to wear it. Cowboy type."

The man had looked in the glove compartment where Sonny carried the truck's registration and his Bisabuelo's Colt .45. And loaded in the pistol the one bullet made by a brujo. The bullet that could kill Raven.

"You must be a mind reader," Sonny said sarcastically.

The Santo Domingo man smiled. "You walk with spirits," he said with a slight nod of his head, meaning he had sensed the old man.

"And you?" Sonny asked.

"I'm José Calabasa," he said, reaching out to touch Sonny's hand. "Yeah, I pray to the holy people." He looked at Chica. "Dream dog?"

Sonny started the truck and headed down the road. So what do you want, José? he felt like asking; instead he said, "Nam."

"Yeah," José said softly. "Seems so long ago. Now it's Iraq and the terrorists. Shit, what did we expect? We brag about being number-one super power. We forgot, nobody likes number one, especially when we're consuming the wealth of the world."

"And the governor?"

"He had it coming."

"Why?"

"God, you should know."

"Pretend I don't."

"The governor had plans to be a Senator, so he joined up with Dominic. A scheme to get water rights. When he smelled the pile of caca Dominic was cooking up, he got cold feet."

"So they killed him. Had him killed."

"Yeah. You heard about Santa Fe Woman?"

Sonny nodded. A year ago while digging into the Santa Fe Mesa for a multi-million-dollar development they found the skull of a woman. Anthropologists declared the skull was Caucasian, not Native American, and the carbon dating showed it predated all Pueblo Indian settlements in the area, including Mesa Verde and Chaco Canyon. The find became the most explosive discovery since Sandia Man. Every anchor man or woman from the national television stations had done a story on Santa Fe Woman.

The discovery had ramifications far beyond the anthropological arguments; it raised all sorts of social and political issues. If Santa Fe Woman, a Caucasian, was a resident in the area long before the Pueblo Indians moved into the Rio Grande Valley, then the Pueblos were not "first in place," and if they weren't there first then their claim to water rights went out the window.

And sovereignty was an issue. If the ancestors of the pueblos weren't the first on the land then they might not have special nation status. Centuries-old rights were being assailed by Dominic's group.

"Frank Dominic planted it. Salted the site, as they say."

"Yeah," Sonny agreed, "but you have some anthropologists confirming the dates of the skull."

That bothered a lot of people. If science said the skull was pre–Pueblo culture, then it must be so.

"Bullshit. They were hired by Dominic. Where did she come from? How did she die? Why only one skull? How did she get here? And who is she?"

All the same questions being asked in public. The old men who met daily in the Santa Fe Plaza to gossip had named her Santa Fe Woman. They smelled a scam. Where did she come from? Well, they surmised, she is from one of the lost tribes of Israel who wandered across the continent. Her people continued on, and she, left behind, died of loneliness.

Some began to call her the Eve of the Desert. This was the first mother, and if they dug deep enough they would find the bones of Adam. Kick the developers out, preserve the holy site—except, they argued, the chamber of commerce would butt in and make it a tourist attraction. Tourism was Santa Fe's name.

Others, New Age historians, argued that this land was once Atlantis, and the skull belonged to an original inhabitant of the fabled lost continent. This immediately led some to suggest the skull belonged to an alien from a foreign planet whose spaceship had crashed. Where was the spaceship? Don't bother with the details, they said. Roswell's chamber of commerce doesn't. And look how lucrative the aliens have been for them.

But at noon, when the old timers heard their stomachs churn and smelled the beans cooking in their viejas' kitchens, all agreed: "Es el pinche Dominic. He wants to get hold of all the water in New Mexico. He stole a skull from some museum, put some old dirt around it, and buried it where it could be found."

At the end of the day the viejitos weren't dumb. They concluded it was all a sham, but their voices were no obstacle to the weight of scientific evidence being developed to prove Santa Fe Woman had stood on the slope of the Sangre de Cristo Mountains long before the First Americans, and, gazing west toward the Jemez Mountains, she dreamed that someday the land would be settled by her progeny.

"She had no family," José said. "But they want to prove she's Caucasian so they can take our water. And you Hispanics who still farm are not far behind. You have trees in the Jemez, don't you?"

"Apple. I plant a little corn."

"Did you hear about the Santa Fe gallery that borrowed the skull? They put it on a mannequin, with a wide-brimmed blue felt hat with a silver and turquoise hat band, and those long skirts the California and Texas women wear when they visit the plaza. Loaded her with squash-blossom necklaces, thick silver bracelets with big turquoise stones, the whole shebang. Santa Fe style. She's on display. Looks like la muerte staring at us."

Sonny waited for the story to end. Right then he was more interested in Raven's path.

"You were up on the mountain with Bear."

José nodded. "You almost got yourself killed," he said.

"So you know about Raven."

"We've known about him for a long time. First he comes around saying he's on our side. Wants to stop radioactive waste shipments from crossing Indian land. Then he ties in with Dominic. They want our water. Then the land. If they get their Supreme Court justices in, they will start questioning Indian sovereignty. It's all about water. Without water our fields die, we die. We become the West Bank Palestinians."

"And in ten years we pay through the nose," Sonny said.

"Right. This country's falling apart, Sonny. Crooks in every corner. Corporation CEOs making millions while the poor go down the drain. How can a government allow them to milk the corporations and let the retirement accounts of the workers disappear? No morality. First sign of collapse if you ask me."

Sonny nodded. Yeah, the ship was overrun with rats, rats with power. The selfish instincts of men would sooner or later consume everyone in chaos.

"Where's Raven?"

"He was up on the mountain. We got off a few shots. You know, it's harder than hell to kill a Raven. Have you ever seen them fly up on the mountain meadows? They dance like ballerinas. People think they're awkward, but these birds can fly and swirl and dive like modern dancers. No wonder this guy picked the raven to imitate. The women like him. Anyway, we almost had the sonofabitch, but the police helicopter spotted us. Bet now they blame us for placing the bomb. I caught a ride out of Ponderosa. Did Bear pick up Naomi?"

Sonny nodded. "Raven turns on his partners," he said.

"You better believe it. Now he's courting the politicians."

"Did he kill the governor?"

"Probably. Or hired someone to do it. It's a big plot, Sonny, with a lot of money behind it. They bought the governor, and when he wouldn't play ball with them they got rid of him. All we want to do is protect our way of life. "

A blast of wind made the truck shudder.

"What Raven really wants is you," José said. "He suckered you into going up the mountain."

"I trusted Augie—"

"You can't trust anyone. Raven will use them to get at you. Get the Zia medallion you wear. The elders are telling the story of how you got it. I'm surprised you're not a dead coyote on the road to Los Alamos. Raven's here, all right. He's following us right now."

Sonny touched the Zia medallion sitting warmly on his chest. Yes, no matter how complicated the plot, it boiled down to Raven coming back for the amulet and its power.

"He gets you, then he goes after the Sun Stone. It's all tied together. You, the Zia medallion, the Sun Stone. The old people say the stone marks the boundaries of our world, the sacred mountains.

As long as we know our universe, we're okay. But if you destroy the boundaries then everything becomes fluid, we slip away into the white man's world. Santa Fe Woman is going to kill us."

He laughed. "Get it? Killed by an old skull a dog dug up. Hey, you got any more tacos?"

"No."

"Let's stop at the Sonic in Bernalillo. I haven't eaten in two days."

Again Sonny fingered the Zia medallion. Like an ancient astrolabe, a navigational instrument like that used by Odysseus on his way from Troy, it kept Sonny on the Path of Light. A personal compass.

"Is the Zia Stone only for the pueblos?" he asked.

"Should be for everyone, don't you think?" José answered. "There's a lot of pain in the world. Cultures falling apart. People need something or someone to believe in."

Sonny agreed. Truth and its revelations had to be for more than a chosen group.

"Maybe it's already happening," José continued. "Our kids are losing touch. Don't want to farm, don't want to dance."

Sonny tried his cell phone again. "Nada."

"Yeah. Bear couldn't get through to Burque. It's Raven. He probably hired a bunch of hackers. Scrambled the software."

He's right, Sonny thought. Hackers love anarchy, they would work for Raven. For the sheer feeling of power they spread viruses. They could hit anything. They had already scrambled banks, the Pentagon, AT&T. Now Raven's sicced them on the cell phones. How many regions of the country could they take down?

"If he can keep the cell phones dead for a few days, western civilization will collapse," José said. "The powers that be will come to him on their knees. Serves the greedy bastards right."

Sonny nodded. "So what now?"

"Check in at Algodones. Then I have to get back to the pueblo. One of the local stations broadcast pictures of the bomb. Won't be long before the national news media starts dropping in. Dan Rather and those guys. They love publicity. God, I bet Los Alamos is an armed camp. That crazy Bin Laden played right into their hands. They blame everything on Al Qaeda. Everybody needs points, even the president. Saving the national labs from being blown to smithereens would win any election. No slippery chads, just good police work. Shit."

"What do you think?"

"It's all smoke and mirrors."

"Raven might hire out, but in the end they can't control him. He does his own thing."

"You got that right," José said. "So let's get Raven."

"I'll get to Raven on my own terms," Sonny replied.

"Don't play the fool, Sonny. You can't see everything."

A fool has limited vision, Sonny thought, just like a one-eyed dog. He rubbed Chica's neck. She had accepted José, a good sign.

He turned on the radio, but it was garbled static.

"You're cut off from the world, Sonny."

Cut off from Rita, he thought. He would try a phone when they got to Bernalillo.

"That's how we felt in Nam," José said, and in a quiet voice he mentioned places with Vietnamese names and recited the names of guys in the squad. He talked about never-ending reconnaissance patrols, calling in coordinates, taking sniper fire, living in the jungle for days on end, wet and rotting.

Then he fell silent, listening to the wind howling its last curse at the people of the Cabezon llano and the people of the valley.

Overhead, the energy of the wind had formed a giant dust devil, a whirlwind such as Pecos Bill might have saddled and ridden like a wild bronco, except this swirling mass came curling down the desolate mesa like a Chinese dragon, a venomous dragon with no pity in its heart. Whipping up dust and trash, the huge funnel rose into the womb of the dry sky, and as they watched it bear down on them, Sonny remembered that the Devil rode inside the dust devil. That's what the old people said, and they had taught him to ward off the evil by making the sign of the cross with his fingers, and so he stuck his arm out the window and made the sign of the cross to ward off the evil that came slapping at the truck, but even the holy sign, the rock of ages, could not turn away the howling fiery dragon.

Its hissing awakened the old man in the back, who also crossed his thumb over his index finger and started humming, "Bendito, bendito, bendito sea Dios . . . los ángeles cantan y alaban a Dios."

"Raven!" José cried above the roar of the wind as the truck shuddered, caught in the blast of the rotating funnel. He reached for the Colt .45 in the glove compartment, opened the window, and felt the vacuum in the truck sucked out as the dust devil stuck its blistering tongue into the interior, blinding them with heat and sand, rattling and shaking the truck.

"No!" Sonny shouted as the eye of the terrible wind bore down on them, and he fought to keep the truck on the road. But too late.

"Fuck you, devil!" José cursed, aimed up at the heart of the dark swirl, and fired.

The report of the pistol was almost lost in the shrill cry of the wounded wind, which—screaming and hollering—struck one final blow against the truck. Then, like a snake shot through the head, the dust devil unfurled and fell sideways, thrashing but spent, its energy lost.

They watched as the dust, trash, and tumbleweeds settled to the earth, the demon dead.

The old man gave thanks. Gracias a Dios. He looked at José. Damn, they are going to call him Shoot Dust Devil Calabasa from now on. He had never seen an Indian kill a dust devil before, but he knew there were many things yet to be revealed, in life and death.

Sonny breathed a sigh of relief as he steadied the truck.

That was the bullet meant for Raven. Now he would have to go into the dream world and drag Raven screaming into the light. Or drown him in holy water and let the element dissolve the very energy it once engendered, for all aspects of the psyche were born in water. Or hit him again with the dreamcatcher, the mandala with a hole in the middle, the hole in the universe. But in the end, nothing could really kill Raven. Violence would only dissolve him into a deeper chaos, for the moment.

Raven thrived in the dark recesses of the soul, corners of the unconscious so old the smell of dinosaur scat, methane gas oozing from the marshes, and the putrid smell of rotting primeval forests still lingered there. Raven lorded over that nubbin of a brain formed in the cosmic sea.

José looked at the pistol, then placed it back in the glove compartment. "Has quite a kick," he said. The demons of Nam awakened by the smell of cordite lay heavy on his heart. Memories locked in his brain cells announced once again that he could never forget the war and its atrocities. He fell silent.

Sonny drove down the long thigh of the hill that spread languorously toward the valley and Bernalillo, the air pleasant after the last gasps of wind whooshed up the face of the Sandias and fell like a spent lover over the Estancia Valley.

A deep quiet fell over the Rio Grande, silent and peaceful. The storm had passed, leaving the last of its caresses playing on the stems of chamisa and dry grass that dotted the mesa. In New Mexico the wind never died. It whimpered to a gentle breeze that cooled the foreheads of those who worked outdoors. Like earth, sky, and clouds, the breeze was a constant friend, a compañero, vigilant over the land. Its strength rose and fell, carrying the whimper of a woman betrayed, or the rage of La Llorona.

The valley actually looked inviting. It was not yet in bloom, but the ochre sheen of spring buds rested on dry branches, on the russet buds on the river alamos, and here and there a globe willow ballooned in bright lime green. Flowering apricot trees graced a few front yards, as did purple plum and redbud trees.

Across the way the turtle hump of the Sandias rose, a faint outline etched against the eastern sky, a turtle on its way to some meeting of mountains, its granite feet leathery, bound to the foothills. In the light of the garish sun the turtle seemed to move. The pattern of light and shadow, deep ravines and outcropping of granite boulders, and the shawl of white limestone along the crest reflected the light, and it was the light that was the breath of the mountain. Deep below the granite exterior, the pounding heart.

"Old turtle," Sonny whispered.

"Alive," José answered.

Sonny's tension dissipated when he made contact with the mountain. For the people of the valley, the Sandias were a force of positive energy. As a lightning rod collects the ever-present energies of thunderstorms, the mountain collected the chi energy of the solar system, gathered it into its bosom and spread it outward, throughout the land. Those whose feet were made of mud could feel the chi rising from the earth to comfort the seven chakras, until even old men's curved spines felt renewed, and women suffering from osteoporosis felt like dancing. Chi for crooked backs and arthritic hands, water for the tree of life, the twisted serpentine spine, the energy of the mountain massaged fibers and flesh, and renewed the soul.

"You don't have to live on the mountain to benefit," José said. "We Pueblo people need the land and water of the valley for our crops. But we honor the mountain. It provides deer, green trees, a spirit. Up there you feel you're close to the Creator."

The true Creator who still imbues the earth with its power, it soul fire, its light.

Yes, Sonny agreed. But he could not enjoy the raw beauty of the land as he used to. The image of the fetus in the jar of water haunted him. Why had he seen two? In the winter-solstice dream, he had seen a light, the soul of Rita's child, blinding Raven for that crucial instant that allowed Sonny to strike with the dreamcatcher. When he recalled the image of the dream he saw it split in two. Twins? It was possible. There was a history of twins in his mother's family. She had a twin sister, and he and Armando were twins.

Raven had killed Rita's twins. No, not killed, was holding them captive. Sonny was sure he could go there, and bring back to life what Raven had taken from him.

12

He pulled into the Sonic Drive-In to phone Rita.

"Sonny, where are you? Have you seen Lorenza?"

"I'm on my way—"

"Are you all right? The cell phones still aren't working. The place is going crazy."

"I'm okay. In Bernalillo."

"There's an important call for you. Augememnon from the state police. He wants you to call him. He left a number—"

She read the number and he penned it on the wall of the phone cubicle.

"I'll call him. How are you?"

"I'm fine. I kept the restaurant open. Brought out the TV set. Everyone is glued to it."

"Everyone?"

"Guys. The place is packed. No one's going to work. They're sitting here drinking coffee and watching the news on TV."

Guys, Sonny thought. Working stiffs from the North Valley. They loved Rita's home-cooked breakfasts, the best red and green chile in the city, and, he knew, they liked to linger and enjoy her presence.

"You're not the jealous type," she said once.

He was, but he said nothing. She was a beautiful woman.

He knew if he was gone all day, by closing time one of the young studs might be tempted to ask to take her home after work. Not that Rita would accept, they all knew that, but they liked to push the envelope. Yeah, he knew his raza, every Chicano a suitor in the heart, always on la movida. It was bred in the bone from day one. Mama Nature had laid one of her hot chile genes in the pants.

He smiled. Yeah, hot chile genes, a hormone gene not yet traced on the DNA molecule, but it was there, waiting to be roasted, peeled, and sandwiched. All's fair in love and war, and the bachelors hanging around Rita's place would just love to score.

Gotta get home before I'm dead, Sonny thought.

"What about the bomb on the mountain?" Rita asked. "Most don't believe it's real. Is it?"

"Nothing to worry about. They have the lab boys out there. I'm sure they will take care of things."

"I hope so. Did you eat?"

"Yes, Chica and I had a great lunch. The tacos were great."

"You didn't give her carne adovada, did you? I put a chicken taco in for her."

Chicken taco sin salsa. The taco he gave José.

"Ah . . . no, she's fine."

"And don Eliseo?" She was hesitant, but she asked anyway.

Sonny turned and looked at the truck.

"Everything's cool. I'll be home in no time."

"I know you, Sonny Baca. You get tied up with Raven and you're a bulldog. He's dangerous, especially if—"

Especially if he messes with my mind, Sonny thought.

"I'm okay. Really."

"Bueno. Just don't go chasing wild horses. I love you."

Wild horses, he thought. The white, the red, the black, and the pale horses of the Bible, and the pale horse carried death, the penitentes said it pulled Doña Sebastiana's cart, la comadre, la muerte.

Why was it that every word became an image? Sound moved into picture, as light moved into time, forming symbols from the world of vibrations. And symbols became story, playing like a concert in his mind.

Today's story had started with the snake. Yes, the snake was a sign on the road. So was running into Bear and Naomi at Red Rocks. The dead governor floating in the tub. The bomb, the helicopter ride. He could see the signs, but he couldn't change their consequences as their ripples moved out in the pond that was the day.

It had always been like this. Waking or dreaming, an idea, a thing, a person, or a word announced itself, became an image in neural fluids, but always the image stood for something else, and the something else it stood for was as nebulous as the original germ. Could even the Logos be trusted to remain static? To mean something? Or had its progeny become just more images floating in a sea of images?

Was the shaman's world a world of symbols? Was this part of the training received from don Eliseo? Something stood for something else, and so it went to the last syllable of recorded time, and there was no way to get at the reality of things, the truth, the essence. Was the world nothing but Vishnu's dream? A world of illusion.

"I love you, querida. Just keep those guys at arm's length."

She laughed. "Maybe if I make you jealous you'll come quicker."

Come quicker. Her words were always playful and suggestive, teasing. Just last week they had driven to the Sandia Casino to a mariachi concert. On the way she heard "Las Mañanitas" on the radio and she turned and told him when she heard the song it made her want to make love to him. The more he bonded to her the more he felt that in the depth of her soul there resided the light of her spirit and the sex of her flesh. It was one.

"I'll be there anyway and kick them all out. And—"

"And what?"

"You know."

"Sonny, we can't make love while someone is blowing up half the state."

"Think of the blast."

She laughed again. "Okay. Just hurry."

"Un beso." She blew a kiss into the phone, and he blew one back. He hung up the phone and lingered there, trying to feel his way through the phone wires to touch her, to make sure things were all right with her. Her laughter swirled in the small booth, an apple-blossom fragrance. Yes, she was okay.

He dialed Augie's number.

"Augie. Sonny."

"Sonny, damn glad you got back to me. Where are you?"

"Bernalillo. And you?"

"Never mind. I need to see you, Sonny."

"What's up?"

"Have you found Raven?"

"No."

"Is Naomi with you?"

"No."

"She disappeared with a gang of Indians. She's the one who led the governor to the Bath House. She's in with Raven."

Sonny shook his head. The medallion on his chest felt warm. Raven was near. Sonny looked at the truck. Something stirred under the tarp.

"Either way, I'm in deep caca. The chief has called out every officer available. He thinks I'm involved. Imagine, me, a suspect! I'm supposed to be guarding the governor and he's dead."

"What about the Al Qaeda suspect?"

"Gone."

"What do you mean 'gone'?"

"The FBI took him. He's gone."

"Where?"

"Sonny, Sonny, Sonny. He's gone. Don't you get it? Gone!"

"And the professors?"

"I let them go. What do they do? Read books! For crying out loud, nobody reads books anymore! They'll be deported. I don't give a holy hill of beans about them, I'm talking about getting Raven! I need to clear myself."

"Where are you?"

Crisply, as if a knife had sliced through the air and cut the wire, Augie hung up.

Sonny cradled the old black phone, a relic of a prior time, almost a museum piece in a world headed toward complete wireless transmission. A few short years ago everyone depended on the telephone, and telephone booths were part of growing up, where you went to call your girlfriend, or call home if you were going to be late. The booth in the movies where someone always made a desperate call. An entire culture had grown up around telephone booths, and now the men in black used cell phones, so did Tom Cruise and Jennifer Lopez, and all the brokers in the world, generals calling in bomb strikes, on and on. Gone wireless and at the mercy of cell towers dotted around the country, satellites circling the earth. In your car with your cell phone you could reach everyone in the world, and still remain isolated.

Sonny looked at the phone cubicle, intimate, with enough room to hold the phone and a tattered phone book, the walls scratched with the graffiti of all the lost souls who in time of need had come to this shrine, to call out, to reach out, to talk to someone. Littered with phone numbers and names, gang signs, modern glyphs, cousins to the petroglyphs the Anasazi had etched on desert boulders. These glyphs were penciled on the walls of the booth, on the tattered phone book, the rock of ages.

He looked closely at the dozens of numbers and messages written on the walls of the cubicle. Maybe this is the Zia Stone of our time, he thought, for here are encoded the encrypted messages of the community. If I could just read the meaning, not the individual messages, but the gestalt, the pattern, find meaning in the scribbles, decipher the names, the lines that lead from one sacred direction to the next, pagan, plaintive cries of crisis, of hope and of sadness, for there, handsomely penciled next to a sad tree, the message, *Christmas day, she left me, estoy en el rincon de una cantina . . .*

The graffiti resounded with a forlorn cry, a canto hondo from deep in the soul. Cries of unrequited love, lust seeking its fulfillment. A crude drawing of a full-bosomed, big-hipped woman holding a very large penis.

The old and smelly phone booth became the cave of Lascaux. There, prehistoric man had painted the mastodon to gain power over the hairy mammoth and be able to kill it. Here, the drawing of the naked woman represented a mad, hopeless desire.

Perhaps the hurried scrawls of body parts that adorned the walls of sleazy bar bathrooms also had a purpose. Neanderthal on the make had to draw the object of his desire. Sex and its need, sometimes a true longing, sometimes perverse.

Sonny studied the names, cryptic messages, lipstick red, Sharpie black, knife scratches, hearts pledging love, fuck-you's, numbers to call for help. For good dope call. Terry loves Flaco. Chuy rules. Darwin. A fish with four legs. And the strangest one, written in seraphim script, at the bottom of the cubicle: *Come to Macedonia and help us.*

Was there a town called Macedonia in New Mexico? A place in desperate need? Sonny scratched his head. Riffing through his memory bank he found the image of the book a Professor Pearce had written long ago, a listing of all the towns and places in New Mexico, a work of love, but then it was teachers like him and George Arms and Dame Edith who had taught a generation of students long before Sonny got to UNM. Professors whose names still rang in the halls of the English Department where he had matriculated. But no, he couldn't recall a Macedonia.

The war in Croatia? Ethnic cleansing? Was the plea for help a call to those who would sit on the fence while entire populations were massacred simply because of their ethnicity? What did *ethnic* mean? Cultural patterns? Or the fear of a different kind of blood? Fear of mestizos? How could one blood be different from another? If a blood transfusion would save your life, you weren't going to ask its ethnicity. The color.

As the center of the world fell apart the guilty would also be those who did not go to help, and their names would be called when Armageddon fell on the fertile fields of Macedonia. The Third World War had already begun, in Iraq, Croatia, in Palestine, Ireland, North Korea, the jeweled Persia of old, Kashmir, Tibet where the Chinese overran ancient monasteries, wherever neighbor turned against neighbor the world shattered. 9-11 was the tolling bell of the new millennium. And who would send to ask for whom it tolled?

The center of the world fell apart when the center of each individual cracked, Sonny thought. It's the soul that must be kept intact. The center of the world rests in each person. We have to go to Macedonia before it's too late!

All the messages begged to be heard, for that was the essence of the phone booth, a Web page before Web pages, the internet of prior generations.

For a good time call Krystal caught his eye. In every phone booth in the world, on every bar bathroom wall, always the name of a woman to call, written not by her but by her avenger.

Testosterone punishes, Sonny thought. A gathering of male hormones creates a violent chi, an angry energy that disrupts the harmonious flow of the psyche.

When he sat with Rita in her garden he felt whole. The fragrance of her flowers and herbs uplifted the spirit, settled the flow of lust into a love that did not need to thrust itself violently into the other to attain completion.

He shrugged, as Atlas must have shrugged upon taking the world on his shoulders, one last deep breath, knowing thereafter he was slave to the gross, material world, bent under its weight so he could never again look up to the heavens, never converse with Zeus or Athena, enslaved as Sisyphus, the poor dope chained to the boulder he had to push up the mountain. The original rolling stone. Atlas and Sisyphus caught in the world of matter, heroes who could not help others, hardly help themselves. Beyond the help of the goddess.

As the old world collapsed the dispossessed looked for heroes, created new legends. Some were false myths totally unconnected to the primal tales of gods and goddesses. Some were fantasies created by Hollywood, rituals splattered on the big screens, composed with gain in sight, not the ordering of a new universe.

Krystal? Was this the sylph in his dream? The anima who protected him?

He dropped his coins into the phone slot and dialed Krystal's number. A long, soft "Hiiiii" answered. "We're open, come on over," said the sweet voice of a siren.

The sirens' house somewhere along the river bosque was open, had always been open, pleasures waited in every room, even as the spring-equinox sun stood poised over the town of Bernalillo, even as the slot machines of the Pueblo casinos kept ringing, enticing the poor with their clink-clanging song; such were the promises of the age that denied dog dreams. The new deal was to offer pleasure or riches, or both, dark illusions of a new illusive mythology.

"I . . . I was just checking the phone—"

"What do you mean checking the phone?"

"It's working."

"Of course it's working. It's the cell phones that are screwed up. Come on, Sonny, quit fucking around. Just come over. You know I'm good."

The words attacked him like a yellow jacket's sting, deep into his flesh, burning down the seven chakras, and he jerked back, hung up the phone, and backed out of the booth. Just what in the hell was happening? The rest of the world wasn't receiving messages, and he was getting more than he bargained for. But what sense did they make? How did Krystal, whoever she was, know it was he? Coincidence? Synchronicity? Yeah, syn-Chronos, the god of Time calling. Yeah, time was turning around the earth, the cotidal sun was in its heaven, and measured time was bearing down on the valley, on him.

In the end this is how it will be, time will touch the soul, become the light within, it will seek its sacred geography, which is after all the inner heart of man and woman, and for an instant everything will make sense. Complete sense.

"I'm not dying," Sonny insisted. It's a coincidence.

He turned and heard the old man. Damn you, Sonny, how many times have I told you, there are no coincidences! It's all part of a beautiful plan. Everything revolves in the Light, and so one name is like another. Crystal simply refracts the light. You call her and you hear the whore next door, or an angel in heaven. What difference does it make?

"I'm not sure," Sonny mumbled. The terrible tension that had been building since he dropped the egg in the glass of water was now a buzz. A headache.

He was irritated at himself and at the old man. Sweat broke out on his forehead, under his arms, pasted his shirt to his back.

"Hey, Sonny!" José called. "Let's go."

He pointed at a half-dozen low-rider cars that were pulling into the drive-in like crows circling roadkill, the customized cars, shining like the chariots of God's angels, decals offering the proof of life, glistening images of la Virgen de Guadalupe on one hood, the Baby Doll with luxurious breasts on the other, bouncing up and down to the rhythm of blaring boom boxes, the thunder of dharma bums, rapping in black and brown, the dark faces of the vatos hidden behind black sunglasses, and at their side lovely, nubile jainas, brown-skinned teenies, faces radiant with paint, a war party into whose arms any opponent would gladly fall, to rest on not-so-virgin breasts.

"Ese vato," one of the locos hissed.

Why aren't they in school? thought Sonny.

José waved. Come on, let's get the hell out of here!

Sonny made his way through the line of cars.

"Ese!" The hiss again. "Forget your past, they're going to bomb you anyway."

They called to him, but he paid no heed, walked through the line of fire, the boom boxes blaring a rap he did not recognize, unless it was an ancient song from Macedonia. He neither acknowledged nor denied the presence of the homeboys, whoever they were.

"Órale! Cuídate."

"El Coco will get you!"

"La Llorona."

Laughter.

Maybe this is Macedonia, he thought, as he got in the truck, started it, and slowly edged out of the lot onto the street.

"Who?"

"I don't know, but they look like crows circling roadkill."

A chill ran up Sonny's spine. Raven was everywhere.

13 »

José pointed, and following a narrow, sandy road they entered the river bosque and drove until José signaled. Sonny stopped the truck, and José got out and looked at the ground.

I've been here before, Sonny thought. But he couldn't remember when or why.

"The house is just down the path, but we're late. All the tracks lead out. The elders are going back to the pueblos to declare war on Dominic."

"What now?"

José got back in the truck. "Your call. Maybe Lorenza's still around. Sure as hell Raven's here."

Sonny followed his gaze, staring into the ominous silence of the brush. Chica whined. Yes, Raven was here.

The bare, gnarled branches of the cottonwoods reached toward the eye of heaven, begging for rain from a sky now glazed with the lingering smoke of distant forest fires.

Sonny shivered. He felt he had come unprepared to Raven's lair. He started to reach for the pistol and remembered José had used the bullet he had prepared for Raven. What weapon did he have left? The dreamcatcher.

He looked up at the towering alamos. The trees were pregnant with thick, dark buds, crust-like chrysalises guarding the seeds within. The leaves and pods would sprout in a month.

His troubled mind retrieved images of elementary school days when he and his friends gathered tetones, the clusters of green pods birthed by the female cottonwood trees. Ammunition. Each pea-sized teton became a stinging missile when shot from the end of a popsicle stick. They pestered the girls and drove teachers mad. Those same green pods ripened and exploded in late May, parachuting the seed-bearing cotton to the earth below. The spring winds drove the cotton like snow. Each cotton fluff carried a seed even to the shores of lands unknown. All of life revolved around the mystery in the seed.

Isn't my soul also like a seed? Seed of mind, seed of body. The body rises up the spinal column, destined to be straight or crooked. And the seven seals of life were locked in the spine. The seals determined the person.

Trees, too, were energized by spirit. Perhaps not the same electric acid that flowed in human nerves, but energized by the earth, sun, and water. The tree lived in a forest of spirits, as the person lived in a community of spirits.

Sonny thought of the biblical cry: "Like a cedar I am exalted in Lebanon, like a cypress on Mount Zion."

But I am a Nuevomexicano, and so like a cottonwood tree I grow in the Rio Grande Valley.

He turned to look at José, who stared straight ahead into the brush.

A strange calm lay over the bosque. Heavy and oppressive. It settled over Sonny. Like José he could only stare at trees. The silence kept him immobile in his thoughts.

He remembered witnessing the miracle of seed. He and Rita sat under a giant cottonwood one still day. Heat from the trees rose up into the sky, creating softly swirling thermal waves, heat usually invisible to the eye, but that day, outlined against the glowing sunlight and bright blue sky the cottonwood was letting go of its seed, and that breezeless day the weightless cotton wasn't falling to the ground, it was rising into the sky like a sudden ejaculation of sperm, the tree fertilizing the sky, a column of cotton fluff rising into the glorious light, a fireworks display without sound, with only the blessing of the tree's terrible desire to propagate itself, to scatter a million seeds to grow one tree. Up and up the cloud of seeds spiraled, whooshing into the sky, the desire of the tree so intense and the rising heat so hot it could be no other way.

Sperm, Sonny had said. Ovum, Rita whispered.

The tree that gave forth its seed was female, the outpouring from its green belly the seeds of potential.

He had taken her hand, standing in awe, humble witnesses to the display of the tree's yearning to be. Miles away the tiny, delicate seeds wrapped in their parasails of cotton would fall to earth, and if the universe conspired, a tree would take hold there. The chances of its sprouting were slim to none, but the green belly of the tree cared not, it flung its seeds into the existential maw of the sky, shouting *I will be!*

The sweat from their joined hands grew hot and slippery as tree sperm.

"Seeds," he said.

José looked quizzically at him. "Come on, Sonny. We can't just sit here. Raven's here!"

"I know." Sonny realized Raven was near, but a new emotion had crept into his heart. What if Raven was too strong? What if he had made so many deals with Dominic's group that he was protected? If they could murder the governor they could get anyone.

The old man had been an alamo, tough bark and green veins, fed by the earth and water of the valley, but trees fall and he had fallen. Some trees are cut before their time, and the old man had been brought down, dashed to the ground by Raven's terrible sword. Scimitar of evil.

"He's waiting for you," José said.

Deep in this forest primeval, without even the sound of a lonely bird crying for its mate, they heard a raven call.

A low growl rose in Chica's throat, and her hackles prickled. Sonny felt goosebumps on the back of his neck.

"Raven," José whispered, and went for the pistol.

"Won't do you any good."

"Why?"

"You used the bullet on the whirlwind—"

José checked the pistol. "Still plenty of bullets left," he said.

Sonny reached for the dreamcatcher hanging on the rifle rack.

José sneered. "Sheeee—." In an instant he was out of the truck and into the bosque, disappearing in a flash.

Sonny looked at Chica. "Quédate aquí," he whispered, and rubbed her neck and stepped out of the truck. She would be safer in the truck than in the bosque.

Raven had been following him all day, and he had chosen this spot to make his move. So be it.

Sonny sniffed the air, separated the smells. On the sandy road lay the scent of a fox that had hunted here last night and left behind a few russet feathers of the pheasant it had killed. Also, a badger had come from the river, perhaps to grub for roots, and a family of skunks had also left their scent, a lingering cloud along the path. Under a tree lay a plastic bread-loaf wrapper. Just recently someone had made sandwiches, perhaps lovers on a picnic, and why not? It was spring and spending a quiet day along the river under the canopy of trees seemed the thing to do.

But not today. Raven's smell also lingered on the trail.

To his left Sonny heard the slight murmur of water, the river flowing south. He moved cautiously, not stepping on twigs, careful because here the bosque was a thicket of alamo, tamarisk, and river willow. The path narrowed, and up ahead he spied the outline of a small house.

He hadn't gone twenty feet when the instinct that keeps men alive told him to hit the ground. As he dove, a bullet whizzed overhead, embedding itself in the trunk of a nearby tree.

A second instinctual wave told him the bullet was a distraction, the smell of Raven was so close. He jumped to his feet, but too late. A heavy club struck him across the forehead, and he went down, grabbing at the enemy, whose odious laughter was followed by a whooping cry of "coup."

Perhaps it was the hot blood blinding him, or the rubble in the path as he was dragged along, but before he passed out he smelled a new scent, the unforgiving smell of pigs.

Very well, he thought, if the sounds and images of semi-darkness can be called thoughts, let this be the darkness in which I kill that sonofabitch and take back my child!

Bravo! Raven croaked. Always the hero!

The brain traumatized, whether from a blow to the skull at work or play, or from excessive passion that burns it to a crisp, or from strong narcotics, demonic lust or booze that numbs, suddenly loses its sense of time, for the blood is now interested in self-preservation, not the tick-tock of the day. A few images come and go, but the brain is concerned only with getting enough oxygen to stay alive.

Sonny breathed deep, felt a light burn as one eye fluttered open. His left eye was closed, full of blood that dripped from where the club had grazed his forehead.

He strained to get his bearing, but the dark room swirled around him. Someone had brought him inside the building. A young woman, a sylph-like creature, stood in front of him.

What's your name? the sylph asked, she of the constellation Hydra, probably gorgon in nature for her silken hair, like burnished gold, oscillated like eels or snakes, not frightening but alluring.

This is a dream of desire, he thought, looking into the face of the exquisite angel, eyes that shone with the fire of amethyst, lips painted with henna, gold rings adorning her eyebrows. The airy creature must be an angel because to her belongs the music of cascading water, like a choir of angels falling from heaven, their silken wings fluttering, filling the room.

Ah, but I'm in the world of the trickster, he thought, and I know enough of survival not to trust Raven's angels. Through ooze of blood he faked a smile.

You know, he replied.

The sylph returned his smile. Dressed in a diaphanous gown strung with threads of gold, so sheer and airy the outline of her svelte body was clearly visible. He could not help but admire her exquisite breasts, so perfectly formed they would stop the musing of any philosopher. The soft cleft between her breasts, where lingered the aroma of freshly baked apples coated with cinnamon and sugar, formed a line down to a belly button adorned with more gold rings, the line continuing down to her virgin sex and slender legs.

Sonny's nostrils quivered with the fragrance that rose from between her breasts, for with each slight movement the aroma changed; now it was the sweet heat of dark figs, next the flowers of the date palm, a smell as ancient as the deserts of Egypt, green fronds nourished by the secret waters of the oasis, water that soothed the desert heat. Date palm flowers blooming as sweet as the dark fruit they bore, so deep and thirst-quenching that Sonny felt a deep need within responding. To what? Her body or the aromas it offered?

Obviously, the sylph practiced aroma therapy, which as all wise men know, is nature's way.

Ah, Raven, you really know how to do a guy in. Funny how a man could be in the deepest of trouble and still respond to that sweet perfume that rose from between a woman's breasts.

But why so suspicious? Surely she means me no harm, he thought, shaking his head to get rid of the pain that rang in his head. He tried to rise from the chair, but felt his arms tied behind his back.

Nymph. Free me.

You are too beautiful to be set free. Make love to me first and make me mortal. She laughed, the tinkling sound of an altar bell, or camel bells as the plodding animals arrived at the oasis. Her touch was so exquisite he almost groaned, not in pain but with the satisfaction that time and again makes the world of men slippery and wet.

Only a mortal could have hit me as hard as you did, he said, controlling the surging energy that seemed to have a life of its own, the same kind of deceptive desire he had once known with Tamara.

The sylph wanted to have her way with him because only by copulating with a mortal could she descend from the dream ambience and become a nymph of the earth. She desired the earth energy, which is nothing but sex energy, the stuff of procreation, endowing all of nature with its impulse, driving it into parasites, bacteria, mammal and bird, insects, even the fungus that grows beneath the wet leaves and compost of winter. Every form of life, organic or rock, everything, obeyed nature's common rule: *Do it!* I don't care how you do it, just do it!

One spring she had drunk mandrake wine with a Pan-like creature who appeared, one of those transients that use the river as a highway to Mexico. But to no avail.

He tried not to listen to her sylph's song. He knew sirens too well, knew the stories his grandparents told of La Llorona, the crying woman who roamed the river's edge looking for the children she had drowned. Why squander his mortality? Why spend his seed in this dry dream? He turned away from her healing hands, the stars on her breasts, the fire in her thighs, and tried as innocently as he could to let go of the urge that might overwhelm him.

The girl had not dragged him here, air spirit that she was. Raven had. But where was he?

I wouldn't hurt you, she said. If you don't want to, I know why. She lifted a blue porcelain bowl filled with the healing water of the river, a dark water in which floated pomegranate seeds and eucalyptus leaves, and with a soft cloth she began wiping away the blood.

She stood so close her forest fragrance touched his nostrils, the rotting leaves of winter, the spice of buds, rabbits in fever, the sharp metallic smell of a snake before it sheds its skin.

She brushed against him as she finished wiping away the blood, her every move suggestive. She desperately sought mortality, as if it were an answer to the prison of her dream.

We have time, she said, kissing him lightly on the forehead, spreading the essence of unnamed aromas, herbs from faraway places.

I don't know your name, he said.

Sibyl Sosostris, she answered, pushing him away.

Damn! Sonny thought, I knew Chicanitas were into designer names, calling themselves Kimberlee and LayLani and all sorts of combinations, but Sibyl Sosostris was too much.

What do you do?

I read tarot cards, for I am mystic. Get it? Mystic. A nymph of the woods. Like Robin Hood's little green men, we were waiting for you. She took the bowl away and returned with a cigarette and a pack of tarot cards.

She lit a match and took a deep drag from the cigarette. Want some?

Sonny shook his head. What's your real name?

Sylvia Sanchez, she said. I grew up on a farm near Belen. When I was little my parents would tie me to a tree by the river while they took care of their garden. I grew to love that tree, to make love to it. Good God, I get off on trees.

She spread the cards on the small table in front of him.

You are a Fool, she said, pointing to the jester's card. You walked right into it. She laughed, took another drag and flipped another card.

The Lovers. Not bad. We could be lovers, if only you let go of the past, which is a web. The Fool who doesn't let go of the past is doomed to repeat it, as Benito Juarez said long ago.

The past can also be a garment of many colors I wear, and therefore I know myself, Sonny countered. When I look in the mirror I know who I am.

She was obviously enjoying her game, flirting and letting her small breasts bounce in front of him.

She was no Madame Sosostris but one of Raven's women, trained in the art of seduction, Sonny knew.

He remembered the poor, deranged women Raven had hired last summer, the summer the people of the valley called Zia Summer. They had killed a goat for their summer-solstice ceremony, and they were ready to kill Sonny before don Eliseo and Rita rescued him.

But Raven had grown in power and intelligence, and this was no cult lady hired to do his dirty work. This could be his anima, as dark a lady as ever rose from the deep well of the mind, and why not? There is an anima of beauty even in the bad guy's dreams.

Twins, she said, turning the card. To be lovers we must become one, as twins are one.

Twins. The soul of the child Rita lost was one soul ready to split into two. Twins. He and Armando were twins. He and Raven were twins.

You're getting ahead of yourself, she said. Pay attention. Don't play the Fool!

She flipped another card. The Sun. Ah, you are a child of the Sun, but it has blinded you. You thought being keeper of the Zia medallion would save you, now look at you.

She opened his shirt and removed the gold medallion, turned, and offered it to the man who sat on the Zia Stone.

The man dressed in black received the medallion, the eternal prize.

Sonny, Sonny, Sonny, Raven said. You've lost it all. Fell for the oldest trick in the book, and now look at you.

His laughter filled the dark, folded shadows of the room.

14 »

THE SYLPH DISAPPEARED INTO THE AIR, or into the silken, feathery shadows that fluttered nervously in the room.

Sonny looked at Raven. There he sat, as handsome and full of temptation as ever, a guy that could win over the heart of any woman with one of his dark, devastating Pedro Infante glances, and win the hearts of men with his visions of freedom. A chaos he called freedom.

You're back, Sonny managed.

I was never gone, Raven replied, that thin smile that was half sneer on his lips. And why not? He had the upper hand—cupped in one hand was the Zia medallion, the Medal of the Sun, which he so coveted, willing to break all the commandments of Moses to wear it on his chest. Now his mojo power.

The other hand held Sonny's dreamcatcher, the weapon don Eliseo had forged and blessed. Raven feared the dreamcatcher, for if it struck him at just the right angle he, like a bad dream, would disappear through the hole in the middle. But bad dreams return, as Raven just said, surfacing from the unconscious, for, as everyone knows, mythic imagery is universal, it lives in that elusive state of being called the psyche. There's more if one is willing to believe. What if the memory of those primal images is ingrained in every cell in the body, from spleen to liver to toenails?

The devil works in history. Yes, one can't get away with claiming only the angels toil, one has to claim the whole caboodle. The whole enchilada, Chicanos would say. You eat bean burritos and you're going to get some gas. You dream and you get Blake's angels—and his demons.

The mind is not a house of neat rooms, rather it flows like a stream from primal memory, like a river seeking its home in the brilliant sea, its currents thick with the hidden waters of the primeval jungle, as well as the holy waters of Eden's four rivers. Dream images surface into the light of waking, there where the expert shaman works to interpret the signs and convert the symbols into useful myth or story, so—any shrink will explain—the dreamer might better know himself.

But there's a rub. Every dreamer is a storyteller, and so from those bubbling images a story is composed, and even the most expert shaman cannot distinguish between the true image, if there is such a thing, and the story composed by the dreamer from the dream's images. So who's in charge? Is life simply story piled on story?

Who's in charge? Who's on third? don Eliseo would say. What's on second?

Sonny knew the ambiguity of dreams. So did Raven.

The medallion, which Raven swung like a hypnotist's pendulum, caught intimations of the dim light in the room, gathering it into one bright center, then exploding in a rainbow of possibilities.

But where, oh where, was the source of the light? Sonny's swirling mind was as dark as a web spun by Arachne.

No, you can't get rid of me that easy, Raven intoned. What would the world be like if there were no shadows? Get it? I am your shadow.

Tell him to get behind you, the old man whispered, and Sonny breathed a sigh of relief. The old man, the only trump card he held, was still around.

You solipsist sonofabitch!

The curse was not strong enough; in fact, Raven ate it up. A compliment.

Abaddon! Sonny shouted, trying a new tactic, knowing if this didn't get Raven's goat he was in deep trouble, for curses only come in threes.

It worked. Raven cringed. Sonny had never called him one of Satan's minions. The name was like a slap in the face, an insult, for Raven considered himself Sonny's equal. If there is such a thing as metempsychosis, if the soul passes from form to form, from one generation to the next, then Sonny and Raven were twins from an ancient time, coming down through the eons, battling each other for ascendancy, now one having the upper hand, now the other, and just when civilization thought it had seen the light a spontaneous massacre of innocents or a world war erupted. Or a Holocaust with its indescribable horror descended on the world.

This everyone knew, but Sonny had never called him a cohort of El Diablo.

Sonny, Raven said softly, recovering from the insult. You disappoint me. I am not the Satan of the world, I am not the anti-Christ.

He paused and looked Sonny in the eye. Do you still not get it? I am the shadow that lives within the hidden self. You need me as I need you. Without me there is nothing to reveal of the myth you once knew by heart, and without the original story you will never know yourself. That's what it's all about, Sonny, knowing yourself. Without struggle there is no life, and without the existential tension within the psyche, there are no signs to light the way.

Sonny shivered. He knew the psyche was a bottomless pit, a wide, dark lake. Voices spoke across the waters. Images appeared.

Raven continued. The masses are born, live, and work in darkness. They die while sleepwalking. The masters who command are no better off. They amass gold coins and power. To what end? With all that baggage they can't get through the eye of a needle. But you, Sonny, you could be different. If only you opened your eyes.

Sonny looked to the old man for advice, but he turned away, a tired, sagging look on his face.

I don't feel too good, he said. Try something else. Get him to talk about the bomb on the mountain.

The old man wasn't going to be much help. His time was crumbling down on him; perhaps his vision was already on the next karmic road, a new dream.

Devil or terrorist, it's all the same, Sonny said. He knew Raven would talk for a while, but sooner or later he would strike with his sharp beak-like scimitar. Death was close by.

Raven shook his head in disbelief.

You think me a common terrorist? Is that it? Maybe I will blow up the Jemez. Just to teach you a lesson. Destroy the Los Alamos labs! Blow it up and have your government blame Al Qaeda, blame Osama Bin Laden, blame anyone. It's much easier to blame the immigrants, the Commies, terrorists! But the real enemy is within! It's the beginning of the end.

Sonny tugged at his ropes. He wanted to get free and choke the life out of Raven, make him return the child of Rita's dream.

You're seething with anger, Sonny. That's no good.

Sonny relaxed and rested his burned wrists. Yes, the strong emotion he felt wouldn't solve his predicament. He was dealing with a trickster, an entity that had the power to drive him mad and bring down the seven seals. He had to think, to be cautious like a coyote, to plot his way, but in such a dismal state, where was there to go?

You tried to kill me.

Raven shook his head. Me? No, no, Sonny. When I cut a heart in two it stays cut.

Then who?

You should know, Sonny. The government thinks you know too much. If you find out who really killed the governor a lot of very important people will go to jail. Yes, we were waiting for you, but so were others. Could it have been my friend Augie? He blames you for things falling apart. Or could it have been the man they call Bear?

He thinks you're interested in his woman. That kind uses guns; I work in subtle ways.

Sonny laughed. Bullshit! You call the bomb subtle?

Raven shrugged. You have a point. Sometimes the only way to win the hearts of weaklings is to create panic. Panic leads to fear, and with enough fear I can lead your good people back to the Dark Ages. Isn't it appropriate that the last World War start here, in the mountain where the first atomic bomb was developed, in the state where at Trinity Site it was exploded?

You want complete control?

Yes.

Let him talk, the old man advised. Talking is the first step toward tripping yourself. It's what he means behind the words you have to listen to.

I have what I want, Raven said. The Zia medallion. Now I am its keeper. And I have your dreamcatcher, which is worthless. I'll use it as a hula hoop and pass back and forth from one dream to the other.

He tossed the dreamcatcher aside, and the sylph came forth from under the wet cottonwood leaves to retrieve it, her once silken, airy gown now covered with nature's wet ooze. She looked at it, sighed, then placed it on the table with the tarot cards.

What he wants is your soul, the old man warned.

Ah yes, Raven said. Let's cut to the quick. It is your soul I seek. You were taught by your mentor, and by all those modern psychologists who still search after the philosopher's stone. They preach they can cure unsettled minds. Turn dross metal into gold. They preach I must come to you. Assholes! Don't they know, it is you who must come to me? That, in a nutshell, is what I want. You, begging for sanity, at my feet. And we're almost there.

No! Sonny cried.

Oh yes! You're sitting in a darkness that holds you immobile. You can't think straight. Those who set out to help you only led you deeper into despair. The potter warned you. What she predicts is never believed!

I believe in myself, you sonofabitch! Sonny shouted in anger. I went into your dark dream, fought you there, and sent you to hell!

Not before I killed the old man! Raven retorted, rising to his feet. The dreamcatcher worked for the moment. But relief from me is never permanent!

I'll make it permanent! Untie me and I'll show you!

Raven jumped forward and slapped him hard. Shut up!

The sylph let out a faint gasp.

Afraid?

You're in my net! Why should I be afraid?

Sonny relaxed and smiled even though the slap bruised the side of his face. Raven had taken the bait. Roadkill.

Ropes can't hold me, Raven. I'm coming after you. I want my child!

You have no power left, he said, dangling the Zia medallion in Sonny's face.

Sonny smiled, spat out blood, heard the sylph's soft *oooooh.*

The old man—

Damn the old man! He's useless! See him cowering in the shadows! He's useless!

Sonny nodded. Perhaps. But there is another way.

Raven cocked his head, as ravens are wont to do when they sense danger during mealtime, or out of curiosity.

Sonny knew he had taken the bait, poisoned with the coyote's spittle.

What way?

The soul you took from Rita's womb is a spirit of light. As is the soul of every child. You hold my child prisoner, and that's your mistake.

I don't understand, Raven replied, nervously.

The light of my child shines in your darkness. It calls to me. It will guide me.

No! Raven shouted. What's mine is mine! You're misguided. You have no way to enter my circle! He paused, then said, I should be wary, but I'm not. You spoke of trumps. It's time you see mine.

He turned and pulled away the black cloth that covered the seat, revealing a large black boulder.

Iron pyrite, Sonny guessed, fool's gold. Indeed, the stone shimmered with specks of false gold and a blue aura, ecumenical beyond belief.

The Zia Stone! Raven announced proudly. It's mine!

Sonny shook his head. If this were true then Raven held a full hand. The most prized possession!

It can't be.

It is. Look! See the signs. Written in hieroglyphic Hittite, it made its way from Anatolia to Atlantis to Aztlán. See the relationship? A, A, A. In Anatolia this extinct language was first written in cuneiform. Remember the wet clay tablets your sixth-grade teacher made you scribble on? Cuneiform. A secret language from the past.

Bullshit, the old man muttered. Don't listen to him, Sonny.

You doubt? Raven said. Look closely. This stone was taken from Anatolia, across the Nile where it was engraved by the priests of Ra who knew the end of their world was coming. There in the port of Alexandria they placed it in a ship bound for Atlantis. There it sat for a millennium, in the middle of the central plaza, the agora. But Atlantis, too, was doomed. That is the history of civilizations. They are born, rise, die. Before the ocean washed over that ancient civilization the priests shipped the stone west toward the setting sun, past the Pillars of Hercules, to the land of the Olmecs. The priests of Africa visited the Olmec shore. There your ancestors found the stone and brought it to Aztlán, your Chicano homeland, Sonny. It's all there. The sad truth is, now it's mine.

Don't believe a word! the old man warned.

But it made sense, Sonny thought, falling for the oldest trick in the book, the theories of those who said the secrets of life had been revealed only to those civilizations from across the sea, never to the natives of the Americas.

Don't listen, Sonny! the old man shouted. You know better! The stone was carved here in Aztlán, the homeland of the Aztecs, earth of the Anasazi, place of origin for so many of our tribes. It's your story, Sonny. Indio y Español, y todos los demás. Your blood flows from this place, as sure as the springs of the mountain feed the rivers. The Zia Stone was carved by your ancestors.

Sonny struggled to contain his thoughts. The vertigo began to clear. Damn Raven! He could confuse anyone. And why not? That was the power of the unconscious energy that wove its tapestries from a memory so old its warp and woof were the aquatic moss of primeval oceans.

In the darkness a coyote howled. Along the bosque a family of coyotes moved. Their call reminded Sonny that often the best medicine was to laugh at Raven. As a coyote laughs at night when the moon is full and shining through open windows on the moist, glistening flesh of sleeping virgins.

Sonny laughed. A loud howl that scattered the dark shadows.

Why do you laugh? asked Raven.

Because you expect me to believe that story. You forget, our people didn't inscribe wedges in clay. No cuneiform, Raven. And the stone you sit on, it's plain fool's gold.

Damn you! Raven exclaimed, stepping forward and drawing his sword.

What if I cut you loose from your dream? You will never awaken, never know again the world you once knew!

Won't do any good, Sonny replied. I'm coming for you. Wherever you are. You can't hide from me!

You're too late! Raven cursed. You missed the tide! Fox tried to warn you. Give up the dreaming dog.

I give you eternal struggle, Sonny countered. To the bitter end!

No! It ends today! Raven shouted, raising the curved blade, the shining scimitar that could slice a man in two.

The blade hung in the air, caught in that instant in that space of twelve o' clock, the exact equinox moment when the sun teetered on the edge of yes or no, the time on Sonny's broken wristwatch that at least twice a day was correct.

A banging at the door shattered the silence. Raven cocked his head at the loud thumping. Help was on the way.

Someone shouted Sonny's name.

Raven paused. Noetic justice, he whispered.

Sonny heard, neurotic justice.

We need to plan another meeting, Raven said. He knew that sparing Sonny meant sparing himself.

Name the place, Sonny answered.

The movie house. I have things to show you. A new technology that creates dreams.

I'll be there.

The banging rattled the door.

Someone knocking at the door reminds me of a poem, Raven said. He looked at Sonny with a raven's cold eyes, always the teasing trickster. I set sail for Burque where I make my deals. The dream, or nightmare if you prefer, continues. See you at the movies!

And he was off in a flutter of dark wings.

I'll see you in hell, was all Sonny could muster.

15 »

The door of the hut opened with a rush of wind, and the hinges, forged long ago by a Mexican smith at the Estancia de Las Golondrinas near Santa Fe, tore away from their rusty nails, screaming, "Heeeee's gaaawn! Heeeee's gaawn!"

Lorenza rushed in, followed by Augie with his state trooper service revolver drawn. Just like the movies, and just as in the movies the dark shadow of Raven disappeared, leaving in its wake the smell of cobwebs.

Lorenza, who had been with Sonny through the travails and paralysis of the shaman winter, was instantly at his side.

"Dios mío!" she cried.

Sonny nodded toward Raven's tracks on the dusty floor.

Outside in the owl light filtering through the bare cottonwood branches a huge flock of muttering crows rose into the air. Augie, with drawn pistol, dashed out the back door.

"You're hurt," she said, looking at the bruise on Sonny's forehead.

"I'm okay. Untie me."

Lorenza looked down at Sonny's hands. "You're not tied."

Sonny thought for a moment, then brought his hands from behind his back and rubbed his wrists. He was sure he had been tied, but he knew enough of Raven's powers to suspect hypnosis. A very strong type of hypnotic aura, perhaps stronger than dream, came from the deepest recesses of the mind-soul bearing Raven's eternal message: I'm going to give you some of your own medicine, confusing both essence and the body's nervous system.

"Raven," she said.

"Yes. And you?"

"I waited for you. I ran into Augie outside. Why is he here?"

"I'll explain later. How did the meeting go?"

"It didn't last long. There's an agreement to stop Dominic. Code name, 1680. What's going on, Sonny?"

"Augie's covering for Dominic's group, I'm sure. I just don't know how deep he is. Anyway, thanks. You got here in time."

He tried to stand but felt wobbly.

"Sit still awhile," she said. "Let me look at your eye."

Dressed in jeans and turtleneck sweater, Lorenza looked like Rita's double, as beautiful a native Nuevomexicana as walked the valley. Before her earthly beauty the sylph, who now was cursed to remain in the breeze that caressed the highest tree branches, rose and disappeared with a sigh. Her cards tumbled down on the dirt floor. One fell face up: the Fool.

Raven's last message. He was rubbing it in. Raven had led him by the nose as a bull is led by a ring, made him walk right into a kind of waking dream. Dream or not, the bruise above his left eye was real.

"Who hit you?" she asked.

"I don't know," Sonny stammered. And he didn't. Someone had shot at him from a distance, but whoever hit him over the head had been close by.

"Did you see José?" he asked.

"No. Is he here?"

Sonny nodded. "He came with me—"

"Say nothing to Augie. The police are looking for him." She looked out the door where Augie had exited.

She held his head back and peeled up his eyelid. Her owl eyes peered deep into the light cells.

Her body smelled of sweet herbs. Her gentle touch seemed to move into his skull, then down along his spine. He relaxed, knowing she possessed the power of healing.

"It didn't cut the skin, but it's going to swell and close your eye."

She took a small bottle from her curandera pouch and touched a drop of the contents to the bruise. The pain eased away.

"Gracias," he said. She had the healing powers of the owl in her.

"You know the story of Horus," she said as she held a handkerchief to his eye.

"Yeah, the guardian son who while avenging his father lost one eye in a battle with his uncle. Funny you should mention it; I've been thinking of that story today. But it doesn't apply to me."

"Every story taking place in your mind's eye applies," she corrected him.

Yes, she was right. A man carried a bag full of stories. The winged eye was one such primal image. Horus was the falcon god of the ancient Egyptians. Was there a falcon god in the Indian pueblos of New Mexico? There were eagle dancers who in feathered costumes imitated the eagle so gracefully that they transported the viewer into a world in which man became the mediator between the gods and the earth's people. But, no, there were no gods like Horus in the pueblos. Perhaps someday a storyteller would write a poem for Isis, and such a thing would come to pass.

In his metempsychotic dreams Sonny had wandered along the banks of the Nile with his brothers, Osiris and Seth. He understood the Egyptian pantheon, and its stories reached even the shores of the Rio Grande.

"Did you talk to Rita?"

"Yes. She's all right. It's you I worry about."

Sonny knew Lorenza was soul-sister to Rita. Even the preacher Ezekiel, he who had been transported into the realm of God in a flying saucer, knew the power of soul-sisters.

"He took the Zia medallion."

"Damn!" she cursed. "We came too late."

"Not your fault, I walked into it."

I'm sorry, the old man said from the corner where he sat in quilted shadows.

Not your fault either, Sonny replied. He struggled to understand what had happened. He had walked into Raven's circle totally unprepared. And it wasn't just the blow to the forehead that had him off balance. Raven was working a strange new medicine. Would it be possible to enter Raven's night world and rescue Rita's child? The feeling of impotence overwhelmed him.

"What now?" Lorenza asked, stooping to retrieve the dreamcatcher.

"Get it back—"

"Sonny, that's a bad blow you got. You're not—"

"Able," he said, standing. "I'm okay."

He felt uncoordinated. But he had no choice. Raven had thrown the gauntlet. Dared Sonny to go to him. Now he had the Zia medallion. The solar disk. The same symbol carved on a Babylonian stone, twelve centuries before the birth of Christ.

"He wants you like this," Lorenza said. "Weak—Let me go with you."

"This time it's just the two of us," he replied. "I'd feel better if you checked on Rita."

He felt lousy. Stumbling into too many incidents. Unprepared. And the old man seemed unable to help. But why dump his chagrin on the old man? He just had to plant his feet more firmly.

He walked to the boulder Raven claimed was the Zia Stone and kicked it. The soft tufa stone crumbled.

"He never quits."

He can't, the old man said. It's his nature. He loves to play games.

"Yeah, except the bomb on the mountain isn't a game."

"You bet it isn't," said Augie, entering, pistol in hand. "Nothing out there but a flock of crows. Went up in the air like a black cloud."

"What in the hell are you doing here?" Sonny asked.

"Hey, that's a bad bruise you got there. What happened?"

"How did you find me?"

"I followed you."

"To take a shot at me!"

"Shoot you? Why the hell would I—Hey, you're really mixed up. You're not well—"

"Let me check your pistol!" Sonny challenged him.

Augie looked at his pistol, then at Sonny. He shook his head. "Against regulations," he said, smiling. "If it goes off, you might be dead. I'd lose my job. The force doesn't like messy cops."

The two men gauged each other, then Augie's smile turned to a grin. He tossed the pistol for Sonny to catch.

Sonny smelled the barrel. "It hasn't been fired."

"God no," a very satisfied Augie chortled. "Only time I get to fire this baby is on the range. You don't think I'd take a pot shot at you, do you?"

"So why here?" Sonny handed him the pistol.

"I saw your truck leave the drive-in and followed."

"Why?"

"Hell, Sonny, you're driving into the bosque with a wanted felon in your truck and you're asking why I followed?"

"José? A felon?"

"Yup, one José Calabasa. We got him on a misdemeanor. Threatened to blow up Cochiti Dam. He's with those so-called *Green* Indians. Troublemakers is what they are. He was in the Bernalillo jail last night—"

"José?"

"That's right. Broke out early this morning. Hell, everybody breaks out of the Bernalillo jail. He headed up 550. Where did you meet him?"

"Never mind. Have you talked to anyone on the mountain?"

"Nope. I know what you know. It's ticking. Hey, let the lab boys handle that. What I've got is a lot more interesting." He turned to Lorenza. "Nice meeting you. Sorry I couldn't be of more help. But when this thing blows over maybe I can call you."

Lorenza picked up the Fool's card from the floor and handed it to Augie. "Maybe."

He looked at the card. "Yeah, right." He stalked out the door.

Sonny and Lorenza followed him outside. They watched the police car disappear down the dusty road.

"Safe to come out?" José asked, coming from behind a thick tamarisk clump, pistol tucked in his belt. "Whatju find?"

"What do you mean what did I find?" Sonny retorted.

"Did you see Raven?"

"Did you?"

"Saw a flock of crows. Guess he flew." Looking at Lorenza, "Did you tell him?"

"Yes."

"So what now?"

"Who sent you to find me?"

"I did," Lorenza said. "José's on our side. Yes, he was in jail, but the charges are ridiculous. Intimidation. It's Augie doing Dominic's dirty work."

Sonny nodded. The professor had fingered Augie, saw him coming out of the Bath House, but admitted the light was dim; he only thought the man looked like Augie.

"It's a big conspiracy," José said, "but you can't go to the attorney general with a conspiracy theory."

"Yeah." Sonny agreed. The whole thing was murky. Let the good cops find out who murdered the governor. Still, he had a bad feeling that Naomi was in danger. Both the governor and Naomi knew the fringes of Dominic's plan. When the governor backed out, they drowned him. And Raven was playing all sides.

Chica! He would go after Chica!

He turned and sprinted up the dirt path to the truck. The door was open, and Chica was gone.

He looked into the bosque and shouted "Chiiii-ca!" But he knew Raven had struck. Four black feathers rested by the door.

"Damn!"

Other black feathers fluttered in the tree branches, droppings of the whirlwind of crows.

"He took the dog," José said. "Why?"

"To get at Sonny," Lorenza answered.

"I don't have much time," Sonny said, jumping into his truck.

"You better take this." José handed him the pistol.

Sonny tossed the pistol in the glove compartment.

"I'll go by Rita's," Lorenza offered. "You take care—"

"I will," he replied. "You?" he asked José.

"Lorenza can drop me off. Hey, Sonny, I'm sorry. I should have stayed by the truck."

"I'll find her," Sonny said. He started the truck and screeched out of the bosque, following the road back to Bernalillo.

He sped through town and took the old Camino Real to Alburquerque, thinking, the old man is right. I've made too many mistakes. Not thinking straight. But I'm not going to rest till I get that sonofabitch.

Overhead, in the clear spring light of the equinox a swirling cloud of birds swooped over the bosque, and Sonny thought he heard Raven's laugh echo up the slope of the mountain.

But as confused as he felt, he now knew Raven's plan. The events of the day were falling into place. Raven wanted respect, if only momentarily. He would meet with the mayor and the Los Alamos Labs director and promise to clear up everything. The Al Qaeda operative had been planted as the fall guy. The events of the day meant everything had been orchestrated to draw Sonny into Raven's net.

Half a mile from Tramway Boulevard Sonny swerved, the truck skidded sideways, and he brought it to a stop on the shoulder of the road.

A turtle, probably finished with its winter hibernation, had pushed its head up from the riverbed of damp earth and rotting leaves, smelled spring in shoots of grass, and was once again alerted by its reptilian brain. Arise and rumble! Its nature and the mud-ooze of the hidden waters called it to make time. Time to eat and procreate. Spring had dug its fingers of renewal into the flesh beneath the skin of earth.

Sonny jumped out of the truck and ran back to the turtle, which had been sideswiped by a car.

He picked up the wounded creature tenderly, and hot yellow pee squirted out of the shell, a sure sign of trauma. He held it and then slowly the four leathery feet and the small, green head came out of the shell.

From a scratch on one foot oozed a dark green liquid, just starting to form a crust. Although the acrid smell of turtle blood still hung in the air, its sodden, burnished shell had saved it from the blow of the car, which had hurtled it through a space it had not anticipated. The green fragrance of the river shone in the turtle's sad eyes, a plea for help.

The creature opened its amber, unblinking eyes, but one bruised eyelid would not quite lift. A one-eyed turtle, it peered from its reptilian past to gaze into Sonny's eyes, its forlorn look seeming to say, my savior.

16 »

Pobrecita, the old man said.

Sonny looked closely at the tortoise.

It won't make it, out there. . . . He meant on the road where sooner or later crows would settle around it, curious at the find, a roadkill delicacy. The crows would proceed to peck at it, and smelling the blood they would go for the eyes until they completely blinded the creature. Then, taking their time, they would, in bits and pieces, extract the flesh.

Turtles don't die in a hurry, the old man said. Nebuchadnezzar the Babylonian king knew. He hired magicians to interpret his dream. But the old fart didn't tell his wizards his dream. Tell me what I dreamed, he said. They couldn't. So off with their heads. Can you beat that? Imagine. The shrink must know your dreams when you step into his office, or off with his head. But what the devil, we have no Daniels in our world.

Sonny wasn't paying attention to the Nebuchadnezzar story. He had to get to the mayor's office. He had to know what Raven was promising and where.

The one thing we haven't considered, he said, still holding the turtle, Dominic hired Raven.

Yes, the old man replied, but either way Raven will strike out on his own. You know, future wars will be fought over water, not oil. Sure, the GIs beat Saddam's ill-equipped army, and the first thing they took were the oil fields. But just wait till Turkey says it can build dams on the Euphrates. Then you'll see a real fight. Same on the Jordan, in Africa, and here on the Rio Grande. Wherever a river or an aquifer crosses borders, that equals war. Every nation has to feed its people. Corn, soy, and wheat need water.

What do we do with the turtle? Sonny asked. He couldn't leave it. Never leave a wounded animal on the road.

The old man was looking at the mountain. Musing. I read in *National Geography*—

Geographic.

That's it. The ancient Chinese honored turtles. They placed bronze turtles at the entrances of their temples. Those who came to turn the prayer wheel or to light candles and incense for the ancestors paused to rub the front feet of the turtle for good luck. Over the centuries the bronze wore to a polished sheen. Millions of hands had touched the turtle.

Yeah, but now, Sonny said.

Maybe take it to the pueblo, the old man said lamely, for although he had recovered some of his strength, he didn't want to tell Sonny what to do.

Sonny nodded, but he knew he didn't have time. Raven's trail would grow cold.

Take it to the casino, Sonny suggested. He could drive up Tramway and drop the turtle off at the front door.

The old man laughed, a sneer. Damn it, Sonny, you drive up with that wounded creature and those white people the pueblo hires to run their business will kick you out faster than you can fart.

You never gambled?

Life is enough of a gamble, the old man answered. Why go

looking for trouble? Besides, I heard about an elderly woman from Belen who met el diablo—

I heard the story, Sonny interrupted. Maybe the losers tell those stories. But he knew better. The people told stories. Soon a corrido about the woman would be sung. People would report a man in black sitting next to anxious housewives at the slot machines. He watched with burning eyes as would-be winners polished the buttons on the slots on machines that were not lucky turtles.

Sonny held the turtle up to the sky, toward the mountain so that the outline of the creature was the exact outline of the Sandia Mountain. A perfect fit. The mountain itself was a turtle facing north, a living creature, and those who understood turtle dialogue could hear its story.

The old man was in a storytelling mood. He told how long ago Father Sky came to lie on Mother Earth and the weight of Father Sky formed the soft depression that became the great valley of the Rio Grande. All forms of life came into being from that divine connubium. The begetting in the Bible paled before the life forms that sprouted from sperm clouds and earth meeting. Everything was born of that union: trees, grass, flowers, deer, raccoons, beavers, snakes, even the dragonflies and other common insects. But they could not grow because Father Sky continued to press on Mother Earth, continually fertilizing her and yet not allowing growing room for the life they engendered.

So the animals, whose desire was to sprout upward, sent a black bear to lift Father Sky. The bear pushed and grunted, but he wasn't strong enough. Then buffalo was sent, but he couldn't budge the sky. Even the mighty cottonwood tried, lifting its huge arms like a gymnast pumping iron, but even this Tree of Life could not lift the sky. Life was trapped in a claustrophobic atmosphere. Each cell wanted to grow upward on the chain of potential, but they were stifled by the weight of the sky.

Finally the meek turtle, a water creature, volunteered to lift the sky. The other animals laughed. Even the river trees, whose desire to grow exceeded everyone, chortled. How could a mere turtle lift the weight of Father Sky?

The little turtle lifted its small head and announced to Father Sky that in order for life to grow, he must move. Father Sky didn't move, and so the turtle in its knobby shell began to push. It pushed and pushed until slowly but surely, it lifted Father Sky.

Imagine the relief of the plants and animals! They could finally breathe! Every living organism, including the rocks, gasped for air. The turtle rose like a mountain, lifting Father Sky about a mile high. Now our valley people call that turtle Sandia Mountain. It's still holding up Father Sky and allowing all of us the space to breathe and grow.

Divine connubium, Sonny thought, a marriage made in heaven. Stories of the sacred marriage were older than Joseph's marriage to Mary. The sky god Zeus had come to visit good-looking mamasotas on earth, and Isis had lain on the dead body of Osiris. Life blossomed.

Sonny blinked. A second ticked by. The blinking of the eye created time, as did the ticking heart. Count the heartbeats for a minute. Multiply by sixty. Multiply by days, months, and years to arrive at the Source of the First Dream.

Is there such a thing as divine marriage? he wondered. That's what he wanted for himself and Rita.

I like that story, he said, looking up at the granite face of Sandia Mountain, the orienting feature of the valley.

I think it's an Egyptian myth, replied the old man. From the time of the pharaohs. They had their Nile, we have our Rio Grande, so we share stories. The Egyptians don't mind; as you know, most of the pharaohs are dead.

So mountains hold up the sky, Sonny mused, and if one is blown apart the sky will fall. The Chicken Little story has an ominous ring to it.

Mountains have many uses. I read that the Babylonians constructed zig-gu-rats. The Egyptians pyramids. Later those ideas came to our ancestors, the Olmecs, possibly from Chinese and Japanese boat people who landed on the coast of Peru long ago. They spread to the Vera Cruz. From there to other Mexican civilizations. Like Teotihuacan. Those magic mountains are all over, even as mounds in Illinois and Ohio.

If Raven blows up the Jemez, a gaping hole will appear on Mother Earth, a wound from which will seep the hidden waters. Blood of the mountain. A wounded turtle. And a large part of Father Sky will cave in, fall into the vacuum. Everything will be contaminated with radioactivity.

Sonny knew this wasn't science, but it was a way of relating to the natural order of the cosmos. Relate with the wisdom of story, not the microchip. Stories, legends, and myths are what connected the humans to the Eternal Mystery, connected one person to the other, because all shared the same history, the same First Mother, the same First Father.

I'll take the turtle to Rita, he said. In her garden it can eat the succulent herbs and flowers, ripe parsley and turnip greens, chile verde, verdolagas y quelites, bright tulips. Two Lips the turtle.

He tore a clump of wild alfalfa that grew by the side of the road and made a bed for the turtle in the back of the truck. He placed the grateful creature tenderly on the alfalfa. You're going home, he said, then jumped back in the truck and headed with urgency down I-25, the fastest way to get to city hall.

Normally he would drive along Fourth Street, the most interesting street in the city with its sense of history still lingering along the route. Fourth Street was part of the original Route 66. It was once the Camino Real, which connected Nueva España with New Mexico.

Driving into Alburquerque on the interstate he was always struck by the city's continual, painful growth. Large subdivisions spread up the slope of the mountain, and businesses had sprouted along the interstate. Across the river lay the mushrooming Rio Rancho. As usual Sonny's sight, as troubled as it was now by his puffy eyelid, rested on the lava escarpment of the old volcanoes that dotted the West Mesa.

Hundreds of times, 432 by his own count, he had hiked around the volcanoes, looking for the Zia Stone. He knew the major petroglyphs by heart, could stand on the escarpment in the sun and the wind and hear the whisper of the old people who had etched messages from the spirit world on the faces of the dark boulders.

On the extinct volcanic cones the wind was constant. Its refrain played on dry grasses and chamisa. If one stood still, the mantra of the wind resonated to the gurgle of the hidden waters running beneath the ancient lava flow, pure water of ancient ages sizzling as it encountered the boiling magma far below. Somewhere on that lava bed a golden seal might reveal itself.

Affordable land on the West Mesa, he said. Good thing the politicians saved the Petroglyph National Monument.

They do things right—sometimes, the old man said. But if bulldozers cut roads through the lava flow they'll disturb the Zia Stone. A great tragedy if they bury it for another 432 million years. And that's just one day in the life of the eternal dream. One day of eternity.

The sun was past its zenith as Sonny turned on Martin Luther King Boulevard and drove into downtown, with its flashy new court buildings. Center of law, the logos law, that which is written, that which knew very little of Sonny's dream.

Laws were written to be applied equally. But Sonny knew a rich man can buy what a poor man can't.

Why here? the old man asked.

Fox will know what kind of deal they made with Raven.

He screeched to a stop in front of city hall, parking illegally, not heeding the traffic cops who signaled furiously and blew their whistles.

"You can't park there!" was the last threat he heard as he jumped out of the truck and dashed inside, past startled workers rushing out of the building. His boots echoed on the marble floor, and even amidst the confusion in the building, a few well-groomed secretaries turned to admire the tall and slim Sonny Baca.

In long, purposeful strides he made his way quickly to the mayor's office, past the startled city cops, past the secretaries' foyer, where one held up her hand and said, "Hey, you can't go in there!"

"Urgent business," Sonny replied as he burst into the mayor's office. The room was full of embattled city officials and a film crew from CNN interviewing the mayor.

This is it, thought Sonny. Raven mentioned the movies.

"Sonny—" the startled Fox uttered as Sonny reached out and picked him up by the lapels.

"You made a deal with Raven!" Sonny shouted.

"What the hell do you think—" the mayor cried, his face flushing.

"What is it?" Sonny repeated, shoving his face into the mayor's.

"You're crazy!" Fox cried out as two cops grabbed Sonny and jerked him back, flinging him down to the floor where they pressed their knees into his back. They twisted his arms and handcuffed him.

"Is this what you're after? National spotlight?"

The startled film crew had turned their cameras on him and the cops, beaming the picture around the world.

"Damn you, Sonny! I've got the cell phones dead, a bomb on the Jemez, and you charge in here—"

The cops lifted Sonny to his feet. He looked into the Fox's eyes, and the gleam that was always a political plot, in spite of the ever-handy smile, told Sonny more than he needed to know. Raven was a shape shifter, and he had taken on the mayor's mask to play the game. Yes, ravens and foxes were cut from the same cloth, even the wily Odysseus knew this as he made his way home from Troy.

Okay, more than one could play the game.

"I just want to know what you gave him," Sonny whispered.

"Get the cameras out of the room!" Fox waved at his startled aides, and they rushed to hustle the interviewer and camera crew out.

The room settled down and Fox glared at Sonny. "I ought to have them throw you in jail. You just screwed up the biggest interview of my life—"

"My life!" Sonny retorted; the image of himself dangling from the helicopter and the bullets whizzing flared up.

"Okay, okay. Settle down and we'll talk reason."

Sonny glanced around him. He had surprised the politicos gathered in the office, frightened the good-looking secretary so her breath quickened. And for a moment he had startled the police guard. But now he was handcuffed. Best to talk.

"Who do they interview next, Raven?"

"I don't give a damn what happens to that madman," Fox replied, straightening his red-chile-spotted tie. "If I didn't know you better I'd throw the book at you. I just don't need wild cowboys during a national emergency. The cell phones are down, and there's a nuclear device sitting on the Jemez. Gotta keep cool."

"Working for Dominic is keeping cool," Sonny taunted.

"I don't work for Dominic!" Fox shouted. "My concern is water for the city's future! Yes, Frank is buying up water rights, but I'm ahead of his game. I've secured enough water to keep the city afloat! Your grandchildren are going to thank me, Sonny. Not Dominic!"

The men around him nodded. In the end his prophecy might turn out to be true. Had Fox outwitted Dominic? If the city secured enough water rights along the river's basin, there would be precious little for Dominic's cartel.

Fox's gleam disappeared. He's telling the truth, Sonny thought. I'm out on a limb, again. "What did he offer?" he asked.

"He claims to have the code to disarm the bomb. Claims he was the one who took it from the terrorists. Al Qaeda. Can you believe? In New Mexico?"

Here he paused, drew himself up, puffed a little, watching his cronies out of the corner of his eyes. The same pose Mephistopheles must have struck when he swore damnation on the seventh seal.

"What does he want in return?"

"You." Fox chuckled. "He wants us to sit with him on stage and bow. His five minutes of fame in front of the cameras. The cell phone problem is a temporary nuisance. We'll eventually find the hackers and get everything back on line. But the bomb has the Los Alamos scientists scared. We play ball with him and he defuses the bomb. After that, you can have him."

Sonny nodded. He should have guessed. The net was tightening; Raven was at the movies, but not at Fox's interview. The rift was already happening, the politicos were washing their hands of Raven, as the governor tried to do. But there were a dozen movie houses around town. Where?

"Turn me loose."

"On one condition. You stay away from him till he gives up the code we need. After that, he's all yours."

Get Raven, Fox was saying. He's too much trouble for us. The entire Dominic scheme was unraveling and those who could were jumping ship. They hadn't planned on the governor's murder. Raven, they quickly learned, could not be trusted. Make him disappear, Fox was saying to Sonny. We don't care how. We don't want to know.

"We're meeting with him at the Hispanic Cultural Center. Seems he likes the theatrics. Wants to show off in that beautiful new auditorium. The directors didn't want him there, but he holds the trump card. The bomb's code. So, for now, whatever he wants, he gets. And he wants a show. National TV and all that."

For a moment Fox grew serious. "Isn't it funny how the mind works. There's a megalomaniac in all of us . . ."

Genetic drift, Sonny thought.

"Anyway, all we want is the code to disarm the bomb."

"I understand," Sonny said.

"I'm glad you see it our way," Fox said, puffing up his chest. "Take the cuffs off."

The two city cops, big, burly men left over from the Neanderthal age, took the handcuffs off and stepped back. The others in the room breathed a sigh of relief, as did Fox.

Sonny turned and walked out of city hall.

Let Raven have his fun. He's given me the clues I need. I'll be there.

17 »

Sonny, give it up! the old man cried in exasperation, as they fled the labyrinth of city services and city ordinances, the Maze of Laws that was the postmodern pyramid, city hall, the ziggurat of the city council, lobbyists, lawyers, police, burro-crats, wannabes, all sorts of folks suffering from the genetic drift of a quantum universe gone wild.

Sonny didn't listen. He was following the thread of his frustration, a deep ache that told him too many deals had been made for him to trust the makers of social justice. He wasn't the only one who had been sold out by "the system." A lot of people had been bought and sold and the ripping at the seams was the sign the seals were not holding, the structure was falling apart, as sooner or later all social structures run by men of greed are bound to collapse.

People forget: every nation born of human dreams and desire rises and falls. No one can divine history's purpose; in fact history, like evolution, can be said to have no purpose.

The thread of betrayal led Sonny to the exit and the shining light outside, where the frenetic rush and panic-stricken atmosphere reminded him of Dante's inferno, a vociferous circle of lost causes, his own painful need reflected in the cacophony of the city's spiraling down.

Gotta find Chica, he gasped, trying to find purpose in the center, which was slipping away.

It's not just Chica you're after, the old man said, nearly shouting, still trying to get Sonny's attention.

Find Raven.

Raven's playing games all around you! You can't think straight. Get hold of yourself!

Post-9-11 angst? No, I know what I'm doing.

Don't kid me, it's that damn obsession. It's no good, Sonny, you can't bring back the dead.

They're not dead! Raven was able to get into Rita's womb and take the spirit of the child, and we both know he holds prisoners! I need to find him!

He sensed he was shouting, unaware of the rush of women fleeing city hall, gorgeous dolled-up Chicanas who spent half their pay on Lancome cosmetics, or Maybelline if they were on the lower end of the city's pay scale. These modern-day sirens sat in warm offices in winter and air-conditioned in summer, doing the people's work day in and day out, whiling away the time singing siren songs, tales of last weekend's pleasures if they were single, the pressures of family life if they were married, and plans for next weekend, for that's the way time was measured, from weekend to weekend.

But Sonny seemed unaware of the phalanx of women rushing by him, and he didn't smell the sweet plumes of their perfumes, desert currents that any other time would have flared his coyote nose to catch a whiff and turn his head in admiration.

Now he could only sense Alexandria was falling, Ephesus burning, Burque, the City Future on the Rio Grande, was grinding shut. Raven-created panic lay as thick as the smog cloud that fell over the city on winter days when the cold kept the pollution trapped along the valley floor.

Sonny! the old man cried. It's not just the spirit he took. I was there when Rita miscarried. I saw the blood. The flesh is gone. There's nothing to hold the spirit!

Sonny stiffened. A cold chill ran through him.

The old man had hit him as hard as he could with a burning hammer from the forge of truth. The blacksmith is after all an alchemist, one who can shape forms, so dross metal may become Thor's hammer, or Santiago's sword. Either can kill the dragon, and as everyone knows the ancients were misguided dragon slayers. Always thrusting at the projection, never at the dragon within.

Sonny stopped cold, the old man's words ringing in his ears. Around him the blare of sirens announced Fox and his henchmen rushing out of city hall, skipping out, surrounded by cops and media, fleeing to the Hispanic Cultural Center, where Raven was to hold his press conference, where he would bargain with the city fathers as ravens and foxes are wont to do.

The afternoon sun was warm, but the old man's words froze his blood. No, Rita's babies weren't gone. There must be a place where a few ancient heroes had trod, perhaps a heaven of sorts, a Limbo, any hint of a promise where Sonny might yet meet his child, or two if they were twins. That place had to be Raven's lair, and he had to get there.

He had to cling to this hope. It was all he had left, and even the warning of the old man, his mentor these past few years, would not deter him.

But the old man's words took so much out of him that he had to sit down on the steps of the building. His obsession had created a burning energy, but his frustration—realizing he might not know how to get into Raven's circle—depleted his strength.

Was he the Fool on the tarot card? Could he live up to the reputation of his bisabuelo, Elfego Baca, the Chicano lawman of New Mexico who had stood against a gang of bad-ass Texas cowboys? Sonny carried his great-grandfather's Colt 45. in his truck, a family heirloom handed down to the firstborn, like the bow of Odysseus, but everybody knew they just weren't making men like the grandfathers anymore. Was it really the fear of failure that had caught up with the young Sonny Baca?

There is a time in every Chicano's life when he feels the gods and all the universe have conspired against him, and all he can say is *que chinga!* That's what Sonny whispered. "Que chinga!"

He wiped his eyes. This is preposterous, he thought. Cowboys don't cry. What would Rita say? That I've lost it? I'm all right, he told himself, as he sought to control the awful sense of loss that racked body and soul.

You've got to get a hold of yourself, the old man said.

Yeah, Sonny replied.

The rush of workers fleeing city hall skirted him swiftly. Some recognized him. His exploits were well known in the city, but all treated him like a homeless person. All were hurrying home to see if the phones were still working, or to turn on TV sets where they could watch the story of the bomb on the Jemez unfold. CNN was already there! So was Dan Rather! They would tell the truth!

No one stopped ask why Sonny sat so forlorn on the steps. Except one, a young woman. She recognized Sonny. Stout and big-bosomed, her large hips wrapped in a tight Tyrian-purple dress, the indigo of royalty, her tiny fat feet sore from shoes that pinched, her black hair bubbles of curls that rose like an afro teased beyond teasing, a birthmark on her chubby cheek, a gleaming spot she had glued there right after she curled her eyelashes with a mascara as black as her tiny pupils.

She stopped by Sonny and felt a pity in her round heart, which already was pounding with some fear that she would arrive late at her lonely apartment and find Bosque, her dog, had eaten her box of chocolates, the last one on earth if truly the world was ending. She bit her puffy lower lip, a lip glistening with red, greasy lipstick, which she had paused to dab on before she rushed out of the building.

A stout girl had to look her best, no matter what. She had sat at enough singles bars with her thin friends who got picked up and driven to weekend pleasures, while she wound up walking alone across dark parking lots to her beat-up Ford Escort and driving home in that terrible loneliness that only late Saturday nights can lay on the soul. Wasted days and wasted nights, Freddie Fender's elegy.

Doing what humans do when they find someone more bereft of direction than themselves, she lifted her tight skirt just a few inches and sat down beside Sonny, her large, ballooning nalgas immediately warming the cold cement. Soft and motherly, she touched Sonny. The bracelets on her fat arms chimed a sad song, costume bracelets from Dillards, for this was no queen of the desert, no queen of Sheba, this was a city worker who was paid lowly wages and who always tried to look her best.

"Hi," she whispered.

Sonny looked at her and wondered who had stopped to greet him. He glanced at her ample bosom, two large, soft pillows where she had always hoped some seafarer cast on her shore might find a welcoming dock.

Instead, there sat Sonny Baca, in a moment of loneliness she recognized so well.

Sonny welcomed her touch, and thought, is this the sylph who caught a ride in my truck when I wasn't looking? Or the turtle? Yes, that tortoise I picked up could be a bruja who took the form of a turtle. But he knew that in New Mexico folklore there were no recorded stories of witches becoming turtles. And the turtle had given off very little heat while the woman at his side was as hot as a carne adovada enchilada.

Sonny smiled. Her voluptuous breasts gave off the aroma of ripe watermelons, awakening Sonny's memory of childhood afternoons on his grandparents' farm in La Joya, when summer watermelons were lifted from the cold water of the well where they had sat all day, then sliced open with grandma's kitchen knife, splitting the rind with a cracking sound, exposing the red meat, and at the center the dark, seed-spotted heart.

He looked into the woman's small jewel eyes, the glistening beads of perspiration on her forehead, and the beauty spot wet with sweat on her chubby cheek.

"Who are you?" he asked.

"Sophie," she replied.

Sofia, the goddess of wisdom, not Athena, come to guide me, thought Sonny.

"Do I know you?"

"Sophie Valdez. You don't remember me. I used to sit behind you in twelfth-grade English."

Sophie Valdez, of course. She was there, always in the shadows, always in the background of the gung-ho Rio Grande High cheerleaders. Sophie had cheered every pass Sonny ever threw. She attended every game, every assembly where he spoke, every Saturday night dance in the gym. He remembered her sitting quietly by the punch bowl at the senior prom, without a boyfriend, without anyone asking her to dance, so he had asked her to dance, because the preppy cheerleaders and his jock friends had dared him.

"You were so smart, Sonny. God, when you gave the graduation talk I cried. And last summer there you were again. Chasing the bad guys. I clipped all the newspaper stories about you. You stopped the truck full of atomic stuff. Something or other. You saved the city. I've got all your pictures in my scrapbook."

"I remember the prom—"

"You danced with me. The DJ was playing oldies. 'In the Still of the Night.' God, I think of it every day. It was like being in heaven. I play the song every night."

Sonny felt uncomfortable, ashamed of himself. Someone he hadn't noticed during those heyday high-school years had now paused to offer confidence.

"You work here?"

"Yeah. They let us out early because of the bomb. And the cell phones quit working."

"It's been a while," was all Sonny could offer. "What did you do after high school?"

"I got married. You remember Bernie? He was a tecato, used to sell drugs for your primo, Turco. Anyway, he was abusive. Beat me, called me fat, said I deserved it. One night he beat me so bad my cousin Nadine took me to a battered women's shelter. They took care of me for a while, got me into Joy Junction. I took courses at TVI, and now I work here."

She paused. "Let's not talk about me. How about you? Why are you sitting here? You look kinda sad—Oh, I didn't mean it."

"It's okay," Sonny replied. He stood and pulled her to her feet. "It's good to see you, Sophie."

"It's good to see you, Sonny. I always remember you. I never missed a game when you played. God, those were good times, huh?"

"Yeah, good times." Sonny nodded.

He could have kicked himself. Pendejo! What's new? Don't you know, even the lonely living in the backwash of life enjoy the fleeting moments they call good times.

"That's quite a bruise you got. If you want, I can go get—"

"It's nothing. Thanks."

"Well, I gotta go. My dog is home alone. Oh, and I do believe you, Sonny. Dogs do dream. Bosque, that's his name, talks to me. We sit in the afternoon, and I allow myself a glass of wine. I put my feet up, and Bosque sits on my lap and he talks to me, tells me so many things. Dreams of faraway places. You know."

"I'm glad, Sophie. I'm glad."

"I don't know what's going to happen. They let us all go home early. You know, the bomb. Maybe you can help catch whoever's responsible. We trust you, Sonny."

"I'll try, Sophie."

"You're our hero—"

Sonny shrugged. Something in his heart melted. There were people out there depending on him.

"Call me sometime—" she blurted, then quickly corrected herself. "I shouldn't have said that. You're busy—"

"No, no, as soon as this is cleared up I will call you. Maybe we can go to lunch, catch up on high-school days."

"Oh, Sonny—" Her voice caught. "That would be just like heaven."

She hugged him and her rotund warmth revived hope in his tired body. Her moist cheek pressed against his, leaving her beauty mark stuck to his face. Then she turned and fled down the remaining steps, as agile as an angel descending from heaven to touch an unsuspecting heart with her magic wand.

"Bye!" she called.

"See you," Sonny answered, raising his arms, while in the background a mariachi band played his theme song. He straightened his shoulders with new resolve as he watched Sophie disappear into the street that held the rushing workers.

Quite a woman, said the old man, nodding, perhaps remembering his wife had been round and firm, and in their youthful days a lot of woman to handle.

Yeah, Sonny agreed. Funny how we don't notice the beauty in people until they touch us. She was the only one of the hundreds rushing out of city hall who had stopped to lend comfort. In her memories he was a hero.

Sonny looked east to the Sandia Mountain, and although the dry air of March now wafted through Tijeras Canyon, he was sure that in July the monsoon would flow north from Mexico, as it had done from the time of the Toltecs, a giant plume of moisture from the gulf would appear, flowing north, a serpent smashing against the northern Chihuahuan desert of New Mexico and its rugged mountains, delivering to the parched lands the renewing rain, rain laden with the sounds of Mexican corridos, the beauty of mornings in Cuernavaca.

Such July afternoons the clouds would begin to form over the Sandia and Manzano mountains, rising in rounded cloud forms, fat billowing cumulus, which from that day forth would always remind Sonny of Sophie's round calves, her saddlebag thighs, her watermelon tummy pinched in by a thin belt, her swelling breasts. Such clouds grew and grew, expanding with the heat of the day, sensuous forms that excited the fantasies of men who loved clouds, men who praised the bodies of clouds and admired the beautiful faces of clouds whose round, puffy cheeks held puckered lips, lips that blew gentle, cooling winds upon the dry earth. And hair! Medusa-like entanglements of swirling hair, boiling froth of dark cloud moisture, the hair of a wild woman who held in her body the energy of a nuclear explosion.

Reclining in all their glory, clouds with Sophie's shape would rest luxuriously supine over the skies of Alburquerque. They would appear as Paleolithic Venus figures with the super-large breasts, hips, and fruitful yoni, such figures as were found in caves where women were once the shaman of the tribes and their pregnancies analogous to the earth's fecundity. No wonder the myth of Demeter and Persephone still illuminated the daydreams of farmers.

The shapes of clouds were the bodies of women. Women born of the heat of the earth and the Mexican moisture, they were the sex creatures of the summer, scantily covered with dark rebozos whose fringed edges were the dark rain that fell, releasing New Mexicans from the tensions and anxieties of the dry summer. Skirts of dark rain washed across the earth as the clouds came to their natural climax in a bed of ecstasy, the arms of Father Sky. Wise men hurried home to make love under the pelting of raindrops, those first crystal drops that awakened the pores of mother earth and gave forth a sweet perfume, the moisture of a woman making love.

The drops turned into a crescendo, falling in a fury, heavy and immediate, gathering into rivulets, rushing along street gutters, filling arroyos with surging chocolate waters. Cloudbursts finished as quickly as they started. Exhausted by the frenzy, the cloud women picked up their dark skirts and moved on, tumbling east toward Santa Rosa, Clovis, and West Texas, leaving in their wake the freshness of their breath on the land.

The billowing sails of moisture rose into the heart of the blue-bowled sky, and reaching the high, thin atmosphere they began to flatten out, forming the familiar anvil shape, for even as they reached for the highest heavens the clouds transformed themselves into a blacksmith's anvil, and Father Sky, the eternal alchemist, could pound his hammer on the flat surface, casting loose, like Thor or Zeus, bolts of zigzag lightning and booming thunder that shook the land, snake lightning that flashed across the dark sky, adamantine thunderbolts with diamond edges.

High above Mount Taylor, Grandfather Sun would fling his palette across the sky, lighting up the clouds with watermelon reds, brilliant oranges, lilac violets, soft mauves and apricot colors, breathtaking hues.

And Rainbow Woman would run her herd of wild, stomping mares across the sky, sliding down to the verdant Rio Grande Valley, white mares of cloud sinew and muscle, manes of wispy cirrus. Grey mares dripping with sweat that fell sweet to earth, their tails dark showers that fell on the thirst-plagued land.

The people of the valley would give thanks for the holy rain.

Some would thank the saints, or Jesucristo; some would thank the Cloud People, the Holy People who came from the land of the kachinas to bring rain. Some would thank Tlaloc the rain god of the Aztecas, or Vishnu who at the end of time takes the form of a cloud and rains to quench the world's conflagration, flooding the earth as it was once inundated during Noah's time, dissolving everything back into a cosmic sea, then alone on a cloud in that vast eternal ocean Vishnu would sleep, *alone,* aware only of himself.

Sonny was no oceanographer of clouds, but he would think of Sophie when the clouds of summer came north from Mexico. And he would thereafter call the sensuous and sweet-smelling summer clouds *Sophie's Clouds.*

He breathed deep and felt a release of endorphins, chemicals flooding body and soul. He felt renewed.

"Time to get cracking," he said.

Yes, the old man agreed.

"Hey! Where's my truck?"

His truck was gone.

"You're Sonny Baca, aren't you?" a young photographer standing nearby asked.

"Yeah."

"I took some pictures of you at the Kimo. For the *Journal.* Remember?"

Sonny nodded.

"They towed your truck. Everything parked here was towed to the city lot."

His words hung in the air, and just then an SUV jumped the curb and came to a screeching halt a few feet away. Naomi rolled down her window and shouted, "Get in!"

Sonny jumped in, and the photographer clicked a picture, which in some future alchemist's bath would become the photograph that testified to a turning moment of that day's history.

18 »

"WHERE IN THE HELL DID YOU COME FROM?" he asked, and she answered, "That's just it," as she gassed the SUV, jumped the curb, and turned toward Central, swerving around slow-moving cars and groups of people overflowing the sidewalks onto the street.

"Move!" She honked the horn, and the throngs of suddenly freed workers of the city laughed and waved.

"Party time!" they cheered. "Viva la fiesta!" "Viva Annie Oakley!" "Viva Zapata!" They banged on the hood of the SUV.

The annual Spring Arts Crawl scheduled for the day had suddenly and gratuitously been rewarded with party-goers numbering in the thousands. The art galleries along Central flung open their doors, welcoming the gathering, a powwow of revelers.

Central Avenue and Fourth Street were the crossroads of the City Future, a rangy, burgeoning, desert city whose history lay lapping at the shores of the Rio Grande. Here Highway 66 of Anglo America met the old Camino Real of the Mexicanos. Here the east-flowing, English-speaking, Bible-thumping axis met the great meridian that connected Mexico with its northern colonies, creating the center of a Zia sign, the center of a mandala where the Americanos' latitude met the Spanish and Native American longitude, and always at the center there was sure to be trouble as differing world cultures met and clashed, with little knowledge of each other's ways, until a son might be born of these worlds to bind the bloods of antipathy. Or a daughter, a new mestiza.

A block from Central the street was blocked off. A policeman blew his whistle and signaled Naomi to turn. She cursed and shut off the ignition.

"Let's go!" she cried, jumping out of the SUV and diving into the tide of office workers. Workers who had been let out of PNM, city hall, federal and municipal buildings, and lawyers from the offices that filled downtown. The city was awash in attorneys, purveyors of every legal tort imaginable.

Sonny followed her into the crowd.

"Where are we going?" he shouted.

"Follow me!" she replied.

Those lucky enough to be let out of work because of the bomb scare weren't going home at all. The afternoon was warm, and most decided to take advantage of the bars and restaurants that lined Central Avenue. Time to have a brew and a bite and watch TV. On the Jemez crater images of men appeared crawling around the barrel-like contraption the media was calling Fat Boy.

Never mind that the governor was dead; that was politics as usual. The lieutenant governor had already spoken to the masses via TV, assuring the natives that state government would continue to operate on schedule—which only drew moans from lowly taxpayers.

Meanwhile, the noise and laughter echoed along the sidewalk cafes where instant game pools were devised by the Alburquerqueños, who loved to bet on almost anything. Horse races, dog races, duck races, casino slots, Las Vegas blackjack, sports events, the Lobos or the Isotopes—every game was fair game. If a sparrow fell from heaven, none would ask if God saw it; instead a bet would be made on when it would hit the ground. So today, a dollar bought a numbered square on the big board, the numbers corresponding to different times when the bomb might go off. There were also bets on if it was or wasn't a bomb, bets on whether the radioactive cloud would reach Alburkirk if Fat Boy did go off, etc., etc.

As far as Sonny could see from Seventh Street to First Street, and beyond to the railroad tracks, the crowd of revelers resembled a spontaneous Mardi Gras party. Lenten promises were forgotten for the moment. Who was to know you downed a few beers and ate a couple of hamburgers? Besides, if you were Catholic, and there were a lot of those partying, you could go to confession later and be forgiven for the price of a rosary, and on Sunday you could receive the Holy Eucharist and feel whole again. By Easter all the sins would be forgotten. By Easter the governor would be long-buried and forgetfulness would settle into the lives of the one-eyed partygoers.

The fiesta was in full swing. Was it fear, dread, loss of hope or anxiety, or just an afternoon off work that drove the suddenly freed slaves from the machinery of government?

Sonny caught Naomi's arm and stopped her. She looked scared, her complexion ashen.

"What the hell's going on?"

"I'm getting out of town," she replied. "You should too. You're in danger."

"I can take care of Raven."

"And Augie."

Sonny didn't trust Augie, but danger?

"They tried to pin everything on José Calabasa and his group. The ones they call Green Indians. They claim he killed the governor. They're going after him, and me."

"Augie . . ."

"Who else? He's in with Dominic. The plan is to take over the water rights of the pueblos."

"I saw José in Algodones. Augie was there—"

"Is José all right?"

"He's back at the pueblo by now."

"Thank God. Then you know everything."

"I know the governor got cold feet. He wanted out of the scheme, but he knew too much."

"And I'm next in line," Naomi said. "There were secret agents everywhere. In the background. Dominic's group let Augie lead you around. You were in danger up on the mountain. It's a big conspiracy, Sonny. They don't want just Rio Grande water, they want to control the West."

"So they hired Raven. Then he turns around and screws everybody."

"If the Pueblos are threatened, if they think they are going to lose their water rights, which means losing the land, there will be an uprising. Not in the halls of Congress or before the Supreme Court, but a bloody one. Like 1680. José Calabasa is the leader. Like Popé. That's why they want him out of the way."

Sonny understood. They had sent in Raven to rile up the Pueblos, and when José's group shot a government agent or state cop, the U.S. Attorney General would declare a state of emergency, convince the ultra-conservatives in Congress, and most of the country, that the Al Qaeda taken prisoner at Jemez Springs was part of a terrorist plot to bomb the labs. Enough evidence would be planted to implicate José Calabasa's group. The army would move in and take over the pueblos.

"Dominic's behind it all," Sonny said.

"You're in danger. You know too much."

"Who else?"

"A lot of very powerful people. In business and in government. Maybe the mayor—"

"No. He wants water for the city so he can climb the political ladder. He's promised water to the developers. Problem is the aquifer's drying up, so he taps the river. The environmentalists protest, they want water for the silvery minnow. They're fighting each other instead of fighting Dominic."

"The pueblos were first in place. The acequias have been used by our people since—You know."

"So that's Dominic's next gamble."

Naomi nodded.

Sonny felt the press of the partygoers. They weren't aware of Dominic's scheme. He had sold the state a bill of goods, claiming competition would bring down the price. But wherever water rights had been privatized the cost of water had skyrocketed. Sure, the rich will be able to afford water, but if you didn't have the money the faucet would go dry. The chamber of commerce was inviting new businesses to start up in the City Future, and the city was providing all sorts of tax breaks. Development bonds and a free ride on taxes. But not even the San Juan/Chama diversion water would be able to keep up with the demand.

"Why you?" he asked Naomi.

"I dated Augie. I mean, we went dancing a couple of times. Yeah, I know, I have no taste. That's beside the point now. Damn, lonely women do dumb things. It's Bear I care for. Anyway, Augie mentioned the names of people involved in the scheme. Now I'm in the way. Come on. We don't have time! In here."

She pulled him into a bar. Woody's Place.

"Woody's a friend. I need to get out. I think you should too," she said as they entered the dark, dank cavern, reeking with beer and smoke.

Sonny knew the place. Very few self-respecting folks frequented the bar. Pedophiles hung out at Woody's, men who exposed themselves on school grounds. So did drug dealers, crooked CEOs, and their crooked attorneys. And their women. Women who couldn't even get jobs in the so-called massage parlors of the city.

Over the bar a large sign read, "Eggdrasil Beer Served Here. Ice Cold." In the middle of the cigarette butts–laden floor was erected a pile of oak casks, like a tree reaching to the dark ceiling—Woody's weird idea of interior decorating.

A few eyes turned to study Sonny and Naomi as they entered. By now Sonny felt sweaty and beat, but he looked well dressed compared to some in the crowd.

"You know Woody?" Sonny asked.

"Yes," Naomi answered, resigned to her fate. "He's an old friend. He can get me out. If it's not too late," she added.

Woody, the one-eyed man behind the bar, was muscular, with a rugged face cut from Sandia granite, a black patch over one eye. Obviously he had climbed the tree of beer casks more than once. Beside him stood a handsome woman, gypsy-like with red bandanna tied around her hair, long dangly earrings, and eyes that saw through any illusion the world might offer. In short, it was clear she had been around the block more than once. Smoke from the cigarette at her lips wisped upward, creating a blue aura.

"Naomi, cara mia, comed sta," Woody bellowed, coming around the bar and lifting Naomi in a bear embrace.

"Fine, Woody, just fine," Naomi replied. He used the traditional abrazo of the Mexicanos to full advantage. His Spanish was just awful, but in such a place, who cared.

"Woody, a friend of mine, Sonny Baca."

"Sonny Baca! El famoso detective? Bueno, I am Woody, your amigo."

He gave Sonny a bear abrazo, deftly feeling to see if Sonny was carrying a gun.

"It is an honor, soguro," he went on, "and this my exposa, Prajna. Say hello, para mi hita," he boomed, introducing the gypsy lady. "I call her para mi hita, my little daughter, but miralo, she is as beautiful as Jezebel."

Prajna was beautiful, in an ethereal way, not connected to the real world at all. When she took Sonny's hand, she could feel his destiny, as it had been cast in runic characters long ago.

She felt the obsession he carried, the desire and dread of meeting Raven and reclaiming the two lights that were Sonny's blood.

"You are too attached to life," she said cryptically.

"Ah, mi amida," Woody interrupted, saying "amida" for "amada," the Spanish word for beloved. "Do not read his fortuna before he drinks a beer. Come, I have cirvesa that will tickle your fancy."

He motioned them to a round table, but Naomi protested. "Thanks Woody, but we don't have time. You know what's happening."

"Yes, we know, saber, sabeduria." He smiled and winked at his wife. "She knows everything. Sabe todo y mocho. But if you do not have the beer of heaven," he pointed at the tree of beer casks, "you cannot know."

"Prajna, tell him, I'm in a hurry," Naomi pleaded.

Prajna shrugged. She shivered and turned away. As far as she was concerned Naomi's fate was already sealed. She wondered if Sonny's life would be spared, or if his obsession would that very day destroy him.

Woody filled four large cups he called kantharos, and offered one to each, cups with a dark beer whose froth spilled and ponded on the table.

"You see, amigo, each kantharos is a way to heaven. To Dios, as my amigos the Mexicans say. We go to nirvana—"

"It's too late," Prajna protested.

"What do you say?" Woody cried. "No, not too late. I will cast the runes."

He took a leather bag from his shirt's pocket, clay tablets with their cryptic lettering, and threw them on the table, where they splashed on the beer foam and instantly began to dissolve.

"Ah," he said.

"Ah," Prajna said. "A pity."

"Yes."

Woody, with his one brilliant eye, stared at Sonny. "Amigo, you must sacrifice your ego."

Not on your life, Sonny thought. He had played this game before. He knew the cantina was a place of illusions and not even the saddest mariachi love song could make things right. Yes, you could go to nirvana, whether on beer or mota or a high-priced hallucinogen, but when you returned to terra firma you still had to deal with the layers of illusion. The thought that one could escape the world of illusion was an illusion.

Sonny looked up at the beer sign, which now read "Have A Bud." They weren't drinking Eggdrasil beer at all, just plain Budweiser. And the clay tablets dissolving on the table were part of the illusion.

Sonny felt the hair along the back of his neck prickle. Raven was near. He reached across and grabbed Woody's wrist.

"Raven was here!"

Woody winced. "Yes."

Naomi jumped up. "Why didn't you tell us?"

"I'm sorry, I'm sorry, cara mia. He threatened us—" He looked pleadingly at Prajna.

"They knew you would come here," she said. "They threatened Woody. What could we do?"

"Where is he now?" Sonny asked, tightening his grip.

"He goes to his old friend, Tamara."

"And Augie?" Naomi cried. "Where's Augie?"

"He called, he's coming here. Ah, cara mia, you must run. Desaparcida, very quickly. I expect him any moment. He's dangerous—"

"You should have told me!" Naomi cried and bolted for the back door.

"It was a mistake!" Woody cried. "Forgive me!"

"He's here now," Prajna said. The siren outside belonged to a state police car, she was sure.

"Danger!" Woody cried.

Sonny tossed Woody aside and jumped up to follow Naomi, but he tripped into Prajna and they both went down.

"Your obsession will kill you," she whispered as they fell to the floor.

He tried to break her fall, knowing that wisdom was fragile, something to be held onto if once you stumbled into her arms. By the time he got to his feet, a gunshot had exploded in the back room.

He hit the door hard, splintering it and falling forward into the dark wine and beer storeroom musty with cobwebs and the scratching sound of rats scurrying away, a perfect Raven place.

Naomi lay slumped on the floor, and the shadow was already out the door, racing down the littered alley and disappearing as it passed a group of teenagers doing crack.

There was no use following in the congestion, so he turned back to Naomi and knelt beside her. Her eyes fluttered open.

"I'll call an ambulance!" Woody shouted at the door. Prajna entered and stood by Sonny.

"The sonofabitch—" Naomi choked on her words, her complexion gone pale. At her lips appeared an oval tear of ripe blood. "He said I knew too much . . ."

"Take it easy," Sonny said, knowing words fail at such times, the wound on her chest was fatal, the blood already pooling on the floor, the heart hardly pumping.

"Tell Bear . . ." she whispered, ". . . I loved him. I had to screw around the world . . . come home to realize . . . I loved him."

She smiled, her eyes closed, the flame disappeared from her face.

Cihuacoatl, the Aztec's Snake Woman, curled in her death, returning to the depths of the earth to bless the seeds.

Sonny laid her softly on the floor. "Virgen de Guadalupe," he whispered.

Prajna took off her shawl and covered Naomi. Woody returned to stand by them.

"Oh, cara mia," was all he could say. "Sorry . . . sorry. I was afraid for Prajna. They threatened me. We loved Cassie. Such a great artist. Only evil men kill such talent."

"Men who have not washed in the Ganges," added Prajna. "They have no way of letting go of their sins. Go wash in the river," she said to Sonny. "When your day is done, go."

Outside a siren sounded, but the partying along the street was going full blast and the paramedics could be going to any one of a dozen places where the good times were getting out of hand.

"It's the dread of the bomb," Prajna said. "People's fears turn into desire, then back to fear again."

"Take care of her," Sonny said.

"Yes. Do not worry, amigo. We will deliver her to her people."

He hated to leave Naomi, but Woody and Prajna would see to her, and he had a matter of life or death on his hands—much to do before the day drew to a close.

He walked back into the bar, where hardly anyone had taken notice of the commotion or of Naomi's death. The desire, or need, or lust, to be somewhere with someone at this time of inevitability had taken over. It drove the patrons to drink, and with Woody's beer they sank deeper and deeper into the illusion of self, which is why Prajna did her best to warn them that the ego itself is an illusion; in fact, the many egos within the psyche were the most dangerous illusions, for the minute the ego desires the illusions of the world, it becomes the enemy of harmony.

Sonny walked outside where the bright sunshine reminded him there was another reality, the truth of light, the same light that created shadows, forms of illusions that from the shadow's point of view were as real as the light that created them. No light, no shadow. No shadow, no light.

Shadows have their healing properties. The shadow of Jesus of Nazareth was said to heal the sick. And shadows can be mistaken for reality.

He tried the pay phone on the corner, rang Rita.

"Sonny," she answered, "where are you? Are you okay?"

"I'm downtown. I'm fine. How are things there?"

"Settled down, a bit. People are getting used to the bomb. The panic's gone, everyone's taking a holiday."

"The guys left?"

"The guys? The regulars? Oh, no, most of them are taking a day off. We're busy. Things are returning to normal, except the traffic on the street. If people can't use their cell phones they drive. It's incredible. What are you doing downtown?"

"I had to see the mayor."

"And you're okay?"

"Yeah." He didn't tell her he had lost the truck and Chica. Right then he didn't feel like telling her he had been suckered by Raven.

"I need to talk to Diego."

She hesitated, then he heard her call Diego. "You sure you're okay?"

"Fine. I need him for an hour."

"You be careful, Mr. Sonny Baca. I'll stay open till you get home."

"Gracias, amor." He felt a lump in his throat. Maybe he should be home with her, taking care of her, not of the affairs of the world. But catching Raven did have to do with her, if only he could recover her womb seeds. Yes, he had to see it through.

On the phone he told Diego about losing his truck, and said for him not to tell Rita, but to get over to the city impounding lot and get the truck out.

"No problem."

"Park it on Broadway right in front of Alburquerque High."

"Can do," Diego replied.

Sonny knew his friend could do magical things in the city, for he knew its streets and its people.

He remembered the Gilgamesh epic and the loyal servant, Enkidu. He knew he was no Gilgamesh, but when it came to being a camarada, a real compadre, Diego was Enkidu, willing to go to the depths for a friend.

For that Sonny was thankful.

19 »

SONNY ENTERED THE CROWDED STREET, cast into the human sea like a shipwrecked sailor. History has recorded that sailors from the villages of New Mexico have left their loved ones on the docks, the tide sloshing at the ship, the excitement of the adventure written in a last kiss, for who knows when the sailor gone to sea will return, or if he returns at all. Landlocked as it was, New Mexico had sent its warriors abroad, to the fields of Normandy, the trenches of France, Bataan's deadly march, Iwo Jima, San Juan Hill, the frozen hills of Korea, the steaming jungles of Viet Nam, Kosovo, the deserts of Iraq, and other distant places, geographies that became part of the history embedded in the language of the New Mexico paisano. Even in their landlocked nation of mountains, deserts, and muddy rivers, the New Mexicans had sailed with the tide of history.

The same wars had brought strangers to the desert nation, La Nueva Mexico. Foreign languages from Babel had arrived in the City Future, immigrants bringing their food, culture, and their business sense, offering at the foot of Mammon their hard, back-breaking work, just trying to get ahead, be part of the American dream, work so their children need not suffer what they had suffered in their past.

The city prospered as the newcomers gave of their sweat and muscle. Now the city belonged to many cultures, many ethnic groups, many languages, and that gave a new sense of vibrancy and joy to the desert polis, new colors, nuevas idiomas in the air, new songs over the radio, the colorful call of Chihuahuanses laborers building walls, the roughneck call of workers as they completed the Big I, the interchange that had become the city's symbol.

There where interstate I-25 met I-40, a Zia sign had been created. Seen from the air the two roads met and formed a center, a circle from which radiated four lines, roads to eternity. Those who journeyed into the city were flung out from its center to settle with their heavy loads in one of the four quadrants of the burgeoning city: NW, SW, NE, SE. Points from the compass became points in the heart. Home.

The four quadrants reflected the four spaces of the universe, the four ages of life, four humors, four corners of the heart, all as it had been since the city fathers laid a square grid on the city, a quincunx dormant in their souls.

A prophet of the land had declared that each person keeps seven seals, each to be broken as revelations of life at a particular time and place. Each person is destined to break open those seals in one of the four quadrants of life. When the fourth is broken the soul enters the center of the quincunx, the zenith and nadir, the heaven or hell of old legends.

The riddle of the Sphinx, the prophet said, was no riddle at all. It was a giving up of the ego. Only thus could the psyche enter the center.

And so the immigrants settled in the City Future, and learned a sad part of the story, which is also part of the American dream. They learned that every city demands that the newcomer leave his old culture behind, discard it like an old coat. Leave your past behind and become American. Adopt the new image, the American way, a way of life copyrighted and owned by tradition, also by those who hold power. "America: Love it or Leave it" became a new burden, a polis pressure. Either speak the common language and learn the common ways or live on the margin. And Americans hate the margin, the border, the sense of not fitting, and so those who wished to become good citizens made a god of conformity.

Great cities resist this homogenizing of their immigrants, and that is part of their greatness. Such cities thrive on diversity, an ethno- and biodiversity. Great cities remain multicultural. Could the City Future resist the pressure to homogenize the diversity that fed it? Could the children of the immigrants keep the language of their ancestors and their traditional ways? Why were the old ceremonies attended by politicians only when they were on the stump, only when they needed votes?

On Saturday summer nights the city celebrated its ethnic communities at festivals in the city hall mall. When it was Greek night, the denizens of the city went to eat Greek food and hear Greek music. Theme song from *Zorba.*

Some complained. "We found the tub, but we didn't find Diogenes." The Greek philosophers were missing, consigned to menus in a few Greek restaurants around town.

Few could say *we sail with the tide* in Greek.

Was the journey from Ilium so long and torturous they had forgotten their language?

In consolation, the following Saturday nights Hispanics were celebrated, then Germans, then Indians, on and on. Diversity offered in coffee spoons.

The equinox day was multicultural, for there was a sense in the air that if one perished everyone would perish. Singing, dancing, raising steins of cold beer, chewing on fat hamburgers, bean burritos laden with green chile, tacos and tamales steaming hot, Greek salads, Chinese egg rolls, Thai sweet and sour, chutney, you name it, the city was on a roll and hungry, because it wasn't every day the rank and file got an afternoon off from work.

"Viva la bomba!" someone shouted and a loud hurrah went up from a nearby table of revelers.

They were cheering the bomb? Yeah, cheering the cause of their release from work, the cause of their merriment.

Only in Alburquerque, Sonny thought, as the cheer went up again, "Viva la bomba!"

The leader, obviously an out-of-work actor who spent all day bemoaning his outward state because of the few roles available to a fading baritone, and because funding for the arts had hit an all-time low, jumped up and bellowed to the tune of *La Bamba.* "Para explotar la bomba, se necesita una poca de mota! Bomba, bomba . . ."

Others joined in, forming a snake-like line, dancing, swaying hips, a human rope winding down the street, singing and laughing.

Sonny had to smile. Was this the way to face the inevitability of possible death by nuclear fire? Not with a whimper but a fiesta? Why not? Fiesta and ceremony were at the heart of all the cultures of the city. Any excuse for a fiesta. "Mi hija made First Holy Communion." "Pues, let's have a fiesta." "Confirmation." "Let's party!" "Mi hijo graduated from high school." "Let's boogie!" "I wrecked my truck." "Sorry, compadre, so let's drown our sorrows con una fiestecita."

Marriage, a new baby, a matanza, Bar-mitzvah. A Lobo win. Halloween. A mass for the dead. Whatever, let's party!

Even death was celebrated with a fiesta, beer cooling in the coffin of the deceased if it was a hot summer day. After all, one needs to turn personal prayer and grief into community ritual, as the old priests of the clan and the cave had discovered long ago. Praying without ceremony was okay for hermits or monks who preferred to live alone with their thoughts of God, but the community needed ritual to complement each person's story. In short, the people needed fiestas.

And who was drawn to the fiesta? Why, every conceivable angel and devil, which is why Sonny was stalking brother Raven down the main avenue of the City Future. Raven was probably just steps ahead of him. But was it Raven's shadow that had appeared in the dust-streaked window of Woody's Nest? Or Augie's? Naomi knew too much, Augie had said. She knew the names of the conspirators, Dominic's cronies. The net to capture the water rights of the world had been cast wide and deep.

Sonny opened his hand, revealing the four black feathers he had taken from Naomi's side, and with a curse he tossed them in the gutter where they might be trampled into the dust and spilled beer.

Naomi had returned home and found the pueblo again, the circle of her people, and the man she loved. With luck, she might have etched her final revelation onto the fat, round belly of one of her pots, a marriage bowl molded from Jemez Mountain clay on whose shiny surface would be etched the same signs engraved on the Zia Stone. That's how close she had come to understanding what life was all about, the knowledge of the old ones who said you don't have to travel the world to understand the soul's journey and how it came to have the face of your flesh.

Beneath the good times and the journey into the world of white people, there beat in her heart a silent message from the past. This is Mother Earth, this is Father Sky, this is the Sacred Water, here in our circle we keep the ceremonies of harmony.

If justice be trusted, Augie would get his when the whole mess was exposed. Dominic would need a scapegoat. The water cartel would expose him, throw him to the mercy of the court as they tried to save themselves. Or, more likely, he would be made to disappear, a victim of the cartel. And by the time the water rights battle got into the courts it would be too late. The thirsty would be paying through the nose.

But those who dreamed of stealing water would find that they could not carry water in their cupped hands, nor in contracts written on paper. The ink would run. The waters of the Rio Grande would find their own natural course, flow south into the desert, and finally into the sea where they would be healed of contaminants. That is why Prajna said the river was the Ganges. The flow of water cleanses itself of human pollution and finally heals itself, if only the daily poisoning can be stopped.

The law was not all bad, unless you happened to be a poor Black man or a Chicano in LA. In the end one had to trust the good cops would get Augie first, and to save his skin he would give up the plot. In the end the media could cry all it wanted to about the great New Mexico conspiracy to privatize water, and most citizens, not paying attention to the cry, would go on using water as if the tap would never go dry. Swimming pools, golf courses, manicured lawns in the desert country where nature had long ago contrived a more thrifty plan when it came to water.

The plot was complex and Raven was at its center. That's why Sonny hurried up Central to Tamara's.

But Raven was Raven, and he would stop and peck here and there, mess with things at the fiesta, get some people too drunk to drive and increase the DWI carnage on the highways and byways, provide dope for others, a gun here or there, a fatal shooting, always looking for a way to turn the fiesta sour. In moments like this his mind didn't focus on the bigger picture. He would forget the bomb on the mountain simply to stop and play, for never let it be forgotten, he is at heart a trickster. His friends would say, the Ultimate Trickster. And tricksters sometimes play rough.

By now the wise know that getting to Raven is never by walking in a straight line. The heart has no straight lines, only burdensome twists and turns, which those not so wise call emotions. Sonny knew Raven had a history linking him back to Cain, who was not so much a character in that murderous drama as he was a deep dread in the heart. Call that dark emotion Cain, or call it chaos.

"Hey, Sonny, come and have some fun!" a woman shouted, spilling white wine from her crumpled Dixie cup as she grabbed his arm.

Sonny recognized Soledad, an artist, with a gaggle of her friends, artistas, all dressed in revealing summer dresses, for spring is not a season in New Mexico, but a wind, or a series of duststorms, and suddenly the days go from mild winter to summer, a turning point as was happening that eventful day.

And why always good-looking women? Perhaps it was cast in the runes, the alphabet of desire. After all, Alburquerque was a city full of good-looking women. And art. The booths and galleries were replete with world-class art. Never mind Santa Fe, Burque was a whirlwind of creativity, sucking into its center stupendous, hard-working, front-line artists.

"We're selling artwork to send some Chicanitas to college," Soledad said. "Have a glass of wine. Where's Rita? Hey, mujeres, look who's here, Sonny Baca!"

"Sonny Baca!" They flocked around him, artistas. Delilah, Maria Baca, Liz, Bernadette, Anita from Taos, and Valentina, a curandera.

"She started a curandera college, don't you know."

"Our roots," Valentina teased, "so we train curanderas, sweat lodges, holistic osha, all the hierbas our grandmothers used when we got sick. Potato slices soaked in vinegar or the tags from tobacco sacks on your temples for a headache. Maybe something for your eye, Sonny."

"Hijo, that's quite a bruise."

"I'm okay," he said.

"Is the bomb going to make all this passé?" one asked, pushing herself in Sonny's face, a young Chicanita, muy güerita, who had studied French at the university, and she had learned to use her bounty to its fullest.

"It could," Sonny stammered, realizing reality wasn't meshing with reality.

"Hey, let's paint Sonny's portrait and auction the painting!" Amy Cordova suggested.

"Or auction Sonny," the güerita said, staring Sonny in the eye, a devilish look for one so young.

"I can't stay," Sonny made an excuse, "gotta see a man—adios." He turned, waved, and they all shouted "Bye, Bye, Sonny," their voices hanging in the air like a siren's call.

Ah, Sonny Baca, don't you know. Large-hipped, big-bosomed, ample women will be your downfall. Risen from the sea they come on land to populate nations. Never mind the culture or color, these are the mothers of mankind; from their sea-wombs stream the men they call sons, lovers, husbands.

Thinking the old man had spoken, Sonny looked around. No, it wasn't the old man joking as he was wont, it was another voice.

Why my downfall? asked Sonny. I admire big women.

Because you must fall down, deep into the miracle of Rita before you can know yourself. You must enter, it has been said, the flesh, as you have entered the yoni of the mountain. Then you will rise again, washed in the sea-blood, a new man.

A new man, he thought, touching his swollen eyelid. He glanced back at the artistas, who waved at him. Gifted women who could give Frida Kahlo a run for her money. Such beauty and talent. And now one of them lay dead in the back room of a dark bar.

For a moment the artistas had shocked him back into the reality of life. Beauty abounded, and beauty was even at that moment being created. But the voices came to tempt him, as they often did in times of great pressure. It wasn't just the old man who spoke to Sonny. There were others. Ancestors. Old friends. Voices in the breeze.

But he didn't have the time to listen and respond. He had to get to Raven. He was fixed on that.

He pushed against the revelers who packed the street. Around him subliminal instincts were rising to the surface, and the Spring Arts Crawl was turning into an ancient spring bacchanal. Lust and desire floated in the air. Nature, torn loose from her mooring, was having a rip-roaring time, Pan was the god of the moment, frolic was in the air.

A Spring Tide swept through the City Future and washed away the dormant dreams of winter.

A matachines dance troupe came up the street, fiddle and guitar jigging. Sonny recognized the Bernalillo group. Off to the right a booth where santeros sold their bultos and santos. Pueblo people sold pots and storyteller dolls, fry bread, piñon. Navajos sold jewelry. An old weather-beaten farmer sat stoically nearby, advertising an ephah of last year's bean crop from the Estancia Valley. Some were selling last year's ristras from Hatch, last season's apples from Velarde, and in the midst of the melee, Sonny saw more spirits.

His neck hair tickled; he felt a shiver. What was happening to him? He was losing time. The clues were clear. Raven at the movies. Raven at Tamara's. Raven carrying on at the Hispanic Cultural Center. He had to move faster, but the press of the crowd hemmed him in. Or was it the thought of holding Naomi's dead body only minutes ago?

A troupe appeared. At first he thought they were actors celebrating old times in Alburquerque. They looked so real he could smell the cologne on the men and the rich perfumes on the women. But no, these were no thespians; these were ethereal characters from the city's past, spirits walking among the crowd and enjoying the day just as any living person might.

Sonny recognized Clyde Tingley and his wife, Carrie, sharp in 1940s proper dress, smiling and strolling down the avenue as they might have walked when they were alive. And Elfego Baca, Sonny's great-grandfather, El Bisabuelo of his dreams, cane in one hand and a gorgeous First Street prostitute laced around the other. He was the one who spoke of large-hipped, big-bosomed women.

"Abuelo—" Sonny stammered.

El Bisabuelo winked and said, Don't lose it, Sonny. Don't let the Baca name down. Honor above all things. That's our heritage, mi'jo.

Then he walked on, smiling cordially and nodding handsomely at the Tingleys. Other spirits from the city's past followed.

Dick Bills, saddlebags full of beans and jerky; and Mike London, who used to run wrestling matches; Miguel Otero, a former governor handing out "Vote for Me" cards to paisanos who came from Plaza Vieja to join the party. Tom Popejoy, the educator; Dennis Chávez, the famous senator from New Mexico; Erna Fergusson, the writer; Ernie Pyle, the World War II reporter; George Maloof; Julian Garcia; professors from UNM; Uli; and others. All as natural as could be.

Quite a show, the old man said.

Where the devil have you been? asked Sonny.

Around.

What the hell's going on?

A party. The old man laughed.

I'm losing it, Sonny stammered.

Why? Because some of these departed folks show up at the fiesta? Hey, everybody loves a fiesta. Besides, you've seen your Bisabuelo before.

Yeah, but in my dreams.

The biggest mistake those sico-ologists make is to separate dream from reality, the old man said, quite sure of himself, acknowledging his spiritual compadres. La vida es un sueño, y los sueños sueño son.

Sonny shook his head. Why here?

Why not? This is their city. They lived here, created its history, became memorable in the spirit of the city. Just be thankful you have no Nero or Caligula.

Sonny nodded. He had been trained by the old man to be a shaman, to enter the world of dreams as the principal actor, because a shaman cannot be tossed around in a dream, he goes there for a purpose, to help whoever is in need, so maybe something had stuck to him during all those long hours of initiation. He had learned to create his own dream and enter the door of the dream, and he had seen Andres Vaca, one of his 1592 grandfathers, and his Bisabuelo Elfego Baca, and Billy the Kid, Stephen Watts Kearny, the sonofabitch, and Popé, the leader of the Pueblo Revolution against the Nuevomexicano Españoles. He had met four of his own great-great-grandmothers at the origins of New Mexico history.

So why should he doubt, now, the depth of the old man's teaching. The world was full of what some would call magic, but for the ancestors, visiting the place where they once lived was as natural as prayer. So why call it magic, or worse, the "mystical" experience? No, it was as natural as apple pie. The spirits did not go away, as the old man said, and they loved a fiesta.

"Joven!" someone called. "Ephebus!"

Sonny turned.

"Aquí! Aquí!"

Someone dressed as a Cirque du Soleil clown was calling him into the movie house at the corner of Central and Second Street.

"Come on in, but don't lose hope," the clown said, and disappeared into the theatre.

A large group had gathered outside, clamoring to get in, eager to be part of the movie playing inside, a remake of the old classic *Salt of the Earth,* the story of Mexican miners in the Silver City area who had the guts to strike for better wages and housing conditions. These were no Wobblies, no trained union activists, just oppressed Mexican miners and their wives whose humanity was being driven into the copperish dust of the open-pit mine. Theirs was a cry of *Huelga!*

The crowd was not drawn to the story but to the technology. Something called laser projection, far beyond digital or holograms, it was the first true reality film. A series of well-placed laser machines projected the story's images onto an ionized central stage. The characters, projections of congruent light, actually came alive. 3-D. They became players on a stage.

The moviegoer could step right into the center of the action. The union sympathizers could join the miners in huelga, the far right could join the repressive owners. The images evoked in the moviegoers the most primal instinct, the desire to change the outcome of the story.

Science had finally taken the image from its flat surface and made it whole. And he who could control and manipulate images could control the masses. Ancient cavemen knew that. The hunter painted the image of the hairy mammoth on the wall of the cave, then went out and killed the beast. That was the history of the species.

Raven had said, See you at the movies. He was waiting.

Sonny pushed past the mass of kids with spiked, psychedelic hairdos and leather outfits, smoking, gabbing about the philosophy of life, never having read a philosophy book. The girls in very short shorts, the guys in leather jackets with glistening steel studs and chains, all thought themselves artists but they practiced no art, unless it was the art of acting bored with life. Today they would identify with the striking miners and feel socially responsible, even though in ordinary life they had never marched for a good cause.

Sonny searched his wallet, found a twenty-dollar bill, paid the gum-chewing, red-haired girl for a ticket, and entered.

He smelled the dark. Yes, Raven was near. But why here? Did the miner's story have something to do his challenge? It didn't make sense.

He's theatrical, the old man warned. Patron saint of theater. A ham, a misguided actor. That's the role of the trickster, to act out the story. To suck you into his story.

That's where I want to be, Sonny replied. He moved toward the stage. Other dark figures milled around him.

"Raven!" he called.

The machines around the stage buzzed. Pale blue lights subdued the darkness, allowed some light. The movie was starting.

Sonny looked at his hands. They had turned blue.

Was he now only an image projected onto empty, ionized space in which the laser projection reintegrated itself and came alive? Some in the audience walked into the middle of the action. The moviegoer had finally achieved godlike status, become a prime mover who could change the course of the actors' lives.

Repressed emotions flowered on the stage. Lonely hearts could fall in love with the hero. The sociopaths could beat up the minor characters and murder the major characters.

Somewhere in the outer edges of the action Raven laughed. Hullabaloo! he called.

"Raven!" Sonny called again. He reached out to touch one of the actors. The woman flinched. She had not expected Sonny's touch. It wasn't in her script.

Sonny jerked back. He had not expected to feel flesh when his mind told him that the images being projected were composed of light.

He had never backed away from an encounter with Raven, but right then he felt he had fallen into a game that was more than he expected. Raven was in charge again. Raven the director. And Sonny? A petty player on the stage, one to be manipulated by the unfolding story.

Anthrax and smallpox, dirty nuclear bombs, flying airplanes into public buildings, and other atrocities aimed at the destruction of civilization had not worked. But enough images with their latent chaotic message could garble the nervous system. This was clear to Sonny as the audience in the darkened theater dove into the action and disappeared in the void.

Like a dream. But entering the dream without a guide could prove extremely dangerous.

Sonny! Raven called from the middle of his fantasy. Come on in.

Sonny turned and faced Raven. Handsome as the devil on Sunday at church, he presented an imposing figure. The women flocked into his new, light-based reality, thinking they were the anima to his animus, and he the answer to their bewildering dreams. The young men, those lost long ago to the chaos of the world, entered to be warriors at his side.

20 »

On either side of Raven stood two lovely girls dressed in satin white with lace fringes, white gloves, and vaporous veils on heads so innocent and lovely they brought tears to a man's eyes. Each girl held a prayer book in one hand; in the other hung a white mother-of-pearl rosary. They were obviously dressed for their First Holy Communion, and they looked up at Sonny with such longing that their gaze tore through Sonny's heart, deep into his soul, which expressed its grief with a deep sigh, a sigh that startled those waiting to jump into the laser-projected reality.

What has he seen? people whispered. And why does he tremble and grow pale?

My daughters! Sonny cried, a cry that came like the roar of a tiger that had just seen its mate burned alive by hunters who cared naught for transubstantiation, and what that might mean to a person's endlessly wandering soul.

The cry, loud and painful, echoed in the darkened movie house, its reverberations swayed the quantum particles of light, and even Raven's triumphant face for a moment reflected dread.

Sonny had finally seen the images of the two spirits lifted from

Rita's womb, two daughters he would have raised, taken to school and on trips to the sacred ceremonies and magic mountains of the state, playful girls who would run to hug and kiss him after an afternoon of splashing in the water of the river, the Ganges that flowed through the valley, two who would sing and dance into young womanhood, with all the pain and joy that meant. Two to play piano and guitar, hear the cuentos of the ancestors, pray to saint and kachina alike, learn the old ways, and grow to bless his middle years. Two whose future he would watch unfold, even as his hair turned gray and he, abuelito, stooped to pick up his grandchildren.

Two dressed in the innocence of Communion white.

Naomi had pointed the way, prophesying the egg in the water would reveal the daughters who stole his heart. Now it was up to him to take them back.

Beelzebub! Sonny hurled the first insult that came to mind, thinking that if Raven could compose the movie's reality he could also hold the girls prisoners.

A murderous desire filled Sonny. He would kill Raven, even if that meant killing part of his own psyche, images that had hounded him since a time when the deepest seas were crystalline.

Sonny, no! the old man cried. It's a trick!

Of course it was a trick, as had been made clear in all the stories told about Raven. His taunting was to be expected, along with his sick way of drawing Sonny into his circle, just as he was now enticing an entire generation into the world of false images.

But rage clouded Sonny's good sense, and he didn't recognize the tools of the new technology as the same smoking mirrors used by the Aztec gods long ago to present false images. Tezcatlipoca came to mind.

Sonny struck at Raven, but the vampire who sucked not human blood but human energy protected himself by unfurling silken wings and tripping Sonny by stepping on his ankle, the same foot Sonny had broken years ago steer wrestling.

Sonny reached out to grab the girls, his daughters, one in each arm, hoping he was in time to pull them out of the laser fire, which burned like halogen, diatomic molecules gone wild.

But they were gone, evaporated, as the controllers of the projectors, Raven's cronies, expertly changed the scene, and in an instant Sonny was no longer in the midst of the miner's strike, but alone in a wide and empty desert of white sand where the restless wind blowing across the dunes cried like La Llorona as she wandered aimlessly down dry arroyos. Nothing lived in that desolation except a few spindly yucca plants, the lotus of the desert, flowers on which bodhisattvas dared not sit.

Do you like the movie? Raven asked. And where would you like to go next? The Iberian peninsula where some of your most recent ancestors lived, or Mexico where your Indian blood flows, or the court of Peter the Great, Napoleon's France, the Lewis and Clark expedition, the founding of Santa Fe—Ah no, you've been there. I can't think of a place you haven't been in your dreams. Unless it's this new reality.

He gestured at the virtual reality at his command. This is it, Sonny. The new soma holiday. No more of those chemical highs, no more ecstasy drugs, none of that caca the kids learn to mix from the Internet, just the world of images to dazzle you. Think of it, Sonny, the image is now returned to its rightful place as mover of the universe, ahem, as it always was.

Control, Sonny, he continued. This is the way to control the world. I give the kids a new fad every day, violent video games, action movies, images they mistake for knowledge.

Sonny shuddered. If Raven's tricks could move him from scene to scene, where would he wind up next? And why had the beautiful daughters suddenly disappeared? He had seen them, and for that he gave thanks. Now he had to learn to play Raven's game. Be coyote.

You would have me believe you're my brother, he said to Raven. Like the yin and yang enclosed in a circle, or the DNA double helix, the staircase whose genetic sequence has been reduced to four letters. ACTG. The four sacred laws of the dharma wheel.

Or the two snakes that bite each other's tails and become the circle, Raven added, for he loved to play at the analogies of life. The caduceus of Hermes, your guardian angel.

I pray to Santo Menos, Sonny thought, the patron saint of the Chicanos. And to my mother's Virgencita, la Guadalupana. La Wonder Woman of liberated Chicanas.

And Sonny did pray. With a deep breath he asked for guidance from the ancestors. No coyote warrior ever went into battle without asking for help. He did not pray to Santiago, El Matamoros, the blood-letting saint, instead he prayed to San Isidro and La Virgen.

This time you've gone too far, Sonny said, and moved without a sound toward Raven.

Raven placed one hand on his chin. I do what I have to do to gain ascendancy. Once done, the past can't be righted. Not even in the dreams you've learned to control. You see, the shaman is trained to help others. Seeking lost souls, he dares to enter the depths of Hades, the Mictlan of the Mesoamericans, Hell of the Christians, which by any other name are aspects of the psyche. Trained to help others, that's the key, Sonny. But you are not trained to help yourself. And so, I break the seventh seal, and leave you to wander for future eternities in this wasteland, a desert created by the genius of our kind. Here you will sense a time that does not flow, separated from those you love, never again to feel human touch or comfort.

He raised his carved sword, the scimitar that could slice the body of a man in two, create duality from the unity all men seek, for only by destroying wholeness could Raven win.

The question was, Did he have this power or was he bragging?

The soul cannot be erased from the memory of our kind, Sonny answered, and Raven clenched his teeth.

It can!

No, it returns and returns. So I will seek my daughters, he said with confidence.

They are illusions, Raven shouted.

I won't give up.

Your obsession is your death, Raven clearly pronounced.

Was obsession the ego's trap? Prajna had warned him he was too attached to the world, and it was the ego and its power, its desire for worldly goods, that tripped the man. But what of that dark residue beneath the ego, the anima who always visited Sonny, the feminine entity of every man's psyche, the strange and seductive woman of his dreams, analogous to the living flesh, Rita, her warm embrace, her breath hot on his neck, the warm ooze of her sex when they made love.

Was all this illusion? No, there had to be a reality that clothed itself in tree, stone, fish and fowl, and especially a reality that came in the body of the beloved. Else what's a life for?

The Zia Stone, Sonny said, making small talk as he inched ever closer to his dark brother.

It can't help you, Raven chuckled. Even if you had it in front of you, you couldn't read its message.

But there are old men in the pueblos who can, Sonny thought, tiring of the inaction, aware that he was a child of the desert and that in the desert death came quickly.

At least destroy the bomb, he said.

Raven laughed, that awful laugh that said: *You are so dumb. You haven't figured out a single line of the drama and you call yourself a detective!*

Did you believe I would waste the plutonium pit on your sacred mountain? No, I'm giving it as a Christmas present to Al Qaeda. Let the terrorists do the dirty work. Let the masses think they're the enemy, when the real enemy is within. You know this.

You made a deal, Sonny said, resigned.

Of course I made a deal. It's in my nature, as well as yours. Human nature thrives by making deals. Evolution is adaptation. I will give the authorities the code. At the last moment, of course. High drama. The clock ticks down and I call the boys from the Los Alamos Labs. You see, I'm holding a press conference with the mayor and all the local politicians. Coverage by CNN. I'll blame today's favorite target, the terrorists. The Evil Empire boys. Blame

Syria, Iran, Bin Laden, Al Qaeda, North Korea. People are so dumb. They believe the government's message, forgetting evil also lies inherent in the messenger. I love it. So, the cameras will shift from us to the scientists on the mountain as they punch in the code and the ticking goes dead. Cheers galore. I love it!

You're crazy—

I've told you never to say that! Raven shouted, jumping forward and trembling with rage, his face red with laser light, veins bulging along his neck, thunder flashing across the desert space, La Llorona's cry chilling the blood.

Humph, humph, hah, haah, heeee-eee. He laughed, struggling to control his own chaotic essence. You try to get me *mad.* Hatter mad. Doesn't work, Sonny, I am as old as you. I, too, share in the collective memory of the species, share in the protein code of every cell. Damn DNA! I am the building block of the species! Don't you get it? That's how complex I am. I can't be dismissed with a wave of *you're crazy.*

When the going gets tough, Sonny thought, it's coyote nature that must face Raven. Coyote howls and coyote bites.

My dog? he asked.

The little mutt hasn't fallen asleep, Raven replied. But she has to. Half a dog's life is to sleep, perchance to dream—

Here he let out a robust explosion of laughter that echoed to the ceiling. You get it? Perchance to dream, and in that dream of your dog's sleep, I will enter like the assassin I am. You'll be helpless, Sonny. They minute she dreams your image, I strike. Do you understand? The soul is the image of your life's eternity. Killing it will be the end of you, I guarantee.

And this? Sonny asked. What's this for?

This is a game. I wanted you to see what our so-called civilization has come to. Virtual reality. You're on the way out, Sonny. Future anthropologists will find the machines, but they won't find a trace of the makers or those who went to the movies. They won't find Diogenes. You see, my dear boy, we are images in the movie of life. We are projections who strut and fret our hour upon the stage, and then are heard no more. The light will go out, Sonny, the movie will end. You will disappear into a void far beyond virtual reality.

Now! the old man said.

It was time to toss down the gauntlet. His trump.

Tamara knows, he said.

Raven's eyebrows knitted in a scowl. The tramp. She knows nothing!

She knows your plan!

Raven cocked his head. Have you talked to her?

No, but I'm on my way.

Damn her! Raven cursed, shaking violently. She has the hots for you! She'll give you any secret to get in your pants!

Sonny pressed the point. Maybe in your sleep you've confessed to her, a word here, a word there, and you let slip the way for me to find you in my dream. Find my daughters.

Your obsession will kill you, Raven screeched. Your soul is already dissolving in the river of memory!

My river is the Rio Grande, Sonny replied. And you're as much afraid of dissolution as anyone.

No, no, Raven protested. There is no river that can erase my energy. You know that.

Let's put it to the test, Sonny challenged. Let's meet there.

Raven grew interested. And make an end of the game, he said.

Sonny shrugged. Why not? I win or you win.

Sonny was suggesting the denouement. Not the OK-Corral shootout, but a duel to the end on the banks of the holy river, the muddy Nile, Prajna's Ganges, China's Yangtze, actually New Mexico's Rio Grande, which was always too thin to plow and too thick to drink.

By the Barelas Bridge, Raven said.

Done, Sonny agreed.

By now he had circled in on the unsuspecting Raven, using his wily dialogue to lull Raven into false security, and he was close enough to lunge forward and rip the Zia medallion from Raven's neck.

Ah-ha! Sonny cried, holding up the prize.

Oh-no! Raven countered, his grin as big as a watermelon slice. He signaled, a light of one of the laser projectors died instantly, and the Zia medallion disappeared from Sonny's fingers. Sonny was left holding thin air.

I see you believe in illusions, Raven scoffed.

Of course Sonny believed in illusions. He and Rita liked to take in a Saturday-night movie once in a while, or rent a video and watch it at her place, where after a long and tiring day at Rita's Cocina a beer and a good movie was a prelude to making love. Movies as foreplay.

I honor the art of image making, Sonny replied, looking at his empty fingers. The image is holy. But you and the producers of illusion have taken our myths and made them vulgar.

Vulgar is as vulgar does, Raven said, pointing at the hundreds of moviegoers ready to enter the movie in which they could participate. $Millions$ $Millions$ The masses are so bored with their ordinary lives they flock to the screen. Hollywood offers psychic relief for the lumpen. Our producers offer escape from reality, and the masses lap it up. Look!

He flashed a signal and created a new dimension, a time-space so distanced from human conception that it became the archetypal Armageddon, the end of the world, Ezekiel's vision, a scene so murderous it drove fear into those who watched, terrifying the moviegoers and sending them screaming and scurrying for the exits.

Another light went out, the light that embodied Raven, and he disappeared with a Tra-la-la. The river at 6:00.

Sonny exited, leaving the now-bare stage, walking hurriedly through the lobby and into the bright sunlight of the pleasant March afternoon.

He squinted, blinded as he was, and had not yet cleared his vision when someone grabbed him by the collar and slammed him against the wall. He felt a hunting knife prick just beneath his ribcage.

A furious Bear pressed his face against Sonny's.

"Where is he?"

"I don't know—" Sonny managed, and felt the knife press deeper into his flesh.

"Where is he?" Bear repeated, his full-blown rage smothering Sonny, the knife ready to pierce straight into the liver, as Jesus had once been pierced, allowing the blood to flow, creating in that horrendous act a new river, one the Roman soldiers had no way of knowing would flow into the future.

The enraged Bear was too strong to push away, the knife too sharp to evade. Coyote sense might get him out of the jam, not brute strength.

"The sonofabitch killed Naomi!"

"Let me handle Raven—"

"I'll do it my way! First Raven, then Augie! Where are they?"

"Ease up . . ."

Bear, breathing like a wounded animal, pulled back a fraction.

"No tricks, Sonny, no tricks or I swear I'll cut you open!"

"Augie's going to get his, sooner or later. You've got to let me take care of Raven."

"Because of his witchcraft? Because he can fly? I'm not afraid of that. I'll get him or die trying. Where is he?"

The crowd around them pressed forward, thinking this was part of the movie, or a staged act to incite them further: foreplay. These big men were gladiators, the Indian obviously had the upper hand, and now they had to choose if Sonny lived or died. "Kill him!" some jeered, thumbs down. Others shouted, "Give him a weapon to defend himself!"

"I don't know," Sonny replied. "I lost his trail . . ."

"I just left her . . . held her in my arms. The sonofabitch didn't have to kill her. I blame myself for letting her go. She was afraid of him, needed to get out of town, she said. He led her along, told her about the big scheme to siphon Indian water rights. They needed her out of the way."

"I'm sorry," was all Sonny could say.

Sorry for the killing going on in the world. Sorry for Naomi. She was Snake Woman, one whose earth energy was aligned with a deep wisdom, for as has been told in many stories, wisdom did not rain from the sky but came from the earth. The snake did not tempt Eve; it came to deliver her and the man from the bondage of ignorance, a whispered message that they should disobey the lesser god.

Hadn't Moses lifted up the healing serpent? And wasn't the wisdom of the serpent written in all the ophidian mysteries, imaged even onto the cross?

"Oh God, she's dead . . . never told her story."

"She said to tell you she loved you."

Bear nodded. Tears filled his eyes. "We grew up in the pueblo. I was in love with her from the time we were kids. But she had to find her way."

"Take Naomi home. Leave Raven to me."

Bear pulled away. "You do it your way, I'll do it mine," he said, turning and disappearing into the crowd, which booed and jeered him for not killing Sonny.

A young woman stepped up and placed her tepid fingers on the spot of blood on Sonny's shirt.

"You're real," she gasped, drawing back.

"Yes."

"We thought it was part of the movie. He could have killed you."

Sonny nodded. A slight push and the hunting knife would have pierced heart or liver. In seconds Sonny's blood would have run in the gutters of the Alburquerque streets, mixing with the beer and trash of the boisterous crowd.

Private investigators dying in the streets was for the movies, not for Sonny. I want to die at home, he thought, comfortable in my old age, on a soft bed surrounded by images of the saints, my father and mother's pictures, candles lit and copal incense burning, with Rita holding my hand as I totter off into a heaven where I will have many books to read, and wise people with whom to discuss the meaning of life. Not on the street.

"I'm sorry," the young woman said, wiping her finger on her midriff where hung a ring, gold emblazoned with the Zia sign. She went back to the waiting line.

The sylph, Sonny thought, come to the movies.

He pushed through the crowd, holding his left side, punctured by the knife, tired now, limping from the pain in his ankle, which Raven had kicked. He didn't look like much of a hero as he hurried up Central, rushing because the sun had already started on its downward spiral and in three hours it would be behind Mount Taylor, the western sacred mountain.

And there was a lot still to be done if Sonny was to find the daughters he had seen in Raven's movie.

Aren't you convinced by now, it was an illusion? the old man said, hurrying after Sonny.

Because the medallion disappeared?

Yes! the old man said forcefully, trying to get through to Sonny's coyote spirit, where he might understand survival, and the truth of survival.

How can I deny I saw my daughters? Sonny spat out.

People turned to look at him, thinking perhaps he was one of the homeless who roamed the downtown by day, asking for this or that gift, living out internal fantasies that sprang from bottles of cheap wine hidden in paper sacks.

Sonny, the mind can conjure up anything it desires! When it fixes on one thing, that's obsession. The paranoid hear voices. The psychotic act on those voices. Schizophrenics hear God!

You think I'm losing it?

If you go meet Raven, unprepared as you are. . . . He didn't finish.

They had crossed the railroad underpass. Here the crowd was thin, mostly small groups of homeless men and women waiting for the dinner the Baptist church served.

In front of him, on the corner of Broadway and Central, loomed the three-story Lofts, the old Alburquerque High renovated into an apartment building. His parents had attended AHS, and they remained loyal alumni. His dad used to go to all the games, wear his green Bulldog jacket proudly.

Sonny glanced up at a window and saw the shadow of a lovely woman behind the sheer curtain that turned in the breeze.

Tamara beckoned.

21»

Anybody who was anybody in the City Future knew Tamara Dubronsky's history. It was scattered all over the internet, *la Red* in Spanish, the World Wide Web spun not by Arachne, but by a business world as infected as a hangnail in Adam's toe, the new digital reality served up with loads of spam and enough games to drive the kids into schizophrenia. Or pornography.

But Tamara certainly was *not* spam. She was one of the best-looking women in Burque. A svelte, vampish, émigré type with a Russian accent, who, as one story told it, had cavorted with the leaders of the Soviet Union when they tore down the walls and declared democracies. She had smacked her lips on caviar from the Black Sea in parties that lasted all night as the up-and-coming Russian mafia bargained for a position of power in the new capitalistic empire. So what if Marx and Lenin were turning over in their graves? Any revolution is heady, and Tamara had, purportedly, been there.

The CIA and FBI files contained fat dossiers on her. A few had been released to a university professor under the Freedom of Information Act, including photos. In one picture she is standing next to Boris Yeltsin on top of a tank, defending the new democracy. Well, there is a thin young woman in a beret next to him, and CIA operatives in Moscow claim it's Tamara. Who can believe photos in the digital age? They can be doctored to produce any image one desires. Therein lies the problem: so many of the images are make-believe.

Was Tamara Russian? No one knew. Sometimes her accent changed to Polish, then German. Whatever the accent, she could charm a snake, or a wily coyote. She read tarot cards and claimed a psychic personality. Was she one more personality of the sylphs of the world?

One story on the Internet reported that Frank Dominic had found her in La Fonda in Santa Fe reading palms for a hundred dollars a throw, relating destiny to unsuspecting California tourists who thought part of the Santa Fe style included finding a psychic guide who would take them to an "energy place" in the foothills of the Sangre de Cristo where they could Oooooommm and Ahhhhhhh and get in touch with the spirits of the Native Americans long gone to the happy hunting grounds. The same Indians pierced with cannon shrapnel during ancient battles with the same tourists' Anglo ancestors.

The Chicanos in the city, those workers who lived in the mobile-home parks where they could afford the rent, those same workers who often appeared as "quaint" background fodder in videos taken by the tourists, paid no attention to the psychic-phenomena ladies, whores of the New Age, whom nobody blamed for making a living because usually they had four or five snotty kids to feed, were behind on the rent, and the ex was not paying the alimony.

There was a strange relationship between being psychic and the number of kids those ladies produced, some said, because it followed that some went all the way when they got into the past lives of disturbed men. The digital age had also perfected psychic masturbation.

Santa Fe Chicanos, who had been displaced by newcomers with money who could afford million-dollar homes with their accompanying taxes, knew about survival, so they tolerated the women who could read your fortune and who could for a hundred extra bucks take you to a "place of power."

"You want a place of power," the workers joked, "cut firewood for the winter."

"Hoe the chile plot."

"Try making beds and cleaning dirty toilets all day. That's virtual reality. Muy pronto."

"Try raising a family on six bucks an hour."

"Time for huelga!"

The truth is, it wasn't Frank Dominic who found Tamara, it was Raven. Raven could read beauty, especially beauty with money. He courted Tamara and led her into his cult, the cult of chaos, which in their twisted way they called the Zia Cult, convincing her that the world needed to be shaken out of its misery. A nuclear accident would do, or an attack on a major city with anthrax or smallpox.

Tamara fell for Raven's line; she gave him her fortune and lost her big home in Los Ranchos. Why? That was the big question. Was it because she was a child of postwar chaos? Or was it just something to do in a city she considered dull and dreary? Whatever, she wound up in a Santa Fe sanatorium to escape prosecution for the murder of Frank Dominic's wife. Tamara was somehow involved in the chaotic evildoings of Raven and his gang, but she hadn't even been indicted. Now she was living in a modest apartment in the Alburquerque High Lofts, looking down on the heart of the city from her window, and waiting for Sonny.

He didn't need to knock. When he held up his fist, the door opened and there stood Tamara in all her glory, breathtaking in a vaporous chiffon gown so thin and sheer it would excite any healthy male. Titillating. That was Tamara's way. The ophidian seduction always began with subtlety. Enticement with the slightest movement of her finely shaped body. Food for the weary warrior. And so Tamara swayed, as a charmed snake might sway in front of the bird it's about to strike.

When she spoke there was a song in her speech, vowels intimating intimacies, consonants that created images of sweating bodies curved in lovemaking. Just so a spider weaves a web, and only when the fly is immobile in the gossamer thread does she descend to suck out the sweet juices.

Tamara smiled, the curves of her body in a classic pose, becoming for the tired and wounded Sonny Baca a port where he could rest from the tossing sea, a sea no longer pristine but awash with the tragedy of the afternoon.

"Sawwww-ny," her soft, syrupy voice greeted him. "I am so glad to see you. Come in." She stood on tiptoe to kiss first one cheek, then the other.

Her small breasts brushed against him, her lilac cologne, a touch of hoped-for spring, reminding Sonny of the summer morning when he stepped into his cousin Gloria's bedroom and found her lying on the bed, peaceful in her death, that lilac fragrance permeating the room.

"You do not need this beauty spot to adorn your handsome face," she said, and peeled off the false mole Sophie had left pasted on his cheek when she kissed him.

"And we need to take care of this wound," she added, placing her hand where Bear's knife had pierced the skin. "Come in." She closed the door behind them, revealing a modest one-bedroom condo, a gold-embroidered divan facing the window, Egyptian reproductions on the walls. One showed Isis mending the torn body of Osiris.

Tamara believed she was the reincarnation of the goddess Isis, and since Osiris had been cut up into many pieces her obsession was to sew the pieces together. Compose the man. Not a Frankenstein, but a man worthy of her orgiastic pleasures. New Mexico and its Rio Grande were far from Egypt and its Nile, but she had read the poem of a well-known poet who wrote that somehow the penis of Osiris washed from the Nile across the sea into the Rio Grande. Obsessed, Tamara was determined to find the organ. But that's another story.

The room felt stifling, the lilac perfume oozing from a vase full of deep purple flowers.

"It's nothing," Sonny protested.

"A knife carries the memory of blood it has shed. The wound must be cleaned."

She led him toward the bathroom.

Sonny stopped. "Raven was here."

"Don't mind him, Saw-ny. He's crazy, as you well know. He's everywhere, first the silly bomb, then the phones, next—"

Sonny squeezed her hand.

"Where?"

Her green gypsy eyes looked into Sonny's, wet with tears, her cat-and-mouse mood suddenly aroused by the erotic pleasure of his firm grip.

"Who knows? Yes. Moments ago he was here. He's jealous, Sonny. He knows I would rather make love to you than any man on earth. But you're safe here. You're safe with me."

"Is he—"

"Androgynous? Hermaphrodite? Transvestite? Yes and no, he's all of the above and much more. At his worst moments his energy is pure libido. Do you understand? Sometimes he loses control."

Sonny nodded. He knew.

"He's dangerous, Sonny. He has acquired a tremendous power. And what does he do with it? Play games. Unchecked libido impulse. He has forsaken ritual. But I haven't, my dear Sonny. That's what I can give you."

She touched his cheek. Her perfume was a desert scent, sweet and intoxicating.

"Raven wants to end it," he said. "Is he for real?"

A frown crossed her forehead. "Let's not talk about Raven. He's a votary of the cults of the bull. He has an energy any man would die for. But it's uncontrolled. He comes on strong, like the toro, full of fury, demanding, like the male child who has his first erection and seeks immediate satisfaction."

What in the hell am I doing here? Sonny thought. What she knows she won't reveal. Am I now making deals? What's the payoff?

"You're not like that," she continued, putting her arms around him, pressing close to feel the pounding of his heart, the same rhythm that she could, by the slightest movements of her body, move to his pelvic region and create the stirring of a sea responding to the moon, a midnight tide that could turn into a storm.

But she was too studied in the art of love to rush. As quickly as she began to play she backed away and opened the door of the bathroom.

"You know, I wait for you. You and your dream dog. Oh, Sonny, that was perfect. The dream dog."

"Did Raven have my dog?"

"A small red dachshund. Yes. Showing the bitch off like it was his prize, and the poor thing kept growling at him."

She unsnapped the pearl buttons of his cowboy shirt, and breathed deep his aroma, softly running her hands over his chest, creating a tingle Sonny felt to his toes.

She smiled. "As always, you are the prude." She laughed softly. "How many women dream of having you, and you have a one-track mind for your Penelope."

"Look, I'm going after him. That's a done deal. But he was coming here first. That means he was going to give you a clue, anything that might help me."

Tamara smiled. She had Sonny where she wanted him. He had come to her, not she to him. "Let's take care of this, then we talk."

She dabbed a cotton ball in Betadine, cleaned the wound, then taped it.

"If I were a spider I would sew it, but this will have to do. Put on this robe."

The robe hanging on the door was a prize, Chinese silk from some forgotten dynasty, colorful enough to make a man yearn for a languorous afternoon in the Forbidden City. Movida time!

"I don't have time. You know nothing—"

"Oh, don't bet on that! Come now, don't protest! Put it on."

She stepped out, shutting the door behind her. Sonny took off his shirt. He looked at himself in the mirror, hardly recognizing the man he had met there earlier that day. Had Prajna's wisdom rubbed off on him? The tragedy of Naomi's death? The violent need he felt to get to Raven?

A strange frenzy had settled over the city. Tamara would say it was the sex drive of spring. Raven had picked the perfect time to strike. All of the northern hemisphere was groaning and coming alive with the return of the sun, and its promise was also its confusion. Could it be its downfall?

He splashed water on his face and felt the miracle of its caress. Without water man was nothing. Without water the tides in the woman would not respond to the moon, blood would not flow, the future would not unfold.

He dried himself, put on the robe, walked out to meet the Russian gypsy who fancied herself a Nefertiti of the desert, secluded now, not in a tent, but reduced to a simple apartment in the heart of the city.

She sat on the divan, her fine legs outstretched, a smile on her face, waiting for him with drink in hand, a special concoction that could make a man forget his past.

"Ah, darling, now you are my prize again," she crooned. "I know you have had a difficult day. Come sit by my side and rest."

"I need to know about Raven."

"First drink."

She handed him the delicate kantharos, so intricately carved that Sonny felt pleasure as his fingers wrapped around the dancing Greek maidens decorating the sides of the cup. He drank, knowing he could not rush Tamara, she would give up what she knew in her own time. She needed to play a game, as always. His coyote sense told him to play back. Be wily.

The ambrosia flowed like a honey liquor the gods might drink, awakening his senses as it was absorbed quickly into the bloodstream, racing to the brain where it mushroomed, as a lotus blossom might open, a thousand colorful blossoms. A drink obviously outlawed in Red China.

"What is it?"

"Datura and hibiscus flowers in a secret blend."

Sonny smiled. "I feel exalted," he said, the kind of words Tamara loved to hear.

Exalted? His buddies at Sal's Bar would hassle him for months if they heard him say *he felt exalted.* Especially since he had started drinking only soft drinks. Dr. Pepper? Damn, no self-respecting Chicano drank Dr. Pepper with his amigos. A soda couldn't really wet your whistle, and it sure as hell couldn't make you feel exalted.

"I mean good . . ." he muttered.

"You have the gift of dream," she said, taking the empty cup from his hand. "Seek Raven there."

"We've moved onto a new plane," Sonny replied, nearly adding it was a new plane of illusion. Raven was playing new tricks, far more powerful and dangerous tricks than practiced before.

"I understand," Tamara murmured. "You two have been at this struggle since long before the first stone was laid for the pyramid of Giza. Neither can gain the upper hand, and yet in the struggle is the evolution of the psyche. Our evolution. You know this, and he knows it, two snakes clinging to the same tree, the yin and yang. The masses I watch from my window know nothing. They are trapped in cycles of unredeeming work. They are not conscious of their work. Millions and millions of our species who do not understand they could make quantum leaps in the ladder of evolution, if only they understood the psyche's role. If only they could harness the energy and make whole again the dualities that tear each person apart."

She paused, and they both looked out the window down Central Avenue, where the wild fiesta continued, a rending apart of the human spirit, which sought its wholeness behind the mask of the fiesta, under the influence of booze, cocaine, ecstasy, and lust, only to find the following morning, after a night of riotous revelry, that each had to return to the wheel of unredeeming work.

"Our hope is in you and Raven," she whispered, touching his hand. "Because you have knowledge of previous existences, those times and places that come in your dreams, you have already achieved the first step of the Fourfold Way. Also, you have knowledge of the divine eye, which is your Zia medallion."

"Raven has it," a very relaxed Sonny said, yawning, aware her presence was growing luminous, the image of a woman he had long desired to reach out and touch, and her voice a melody that called from a distant shore.

"You'll have it before the day is done," she prophesied. "The problem is not the Zia medallion or the sacred Zia Stone you seek."

"What then?" Sonny reached for her, felt her warm breath on his face, the beginning of her journey into his body, her path of orgiastic pleasure.

She was no sylph, but a real woman, an enchantress, Sonny knew that. The length of her body exuded the aura of a woman the ancients had called the salacious virgin, a woman who could please a thousand men without losing her virginity. The light in the room became the hue of desire, a royal purple, and as desire yearns to come to life by touching the object it needs, she ever so lightly brushed her gold-ringed hand across his thigh.

"You are tied to the wheel of causation. You have already cut away some of the twelve knots, but you still have a way to go before you arrive at the fourth step."

"The fourth step," he repeated.

At this point it was impossible to tell what was lost in Sonny's plan, or gained. He was staring into her sparkling eyes, liquid pools of green whose tides pulled him toward her as the full moon draws the blood of ready men and women.

Perhaps he was hypnotized by the long, gold earrings that dangled from her small ears, the diamond's glitter refracting light like a prism, creating rainbows on the walls, or was it the tinkling sound of the Egyptian bracelets on the soft curve of her wrists?

"The fourth step is complete awareness. Knowledge of the universal light. A blending into cosmic energy."

Sonny thought of the Path of Light don Eliseo had taught him. That's all he needed. But perhaps he had been negligent. Not fully understood its possibilities.

"There is another way," she said softly, reminding Sonny of his mother's call to dinner, afternoons when he and his brother played with the neighborhood kids, and the call to eat was like an angel's call to heaven's feast.

Her breath wafted ambrosial sweet on his face; the most imperceptible tremor moved the curves of her body toward her goal.

"What?"

"I offer the way of love."

"Tell me." Sonny grinned, a stupid grin.

"As you know, each chakra is a lotus blossom waiting to be opened. Opening the chakras is a way to enlightenment."

"Yeah," Sonny agreed, except that in New Mexico the lotus was the yucca with its stalk of white blossoms and sharp spears, which explained why so few New Mexicans had ever attained enlightenment.

"It is the way of kundalini," her voice whispered from another shore, where the sloshing sea grew still. "At the base of the spine lies the blissful serpent. Asleep. Yoga teaches us how to arouse each of the chakras, beginning with the first and traveling up the tree of the spine, a seven-stepped ladder to the crown of the head. When all are opened and blossoming you are awakened to spiritual consciousness."

"I could use a little of that," Sonny said, aware that his mind was playing tricks on him. He was falling for her line. Was it the drink, or was it his coyote spirit, tired of craftiness, ready to have fun? The mariachi music from the streets wafted through the window.

"Let us began," she said, "a chant of syllables. Each *aum* will be a petal from the lotus flower, beginning at the cave of the sleeping serpent and moving upward as we breathe life into our kundalini energy."

She chanted. *Vam, sam, sham, sam, bam, bham, mam, yam, ram, lam, dam, dham, nam, tam, tham, dam, dham, nam, pam, pham, kam, kham, gam, gham, ngam, cham, chham, jam, jham, nyam, tam, tham . . .*

". . . thus I will open each leaf of the lotus blossom, from the first to the crown, each leaf is a syllable. Let me continue."

"First, Raven."

"He meets with his witches at six."

"Where?"

"There, by your bridge."

The Barelas Bridge. Raven wasn't fooling. It was showdown time.

"Is that it?"

"Make love to me. Leave your seed in flesh, not in dream . . ." Then she whispered, "Don't be a slave to only one reality."

He felt her warm hands on his stomach. From the foreign and distant shore of the kama sutra, he heard her song, the siren's plaintive song. La Llorona's call.

The ambrosial drink tasted bitter in his mouth. He wasn't a datura/hibiscus man. "Yoga takes years to learn. All those syllables. Take me years to repeat."

"Not if I become your guide," Tamara whispered.

"Sorry, I don't have time. I have a date with Raven."

"Damn Raven," she sputtered, feeling him slipping away.

From the street below a car horn sounded. Sonny recognized it.

"Mi troca!" he said, and stood to look out the window.

"Troika!" a frustrated and steaming Tamara cried, stumbling from the divan to have a look.

22

On the street below, Diego was standing beside Sonny's truck.

"Gotta go," Sonny said, flinging the colorful robe aside.

"No," Tamara gasped, clutching at Sonny, her eyes pleading as she reached out. "Stay awhile—"

"Don't have time," Sonny said. He really meant that whatever she was promising just wasn't in the cards. It never had been.

"Damn Raven!" she cursed. "Never mind the chakras. Just stay. I promise—" She ran her tongue across her burning lips. "Raven will always be there. But this afternoon could be so special."

"Some spiritual enlightenments just aren't meant to be," Sonny said.

"Go then," she cried. "Yes. Raven waits for you. But he's dangerous! He's leading you into a trap. Don't you understand?"

"I have to try," Sonny replied.

"Or die trying, as the saying goes," she said, and stood on tiptoe to kiss him. "I wish there was some way I could make you stay. If you go, I'm afraid it's the last time—"

"It's what I wanted," Sonny said, "for Raven to lead me to his place. The river's as much mine as his. The water—"

He didn't finish but walked briskly to the bathroom, picked up his shirt, and went to the door.

"He's been playing tricks all day!" she called.

"I know," Sonny answered.

He shut the door softly behind him, then flew down the stairs while pulling on his fluttering shirt, arms outstretched like an airplane, letting out the shout of a boy playing with a homemade airplane, "Baaa-rooooooommm," the sound of flight contained in the joyful and untutored *ommmmmmm* of childhood, learned not in the long and tiring regimen of yoga, or in Tamara's kama sutra, but from the natural burst of air that explodes from innocent lungs.

Sonny burst out the door and ran across the street.

"Hey, bro, what's happening?" Diego asked, pursing his lips toward the building. He guessed Tamara lived there, and here was Sonny buttoning his shirt. "Man, did she punch your eye?"

"Nada," Sonny replied, "pura nada. Thanks for finding my troca. Was there any sign of Chica?"

"No. She's not with you?"

"Raven—"

"Raven? Ah, que chinga."

"I don't have time to explain. How's Rita?"

"Everything's cool. Y tú?"

"Gotta see the man."

"Want me to go with you?"

"I'm okay. Stay with Rita."

"You sure?" Diego asked. He knew of Raven's power.

"It's gotta be," Sonny replied.

"The pinche is holding a big press conference at the Hispanic Cultural Center. He's got everybody acting like this whole thing is a game. The guys hanging out at the cafe are taking bets—"

"What kind of bets?"

"Ah, you know la plebe. Pura cábula."

"Come on, what kind of bets?"

"Tú sabes, bets you won't make it back. Kidding around, telling Rita if you don't check in by closing time one of them gets to take her home—"

"Some friends," Sonny said through clenched teeth. "You tell Rita I'll be there."

For a moment he thought of turning home. Maybe resisting Tamara had been the last test. But no—he had to get over to the Hispanic Cultural Center. Raven had called the shots. Told him to be there. He had to rescue his daughters, the images he had seen at the theater, and take from Raven all that belonged to him. Or die trying.

"Suave, bro, suave. Keep the faith. You gotta do what you gotta do, like the old pachuco said. Don't worry, things are okay at the cafe."

Sonny took his clean jacket from the plastic bag and put it on.

"Hijo, bro, cool. Man, you show up in that and those guys will scatter like gallinas."

He checked the glove compartment, took out Elfego Baca's Colt .45, loaded it, and tucked it in his belt.

"It could have been lifted at the city lot," Diego said, "pero tú sabes, la plebe takes care of their own."

Sonny understood. Sometimes la raza surprised you. A pistol like this was worth its weight in history. Maybe he would use it to scare the hell out of the guys hanging around Rita. Shoot their asses. Show them he meant business. No, he knew better than that. The old pistol had served only on the side of law and order, and today it had shot down a demon wind. Time for it to be retired.

Besides, he had never used it in anger, never shot a man with it, so why carry it and tempt fate? In the time of chaos it was time to put away the guns, make love not war, create a balance of power through cooperation not competition, heal the wounds of the world, green vegetables for all the children, massage therapy for all the senior citizens and those stiff and weary from life.

Yeah, it was time to put the old pistol in a glass case, save it so he could tell his grandchildren how José Calabasa had killed a giant dust devil with it.

But why was he carrying it hidden under his jacket? Did he still believe, in spite of everything don Eliseo had taught him, that he could shoot Raven? Was it some quirk in his psyche telling him that he really could put a fatal and final bullet in Raven?

There it was, the seed laid in the brain of man from the time he first stood upright. Stood up to piss and shivered. The sabre-tooth tiger lurking in the savannah grass was always nearby. No matter how much a person tried to put aside violence, revenge reared its head. Would it never end?

"Can you catch a ride?"

"No problem. The buses are running. Cuídate."

"Tú también," Sonny said, "y gracias."

"What's a compa for?" Diego replied, saluting.

Sonny started the truck, and drove across Central toward Cesar Chavez Boulevard. Raven's big meeting with the city fathers and the Los Alamos scientists was about to begin.

In the west the sun was one of those glorious fat sunflowers people raise in their backyards, brilliant yellow petals pasting themselves on the sky turning gray, the end of the equinox day. A knot of clouds in the west gathered to form the dark center of the flower.

Today the one dark seed in Sonny's path was Raven. All around, afternoon shadows crawled from buildings and trees to claim their own essence, sisters of the falling dusk, brothers to the night.

The blooming sunflower didn't last, it wilted, the doom of time bending the stalk until the yellow petals bowed and settled into the western horizon and all that was left was a pale glow lighting up the azure sky.

How long was I with Tamara?

Yo no llego ni temprano ni tarde, the old man said.

What does that mean? Sonny asked.

It means God was always there. I am who I am. In his world there was no time. Same could be said of a passionate woman.

So you were there?

No, I stay away from sex scenes. He laughed.

There was no sex, Sonny explained.

Yeah, right.

I tell you, no s-e-x.

With a woman like that, and you didn't—

See! I can't win. If I'd taken advantage I'd be a heel. Because I didn't, you doubt my virility.

Well, Sonny, the old man continued, knowing he had just pulled Sonny's coyote beard. What are your compañeros going to say when they find out she was hot to trot and you left her hanging?

She had herself hot to trot! Her and her mumbo jumbo. Humming *wham, bam, thank you ma'am.* Bull. Besides, who's going to tell them?

My lips are sealed, the old man answered, grinning like the Cheshire Cat.

The passage of time bothered Sonny. Was it the drink she had offered that caused the hands of the clock to collapse like they did in a Dalí painting? Or had it been like that all day, time moving back and forth, not in a straight line? In the Algodones hut, in the theater, Raven seemed in control of time. Maybe in control of Sonny's fate. Or was time itself the final illusion, a straight line invented around the cycles of nature, the squaring of the circle?

The South Broadway barrio seemed peaceful enough, dark in the crumbling light. Workers hurried home, old men bundled in well-worn jackets, urban men whose grandfathers had once worked the fields of corn and chile in Puerto de Luna, Chimayo, Peralta, Mesilla, all the traditional villages of the state. They had fled the earth of their birth to migrate to the City Future, and this was their reward, the falling night.

Sonny knew the barrio. He had briefly dated a girl from Sanjo when he was in high school. Other friends from the South Valley drove into the dangerous territory to court the girls. The guys from South Broadway and Sanjo didn't like vatos from other barrios messing with their women, so there were a few fights, but nobody was ever seriously hurt.

The grandchildren of Black railroad workers lived here, porters for the Santa Fe railroad who had settled along Broadway. Now these were the streets of immigrant Mexicanos, and they rang with new sounds.

Todo cambia, as the old people said. The barrios of the city were in constant motion as one group layered on the other. Chihuahuenses were moving into the old Chicano neighborhoods, and the Chicanos, who now called themselves Hispanics, had saved enough to afford new houses on the West Mesa. The city was continually shifting, like a snake thrashing as it sloughed off its old skin, swallowing the unrecorded lives of the poor.

Sonny turned south on Fourth Street and into the Hispanic Cultural Center parking lot, which was filled to the brim and ringed with dozens of police cars and TV vans.

The happily drunken, festive crowd from downtown had poured into the center. The news had spread, someone called Raven had killed a bunch of Al Qaeda terrorists single-handed in Jemez Springs and recovered the code that would defuse the bomb. This was reality TV in the making! Why go home?

Sonny parked, got out, and headed for the center.

"Hey!" A cop called, confronting Sonny. "It's full! They're not letting anybody in."

"Aren't you Sonny Baca?" his partner asked.

"Any chance I can get in?" Sonny asked.

"We can let you through, but they're going to stop you at the door. FBI's got the doors covered."

"Thanks," he offered, and hurried toward the main entrance, where dozens of FBI agents who weren't from the Alburquerque office stood surveying the crowd.

The attorney general has sent in his own guns, Sonny guessed. Dominic's mess has spread beyond our little corner of the world. Probably a few CIA agents also working the scene.

He walked around the plaza toward the back of the theater. Someone called. "Phssst! Hey Sonny!"

He turned and recognized Lucinda and Patricia, two ladies who had helped him and Rita do some genealogy research in the library.

"You're late. Doors are closed."

"You want in?"

Sonny nodded.

"Come with us."

They led him around the back. Sonny paused and sniffed the air. The scent coming from the river bosque reminded him of wet Raven feathers, or diatomic molecules laid down during the last ice age, but no, it was distinctly pigs.

"Pigs?"

Lucinda explained. "We have a program to teach the kids the old traditional ways our ancestors farmed. The river's ecosystem. Acequias and all that. The kids are supposed to raise animals."

"Today they were supposed to bring us some sheep," Patricia added, "But they brought pigs. We put them in a pen near the ditch. Hijo, they smell."

"We were going to have a matanza in the fall. Teach the kids where pork chops come from."

"But the pinche pigs got loose. They ran to the river and no one on our board of directors wants to go after them."

"There's a big black sow. Very mean. She knocked over a maintenance man, nearly killed him."

"Pinche marrana. Hope they make her into chicharrones."

They opened a back door just far enough for Sonny to slip in.

"Be careful."

"Cuídate."

The steamy air of the overflowing crowd met Sonny as he squeezed into the theater. He made his way backstage, around the curtains to the side. From there he had a perfect view of the brightly lighted stage.

Frank Dominic stood at the lectern. Seated behind him, dressed in shimmering black, a frustrated Raven. The board of directors had boycotted the meeting. A smart bunch who had built one of the most beautiful cultural centers in the nation, they had washed their hands of Raven. They had to rent the space because of Dominic's political pressure, but they didn't have to attend.

In fact, very few of the dignitaries Raven was courting were in attendance. In the front row sat Fox. He had to be there as representative for the city. After all, a bomb was ticking away in the Jemez, and only Raven had the code that would defuse it. And time was running out.

Sweat glistened on Dominic's forehead as he spoke. "I want to thank all of you for coming. Today we have lived through a day of infamy—"

The crowd, now sullen and tired from the afternoon's partying, was in no mood for political speeches.

A young woman stood and held up her useless phone. "You promised to get our cell phones working!" she shouted.

"Cell phones! Cell phones!" the cheer went up.

Raven jumped to his feet. "I can and I will!"

"Please!" Dominic shouted into the microphone. "Let's conduct this meeting in an orderly fashion. Please sit. Your questions will be answered."

Raven sat and the audience settled down.

"That's better. We can't waste time. Most of you don't realize, but today we went through one of the most serious emergencies our state has ever faced. Our social fabric was tested. Our morality was—"

A few boos and hoots sounded in the audience. Dominic preaching morality was like the devil giving Sunday's sermon at church.

He knew enough to change the subject. "Thanks to outstanding work by our law enforcement officers we have come through. As you know, the governor was murdered this morning—"

A wave of oh's rippled through the audience. The news of the governor's death had already leaked out. Now everyone wanted to know the details.

"Who did it?" someone shouted.

"The Republicans!" a voice answered, and laughter broke out.

"Is the bomb real?" another asked.

"Please, all in due time," Dominic continued. "A terrorist plot to bomb the Los Alamos labs was intercepted by the FBI working in conjunction with the CIA, and our local law enforcement. At great cost, I might add. The governor, whom we all loved as an honest and courageous man, learned of the plot. That's why he was killed. Informants were able to leak the name of the Al Qaeda terrorist to the governor. And as he was about to deliver this information to the police he was murdered in cold blood."

A wave of whispers swept the audience. The Catholics in the audience made the sign of the cross. "Pobrecito." "Que descanse en paz."

Dominic turned and looked nervously at Raven. "Were it not for our friend Raven we would never have identified those responsible. A man known only as Bear is at this very moment being chased down as the ringleader. Bear is the leader of a small renegade group of Indians who call themselves Green—Green is a misnomer, because this small group has connections to Al Qaeda."

The audience stirred uneasily. They weren't dumb. They knew Dominic was positioning himself as water czar for the region.

"As you know, this group of Indians refuse to admit that Santa Fe Woman was here long before any Indian settlements. But they are wrong. Science will prove that Santa Fe Woman was here long before our Indian friends of the pueblos. But I want to make one thing perfectly clear. The vast majority of our Indian friends have distanced themselves from these so-called Green Indians. There is enough water for all of us, if we plan wisely. That is why my corporation, Water Everywhere—"

He paused and looked at the Hispano Chamber of Commerce representative. "As we say in Spanish, 'Agua Para Todos.'"

He smiled, got no applause, and the smile turned into a grin. "I assure you, we will proceed with the purchase of water rights. Believe me, this is the wave of the future. But I pledge on my honor, as we consolidate the water rights of the entire Rio Grande Basin, we will work closely with all the Indian and Hispanic farmers in the valley. And we will save the silvery minnow."

One environmentalist clapped, but most shook their heads, some whispering an audible "bullshit." They knew Dominic's way. Placing water rights in a private corporation run by him was like giving up the baby with the tub. Giving up Diogenes.

Fox shook his head. Apparently he hadn't planned on being used as an accomplice. He stood as if to speak, but one of Dominic's aides pushed him back down.

The same man gestured at Dominic, pointing to his watch. Dominic nodded.

"Water Everywhere will represent the state and every agency which deals with water. We will serve you, the people. The major lakes, Cochiti, Elephant Butte, and Caballo Reservoir will be emptied into our underground aquifers, thus preventing loss by evaporation. We presently lose two thirds of the water stored in those reservoirs to evaporation. By storing water underground we will have enough to serve you, the people, for the next ten centuries. The present water rights of farmers, cities, and the pueblos will remain in current usage. Of course, half of those rights will be purchased by my corporation. Excuse me. It is not my corporation. It is ours. Stock will be sold. You can be owners. It's a fail-safe way of dealing with the issue. By privatizing all the water rights of the Rio Grande Basin, we can assure the people of this great state that their children, and their children's children, will have safe, clean water to drink."

Only his corporate friends clapped. It was obvious the rest had not bought into his plan. Again the assistant pointed at the clock.

"Yes, yes. We have an immediate problem at hand. A nuclear bomb has been planted on the Jemez Mountain with the intent of destroying Los Alamos National Labs. In the interest of time, I have the pleasure of introducing the man who fought the Al Qaeda terrorists on the mountain and recovered the code to defuse the bomb. Our hero of the day, Raven."

Around the stage a ring of laser projectors fired up, a cloud of ionized space exploded in light, and the image of Raven stepped forward to the microphone.

Some in the crowd clapped politely.

Raven eyes flashed as his gaze found Sonny in the wings. You're too late, his sneer said.

Sonny tightened his grip on the pistol tucked under his jacket. Should he shoot now, take a chance on blasting Raven to hell, or wait until the appointed time?

Won't do no good, the old man said. Look.

Sonny looked at the laser projectors. Was the Raven standing at the podium real or illusion? As long as Sonny could remember, Raven had only once or twice appeared before large groups. He loved the recesses, the shadows, the wisps of mists that rose from dark dreams.

Real or not, Raven's booming voice filled the theater. "As you know, I am an alchemist who can change light to dark. I offer proof by first restoring use of your cell phones!"

"Prove it!" a barrio poet shouted.

"Show us the way!" a lone follower planted in the audience responded.

Raven smiled. He was back in the saddle. He popped his cell phone from his pocket and shouted, "The cell phones were disabled by the Al Qaeda terrorists! My people have fixed the problem. Go on, use your phones. They're working!"

Many in the theater reached into their pockets or purses and clicked on their cell phones. Hundreds of messages went out simultaneously. Calls to husbands, wives, kids home alone, lovers, ex's, dope dealers, brokers, restaurants for reservations, friends, hospital rooms where friends lay dying, prisons, the Weather Channel, vacation confirmations, Amazon.com, E-bay, credit card companies, and so on and on.

"Can you hear me now?" Raven joked, and many shouted "Yes!" Their calls had been answered! The cell phones were working. A murmur of thanks filled the space, as if connection to a greater power had just been made.

"They're working!" Raven's crony shouted.

The audience, cynical until now, cheered. The gut-riveting fear of not having a working cell phone was suddenly dispelled. Being able to phone created a mass psychic release. Technology triumphed. The digital age was real, not illusion. The naysayers would be branded skeptics.

"Viva Raven!" someone shouted, and the theater resounded with "Viva Raven" calls as people hugged each other and gave thanks.

In the river bosque, dark now with the shadows of dusk, the pigs who had fled their pens lifted their snouts from rooting in the leafy earth and heard the cry. The huge black sow grunted, calling her brethren down a dark path latticed by Russian olive trees. Someone was coming, a god perhaps, or a man raised from the dead or from the world of illusion.

And men who awaken must be baptized in blood or water.

"There you have it!" Raven cawed triumphantly. "I am the Restorer, not Mephistopheles!"

The audience, some with tears in their eyes, fell quiet, cell phones were ceremoniously put away, all sat back down. The man had proven himself. Let him continue.

23 »

"That's the easy part," Raven continued, the joy of a dark dream reverberating in his voice. "All of you know the terrorists planted a bomb on the Valles caldera, that mountain that I love as a mother . . ." He paused and touched a black silk handkerchief to his eyes, glancing sideways to make sure he was being observed.

Again, Sonny resisted pulling out the pistol. An ordinary bullet couldn't kill Raven, and the bullet molded by the magician had been used by José on the whirlwind.

"In the past you have trusted Sonny Baca. He would have you believe I planted the bomb," Raven whispered, gazing at Sonny and fixing him with a stare. "But you know better. You know terrorists have infiltrated our national labs. They wish to destroy our capability for waging war. They are intent on raining down a nuclear fire on our unique capital, Byzantium, our City Different. They want to destroy the work of our alchemists, our scientists who can turn plutonium into fire. I will not let that happen!"

His voice rose in oratorical flourish, as any war-mongering

dictator, or president, might rouse the masses, with one hand crossed over his heart, staring at the American flag on the wall.

A smattering of applause broke out in the audience.

"Fire," he continued, "the transforming element, the element we most fear, can be controlled. We know the earth can perish in water as it did during the flood of Noah, or it can end in fire. Armageddon! And no phoenix will rise from those ashes! The terrorists who planted the bomb want to create a nuclear holocaust! I fought those terrorists! I nearly lost my life taking the code from them! Now I will defuse the bomb! Our children and our children's children will once again romp in the verdant forests of the Jemez Mountain!"

Nearby, in the dark, the old man groaned. He couldn't take the bullshit any longer. I'm outta here, he said.

Where? Sonny asked.

Anywhere to save my sanity. You listen to that caca for too long and it can kill you. With that he exited.

"I'm calling Mr. Sturluson, the chief scientist on the mountain," Raven explained to the audience.

He punched his cell phone, which was attached to the sound system. Everyone in the theater heard the beeps, then a sleepy voice answered. "This is Sturluson."

"Are you ready?" Raven asked.

"We've been waiting for your call," Sturluson answered.

"Have you been able to defuse the bomb?"

"No."

"Why?"

"Too complicated. The experts we need are flying in as we speak. But they may be too late."

"Why?"

"There's a clock. Clearly marked six o'clock."

"The bomb will go off at six?"

"That's the only reason a timer would be wired to the detonators. The thing is ticking."

A gasp of fear filled the auditorium. All faces turned to the clock on the wall. Minutes before six.

"Punch in 1776," Raven said coolly.

There was a pause, then Sturluson said, "I can't."

"Why?"

"If it's the wrong number. . . . Well, whoever wired this knew what he was doing. There are several circuits . . . if the wrong number is entered it could set off the explosives."

More gasps.

Raven smiled. "You have no choice, do you? Use my code, or wait a few minutes to be vaporized along with the entire top of the mountain."

There ensued a long pause, voices and garbled static on the sound system, the audience waiting with bated breath, then finally, after what seemed a thousand heartbeats, Sturluson's shout, "It stopped! The ticking stopped! All clear!"

A sinusoidal vibration ebbed through the crowd, the release of tension, a harmonics of vibrating strings, and all at once the audience rose to its feet, cheering Raven. The skeptics became believers as the emotional tension lifted. The bomb no longer a threat!

Some pressed forward to thank Raven, but in an instant he was gone, evaporated as the laser projectors on the stage went dark, leaving a warp in the ionized time-space Raven had just occupied. He was out the back door. As was Sonny, who fought the crowd to get outside and head for the river bosque, which was now engulfed in shadows and the terrifying wail of the Crying Woman, La Llorona.

The people of Barelas believed the cry was not that of a river sylph, but the spirit of a young girl from the barrio. During the First World War she fell in love with a doughboy, a young man from la merced de Atrisco, who left her pregnant before he shipped overseas. Two years later he was gassed in the front-line trenches, and lungs burning, crying for air, he died. When the girl received the news she went to the Barelas Bridge. The churning muddy waters below sounded like the call of her lover, her daughter's father, and in that hypnotic state she jumped and drowned herself and the baby.

A corrido, a ballad, had been composed for the young woman whose cry was heard on many a summer evening. The people of the barrio said that when the full moon reflected on the sheen of river water it was the girl's face that appeared, not the face of Mother Moon.

This is the cry that greeted Raven as he hopped and jumped over dead limbs, branches of trees that stuck up from the mud like the bleached bones of La Llorona's child, the same cry that Sonny heard as he crashed through the burnt, winter-dry trees after his shadow.

Overhead the drone of a jet that had just taken off from the Sunport, Southwest to Phoenix on time, momentarily drowned out the cry of the river spirits; and when the gleaming plane had disappeared in the last glare of the one-eyed Sun, the silence returned. The presence of the river felt complete in the heavy dusk, a curtain falling to envelope the witching hour; time when all good men should be home with their families, attending to dinner in lighted kitchens, small dots of warmth and safety where the stories of the day's activities would be told.

In the river bosque the Crying Woman gathered her muddied skirts and moved south, away from the evil she sensed in the grunting of the pigs and Raven's fire. Even El Kookoóee deserted the place of dank humors, preferring to go north, past the Oxbow, maybe to the Alameda Bridge where he might frighten young lovers parked in cars along the conservancy road, those guys drinking whiskey and rye, singing corridos of forsaken love.

In the dark, the eyes of the six-hundred-pound sow glowed with a desire for life, her mangy ears twitched as she heard Sonny's rush, and she turned with a low grunt and barreled down the narrow trail, fast as a pig can run when on a mission, because something about gods who die and are reborn buzzed in her small pig brain and told her that before rebirth can occur there must be death, and so the man hurrying toward her must die. For a man to accept the truth of his life he must die first.

Sonny heard the squeal of the sow, but he could not see the animal in the dark; he did not know her origins. Was she, perhaps, one of the herd Naomi had driven toward the river? Or was she part of a memory hidden in myths already forgotten?

She trampled the brush in her mad rush, bared her teeth, exposing tusks as mean as those of a sabre-tooth tiger, tusks that could cut through human flesh.

Her eyes of fire shone in the dark. Her warrior cry filled the air, and Sonny had only a split second to draw his pistol and fire. There was no time to run or climb a tree, and as pigs were killed long ago by both Christians and Sephardic Hispanos de la Nueva Mexico when they prepared lard and chicharrones for the winter, the bullet entered the pig's skull between the eyes, in the forehead's third eye where the light, however dim in the pig's brain, suddenly went out and the entire weight of the sow charged into Sonny and sent him crashing to the moldy earth.

Sonny's last instinct was to gather the sow in his arms as he fell back, somehow comforting the black mother he had not wanted, nor meant, to kill.

Not the Blood of the Lamb, but the blood of the marrano spurted on his face, baptizing him anew in the name of those forgotten gods who long ago had their images engraved with boars on temple walls, in the name of all those who for centuries in New Mexico had eaten sangre, the blood of a just-butchered pig fried with onions and flavored with red chile de ristra and scooped up with tortillas during the ceremony of la matanza, and finally, in the name of the blood of all creatures who die and give sustenance to the living.

The weight of the sow rested on an unconscious Sonny, as a woman might rest on her lover after the energy of love is spent and both rest entwined in sleep, dreaming of the immortality the brief climax offers, the impartiality that sleep, and dream, and death offer.

The sow slamming against him and falling on top of him had knocked him out, but he was alive and breathing, and with his primeval senses he could smell the pig, feel the thick bristles prick his skin, hear the last breath of the sow, which by law should now be bled, her throat cut and the blood saved, but this wasn't a matanza with family and vecinos helping, this was Sonny lying in the dark forest of the river where the spring flood released from Cochiti Dam played the eternal song of spring, water surging down the riverbed, a flood covering winter's sandbars, entering the mother ditches for farmers to use.

This was the song of the river: the cry of La Llorona withdrawing, frightened by the violence of the killing, El Kookoóee rushing away madly, the algae green of winter covering his face and arms so any malcriado running into him would see a terrified green man, and that bad boy was sure to shit in his pants at the sight, and, if Catholic, make his last Act of Contrition. The memory of meeting El Coco would keep until years later when in study for the priesthood, or in a monk's cell in the Mosque at Abiquiu, he might meditate the rest of his life on the green man's appearance.

The birds roosting in the tree branches were startled by the report of the pistol, and flapping dry wings they rose in a screeching flutter, then settled down again into a waiting stillness.

In the dark there were other sounds. River coyotes began to yip-yap and call to each other, and they came cautiously down the trail to gather around Sonny. Also, deep in the bosque the sound of a crackling fire could be heard, Raven's circle. And Chica's faint bark.

Sonny heard it all as if in a dream. Then he felt the sow being pushed aside and images from the unconscious dragged him toward the looming presence of the Barelas Bridge, the concrete arms that connected Alburquerque to the South Valley, the span linking the city's urban barrios to the old agricultural valley, not exactly the Brooklyn Bridge or the Golden Gate but a bridge for the people nevertheless.

The road crossing the bridge was the old Camino Real and so

its path resonated with the sounds of history, the creaking of carretas that in prior centuries lumbered up from Old Mexico carrying iron goods to exchange for New Mexican wool, buffalo hides, and tons of nuts from the stately piñon trees before those forests lay in ruins; carretas crossing the river at this ford long before the concrete bridge was raised; a century later, horse-drawn wagons carrying produce from the South Valley to sell in the City Future as it grew and expanded. The bridge connected the city to the people of Isleta Pueblo long before I-25 circled the valley.

In the middle of Raven's circle Chica slept, probably an induced, restless sleep, for she whimpered and her small body trembled. The images she saw were worthy of Dante's *Inferno,* and just as terrifying, a spiraling staircase down to hellish doom, epicycles of the psyche, each circle sealed with cast-iron doors. Around her appeared grotesque gargoyles, demon bats, blood-sucking vampires, neurotic fantasies, psychotic dramas, and noises as horrifying to the ear as the street sounds of any city, blasts of hot air, and everywhere a transforming fire roaring and sizzling, a feverish pitch.

Sonny stirred, felt every part of his body sore from the sow's blow, his bruised eye barely open, his ankle throbbing, all signs of death and rebirth.

The March night had suddenly grown cold in the depression of the river, flowing as it was with the flood of winter water, gurgling and sucking and twisting with restless energy, the holy water as tormented as Chica's dream.

An icy breeze whispered in the tree branches, a wind that embraced the dark buds like killing frost. Sounds from the city were like distant cries, the torture of the spring night settling over the city. The homeless hurried to the shelters to get away from the cold night's temperatures descending on the valley. Those with families ate their meals in silence and watched TV. The bomb had been defused, but there were other ominous signs in the air. Hints of the demise of an empire committed to war, leaders committed to greed.

But at the river, what was the sound that coasted across the wide waters? It was like the bellowing shophar announcing the Jewish New Year. It is well known that centuries ago Sephardic families came to settle in la Nueva Mexico; escaping the Inquisition in Mexico they fled north and the Rio Grande became their Edenic stream. Or was it the ram's horn announcing a coming battle? Perhaps the sound was the essence of a thousand didgeridoos mourning the death of winter, as if a lost tribe of Maori were blowing into their ancestral instruments, awakening the new season from its winter sleep. There can be no resurrection without death.

In the warmth of Rita's Cafe the young bachelors who lusted after Rita's body as she moved back and forth pouring coffee for them stood ready to claim her, or at least one of them would make the move because the clock on the wall said it was already after six and the bomb on the mountain had been defused and Sonny wasn't home, so, maybe he didn't make it. Maybe he was one of the bodies that would freeze to death that night up on the mountain.

Don't believe them, Diego had whispered to her as he locked up the kitchen and prepared to leave. I saw him. He was wearing that nice jacket you bought him. He's coming. He's coming.

Rita's constant thoughts were with Sonny, and shortly after six she suddenly saw him fall to the ground. Then, as lovers' minds and hearts are connected with a telepathic energy that allows them to see each other across time and space, a flash of insight, a shower of light illuminated Sonny sitting with Raven by a campfire, and she felt like running out, getting in the car, and going to him. But where was she to search?

She turned to the nicho on the wall that held La Virgen de Guadalupe, and she said a silent prayer. *Virgencita, return him to me. Keep him safe from Raven's claws.*

What did Raven say? The sonofabitch said, "It's been a tough day, Sonny." He sat on an old cottonwood stump, stirring the fire, his dark cloak gathered around his shoulders to ward off the chill.

24 »

Sonny looked up, understood it was his shadow that had led him to this night camp at the river's edge, a river whose seasons he knew well, for he had spent his childhood summers exploring its bosque, in the time when the river was a fuse sparkling with summer-green currents, and huge carp plowed the muddy waters.

He and childhood friends ran along the sandbars they called playas, swimming and fishing in the holes the floods created, lairs of big, fat catfish, which he caught and gutted, casting the vital organs back into the river and taking the string of fish home for his mother to cover with cornmeal and fry.

And he knew late summer when the vatos, mostly young men from the Barelas, Martineztown, and Sanjo barrios, and also some locos and veteranos, parked their low-rider ranflas on the conservancy road at the river's edge, drank beer, smoked, played the lira, sang, and swore they would die for their turf and their baby dolls. Summer rolled by on the wings of mota smoke, swirls of laughter, and sometimes explosions as rival gangs fought each other.

In late summer the water slowed to a trickle and Sonny and his compas could walk across the river, "like Christ on water," his friend Chelo used to say.

Sonny felt haunted by the waters of the river, yesterday's voices, which even now played on the trees. The voices of the river were never silent.

But that was in another time. Now he looked at Chica. He wanted to pick her up and comfort her, but he knew he had to watch Raven carefully. A misstep with Raven tonight could lead him into Raven's vortex, where the voices claiming to be from the mouths of false gods spoke.

"She's dreaming," Raven said in a goading voice.

"In a nightmare," Sonny corrected.

"Whatever." Raven shrugged.

"What did you give her?" Sonny asked and knelt to rub Chica's soft fur. She whimpered softly, recognizing her master.

"A little Raven medicine," Raven replied, tossing a log into the roaring fire. "Datura and hibiscus in a special blend. Dream medicine. But she resisted, wouldn't fall asleep, a loyal dog trying to protect her master, but finally the Lethe drink knocked her out. I followed her dream back to—and by the way Sonny, we can now let the public know, dogs do dream, but their dreams are ancestral dreams, dreams of forest freedoms before they came to beg at our doors—Where was I? Ah, she led me to a dark Germanic forest in a time when her progenitors were as large as wolves and as ferocious, before man bred her down to size. But in the end she revealed your fatal flaw. After all, Sonny, you are a tragic hero."

A tragic hero, Sonny mused. He's trying to draw me out, perhaps put a mask on me I do not need. The mask of an ancient Greek king, or a fool.

"Dogs sense things about us we don't even know," Sonny said, feeling Chica's heartbeat. She would recover from the drug.

"Ah, yes," Raven agreed. "So do coyotes."

"She's innocent," Sonny said, shading his eyes from the fire's dancing light, glancing around, sensing Raven's demon birds guarding the circle, those same vampires who often came at midnight to drag him to their master's nightmarish circle. Where was Lady Anima when he needed her?

He dared not pick up Chica and make a run for it. Where was there to run? Can a man escape his own creation?

Everyone knows, it's easier to fall into the clutches of the shadow than it is to break free. Besides, he had come to claim his daughters, the two souls he had seen by Raven's side at the theater. They were here, in the circle, he could sense them.

"Why do you haunt the innocent?" Sonny asked.

"So they learn they don't live alone in this world," Raven answered, and laughed. "Isn't that a great answer? Don't you see, the lonely at least have me, the spirit voice they often mistake for God's. I've been around a long time. Some say haunting mankind, I say delivering them. But let's talk about you, and your tragic flaw."

There he goes again, Sonny thought. Okay, let's play the game to the end. "Which is?"

"Obsession. You are an obsessed man, Mr. Sonny Baca. Like Agamemnon, Oedipus, Othello, King Lear, Don Quixote, or the weak and floundering Hamlet. And the worst of the lot, Captain Ahab! All obsessed with the bride of their dreams, a need that drives them to—you know, you once taught literature—drives them to tragic ends."

"Bullshit," Sonny said. "Coming to claim what's mine is real, not obsession."

"That's just it! Precisely! Claiming what's yours is your mistake! You've been dreaming all day, wandering in a world of illusions, warned by sylphs, oracles, and fortune tellers—and you paid no heed! You saw how I can threaten the world with nuclear fire, and you still believe in yourself!"

"I dream, therefore I am," Sonny answered, his coyote sense awakening to his surroundings, casing the joint like a coyote around the hen house, planning how to move liquid-like in and out of Raven's mandala, the fluid circle of yin and yang.

He spied the old man standing outside the circle, a dappled shadow in the brush, the light of the flickering fire illuminating him as a tree, crusty with wrinkled bark, his arms dangling like useless tree branches. He didn't have the strength to enter the circle, he couldn't help.

"Your dream is my dream!" Raven insisted. "I'm in control here! Not you! You can't even take care of your waking consciousness! You've floundered all day and what have you got for your troubles? Nothing! Nada! Zero! And I have grown in power. I hold your fate in my hands. Kneel before your Lord of Night!"

"Lord of dead pigs," Sonny scoffed.

Raven stood, ruffling his cape furiously. "Don't you dare call me—" He stopped short, grinned, and nodded, looking through pale yellow eyes at Sonny.

"You always try to get me mad. Get my goat."

"Mad is as mad does."

"You're a fool, Sonny."

"So is the Buddha a great fool."

"Then kill the Buddha."

"Yes." Sonny smiled. "Kill the Buddha."

Raven hesitated. "To kill the fool is to bring out his greater Buddha nature. In you that means your shaman nature. No, you can't have it that easy."

"Then you remain the trickster and I the fool. That's what I've been today," Sonny said, "a surviving fool."

"Okay. I agree. There's madness in both of us. Just as insanity feeds a government that believes it can rule the world. The doom of your kind is just around the corner, and it's brought to you courtesy of some of your so-called rational minds."

He laughed, a dry laugh that made the cold tree branches shudder.

"Look, Raven, we're in this together. Why split ourselves in two? Why continue the old duality?" Sonny said, knowing peace with Raven had not proven true since man's ancestors crawled from the ooze of the sea.

"An offer of peace?" Raven cocked his head.

"Why not?"

"Its too late. I'm tired of sharing space and time with you. Don't you know, it's time for the final Apocalypse, the end of the world, the dream of Vishnu, God's experiment, call it what you want, this is my time. It's written, Sonny, written in the Bible, written on the Zia Stone you seek, I'm sure. This story of obsession has to end! I shall call my book *Mankind Obsessed.* The end of the world! A doxology of chaos!"

"It's not your world to end!" Sonny retorted, knowing he shouldn't show fear in front of Raven.

"Yes, mine!" Raven cackled. "My need to return to chaos, the formless ocean before God spoke, a swirling mist that can be dream or nightmare, the cosmic sea before the planets were born. And I will take all human perception with me. I will take Lady Virtue with me. I will take your Sofia! End it in a glorious bang! Not a whimper but a bang! An orgasm! End of so-called civilization! Climax! Total enlightenment! It's what every god has experienced at the end of time."

"You alone?" asked Sonny.

"Yes! Me!"

"And Tamara."

Raven paused, catching his breath. "She believes in the body, the flesh, hot blood, getting you there with her kama sutra tricks, but she's harmless. I believe in an orgasm that leads to nothingness. What every philosopher dreams of but dares not utter. The alchemist's final trick."

"That kind of bang only lasts a few seconds," Sonny reminded him.

"I could say *who cares?* The terrorist who murders thousands of human souls with his final act feels, during those precious seconds, like a god. Complete power. The most potent aphrodisiac. But there's method to my madness. Here's the rub. One beautiful self will be left after the holocaust. Me! That's my secret! I will be Lord of Chaos! King of Chaos! I cannot be destroyed! I plan to rule in that unspeakable world *we* create."

"We?"

"Why, Sonny, you surprise me. Don't you remember? I live in the heart of every man. Ah, I know what you're thinking. Only those who run stark, raving mad down the street are possessed. No, Sonny, every man is my host, my brother. Sometimes my work is so easy I sit back and laugh. Man is his own worst enemy. But you know that. Come now." He held out a silver kantharos. "Have a drink before you die."

Go ahead, the old man said from beyond the circle. Play his game until you get to a good psychiatrist.

I don't need a head shrinker! Sonny replied, angry the old man could joke at a time like this. I know what I'm doing.

But the story was not yet finished, and the psyche knows little of predestination, or if the fate of every creature is simply a dream in the Big God's mind, if it's anything.

"There's just one problem," Sonny said, a smirk on his face, his lips curled just enough to get Raven's goat.

"What?"

"There can be no king in chaos. No Lord of Chaos."

"What are you getting at?"

"You've tripped yourself, Raven. You know that chaos is formless. Nothingness. It's the primordial sea before the Word. There exists no *being* in chaos, no reality, no center on which to stand. You take a dive into chaos and you become the mist before time and space existed."

"You're wrong!" Raven cried, deep furrows appearing on his godlike forehead.

Sonny smiled. Nothing like getting Raven mad. Nothing like reminding him that the primordial sea that beckoned him was an ocean of formlessness. There existed no reality on the face of that ancient and brooding mother.

"You know I'm right," Sonny said softly. "I may be an obsessed man, but so are you. The desire to return to chaos is your death wish—"

"Don't give me that Freudian crap! Death wish, sloosh wish!

What did the old man teach you? That people want to die because they're sick or old or crazy? My desire is deeper than that! It hasn't been named by those so-called psychologists!"

"Let there be light," Sonny said, teasing the very agitated Raven. "You dissolve into that chaos and I'm not going to pull you out."

Pull him out. Ah, it suddenly dawned on Raven. Sonny, as disoriented as he seemed that day, still had the power to pull his shadow into the light. This was his secret. In his gut, within the root of his soul, Sonny knew the yin was as strong as the yang. Complementary, my dear Watson, a former PI might say.

"Damn you, Sonny Baca! You knew this all along!"

"Of course. Everyone intuits there was a formless mist before God spoke. Read the Bible. It's in Genesis. It's in the stories of many cultures. The gods speak and the creation comes into being. The sperm, some say the word, of Father Sky fell on Mother Ocean, and there you are. A universe. Expanding. A miracle, no doubt. Imagine the universe as a mere particle, and from its explosion everything came into being. Was that atom the Word, or a Seed?"

"What are you getting at?" a frustrated Raven cried, his voice a pained echo across the river's churning waters.

"The point is, your obsession is to return to that godless sea, to non-being. An Oedipal desire to return to the womb of the mother. Go on, be my guest."

Raven trembled, at first in rage and then in fear. When the shaking fit subsided he grew sad. Sonny had called his bluff. What would Sonny do now? Tell the world. Let everyone know there was a part of the psyche pulling them down to chaos, that ocean without a port. Chaos, where space-time did not exist. Nothingness.

Would he also tell the *real* secret, that the strongest part of the soul was a light stronger than darkness? At the end of day even the most distressed could find help. Man's soul, composed of chaos, was also composed of light. There were those, call them the saints or good people or helpers, who could help the sick and tortured unto a Path of Light, a Path of Hope. With the help of good and honest people mankind could resist the ancient call that threatened to overwhelm the world's soul.

"Here's to you," Sonny said, taking the goblet and drinking down its dark contents, remembering as the bitter liquid touched his lips that he owed Diego twenty bucks to pay for a rooster, one he had saved from certain death at a corrida de gallos in Bernalillo last summer.

The world was emptying of blood, and those who stood quietly on the sidelines would never wash themselves in the blood of the lamb, or the pig.

"Illusion," Raven said.

"Screw your illusion," Sonny answered. "I see my face in the mirror!" he shouted, confronting Raven. "I know who I am!"

He tossed the cup in the fire, where it melted to a sizzle.

"Damn you!" an angry Raven retorted. "I claim the Zia Stone!"

"I claim my daughters!" Sonny countered.

"Your obsession!"

"Yes!"

"You've been misled!" Raven cried. "Look!"

He unfurled his cloak and the two girls appeared in the light of the dancing flames, glorious in their Communion white and as lovely as the first roses of spring. Smiling, they threw their flower bouquets at Sonny's feet.

Sonny picked up the flowers and smelled their sweetness, aroma therapy that broke his heart. He reached out to touch the smiling girls, daughters of his and Rita's dream.

"Don't you know by now? They're illusions!" Raven chortled.

Sonny hesitated. Ah, yes, he knew the truth. But why do men who know the truth refuse to acknowledge it? Be virtuous and truthful, his parents had told him, and you will be a good man. But even good men deny the truth when their need is great.

"Mine," Sonny whispered, tears in his eyes, not from the smoke that rose from the dying embers of the cottonwood logs, but from a deep emotion he felt. He could not take his gaze from the terrible lightness of beauty, the auras of the daughters he had dreamed into existence.

"Yes!" Raven cried. "They are yours! You gave them life in your dream. They are images created by your obsession! The blood that flowed from your woman's womb was their flesh, blood aborted. But you retained the image of your daughters—Wait. Let's speak frankly. You *created* the images. You dreamt these two angels into existence."

There it was, the truth! A man creates, in flesh or dream, what he needs to struggle through life.

"You took them from me!" Sonny cried, an anguished cry.

"Sonny, Sonny, Sonny. You know so little of the workings of the soul. If it weren't for *your* desire to have daughters by your side, I wouldn't have them. You see, the innocent images in the soul may be plundered by the psyche's ancient powers."

Was Raven angry? Deceiving? No, he was speaking the truth. As everyone knows, obsession and desire create the image, the object of need, and once created the image is subject to the will of both the angels and the demons of the psyche. The soul can lift itself to the highest empyrean and commune with the gods, or it can create the despair of hell.

"You can have them back!" Raven said, and pushed the two innocent forms forward. "You can have the images of your two sweet daughters. . . . But that's all you can have, the images. Not the flesh."

Sonny reached for the spirits that once had inhabited the womb of his beloved. He understood now that he could take the two spirits with him, for the soul was a constellation of images. The mind could hold memories of experiences and ideas, the workings of the brain, but it was the psyche that held the images of mankind's history, or one man's loss.

"Yes," Raven said. "Every man is haunted by his dreams. Some hear the voices of ghosts and commit murder in their name, some write great symphonies. The psychotic and schizophrenic run in the streets of our cities, shouting the names of the images that haunt and speak to them. You cannot erase the image. It is with you always."

The old man had warned him, as Raven warned him, that his obsession was unnatural, an illusion of his psyche's pain, but it was unnatural only because he desired the blood of the daughters growing again in Rita's womb, yearned to be part of the evolution of their flesh. This was his god-awful sin, his obsession to bring them back from the dead, back from a land whose landscape was the uncharted geography of his own soul.

Perhaps he needed to come to this point, to learn for himself what for others was common sense: you can't bring back the departed. They have their own journey to continue, their own stories to tell in other dimensions, but insofar as the dreamer keeps the image of the dead, then those he loved in ordinary time may still keep him company. Yes, Sonny could keep the images of his daughters with him forever.

"Oh, God," he moaned and fell to his knees. The painful revelation spilled out in bitter tears, the tears a man sheds when he realizes he has deluded himself.

Exactly where Raven wanted him, groveling in pain on the wet earth of the river. The evolution of two brothers, as it were, come to speak to each other as eternal reflections of one soul, all this under the looming presence of the Barelas Bridge.

Raven raised his sword over Sonny's head. The soul of Sonny Baca would soon wash away in the muddy current, beginning a completely new chapter, for souls are like books that can be read over and over through the centuries until they crumble into the dust of their own nirvana.

The beak-like sword shimmered with life, reflecting history, analogous to the curved blade that once cut the Gordian knot, the dagger Abraham held over his son, the sword King Arthur withdrew from the stone, the switchblade of the old pachucos. Now the awful instrument that could cut the ribbon of a man's fate was Raven's beak, sharp and polished to a sheen, like the tongue of a snake, two-edged.

It was all Sonny could do to raise his arm and ward off the blow, and as he did he reached out and tore the Zia medallion from Raven's neck.

The eerie sound of a bullroarer rumbled across the turbulent waters of the river, like the buzz of a million bees instinctively wrapping themselves around their queen as she flew into the blue sky to receive that one, fertilizing seed.

"Damn you!" Raven cursed.

Some of his power was diminished now that Sonny held the Zia medal, but in reaching out for the medallion Sonny had fallen flat on his face, and as he looked up he saw a death mask, a revenge of ages that Raven could end with the raised scimitar.

The deafening bellow of the bullroarer became a crashing of trees as Bear, crying like a wounded animal, plowed through the brush like an ancient spirit, scattering the coals of the dying fire. The cry for the woman he had loved ripping from his throat, he charged at Raven, and the force of the attack sent them both tumbling into the river.

Raven cried out, a curse, an explosion of breath as he went flying through the air into the water, the sharp sword still in his hand, his last glance plaintively cast at Sonny, whom, in one more split second, he would have beheaded.

The splash of the two bodies hitting the water was like the closing of a tomb, a heavy stone door slamming shut, encasing the mummies inside in eternal rest, not in a sarcophagus in a dry, desert tomb, but in the waters of the holy river.

Sonny jumped up and rushed to the spot where the two had disappeared. Wading into the dark water he reached out, hoping to hook the two floundering men, who bobbed up and down in the swift current, disappearing then rising to the surface until the watery fingers of the icy stream sucked them under and they were seen no more.

Gasping for breath, clutching at tree roots, Sonny pulled himself back onto the bank, wet and muddied, shivering from the cold, which now was near freezing. He had not wanted it to end this way, but Bear would not be denied his revenge. He loved Naomi, and knowing only revenge could cure his broken heart he took the law into his own hands. He drowned Raven in the river, washed all his sins away, as any river can do, call it the Rio Grande, the Ganges, the Nile, the Yangtze. A river by any name is an instrument of God. It's all the same: from water we come and to water we return. The cleansing was done, the shadow god baptized again, for the moment, for it is not the night that casts shadows, but the light of the sun, and at the end of the spring-equinox night the sun was destined to rise again.

"Yeah," Sonny said to himself, his voice that of a man cutting through the sound of lapping water. The river was not the arm of an angry god, but a presence accustomed to carrying away the souls of the departed. There was no boat with ready helmsman nearby, no skiff of Charon nor bark of Isis, for this was the land where sailing with the tide meant the tides of the heart. The sloshing of water was the moving blood of a land loved dearly by the old paisanos, the cry of the wind its soul.

Raven baptized again. He would return.

But from where? The current was swift, the night dark, submerged brambles and branches of rotting trees reached out, old steel jetties with barbed-wire fingers lay ahead, hungry fish would nibble at flesh, and in the end the bodies would not be found. But where was the spirit, Sonny's shadow? Was he gone forever, or for a moment? And how does a man lose his shadow?

Those involved in the story know that as Sonny was baptized in the blood of the sow, Raven would be renewed in Rio Grande water. Water is blood, say the old farmers; nothing disappears but makes it way back in the cycle of life and death. There is no death, triumphant prophets far wiser than any of the characters in the story have said. Go out and make up your own mind whether the world is real or illusion, whether men are good or troubled, whether or not the soul can be broken down. Even broken souls return home. This much the old prophets knew.

It was time to go home. Sonny peered into the dark waters one last time, then he turned and sloshed out of the mud up to the sandy bank where he picked up a shivering Chica.

The burning logs sputtered, dying down to red embers as he made his way back through the brush to the Center and his truck.

Over the Barelas Bridge moved a slow trickle of traffic, the lights of cars, honest-to-goodness live people going into town or going home, as a normal evening returned to the city.

In the dark Raven's crows shook their feathers and fell into a troubled sleep. Coyotes cried. No need to return and bury the sow, Sonny thought, the coyotes would feast tonight. Nothing is lost. Even the bones would eventually compost, food for trees and grass.

Nothing ever ends, does it?

You got that right, the old man said, putting his arm around his young friend and walking with him in the dark.

25 »

SONNY WAS SHIVERING BY THE TIME he got to his truck. The Center was closed, the dozens of cars and television crews gone. Traffic flowed on Cesar Chavez Boulevard and on Fourth Street, coming from or going to the South Valley. If an alien from the sea, the progeny of the ancient Atlantians, happened to be observing the City Future, it would report a quiet, normal spring night. The frenzy of the bomb threat had settled into the slower pace Alburquerqueans loved so well.

Every TV set in the city and the state would be tuned to the news of the governor's death, and as they ate their suppers the New Mexicans would wonder what it meant. Enough theories would erupt to feed la plática and mitote for months to come.

Sonny wrapped Chica in the seat cover, an old serape from Juárez. He started the truck, and turned on the heater. Chica opened her eyes, looked up at her master, and licked his hand.

"Let's go home. I know Rita has a chicken taco waiting for you. How's that?"

That's fine with me, she wagged her tail, and laid her head on the seat in contentment. The induced Raven-dream had tired her. She had seen things never imagined, foreign places and animals, screams of pain, a primeval dream time where survival was the order of the night, Raven's shadow following her every step, goading her to reveal Sonny's weakness, his tragic flaw. But she refused to give in to his desire and in a fit, quite unknown for peaceful dachshunds, she snarled and cried, "He is a good and virtuous man. Get thee behind me, Raven!"

Raven had hit her with a stick for that. He did not like being associated with anything that smacked of the devil. He did his best to keep away from that Middle Ages stuff, the witch trials of Salem spoofery, Inquisition tortures, and old religious doctrines that denied belief in the possibility of metempsychosis.

The newest psychoanalytic theories hardly covered Raven's thick shadow. He had read the true alchemical formulas, which he understood were all about transforming the soul, not gross metal. For Raven, transformation meant turning light into darkness. This was Raven's New Age goal, as it had been from the beginning of human time.

A while longer in Raven's nightmare would have done Chica in, she would have completely entered the world of dream, but her master appeared in time and saved her from that final step into Raven's whirlpool from which there is scarce return. Now it was home to a chicken taco spiced with just a dab of Rita's salsa.

What about me? the old man asked.

You hungry?

It's been a long day.

Yeah. So, where do we go from here?

We? Reminds me of a Lone Ranger and Tonto joke. When surrounded by enemies Tonto says, What do you mean *we,* paleface?

Skip the joke; are you going to stick around?

I don't know.

Shivering and with a note of sadness, Sonny said, You mean you don't know how much longer you'll be here.

I'll be around as long as you're around. The old man chuckled.

Sonny smiled. He felt drained emotionally. After all, he had just acknowledged that his daughters were figments of his need. Could they exist without him, or were they on their own journey? Were they young souls destined for a place in heaven, like Limbo, but much more beautiful, where they could play with other like souls, enjoying the contemplation of a Universal Spirit and the music of the spheres, the same harmonic vibrations that force-field physicists pondered and admired? Did they not deserve celestial bliss?

Sonny had to give them up. Well, not exactly, because he could still dream about them, that is, image them in his mind and run with them in those blissful gardens where the grass was always green and the flowers always in bloom, where the lion frolicked with the lamb. And he could dream of doing all the things a father would do for his daughters, raising them to be fine young women. All of this was still available to him, if not in the flesh.

In prior times, before her miscarriage, Rita had talked about the life growing in her womb. They sat in her garden where the perfume of earth and flowers was as close to heaven as a man can get. They drank Rita's blend of herbal tea and watched the sun set in the west. The desert breeze whispered of possibilities. On such an afternoon he would tell her what he had seen.

Don't forget the dead, the elders said. Ancestor worship? Call it what you want, it's part of our heritage. Say masses, light candles, erect shrines by the side of the road, descansos to be visited because the soul was eternal and oftentimes restless, as everyone who had ever lived in the culture or read its cuentos knew. Some scoffed at this. Bah! Prayers for the dead! That's for the Chinese, the Koreans, the old Aztecs and Mayas. But get a life, this was the twenty-first century, the Digital Age. Ghosts? Spirits? Wasn't that for Hollywood? After all, this was the age of quantum psychology. Forget Freud!

No, replied the old Hispanos in the wisdom of their mestizo heritage. They're here. We can feel them. Leave a glass of water under your bed at night, for the dead feel thirst. This way they don't wake you up. Pray for them, they are on a journey. And just who do you think the santos are? The saints are our old people who have died. Our ancestors! We pray to them to help us. Santa mamá. Santo papá. Santo Abuelito. Santa Abuelita. Santo Tío, Santa Tía. Those you loved and who loved you in life became santos. So there! Period!

Yes, we let them go, and yet they remain. What is memory but the psyche's library where everything is stored? Sometimes it's like a tomb for quiet, contemplative times. Sometimes it's like a wild party. A fiesta! Let's drink and dance as they loved to drink and dance! We remember! We remember! As long as we remember, they live. So don't act like you know it all, Mr. Smarty Pants!

That's the way it is, Sonny thought. The tenses of time blended into each other, not only in the dream time, but also in that time known as ordinary time. The creative mind was always at work, blending its thoughts into the soul's growth. That's why so many people were attracted to the land of the Pueblos, because here the geography was still sacred, and one could watch the clouds on summer days and let time dissolve into its purer essence. The earth and sky were the true alchemists. So always remember to watch the clouds.

The old man saying that he would be around as long as Sonny was around was the promise of a real friend, compromiso de fé, and such a commitment elevated Sonny and made him feel he had bonded with don Eliseo during his stay on earth, made him understand a loving relationship is the miracle of life. The bell tolled for the departed as well as for those left on this side, as the poet said, and it rang at odd times when the heart swayed and trembled and remembered those now gone.

The old man's promise reminded him of his responsibility to all of life, flesh or spirit, for if a friend so loved his companion that even after death he would be there to lend a hand, one had to live a good life.

Go home to Rita, the old man said. Get rid of those pesky suitors who are hanging around the cafe. They're making goo-goo eyes at Rita like lovesick calves. Philanderers! Don't worry about me, I'm going to hang around for a while. There are a lot of interesting spirits in this city, like the old timers we met on Central. On

Saturday afternoons when they promenade downtown I'll join them. Think of it, mihito, me sauntering down Central Avenue with Clyde Tingley and Ernie Pyle. Cool, huh?

Sonny laughed. "Yeah, cool."

He drove north on Fourth Street, funky Fourth, an avenue he loved, into the heart of downtown where the revelry of the afternoon had died down. Those workers who had partied hard had been called on their cell phones to get home to supper, the kids' homework, family affairs, late payment of the rent or alimony, plugged toilets, all the diurnal necessities of the cotidal day.

Now, those walking the gaily lighted streets were mostly yuppies who came downtown to enjoy the Spring Arts Crawl evening. They went from gallery to gallery, exclaiming, "yes," and "ah" and "well done." They strolled hand in hand in the friendly evening air and entered to taste the offered wine, small chalices they quaffed as they spoke of Michelangelo. These art lovers were joined by university students who were feeling the pressure of the semester winding down and exams coming, and so, many a kantharos of beer was quaffed in the hoot and hollering night.

And always, the homeless roaming the streets, like the silvery minnows of the river with no still waters in which to rest. There were shelters and food at the Baptist church on Broadway and at Joy Junction, and various other places, but a spring restlessness drove them through the streets, lonely and often desperate fish in the stream of life.

And even they could say at end of day, all's well that ends well.

Sonny drove around downtown then back onto Fourth, past the new modern courthouses. Visions for the new Alburquerque took the form of steel and concrete, and the movers and shakers of the city smiled. The City Future was on a sailor's holiday, heady with growth, building, singing, playing politics, hustling for money, all the necessary trappings needed to define itself in the new century. Four flags had flown over the city in the past: Spanish, Mexican, American, Confederate. The fifth yet to be designed would emblazon the logo, City Future, in a glorious, rising sun. Five flags over Burque.

A sense of relief washed over Sonny as he drove up the familiar street. The day was done. The coming night was a welcome relief. His stomach growled for a hot plate of enchiladas, refried beans, and rice, all covered with Rita's red chile, and piping-hot, puffy sopaipillas that melted in his mouth, and perhaps a beer with dinner.

But here's the tricky part. An adventurer about to touch on the shore he left long ago at once welcomes the sight of the port where loved ones wait, and at the same time wonders if the future yet holds another journey, images of tantalizing places he has not seen.

So Sonny wondered. He had gone into the four seasons in search of Raven, explored the four quadrants, entered the fourth dimension and learned that in other universes there might yet be eleven or twelve more dimensions to explore, depending on who did the defining. But for now, four was the parameter, the cosmology that maps a man's life, his heart, his humors, his family, his neighborhood, the city, the country, the universe.

If the four quadrants are laid to rest on a flat plane then the Tree of Life, that same tree where Adam and Eve met the charmed snake and began their adventures, rests right at the center. But a flat geography does not satisfy the adventurer. Curve the flat surface and the picture becomes clearer. There is always someone coming from or going to ill-fated Ilium. America becoming Latino. Chinese. Korean. America becoming Woman.

When will is not enough, destiny pushes the adventurers forward to describe their needs and geography. And in every man and woman there is a call to approach the tree and test the branches that stretch into the heart of heaven, the zenith, and, if need be, to explore its roots into the pit of the underworld, nadir of the soul.

Perhaps Sonny yet had to climb the tree, unify the four directions with the fifth, the up and down, climbing upward into the branches where, as if climbing a family tree, he would meet the damnedest ancestors and the role they once played in his coming into being. And he would descend into the roots, the four main tap roots, each with its tentacles digging into the dark earth, the blood of his body that nourished him. Like Dante descending into inferno, he might search the bowels of soul for meaning, and likewise, also meet there the *damnedest ancestors.*

That's what the whole chingadera was about, as far as Sonny could make out. Make unity of light and shadow, unity of self.

Perhaps there was another season. A fifth season, the call to understand the Tree of Life, the middle, unifying ground. Everyone should know by now that the tree is anchored in the soul. To climb or descend is to explore the psyche, one's inner self, the essence that in daily life most hardly notice, until life presents an overwhelming trauma. Then the injured pilgrim must ask, Who am I? Is this my soul that speaks to me? Why had I not seen this tree before? Why have I not run up and down its fatherly trunk, like a child, exploring the secrets and knowledge it holds of my true self? If this tree planted in my heart is fed by my blood, why am I a stranger to it?

Ah, so many questions left unanswered in one day's story. Many would be disappointed, perhaps want their money back, for a private investigator was supposed to solve hard-core crimes, answer all the questions, not indulge in speculation of life's journey. Such questions are for philosophers, or the idle, or the *inocentes* of the world. Had one day in the life of a PI been twisted too far? Was this for simpler minds, therefore, unacceptable? Who, out in that wide flat world that stretched only as far as his front yard, would be satisfied?

Sonny thought. Yes, the fifth season might prove even more phantasmagorical than today's adventure. Best leave it at that. Best do our daily work in the here and now, but work consciously, praising the Light that arrives each morning with the rising of the sun, praise the saints and kachinas, praise the Lords and Ladies of the Light. Bless all of life.

Ah, he moaned, what a day, and only Rita's arms would make right the day's adventure.

He was tired. It had been a long journey homeward. Not even the glitter of the street aroused him. He only thought of Rita. Perhaps this was his last great adventure, as he had promised the last time.

Maybe when the cops or whoever was in trouble with Raven called the next time he would say no, and mean it. He would stay home, helping Rita, the small cafe would become their bonding place, a place where they could work together, build a life together. And later there would be children, their own or adopted, lots of kids to run around the cafe and grow strong on New Mexican food: frijoles, maize, calabacitas, menudo, carne adovada, tortillas, sopa, natillas, huevos rancheros, tofu and plenty of greens if some became vegetarians.

They would name the cabroncitos after the food they ate. Girls would be Maize and Natillas, boys would be Menudo and Carnitas. The strong boy would be Tortillon, the gay child Sopaipilla.

Happiness is what mattered.

A man cannot help but dream, he thought as he pulled into the parking lot of Rita's Cocina. Usually he parked in the back, but tonight he had to enter through the front door to face the homeboys, the suitors, don Eliseo called them, who had hung around too long. They would feel his fury, smell the blood of the sow on his colorful jacket, smell the muddy river ooze on his boots.

What weapon to use? The battered and torn dreamcatcher, of course. He picked it up. Yes, better than bow and arrows, he could whip a hundred with the magic in the dreamcatcher. Make every mother's son regret he thought Sonny was dead and Rita was ripe for the picking.

He gathered Chica in his arms and walked to the door. The place was rowdy, loud and noisy with the braggarts as they munched on Rita's pastelitos de manzana and washed them down with coffee. They were tired of waiting because it was past six o'clock and, even if the governor was dead, the bomb hadn't blown and the cell phones were working. But still no trace of Sonny Baca.

These were young men Sonny knew. Electricians, plumbers, roofers, guys who worked for the city or the telephone company, a teacher who taught at Taft, a lawyer, and two off-duty cops, all refusing to go home until Rita admitted Sonny wasn't coming, closed up the cafe, and said, *yes, one of you can drive me home.*

Movida time, the Chicanos called such an opportunity. If you're young and horny and Rita's man is not coming home, then you don't waste time. Put the pressure on. Make her say yes. She can't go on stalling them with her sweet apple pies and her blend of coffee that stimulates the blood.

Are you coming with me? he asked the old man.

No, the old man replied. You have new companions. He nodded toward the two spirits who stood by Sonny.

We'll be at your side, father, the girls said in sweet unison, their auras lighting the way.

He looked at his spirit daughters. They stood before him as beautiful and innocent as the bloom on a rose, so harmless they couldn't hurt a fly, but walking at his side they were the courage he needed, uplifting his soul as only a child can do. He felt like crying. Would it never end, this gift life had given him? Was every man so lucky to feel the presence of love at his side, guardian angels protecting every step?

Well, the old Greeks had Athena or Artemis, Zeus and the sea god Poseidon, or other gods to help in time of need. Other people had Thor. Desert people had prophets full of words they took from the mouth of God. The Aztecs had the Winged Serpent, El Señor Quetzalcoatl, he who brought wisdom, and dozens of lesser gods. Dream Time spirits. Kachinas. Catholics had their saints. On and on it went. All the traditional people from every corner of the world had their guardian spirits.

Was this so new? No. Perhaps the uncertainty came because the present age of disbelief had killed the spirit. Science had erased the angels from the monitor screens, forgotten that transformation of the spirit is as important as conquering the physical laws.

Sonny straightened his shoulders. Come then, he said, let us go and make our visit.

He opened the door of the cafe, and all inside turned to look at him.

26 »

"SONNY?" THE ONE CLOSEST TO THE DOOR gasped, looking up as if he'd seen a ghost, questioning in his mind the appearance of the weary hero, eyeing the dreamcatcher that Sonny held like the jawbone of an ass. Was he going to smite the suitors?

The boisterous group were no Chaldeans, no soothsayers whose language the world has forgotten. These were the common laborers of the city who turned to look at the battered and bruised Sonny Baca, the ghost of an ancient mariner risen from the cosmic sea, a man who had washed his sins in the Ganges, trailing seaweed and algae he had returned, one eye nearly closed from a blow received at war, a Greek hero returning home from Troy, if Jemez Springs can be conceived as Troy, and Burque as his Ithaca, and if the world would allow a Chicano to be as heroic as those who fought on the fields of Ilium.

The old men of the northern New Mexico pueblos would say Yes! Seguro que sí! Goddamnit que sí! Porque no? Because in their youth their grandfathers had been at the battle of Embudo, fighting Kearney's Army of the West, and some had been at the deposing of Governor Bent in Taos. Deposing? Well, those first Chicano heroes along with some Taos Pueblo natives did Bent in. Later, their grandchildren had been with Tijerina fighting to keep their land grants, and so went the forgotten battles for survival and for love.

Love? Yes, for as young men these viejitos of el norte had scoured the mountains and the valleys, from Gallina to Tierra Amarilla to San Ysidro to Cabezon and Bernalillo, down to Belen and Socorro, after a hard week's work they rode their horses or drove their old model-T's to the country dances in the most out-of-the-way villages where they courted young women as beautiful as Helen, but more virtuous, brown-eyed Mejicanitas and Inditas who lived in those mountains and whose mestizo heritage engendered them with a beauty born of the earth and sky. Ah, las Inditas de los Pueblos, the way they danced and lifted their skirts to show their ankles made a young man's mouth water. Chicanitas as succulent as a bowl of warm chicharrones.

That's why New Mexican kids came in all colors, some with red hair and blue eyes, some morenitos and dark as the earth, because at this crossroads, at the heart of the quincunx, the bloods had mixed, creating a larger-than-life familia, nature's way of fulfilling her secret destiny.

Yes, Sonny, those elders would say. Goddamnit que sí! You're as good as those who fought at ill-fated Troy. Puro Chicano, you gave it your best shot. Y mañana is another day. And you've got your Rita of the dancing eyes, deep brown eyes whose irises radiate the sacred light of the Zia Sun. It may be you will find the Zia Stone, then again time may scar and humble you and even unto your death you will still be searching. But you gotta keep fighting those cabrones who deny the message of the Sun Stone! You gotta believe the earth is worth saving!

Surprise was too mild a word for the strange looks that crossed the faces of the suitors who all day had argued with each other as to who would drive Rita home. Frowns mixed with gazes of gratitude, scowls because they knew Rita would have no other man at her side, smiles because he was alive, and after all, he was a friend they had known for many years.

Rita turned to look at her Chicano Ulysses home from the war. He sure looked banged up, dressed in his colorful jacket but splattered and reeking of the strange and regenerative blood of the pig, and his boots and pants were caked with mud that smelled of the ooze of the river. He stoutly held the dreamcatcher at his side, the one don Eliseo and the old men of Sandia Pueblo had made for him.

She stood immobile behind the counter, as beautiful after a long day's work as she had been in the morning when he last kissed her and whispered he'd be back. She felt a tremor, her heart suddenly romping to a new beat, a frozen cry in her throat.

Sonny! Gracias a Dios, you're home. Virgen de Guadalupe, gracias. San Judas, gracias.

Perhaps beautiful was too cheap a word to describe her, for those who have felt love deep in their souls know the beloved is like a prism that reflects the soul of the lover, a beacon in the dark that guides home the most weary seaman.

If, as the poet says, the eyes are windows of the soul then the bond between the lover and the beloved is a golden cord that cannot be cut; not even the third fate's final scissor snip can separate the two.

Even those blinded by life, those whose sight has been clouded over by the gods so they may experience with their other senses a deeper essence of life, feel this cord of light, and their love is expressed in touch.

Don Eliseo said: If you shrink from human touch, then you are the lost one. Go forth and touch those you love, a smile, a friendly wave, cómo estás, órale, good to see you, a handshake, a high five, a squeeze, a bear hug, un abrazo.

The caress of the soul is as profound as the orgasm of the flesh.

"Sonny!" Rita cried. I knew, of course I knew.

She started forward, but his look told her to pause and await the outcome of the homecoming.

Chica didn't wait, she jumped from Sonny's arms and dashed to Rita, a bullet whizzing across the floor that Rita caught and held close, feeling in her throbbing heart the dread she and Sonny had been through.

For a long time it seemed as if nobody spoke, then the guy nearest Sonny stood and faced him. The carpenter with his carpenter's belt strapped so it hung low on his waist, like the gun belt Shane strapped on in the movie when he finally had to take up the pistol and face the bad guys.

Okay, he thought, let's get this over with.

He walked up to Sonny and stared him in the eyes, every move guarded, as if measuring his next move.

Then he smiled, and said, "Hey, Sonny, you're back. Good to see you, bro."

Hesitantly he stepped forward and jabbed Sonny on the shoulder. "Hey, you did good, ese. It's in the news. Everything's back to normal."

These were the men of normalcy, and they knew in their hearts, they were no match for Sonny.

The carpenter looked at the dreamcatcher, then back at the other men lined up along the counter and those at the tables.

"Hey, I gotta hit the road. Work tomorrow," he said, threw some bills on the counter to pay his fare, then with head bowed he walked past Sonny and out the door.

"Let's hear it for Sonny," a second man said, a young buck at twenty-five, but tough from construction work, who was always daring Sonny to arm wrestle, trying to beat him in front of Rita and the other vatos, but to date he hadn't.

All clapped and cheered, then one by one they tossed bills on the tables to pay for the pies and coffee, and they began to file out, carrying the tools of their respective professions, each one acknowledging Sonny's presence.

The schoolteacher coughed and made an excuse. "I have to get up early. Kids to teach, gotta grade papers, you know. They might cancel classes because of the governor. Who knows?"

"Governor or no governor, tomorrow's another day," the electrician said. "Gotta wire that new parking lot the city's building. Good night, Rita," he called, secretly cursing his luck, as they all did.

"I gotta help my primo with his roof," the roofer said.

One by one they went out.

"Órale. Ay te wacho."

"Take care, bro. Good to see you. You're the man!"

"Hey, Rita, your lover man's back," one joked, and laughed.

"Did Chica have any dreams today?" another asked. Subdued laughter again.

"How'djuget the black eye? Looks bad."

"Yeah, take care of it."

"He's got his curandera," one answered, glancing back at Rita, sighing, and walking out.

"Better fix that dreamcatcher, or you won't catch any dreams," one said, trying to be cute, touching the tattered totem as a defrocked priest might touch one last time the chalice on the altar.

Sonny acknowledged all with a nod, as a triumphant warrior might look at those beaten in battle, equals in the fray but diminished in the loss.

Perhaps it was the thin smile on Sonny's lips that disconcerted them, for the cars pulling out of the parking lot squealed and burned rubber as the aspirants of the day headed home to one more night of bachelorhood, sadly aware that Rita would rest in Sonny's arms.

Sonny's gaze had never left Rita. Let his friends leave, yes, tomorrow was another day and they'd be back for breakfast, Rita's huevos rancheros, red chile con carne, huevos con chorizo, and homemade tortillas were to die for, manna from heaven, hearty meals to satisfy a man during the long day's work, and her image was one to take away in the heart and compare to other women the lonely bachelors might meet during the day.

"God, Sonny, you're the luckiest guy in the world," the last to exit whispered, glancing furtively at Rita, then ducking out.

A peaceful silence settled into the café; the only sound was the refrigerator's hum, the same mysterious hummmm that had bugged the people of Taos many summers past.

Rita placed Chica on the floor and ran across the room to be gathered in Sonny's arms and held close, both feeling relief from the troubled day, feeling the separation had been too long, longer than the cotidal day, which speeding around the sun had turned into spring. The first day of spring.

"Sonny, Sonny, I'm so glad. . . . Lorenza told me what happened."

She touched the bruise above his eye. "Raven?"

He nodded.

"I'll take care of it," she whispered, and touched her honeyed lips to his, tasting him tenderly, as if for the first time, acknowledging the enormous need they had for each other, an embrace that only the poets of India can describe adequately, for the kiss opened a door into each other's flesh and spirit, and why shouldn't the flesh be rewarded after such a long absence from the lover? Why shouldn't every cell burst forth with all the hormones the body can muster, adding adrenaline for spice, surging in the blood and pounding heart, tingling the nerves, renewing marrow?

Fundamentalists beware! The flesh will outlast you! The cells contain circuits of memory eons long, fibers enclosed in blood as ancient as the earliest stories from India or Mesopotamia, each cell sloshing with the salty water of a cosmic sea in which primordial images float.

He felt Rita's body tremble as she held him tight, the first movement of an orgasm that would evolve into a rainbow of joy, tremors that would last long into the night, blooming colors from the prism of love, a bridge from this world to the next, an arc on which one walked into paradise, the reward of the flesh to the tired soul.

Complete and fulfilling fruition, in whispered moans asking after the first orgasm to be fulfilled again, such is the way of lovers.

The spring sun would blossom into summer, and why stop at one season when the lover and beloved are meant to bond for life? They would nurture each other in the heat of the New Mexico summer, drive together in autumn to Jemez to pick the apples that have grown a delicious yellow and red, wander through the brilliant gold of river cottonwoods and hike up into the aspen groves that dot the green mountainside, then ease into winter's quiet pleasures with fat logs burning in the stove and the first snow of November blanketing the Jemez River Canyon. Those are nights when life stirred again in the womb to awaken in a coming season, such is the way of the birth cycles.

After all, the rhythms of the seasons are the rhythms of love.

"Shakti," he whispered.

"I'm Rita," she said, smiling.

"Shakti means 'my beloved.' I found it in the dictionary."

"You and your books. Think you'll go back to teaching?"

"Maybe. In the meantime—"

"Stay with me."

"Yes."

"Say it again."

"Mi amor. My shakti."

"I love you Sonny Baca."

"I love you Rita de mi corazon."

"Oh—"

"Que?"

"A letter came. You forgot to renew your PI license. They cancelled you today."

"So all day I haven't been a PI?"

"Not according to their rules."

"And I'm not a tragic hero. I'm just me, Sonny Baca. I know the face in the mirror."

His mirror was the shining lapis stone hung on a chain around her neck, the philosopher's stone, perhaps the very Zia Stone he had sought in vain. Could it be the sought-after, transforming Zia Stone?

"You're not tragic at all," she whispered, "but you are my hero."

Sonny nodded then laughed, a hearty laugh that only a man who truly enjoys arriving home can laugh, a man who truly loves the breadth and width of his beloved, whatever the size, whatever the radiance of her, enjoying every aroma that emanates from her body. Rita laughed with him.

I'm sure I'll have my critics, he thought, holding her and looking into her eyes, his blood boiling with a joy that couldn't be bottled. This is just too good to be true, they'll say. Too sweet, too romantic at heart. If they only knew his beating heart resonated to hers. But who cares! Lead on McDuff!

"Ready to go home?"

"Hummm, am I ready," she murmured in his ear, the song of a honey bee echoing in the flower's open petals, the sweet nectar flowing, pollen and wetness on her lips, the probing proboscis, the need to get home to a bed they both knew well, where the mattress sinks and rises to contours of love and the feel of feather pillows eases the tired head to sleep. The luxury of clean sheets waiting to caress the returning warrior.

"It doesn't get any better," Sonny whispered.

"It will," she said.

"Vamos."

"Wait." She picked up a menu and with a lipstick from her apron pocket she penciled in dark red erotic letters: CLOSED FOR THE DAY.

"You're going to close tomorrow," he said. Rita's Cocina was only closed for Christmas, New Years, and Easter. She served comida de cuaresma on Good Friday.

"I'm going to be busy," she answered, her smile tempting enough to launch a thousand ships.

"Órale!" he exclaimed.

She placed the sign on the window and with Chica under her arm they hurried out to Sonny's truck.

She held his hand as they drove, feeling the electric current that flowed from her to him. She looked out the window at a moon that dripped honey, miel virgin, the stuff bees suck from the flower's yoni as they gather the pollen that sticks to their probing, wet tongues, a gooey mixture that needs no cloning, no in-vitro pollinating, just nature working as she always has with her alchemical transformations, making from the sex of the flower the fruit of the table.

In the warmth of the truck she looked at him and squeezed his hand.

"It's a beautiful night," she said. "You're home."

She turned the flame burning in her to low, so as not to rush, enjoying the heat of her sex as they drove into the night. She could wait, because she knew she had to cleanse his bruised eye and feed him. When his ablutions were done they would slowly undress, let fall the grape leaves of Eden, for this is how they allowed their love to grow, unhurried, mature in each others' ways, caressing each other as doors of light opened unto a holy path, illuminations of a lost heaven where once Adam and Eve cavorted.

Their loving would last long into the cotidal night, bringing in spring the way the ancient Druid priests must have celebrated, with orgiastic, dome-shaped pleasures in the light of the moon. Here, the granite face of Sandia Mountain looked down and blessed the lovers, as the giant monoliths of Stonehenge blessed the ritual dances of the Druids long ago, a celebration of love lasting all night and into the new day.

Under the pale moon the trees of the valley glowed blue.

"En el tiempo del hilo azul," he said, remembering his grandmother used to put añil, bluing, in the rinse water to make his abuelo's shirts shine.

"Yes," she replied, for the evening had turned a pale indigo.

A frosty hue clung to bare branches and their buds, but the warmth of spring would soon flood into the valley. It would not freeze, and tomorrow a summer-like day would draw everyone outdoors.

Rita rested her head on Sonny's shoulder.

"Today I wrote in my journal, everything has a character of its own. Every single living organism, and rocks and things we think are not alive, each develops a character and a destiny unlike any other. Up in the Jemez there are a million pine trees, and each one unique.

I could plant a hundred marigolds in my garden, and each plant and leaf and petal would develop its own character."

It was always like this, in the evenings she shared what revelations the day had brought, insights into the worlds of her mind, a true sybil. He loved that about her, her insights into nature, love, the mystery of life.

Her flesh satisfied him beyond any celestial promise the priests might offer, beyond any dream he might enter in his shaman robes, beyond the words the prophets might take from God's mouth, but just as important as satisfying his flesh were the words she spoke of life and its fantastic offerings.

This woman who fed the hungry throngs by day took from its hours a spiritual message, its noumenon, its soul, for every day came with its own character, as she said, there wasn't a single fish, fowl or vegetable, add rocks, planets, suns, and whirling galaxies that did not evolve their own unique character. Knowing the daimon of each thing was God's reward to those who listened and peered into the unfolding of the universe, realm of Light.

But here's the catch, the real mystery. Though each thing sang its uniqueness, beneath the web everything vibrated to harmonic strings pulsing with the same universal energy. There was a sameness in everything.

For her wisdom, he loved her and listened to her wise counsel. This true Sofia.

And she spoke of the everyday. "Diego and I had to get under the sink and unplug the drain. The plumber got drunk when his cell phone went out. I dropped my car off at Leyba's Garage to have the oil changed. Ordered enough food for the week, including extra tortillas. Talked to the accountant and paid my taxes. Called city hall, before it closed, and settled the water account. Water is getting expensive. We need a mayor who can do something about the price of water. Talked to your mom, kept assuring her all day things were all right. Bought lingerie at that little shop Teresa opened recently, a really sexy, silky—well, you'll see, I promise."

"You did all this today and still fed those cabrones hanging around the cafe," Sonny said. Her energy constantly surprised him.

"You did the really dangerous stuff, amor. Suppressing Raven."

Sonny marveled at her words. Suppressing Raven was correct. The sonofabitch wouldn't be gone for long. Bear would hold tight and drown Raven, his revenge for Naomi's death, and the two would dissolve into a soggy mess in the river's pools, sodden bones mixing into the mud, but eventually the river would give up their spirits, as it had since the waters first flowed from Eden's rivers.

"The late news said there was no radioactive core in the bomb he planted on the Jemez. He was playing games with the Los Alamos scientists."

Sonny nodded. Raven still held a trump, a plutonium pit, and he wasn't going to give it up that easily. What he had put in the bomb was radioactive waste material, enough to set off the sensors, enough to make the lab boys think there was something hot in the belly of the beast. Fake wires and timers, enough junk to give him time to get to the river where he waited for Sonny.

He told her what happened at the river.

"Why the river?" she asked.

"Water. Dissolution. Water melts everything away, sooner or later. He thought if he could control the water he could control me. Raven's message repeats itself. Men want control. Over oil, gold, governments, corporations, land, water—"

"Women."

"Yes, women. Those who control enslave."

"I'm glad you're a feminist man," she said, and Sonny blushed. Well, he was trying, but what would the guys at Sal's Bar say? Lordy, Lordy, machismo dies hard.

They arrived home and Rita carried Chica while Sonny took the turtle from the back of the truck.

"A gift."

"Oh, a tortuguita. We'll feed it lettuce."

"Raven said I was obsessed," he blurted.

She squeezed his hand. "You keep right on dreaming, Sonny. To hell with Raven."

So who was obsessed in the end? Can only the dark shadow be blamed for the obsessions of the world, uncontrollable desires that drive one crazy? Isn't the waking mind also full of needs it rationalizes in the name of its progress? Why do religious zealots seek control by imposing their faith? In the end, can anyone control the dark gods within?

"Yes," Sonny whispered as they entered.

"What?"

"I'm glad to be home. Here is where it starts. Your love."

She hugged him. "Go shower."

He took off his boots and the wet, soggy pants in the utility room, took off his splattered jacket and looked at it. It would clean, but the day's memory would live in its threads, as memory lives in the threads of every man's DNA.

He stood in the hot shower a long time, thinking of the day's events that held no quick answer. The privatization of water would continue, the rivers would be bought and sold, the great squeeze was on. The silvery minnow was on the verge of losing its habitat, as were the people of the valley.

But tomorrow was another day, and if enough like-minded people got together they could protect the environment in which they lived. The earth, the air, the water, it's all they had. Those elements were what every person held as faith in life, as had been recorded in all the myths of the past. It was only recently that a transcendent force descended from the heart of the sky; for thousands of years before that the gods sprang from the earth and its elements.

In a warm robe Sonny sat at the table while Rita washed the bruise over his eye with warm osha water. Then they ate, a hot meal of chicken enchiladas smothered in red chile, beans, tortillas, coffee, he gazing at her and she looking into his eyes and realizing how much he had suffered.

Later, as the days went by, the details of what he had learned would emerge as they discussed the politics of the state with friends who came to the cafe. They, the city, and the entire region were caught up in a battle that affected them and generations to come. It wasn't just the war on terrorists, Iraq, or Korea's threat, it was the need to feed starving children all over the world, the need to save the dying cultures. Their own backyard needed saving, for what does a man profit if he topples a dictator only to find the shadow of the dictator in his own heart.

The minnows of the river were as important as corn nourished by water. Enough people coming together could get it right.

But the spring night was for love and the muses of love. She lay in his arms, cradled in his warmth, and he could hear her steady, comfortable breathing. He knew she was in a dream, perhaps in Jemez watering the apple trees while Chica chased the robins that scampered about.

Spring had returned to her dreams, and the love they shared was itself the promise of spring.

There is a footnote that must be added, if the mystery of the life force is to be fully appreciated. It happened the following morning. Sonny awakened to Chica barking outside. He rose quietly and went to the window. In the dazzling sunlight he saw don Eliseo standing by the compost pile. Perhaps the old man was thinking back to his life on earth and all the times he fertilized his cornfield and his wife's flowerbeds. The old man looked at Sonny and winked.

Sonny blinked and rubbed his eyes.

On the lawn Rita's daughters ran and chased Chica. They laughed and cried in joy as the small dog ran back and forth. Their bonnets flew away, exposing long, streaming hair that sparkled like angel hair in the morning light.

They stopped for a moment and looked at him, warm quizzical expressions on their faces, as if to say, *What did you expect? We belong to you.*

Chica agreed, barking at her master, her bright eyes exclaiming, This is the life!

Then the girls waved and they were off again, running round in a circle with Chica happily chasing them.

Sonny smiled. He waved back, then he closed his eyes, faced the sun, and felt its warmth on his face. He held out his hands to cup the light of the sun, and as the Lords and Ladies of the Light came streaming to earth he prayed, a blessing for all of life, in this dimension and in the others.

His prayer blended the essence of light into the essence of his soul, and he felt peace and harmony within.

He opened his eyes, both eyes, fully awakened into the miracle of the new day. Still smiling he returned to the bed and slipped under the covers. Rita turned to receive him.